Good Luck

Also by Whitney Gaskell

PUSHING 30

TRUE LOVE (AND OTHER LIES)

SHE, MYSELF & I

TESTING KATE

MOMMY TRACKED

Good Luck

WHITNEY GASKELL

A Bantam Discovery

GOOD LUCK
A Bantam Discovery Book / November 2008

Published by Bantam Dell
A Division of Random House, Inc.
New York, New York

Cover design by Lynn Andreozzi

Book design by Helene Berinsky

ISBN-13: 978-1-60751-301-8

Printed in the United States of America

For Courtney

One

"YOU'RE *FIRING* ME?"

The morning light filtering into Dr. Johnson's no-nonsense office through the tinted windows suddenly seemed glaringly bright. The typical sounds surrounding the students' arrival at school—chatter, laughter, the occasional shout, the squeak of sneakers on industrial tile—were too loud. Even the office's blandness seemed unusually depressing—the standard-issue faux-cherry executive desk, the fussy gold lamp, the blotter trimmed with leather, framed prints of soulless pastel sailboats hanging on the wall.

Dr. Johnson sighed heavily and set her pen on the desk. Up until a moment ago, when she'd informed me I was losing my job, I'd always liked the principal of Andrews Prep. I'd found her capable, smart, tough, and fair-minded. I was now quickly changing my mind.

"I don't see that I have any choice," she said.

Dr. Johnson was fifty years old—the staff had thrown her a surprise birthday party the previous spring—although she had the sort of gorgeous, slow-to-age black skin that made her look ten years younger. She was a tall, broad-shouldered woman with closely cropped hair and dark, serious eyes. She wore one of the brightly colored suits she favored, this one a mustard yellow with big black buttons down the front.

"Of course you have a choice!" I said, my temper rising up out of the muffled fog of shock.

Dr. Johnson pursed her lips and looked levelly at me. "We take accusations of sexual misconduct most seriously here at Andrews Prep."

"Sexual misconduct?" I could feel the heat in my face, suddenly flaming with anger and outrage. "You know I didn't do anything of the kind! Matt must have made up this ridiculous story in retaliation for the failing grade I gave him last week!"

I had taught English literature at Andrews Prep for the past ten years. Matt Forrester—who was lazy, jaded, smugly self-entitled—was my least favorite sort of student. It wasn't that he couldn't do the work; he chose not to, preferring to spend the time when he wasn't in school or at soccer practice getting stoned with his friends. He hadn't read any of the books I'd assigned for class this year and the previous week had failed a test on William Thackeray's *Vanity Fair,* bringing his current grade down to a solid D.

Andrews Prep's policy of not allowing a student to participate in extracurricular activities unless they maintained at least a 2.5 grade point average meant that Matt had been automatically suspended from the soccer team. Two days earlier, he'd stopped by my classroom after school to argue about his grade and, when that didn't work, begged for a chance to retake the test or do extra-credit work. I'd refused.

Matt had stared at me with indolent blue eyes that drooped slightly at the outer corners. I knew many of the girls at school thought he was good-looking, with his long dirty-blond hair and fine-boned features that were pretty rather than handsome. I didn't see the attraction. I thought Matt's sneering bad-boy act was a bore.

"You'll be sorry," Matt had said. He'd practically spit the words at me, sounding too much like a toddler on the verge of a temper tantrum to be genuinely intimidating.

"Good-bye, Matt," I'd said, dismissing him. I hadn't taken his threat seriously. Most of the students at Andrews Prep were good kids, but it wasn't unheard of for one of the more spoiled ones to fall back on the old favorite from time to time: *Wait until my father hears about this!*

This time, the threat apparently had teeth.

Dr. Johnson cleared her throat and looked down at a yellow lined tablet on which she'd jotted notes. I knew she didn't really need to refer to them to remember the details and was doing so only to avoid eye contact with me.

"Matthew Forrester states that when he petitioned you to change his grade, you told him you would think about it and asked him to come to your classroom after school on Monday. He complied with your request. He claims that you then made a sexually inappropriate comment about the pants he was wearing, saying that you liked the way his"—Dr. Johnson paused and cleared her throat again—"buttocks looked in them."

"What?" I exclaimed. "That's insane! I didn't say that!"

"He states that you told him you'd fantasized about having an affair with a student. He claims you then offered to change his grade to an A if he would have sexual intercourse with you," Dr. Johnson said. She folded her hands together, resting them on her desk, and looked at me again. "We only have his uncorroborated accusation that this happened. I'm assuming you deny these charges."

"Of course I deny them!"

I was practically shouting, but I didn't care. If ever there was a time to shout, this was it.

Dr. Johnson sighed again, and for the first time since I'd arrived for our meeting—I'd been summoned first thing, mere moments after I'd arrived at school that morning—I saw a crack in her stony, professional-at-all-costs facade. She looked tired and, I thought, regretful.

"As I know you're well aware, Andrews Prep has a strict no-tolerance sexual harassment policy," she began.

"But I didn't sexually harass Matt! Or anyone else, for that matter!"

The truth of this was so obvious. I would never hit on one of my students. They're *children*. Even those who'd managed to shed their gawky adolescent bodies for the wider shoulders and hairy jaws of manhood still had the hearts and minds of *children*. The very idea that I'd be attracted to one of them, much less act on such an attraction, was laughable.

"Do you really think I would do something like that?" I demanded.

"This isn't about what I think. It's about what's best for this institution. And we simply cannot take the risk of having someone who's been accused of this sort of behavior around our students," Dr. Johnson said.

I stared at her, feeling sullied by the accusation. Panic began to rise up inside me, closing my throat and constricting my chest.

I drew in a deep breath and tried to keep my voice as calm as possible. "I've taught at this school for ten years. In that time I've had an exemplary record. Two years ago I was named Teacher of the Year. I have a plaque, for God's sake. And now because one troubled and angry boy, who told me I'd regret it if I didn't change his lousy grade, has made up a ridiculous and, frankly, slanderous accusation against me, just like that, I'm fired?"

Dr. Johnson was quiet for a few minutes. I felt an irrational spike of hope that my words had made an impact on her—a hope that was quashed a moment later when she finally spoke.

"Mr. and Mrs. Forrester came to see me yesterday. They're very disturbed by their son's claims. But they've agreed not to take any further legal action against you or against Andrews Prep if we agreed to terminate your employment."

Realization dawned, and suddenly it was all brutally clear. The Forresters were wealthy, even by Andrews Prep standards. Owen Forrester owned several car dealerships. His wife, Cassie, sat on every high-profile charity board in town.

"So that's it, is it?" I asked. "The Forresters have been the biggest contributors to the school for—what is it now?—three years running? I guess money counts more than the truth."

Dr. Johnson didn't reply. But her silence was as good as an admission. The horror of what was happening fully hit me. I was losing my job—no, it was more than that. I was losing my *career*. What school would ever hire a teacher with this sort of blemish on her record? It was the only career I'd ever wanted, and now . . . now it was gone forever. My lungs emptied and my stomach clenched so painfully that it took all of my willpower not to double over.

"Please don't do this to me," I whispered, shaking my head. "Please."

"I'm sorry," Dr. Johnson said. And although she really did sound sorry, her voice held a note of irrevocable finality.

* * *

It was absolutely gorgeous out—a perfect Florida early-autumn morning. The sky was a cloudless azure blue, and the temperature was a balmy seventy-five degrees. I felt betrayed by this idyllic weather. Bad news should summon equally moody weather: steel-gray skies, chill winds, foreboding cracks of thunder, sleet.

My feelings vacillated between numb disbelief and violent shocks of rage that left my hands shaking. I didn't bother going to my classroom to collect my personal items after I left Dr. Johnson's office. I wasn't even sure if I would be allowed to go back there. Shouldn't there be a security guard standing by, ready to escort me from the school? But there wasn't. Instead, I walked out past the school secretary, who was too busy talking to a harried mother dropping off a forgotten sack lunch to notice me, through the office door, past the few students still lingering in the hallway, even though the first bell had already rung, and out into the dazzling sunshine.

My feet seemed to be moving on their own, propelling me toward my ancient yellow Volvo parked in the teachers' lot. I loved my car, even though it was old, temperamental, and rarely had a repair bill under one thousand dollars. At least it was always easy to pick out in a sea of taupe sedans and black SUVs. It was a running joke among both the faculty and student body of Andrews Prep that the teachers' lot looked like a disreputable used-car sales lot in stark contrast to the students' lot, which more closely resembled a luxury-car dealership, full of Mercedeses, BMWs, and the ever-popular Lexus SUV. One student even drove a Bentley, a hand-me-down from her dad when he upgraded.

I never locked my Volvo, figuring no car thief in his right mind would bother with it, so I opened my car door without having to fumble for my keys and climbed in. I sat there for a long time, my hands gripping the steering wheel, my PBS telethon canvas tote bag still hanging on my shoulder. I looked in the rearview mirror once and was startled by what I saw there: My face, usually a pinkish ivory, had blanched to a sickly shade of chalk white, my brown eyes were sunken, the dark corkscrew curls I always struggled to control seemed even wilder than usual. I quickly looked away.

A car pulled in a few spots down from me. I glanced over and saw Mel Hutchinson, the terminally late biology teacher. As he opened the back door and slowly withdrew a battered briefcase, I hunched as far down in my seat as possible, hoping he wouldn't notice me.

Hurry up, I urged him silently. If he turned and saw me, he'd almost certainly stop and ask me why I was sitting there. It was a conversation I deperately didn't want to have. Not now, and certainly not with him.

Once Mel finally walked off toward the school, I started the old Volvo, backed out of my spot, and pulled out of the parking lot, the tires spinning on the gravel. I didn't know where to go. Not home. Elliott wouldn't be there—he'd told me he would be showing houses to a young newlywed couple all morning—and I didn't feel like being alone. I thought about heading to the bookstore, where I could buy an overpriced caffeinated drink and be soothed among the stacks of books. But then, glancing at the clock, I realized it was only eight o'clock. The bookstore wouldn't open for another hour.

Who gets fired before eight in the morning? I wondered. It seemed like an event that should take place over lunch or after the workday was over. Not so early in the day that stores hadn't yet opened.

Maisie, I thought, and impulsively pointed the car toward my best friend's house.

Maisie and I had been friends since her family had moved into the house next door to mine the summer before seventh grade. I'd shyly gone out to meet her when I saw Maisie standing in her driveway, straddling her bicycle as she watched the movers unload her family's possessions off the truck. I liked the look of her immediately. She was wiry and small, with short strawberry-blond hair and an impish, freckled face. We were instant friends in the way that's possible only when you're young and had remained close through our school years and beyond.

Maisie was now a stay-at-home mom to her twin three-year-old boys, Gus and Leo (short for Augustus and Leopold), and since she rarely managed to get everyone dressed and out of the house before ten o'clock, I thought there was a good chance she'd be home.

It took me five minutes to drive over to the new subdivision where Maisie and her family lived in a small three-bedroom house. All of the houses on Maisie's street were identical and packed close together in tight, precise rows. I pulled into her driveway, narrowly missing a faded red plastic tricycle lying on its side, and climbed out of my car. My legs felt stiff beneath me, as though my body had aged on the short drive over.

I could hear sounds of chaotic life inside the house while I was still five steps away from the front door. One of the twins was crying, the other was shouting something, and their dog, a Jack Russell terrier named Fang, was yapping loudly over the cacophony. I had to ring the doorbell twice before anyone heard it.

"Lucy!" Maisie said when she finally answered. She was still wearing her pajamas—red floral bottoms and one of Joe's white V-necked Ts—and already looked exhausted. She hadn't changed all that much since the first time I saw her. She had the same slim angular body, almost unchanged by puberty and pregnancy, the same short fluff of red-blond hair, the same pretty freckled face. Even though I wasn't an especially tall woman—five-five in my stocking feet—I always felt like a giantess next to tiny Maisie. Fang sprang out the door from behind her, leaping toward me, his stubby little tail wagging furiously.

"Hi, Maisie. Hey, Fang," I said faintly. I leaned over to pet the Jack Russell on his head, and he lunged at my hand, licking it in a frenzied display of delight.

Maisie's smile of greeting quickly faded, and her face quirked into a frown.

"What's wrong? You look *awful*. Why are you here? Come on, come inside, I'll get you a coffee," she said, rattling out the words without pausing for breath.

In what seemed like one motion, Maisie pulled me inside the house, closed the door, and slipped the tote bag off my shoulder. Her house was, as usual, a disaster zone. The debris of family life—toy trains, cars, puzzles, action figures, books, T-shirts, shoes, tissues, Fang's chew toys—was scattered everywhere. There was a bench along the wall in the hallway, presumably a place for putting on or taking off your shoes, but it was covered in bags, toys, coloring books, and a mega-size package of disposable Pull-Ups, rendering it impossible to sit on.

Maisie steered me back to the light-filled, noisy kitchen at the rear of the house. It, too, was a mess. Several of the white laminate cupboards and drawers were half open, dirty dishes were stacked in the sink, cereal boxes and apple-juice containers were spread across the counters next to a messy stack of old newspapers that hadn't yet made it into the recycling bin.

The twins were sitting at the table in matching booster

chairs, taking turns blowing loud raspberries at each other and laughing raucously. Whatever storm had caused the upset I'd heard while ringing the doorbell had apparently already blown over. The boys had their father's dark hair and hazel eyes but had inherited their mother's playful, mischievous personality.

"Gus!" Maisie said sharply.

Gus, too busy horsing around with his brother to pay attention, had knocked over his juice glass. Apple juice puddled on the table and dripped onto the floor.

"Sorry, Mama," Gus said breezily, while Leo chortled with delight at the mess.

"If you're done eating, go play in the other room and let Aunt Lucy and I talk," Maisie said.

The boys only then noticed that I, their honorary aunt (Joe and Maisie were both only children, so I took on the role gladly), was standing there behind their mother. I waved and attempted a smile.

"Hey, Wonder Twins," I said.

"Aunt Lucy, Aunt Lucy!" they both shrieked. They jumped down from their booster seats and bounced Tigger-like across the kitchen. As they congregated at my feet, words tumbled out of them as they talked over each other in identical high, sweet voices.

"Aunt Lucy, come play with us!"

"Come play trains!"

"You can be Thomas!"

"No, I'm Thomas. She can be Salty."

"Okay. You can be Salty, Aunt Lucy. I'm James, and James's tender, and the circus cars, and Percy."

"I want the circus cars!"

"No! I want them!"

"Mine!"

"Mine!"

"Boys!" Maisie yelled. She pointed toward the living room. "Go. Play. Now."

The boys exchanged impish grins—as usual, the argument dissipated as quickly as it had erupted—and ran off to the living room, no doubt to hatch a plot that would involve serious injury to the house in some way. The smile I'd contorted my mouth into for the twin's benefit slid away.

"Sorry about that, hon," Maisie said. "Now, what was I doing? Oh, right, coffee. Hey . . . what is it? What's wrong?"

I hadn't been able to stem the tears any longer. They began to drip down my cheeks, and my breath seemed stuck in my chest. When I was finally able to inhale, it was shallow and gasping.

"Sit. Over here," Maisie commanded, taking me by the arm and leading me toward one of the ladder-back kitchen chairs. She sat down beside me and peered intently into my face. "What's going on? Did you and Elliott break up?"

This question startled me. Why would Maisie's first thought be that Elliott and I had broken up? He had just moved in with me two months ago, and I thought he might finally be close to proposing. It had taken three years of on-again, off-again dating to drag him to this point, and I was starting to wonder if it was normal to feel victorious—as opposed to purely happy—that I'd managed to finally wrangle a semipermanent commitment out of him.

"No, of course not. Why would you think that?" I asked. My voice was soggy from the tears.

"I've never seen you this upset," Maisie said. "I thought it must be Elliott-related."

"It's not. I just lost my job," I said.

Maisie gasped and covered her mouth with her hands. "But . . . why? How? I mean . . . why?"

I wiped my tears off my cheeks with the back of my hands. Maisie quickly handed me a paper napkin, and I blew my nose into it.

"Apparently I sexually propositioned a student."

"What? That's the most ridiculous thing I've ever heard," Maisie exploded.

This is why I love Maisie—with no hesitation, no second-guessing, she dismissed the idea out of hand.

As we sat at Maisie's kitchen table, sticky with spilled juice and festooned with soggy Cheerios, I told her about Matt Forrester and the accusation he'd made against me, and how Dr. Johnson had sided with Matt and his donation-heavy parents over me. The telling of the morning's events didn't make it more real for me. In fact, the more I talked about it, the more detached I felt from what had happened. Even my anger, which had been so hot and sharp-edged earlier, now seemed distant. Or maybe it was just that I'd managed to transfer it to Maisie. Because the more I told her, the more furious she became. Her pale skin bloomed red under her freckles, the way it always did when she was feeling a strong emotion, and her lips pinched into such a tight line, it looked like she was holding her breath.

"That little shit," she finally said when I'd finished. "That horrible little cockroach of a child."

"Hardly a child. He's seventeen."

"He's a bastard. Okay, here's what you do: First, you sue him and his asshole parents. Then you sue that godforsaken school."

Motherhood had not softened Maisie's lawyerly instincts. Before she had the twins, Maisie was a prosecutor with the state attorney's office. The job had been a fertile source of anecdotes. Like the time Maisie was in court, prosecuting a burglary. After she finished her opening statement, during which she outlined the pretty much open-and-shut case, the defendant—hulking, tattooed, and nearly three times Maisie's size—had burst out with an angry "Suck my dick, bitch." Before the judge and bailiff could even react, Maisie eyed the defendant coolly and retorted, "Thanks for the offer, but you're really not my type." Everyone in the courtroom—even the judge—burst out laughing.

"What kind of case would that be? It's my word against Matt's. And the school has already made it clear that they're taking his side." I shivered suddenly. "You want to know the really creepy thing? If I didn't know me, and I heard about this on the news—a story about a teacher seducing one of her students—I'd believe it too. What kind of kid makes up a story like that?"

"A really fucked-up kid," Maisie said. She took an angry gulp of coffee. "So what is his story? Did you ever get a weird feeling about him before?"

"That he'd do something like this? Of course not," I said.

"What's he like otherwise? Did you ever get the feeling that he was disturbed? The sort to torture small animals or shoot his parents while they're asleep?"

"No." I shook my head definitely. "He's basically a cartoon of a spoiled rich kid. Strong sense of entitlement, a belief that Daddy's money can buy him out of anything. Hell, he's right, it usually does." I took a sip of coffee. It was awful—bitter and watery. Maisie had always been a terrible cook. She couldn't even make edible instant macaroni and cheese. I set my mug down and nudged it to one side. "I've heard rumors that he's a bit of a partier."

"A drinker or a drugger?" Maisie asked.

I shrugged. "I'd guess both."

"The little shit," Maisie muttered darkly. "So, what are you going to do now?"

Icy fingers of fear gripped at my heart, and I shivered again. I liked it better when I was in shock. Shock has a nice muffling effect on your feelings.

"I have no idea," I said. And then the fear really took hold, and it suddenly felt like I'd been ripped open and was falling inside myself into a deep, bottomless hole. "Oh, my *God*. What *am* I going to do?"

Maisie reached out and grabbed my hand. "It will be all right. You'll be fine."

"I'll never be able to teach again. I'm going to have to find another job. A different career. I'm thirty-two years old. I'm too old to start over again."

Maisie made a *pfft* sound. "You are not too old. People change careers all the time. And a lot of them do it much later in life than you. Think of all the people who've been downsized and suddenly have to become . . ." Her voice trailed off as she struggled to come up with an example that would prove her point. Suddenly her face brightened. "A masseuse! Like Megan Frost's husband. Remember? He did something over at Sunrise Bank but then started going to massage school at night. He ended up opening that day spa downtown."

"But I don't want to be a masseuse!" I said. My voice was shrill. "You know I hate touching strangers! It's why I didn't go to medical school!"

"I thought you didn't go to medical school because the sight of blood makes you feel faint," Maisie said. She had a maddening ability to remember everything anyone had ever said to her. "Don't you remember when we were at track practice in tenth grade, and Kurt Shaw fell and got a rock lodged in his forehead? The blood was just pouring out of him—

really, it was an insane amount of blood for a relatively minor injury, although I guess head wounds do bleed a lot. Anyway. You took one look at him and went all woozy. Coach Miller ended up sending you to the nurse's office."

I shuddered at the memory. "Can we please not talk about this now?"

"You brought it up."

"No, I didn't. I said I didn't go to medical school because I don't like touching people. Although, from where I'm currently sitting, I have to say: really bad move. Because if I was a doctor right now, I wouldn't be an out-of-work teacher with a sexual-harassment charge hanging over my head," I said miserably.

Maisie patted my hand consolingly.

"I guess it's a good thing you and Elliott are living together. He'll be able to help you out financially, right?" Maisie said this as though it was a small point in Elliott's favor.

Maisie was the only person I knew who didn't instantly like Elliott, who was an all-around nice guy and, in many ways, the perfect boyfriend. He's kind, easygoing, faithful, hygienic, gainfully employed. The sort of man little old ladies ask to reach a can of soup off the top shelf at the grocery store and neighbors call when they need to move a piece of heavy furniture.

But Maisie had held a grudge against Elliott for the past two years, ever since he broke up with me on my thirtieth birthday. Unfortunately, he chose to do this an hour before the party Maisie and Joe were throwing for me was due to start, which meant that when I turned up at my own birthday party, I was alone and weeping. Even though we'd later gotten back together, Maisie had never really fully forgiven him.

I'd tried to lobby Maisie on Elliott's behalf. Yes, the birthday-breakup trauma had been an especially low point in our relationship. I wouldn't deny that, nor would Elliott, who had apologized profusely for it. He'd just that day missed out on scoring an exclusive listing for a waterfront mansion—Elliott was a realtor—and that was after learning his sales had been down twenty percent the month before. The combination of these two setbacks—along with his belief that my turning thirty would cause my biological clock to start clanging and turn me into a desperate baby-obsessed cliché—had propelled him straight into an old-fashioned panic attack. Suddenly he wasn't just freaking out about how he was going to make next month's payment on his condo; he was also worrying about how he'd pay for a wedding, the mortgage on a three-bedroom ranch house near a good elementary school, and the lease on a minivan with side air bags. His parents' rocky relationship followed by an ugly divorce when he was ten had scarred him, he'd explained, and made him leery of commitment.

"It's fine," I had assured Elliott the day after the doomed birthday party, as he sat on my couch, clutching my hand in his. His thin face was pale and miserable, and his shoulders were hunched forward. "I don't even want to get engaged right now. Lots of people put off marriage and children until their mid-thirties. There's no rush."

And Elliott had thanked me for being so understanding, had told me he didn't deserve me, and then had asked me if there was any way I'd take him back. Without hesitating, I said yes. Although now, two years later, I was starting to think that It Was Time. Time to move forward—to get engaged, to get married, and, yes, to have children, before my ovaries crapped out. I'd been arrogant enough to think that I was in control of my biological clock. But lately, whenever I saw a baby strapped into a carrier at the grocery store or spent time with Maisie's boys, I felt a pang that was getting harder and harder to ignore. When I'd brought this up to Elliott, he seemed open to the idea.

"It's definitely something we should talk about," he'd said, folding me into his arms. Despite being thin, Elliott was a world-class cuddler. He was the human equivalent of a cozy sweater. "Not right now, of course, not while I'm still getting my business up and running." Elliott had recently left the large realty group he'd worked at for the past seven years to start up his own office. "But soon. Very, very soon." And then he'd leaned back and smiled playfully at me. "Who knows? Maybe it'll be a holly jolly Christmas this year."

"Do you think Santa will bring me something sparkly?" I'd asked, playing along.

"Maybe . . ." Elliott said, raising his eyebrows knowingly. Then he kissed me in a way that I thought sealed the deal.

I hadn't told Maisie about any of this. Any mention of Elliott and the cautious approach he took toward marriage always caused her to roll her eyes and mutter under her breath about commitment-phobic bastards and how I should get the hell out of it before it was too late.

I privately thought that in order to maintain her grudge against him, Maisie was deliberately ignoring all of the wonderful things Elliott had done over the years. Like when I had my tonsils out and he'd filled the freezer with ice cream and brought over his blender to make milk shakes for me. And then there was the time he surprised me by waiting in line at the bookstore on the night the last Harry Potter book came out, so when I woke up it was waiting for me on my nightstand. He had some issues, sure, but who didn't, especially by the time they reached their thirties? And I knew Elliott. At his core, he was a really good guy in all the ways that mattered.

And yet . . . I wasn't at all sure how he would react to the news that I was, in all likelihood, about to be insolvent and unemployable. Of course we were in a committed relationship, especially now that he had finally rented out his condo and moved in with me. But the new living arrangement was taking some getting used to, and I'd thought Elliott had been a bit distant lately. It was probably just nerves, I knew, but I also wasn't thrilled at the idea of adding more stress to our relationship.

I hadn't shared any of this with Maisie, not wanting her already low opinion of him to sink even further. So now I just said, "Hmmm, yeah, good thing."

Maisie gave me a sharp look, but I was saved from prosecutorial interrogation by the sudden and uproarious entrance of Gus and Leo. They came hurtling into the kitchen like twin rockets. Gus was wearing a red superhero cape, and Leo had on a quiver of foam arrows and a toy bow slung over one shoulder.

"You two look like you're expecting trouble," I said.

They giggled in response, and then Leo whispered something in Gus's ear. Gus, always the more vocal of the two, said, "Mama, can we have juice boxes? And crackers?"

"Already? You just finished breakfast ten minutes ago," Maisie said. She shook her head at me. "These two are like bottomless pits. Do you know our grocery bill has tripled since they started on solids? Not doubled. *Tripled.* I can't imagine what our food budget is going to look like when they're teenagers."

"Goldfish crackers, please!" Leo piped up. He waved his

bow around. I privately questioned the decision-making that had gone into arming the boys, even with something as seemingly benign as a plastic bow and foam arrows.

"And juice boxes!" Gus chimed in, quickly adding, "Please!"

"Okay, okay," Maisie said. She stood up, grabbed a giant carton of Goldfish out of the cupboard, and began dispensing the crackers into two green plastic bowls.

I got up too and fetched the promised juice boxes out of the fridge. "Apple or fruit punch?" I asked the boys.

"Punch!" Leo yelled.

"Apple!" shouted Gus.

I distributed the juice boxes, only to have the boys thrust them back at me with orders to unwrap the attached straws for them. It was only when they'd run back out of the kitchen, snacks in hand and making more noise than seemed possible, that I noticed the lottery ticket stuck to the refrigerator door with a plastic banana-shaped magnet.

"A lottery ticket?" I turned around to look at Maisie, my eyebrows arched.

"What?" she asked, trying to sound blasé, although the effect was ruined when she flushed a dark red.

"You've always said the lottery is a tax on stupid people."

"Well, the jackpot is really high this week. Eighty-seven million dollars," Maisie said defensively. "I told you our grocery bill is out of control."

"Eighty-seven million would certainly buy a lot of juice boxes," I said.

"Tell me about it. I don't normally play, and I know you have a better chance of getting struck by lightning than winning the lottery."

"Especially in this state," I said. Late-afternoon thunderstorms were commonplace in south Florida.

"But when the jackpot gets this high . . . Well, I figured why not." Maisie shrugged and refilled her coffee mug from the glass carafe. "I picked the twins' birthday and Joe's and my wedding anniversary as my numbers. I thought they might carry some good juju."

"You're not supposed to play dates," I said.

"Why not?"

"Because everyone plays meaningful dates, which means that there are a disproportionate number of tickets sold where all the numbers are thirty-one or lower."

Bruce Greene, the algebra teacher at Andrews Prep, had once told me this over lunch in the teachers' lounge. Bruce was full of fun facts. He'd also told me that, over a lifetime, the average person swallows eight spiders in their sleep.

"So?"

"So it means there's a higher probability that someone else will pick the same numbers. And then you'll have to share the money with them," I explained.

Maisie snorted. "Half of eighty-seven million dollars? I think I can live with that."

"No kidding. Can you imagine having that kind of money?"

"Yes, I can. We could pay off the house, the credit cards, my student loans, and put aside money for the twins' school tuition. And after all of that, we might just have enough left over to splurge on a few cheeseburgers," Maisie joked.

"Surely things aren't that bad."

"Well, maybe we could afford a couple of steaks instead of the cheeseburgers."

She said this lightly, but I knew Maisie and Joe had been having financial trouble for a while. It started when they hadn't been able to conceive. Maisie's health insurance didn't cover consultations with the fertility specialist, and then it took three rounds of in vitro fertilization before she got pregnant. They'd spent upward of fifty thousand dollars by the time the twins were born, and she and Joe had taken out a second mortgage on their house to pay for it. And then Maisie had opted to stay home with the boys, reasoning that by the time she paid the double child-care costs, her state attorney's salary wouldn't go very far. So now she was a full-time stay-at-home mom, and they were managing on Joe's earnings from the landscape nursery he owned. At least, I'd thought they were managing.

"Maisie," I began, but before I could ask her if their financial troubles were more serious than I'd thought, the twins had stormed the kitchen yet again, roaring for more Goldfish crackers.

"More?" Maisie asked, her face screwed up in comical disbelief. "You ate all of those crackers already? I don't believe it!"

"We did! We ate the crackers!" Leo said, delighted with himself.

Max grinned and nodded. "We did, Mama, we did!"

"Are there holes in your tummies?" Maisie asked teasingly. She picked Leo up and nimbly turned him over, so that his T-shirt fell open, exposing a pale, rounded belly. He laughed uproariously and kicked his legs, while Maisie tickled his stomach and asked, "Is there a hole in there, Mr. Belly Button?"

"Pick me up, Mama, pick me up!" Gus begged, and Maisie set Leo down and swooped Gus up and repeated the gag with him.

And now that the kitchen was full of light and laughter and the screeches of childish pleasure, I didn't have the heart to drag Maisie back to the depressing reality of her financial troubles. Besides, I had my own, more pressing problems to deal with. And remembering this—my sudden unemployment, the accusations that had been made against me, the uncertainty of where I'd go from here—it all hit me anew. There was no escaping the truth: I was in major trouble.

Two

I STAYED FOR LUNCH WITH MAISIE AND THE BOYS—grilled cheese sandwiches with charred crusts and canned tomato soup. When Leo started to yawn and Gus burst into tears when Maisie told him he couldn't have another cookie, Maisie announced it was time for their nap.

"I should get going anyway," I said.

"You don't have to leave," Maisie protested, following me to the front hall, where I gathered up my bag.

"No, I should go. I have to..." Then I stopped, because there was nothing I had to do. By all rights, I should still be at work. I glanced at my watch. It was just after one. Sixth period. My ninth-grade class. We were near the end of the *Romeo and Juliet* unit, and last week I'd broken the class up into pairs and assigned each to memorize one of the scenes from the play. They'd been rehearsing ever since, and today the first few teams were going to present their scenes to the class. It was always a fun project, one the kids really got into. Some even wore costumes and brought props.

I was going to miss it. This realization caused a small stab of pain to puncture my heart. I wondered who was going to sub in for me. Then I remembered that no one would be subbing for *me*. It wasn't my class anymore. Someone else would soon have my job. And the pain I felt at this wasn't at all small; it was more along the lines of an anvil being dropped off a cliff and landing on my head.

"Lucy?" Maisie asked.

I started, suddenly realizing that I hadn't finished my sentence. I was so traumatized and so frightened, I didn't even have the ability to carry on a simple conversation.

"Sorry," I said. "I can't remember what I was saying. I think I'm going to go home and lie down."

"Why don't you stay here? You can nap in our room. The boys will sleep for hours, so they won't bother you," Maisie offered.

"No, thanks. I want to go home," I said. I leaned forward and hugged her. "Thanks for putting up with me today. The company helped."

"Anytime," Maisie said. She leaned back and looked at me, a small frown pulling down at her lips. "Are you sure you're okay to drive?"

"I'm unemployed, not drunk," I said.

"Call me later," Maisie said.

"I will," I promised.

But once I was in my car, headed toward home, I couldn't remember why I'd been in such a hurry to leave the warm, raucous atmosphere of Maisie's house. The loneliness of my predicament was suddenly unbearable.

But I was saved from having to contemplate it further. My Volvo coughed once and then, with an offensive lack of drama, died and rolled to a stop right in the middle of the street. The drivers of the cars behind me immediately began to register their displeasure. One honked, then another, and then several at once. And all the while I desperately turned the key, praying for something, anything to happen. A flicker of lights, a rumble of engine. Anything.

But nothing happened. I had no idea what was wrong. I had just filled up the tank that morning on my way in to work. Or, to be more accurate, on my way in to be fired. If it wasn't gas, what could it be? What would cause a car to suddenly stop working? And what had I been thinking when I took home ec instead of auto shop back in high school? Surely the knowledge of what to do in these situations would have been a more valuable skill set to acquire than learning how to whip up canvas tote bags on a sewing machine.

Honk, went the drivers. *Honk, honk. Honk.*

It was then that I burst into tears. I just sat there, clutching the steering wheel in the ten-and-two position, and sobbed, body-racking sobs, the kind that start in your lungs but spasm outward until your entire body is shaking. I sobbed, I howled, I wailed. I completely and totally lost it.

There was a sharp rap on my window. I started, and looked up. A police officer passing by had stopped and approached my car without my noticing. He was now standing at my window, peering in at me. The officer was overweight, his stomach pushing out against the unrelenting polyester of his uniform, and he had short hair that stood on end like the bristles of a brush. He was wearing the sort of reflective sunglasses I'd always loathed. Seeing myself now reflected in them and being confronted with a distorted view of my red, puffy, tear-streaked face did nothing to change my opinion.

The police officer made a *roll-down-your-window* gesture. I complied.

"What's the problem here?" he asked gruffly.

For a wild moment I wondered if he somehow knew I'd been accused of propositioning a minor, and terror seized me. What if he arrested me? Put me in jail? What if I had to spend the rest of my life trapped behind bars, wearing an orange jumpsuit and being tortured by my fellow prisoners, who would all somehow know—they always did in the movies—what I'd been convicted of?

But, no. Dr. Johnson had told me that Matt's parents had decided to let the matter drop if the school agreed to terminate my employment. And the officer, who had clearly decided that he was dealing with a crazy lady, confirmed this by taking on what he probably thought was a kinder, gentler tone.

"Are you having car trouble, ma'am?" he asked.

"Wha-what?" I hiccupped. "Oh. Um. Yes. I mean, I think so. My car just stopped suddenly. I was hoping it was just taking a moment."

"Taking a moment?" the officer repeated.

"Yes. I thought maybe it just needed to rest a bit. Then it would get over it and start up again," I said.

"Uh-huh," the officer said.

"I'm not crazy," I said defensively. "I just have a very temperamental car."

"Ma'am, please step out of your vehicle," the officer said. He opened the door for me, which I first thought was gallantry and then decided was more likely a concern that I was so deranged, I'd lock myself inside and start waving a gun around at passersby.

I sighed—deeply, unhappily, resignedly—and climbed slowly out of my car.

Forty-five minutes later, my Volvo was hooked up to the back of a tow truck, on its temperamental way to the auto shop, and I was walking home. Officer Drurry, who had turned out to be quite nice and had even thrown a few hard looks at the irate drivers he'd waved around my stalled car while we waited for the tow to arrive, had offered to give me a ride. I'd declined. I was less than a mile from home, and I thought the walk might clear my head.

And it worked. It felt like a big empty bubble had swollen up in my brain, pushing out the sinkhole of worry and anxiety that had been swirling around in there. Maybe it was some sort of post-traumatic stress response. Or maybe something inside me had broken down with my car. Either way, as I trudged along I was able to keep my focus on putting one foot in front of the other and vaguely wondering if the distant hazy grayness meant that it was going to rain later. It was while I was looking up at the darkening sky that I noticed the sign for the local Quik-Rite.

Water, I thought. *That's what I need—a nice, cold bottle of water.*

I headed into the store, grabbed a bottle of spring water from the cooler, and took it to the cash register. The blonde behind the counter looked like she was in her fifties, but maybe she was a decade younger and had just lived a hard life. Her skin certainly had the sort of raw, unhealthy pallor that suggested a diet rich in cigarettes and cheap liquor. It didn't help that all of the color had been peroxided out of her hair, save for two inches of mouse-brown roots. She was wearing a faded peach tank top over sagging breasts, and there was a black and blue tattoo of a unicorn on her shoulder. She lit a cigarette, took a long drag on it, and looked at me with bored indifference.

I set the water down on the counter.

"That all?" she asked.

It was then that I noticed the lit-up display advertising the Florida Lottery. Flashing lights blinked: $87 MILLION!!!!!! PLAY NOW!!!!

"And a lottery ticket," I said impulsively.

"One?"

"Yes."

"Quick pick?"

"What? Um, just the regular lottery, please. The one with the eighty-seven-million-dollar jackpot," I said.

The clerk sighed, as though I were the most annoying customer she had ever had to deal with. As she exhaled, two streams of smoke escaped out her nose, making her look like a dragon. A really mean dragon with a bad dye job. "You know what numbers you want to play, or you want the machine to pick 'em?"

"Oh. Um, I guess it can pick the numbers for me," I said. She moved toward the machine. But suddenly remembering the conversation I'd had with Maisie, I said, "Wait. I want to pick my numbers."

The woman rolled her eyes. "I already pressed the quick-pick ticket," she complained. "If you want to pick your numbers, you'll have to buy another ticket."

"Okay," I said. "That's fine."

"So?"

"So what?"

"So what will your numbers be?" she asked, in a way that made it clear she wouldn't be at all unhappy if a car suddenly burst through the Quik-Rite window and ran me over, killing me instantly. She nodded at a stack of cards standing upright in a Plexiglas box. "You fill in your numbers on a card, and then I put it into the machine here."

"Oh . . . okay," I said. I took a card and a stubby golf pencil. The card had the numbers 1 through 53 printed on it, each in the middle of a little bubble. To select a number, you had to pencil in the bubble. It reminded me suddenly, painfully, of the grading cards the students at Andrews Prep used for multiple-choice tests.

I shook my head, willing away all thoughts of school, and instead tried to focus on which numbers I should pick. Should I play Elliott's and my birthdays? No. I'd just told Maisie that playing dates put you at a statistical disadvantage. Plus, considering how crappily my life was currently going, there was no way my date of birth would be chock full of good luck.

"Ma'am, there are customers waiting," the cashier snapped.

I looked up and glanced wildly around. There were two men standing behind me, both wearing work uniforms with their names embroidered over their left nipples; one of them held a case of beer. They were both giving me hard stares.

"Oh . . . sorry," I said. They didn't respond. I had the feeling they, too, wouldn't be upset to see a runaway car take me out. I quickly filled in the bubbles for 48, 49, 50, 51, 52, and 53—and instantly regretted it. What were the chances that six sequential numbers would be picked? And the last six numbers at that? But before I could change my mind, the cashier whipped the card out of my hand and stuck it into the machine.

"That'll be three seventy-two," she said.

I paid, took my tickets and my bottle of water, and left.

"Sorry about the wait," I heard the cashier say loudly to the workmen, just as the door closed behind me.

Elliott's car, an entry-level BMW he leased, was parked in the driveway. He claimed that it was important to "look successful to be successful." A silver Mercedes SUV was parked behind it. I groaned. That meant Elliott had a client over again, probably to look at listings online or to review a contract. He had a home office set up for client meetings, but I wasn't in the mood for it right now. I wanted to be able to walk into my house—our house, I quickly corrected myself—and change into sweats and veg out on the sofa with a pint of chocolate chocolate-chip ice cream. Or maybe a bottle of wine. Or both. Now I'd have to tiptoe around my own house, staying in the bedroom and discreetly out of view.

But then I remembered: I was out of work, so the success of Elliott's fledgling business was all the more crucial. I'd just have to suck it up and be invisible.

I unlocked the front door, which opened directly into the living room. My French bulldog, Harper Lee, was nowhere to be seen. Elliott had probably closed her up in the kitchen, I thought, which was confirmed a moment later when I heard her high-pitched yip coming from that direction. I decided to change before I went in to greet her.

The bedrooms were off a hallway to the left of the living room. I set my bag down, kicked off my shoes, and padded down the hall. I didn't hear any voices as I passed by the office, but the door was closed, and like many older homes, the walls were fairly thick. The bedroom door was closed too. I turned the knob and pushed the door open.

I was still holding on to the doorknob when I saw them. She was lying on the bed, stark naked except for her jewelry, of which there was quite a bit. Gold, mostly. Heavy chains of it roped around her neck and encircled her wrists. Her breasts were large and, from the way they were standing straight up off her chest, defying all laws of gravity, augmented with implants. The nipples were large too, and very dark. Her hair had been artfully highlighted with streaks of golden blond that perfectly complimented her lightly tanned skin. She didn't have any tan lines.

Elliott was naked too. However, he was standing up. Her legs were wrapped around his waist, and he was holding on to her thighs as he rhythmically rocked his hips into her. He was very thin—too thin, really, with hip bones that jutted out sharply under his skin—and much paler than she was. I'd always thought that Elliott's face was more interesting than it was handsome—the high clear brow, the long nose, the thin lips, the brown hair that flopped appealingly down on his forehead. His eyes were closed, and he started to groan, his breath escaping in small gasping puffs, the way he always did right when he was about to reach orgasm.

The blonde apparently knew the signs too, for she began to encourage him. "Come on, baby, come on. You feel so good inside me," she said in a breathy, bad-porn sort of way that struck me as truly ridiculous. So ridiculous, I snorted. It wasn't a laugh; more a sound of horrified disbelief.

Elliott opened his eyes then and saw me. He halted abruptly, mid-thrust, and the color drained from his face.

"Shit," he said.

The blonde opened her eyes too. "What's wrong, baby? Don't stop now."

I looked from her to him, while my tired brain—already on emotional overload—whirred to process what was happening, to accept that the last shreds of security were being stripped away from me. And then I burst into tears for the third time that day.

Three

I WASN'T SURE WHAT WAS SUPPOSED TO HAPPEN next in this sort of situation. Obviously the blonde had to leave. Elliott too. But as I sat on the living-room couch, clutching a forest-green throw pillow to my chest like a shield, it struck me that it was taking them a ridiculously long time to dress and vacate the bedroom. I'd stopped crying, partly because I was sick of crying and partly because I felt suspended—not in numb disbelief this time, but in sharply edged disappointment.

Elliott was an asshole. An even bigger asshole than Maisie had always thought him to be. And I'd wasted the past three years of my life on this asshole. Three years of trying to coax him along into moving in together, getting engaged, marrying me, having children. Three years of putting up with his excuses and chronic commitment phobia and telling myself over and over again that he'd come around to appreciate the benefits of domesticity. Men always did. Even Joe, who had fallen head over heels in love with Maisie on their first date, had balked when it came time to get engaged. There was a three-month period where every time Maisie said, "I want a ring," Joe would respond by trilling a telephonic "*Riiiinnnngggg.*" Maisie was not amused. The last time Joe did this, she promptly dumped him. He showed up on her doorstep three hours later with a dozen roses, a bottle of champagne, and a diamond engagement ring. Joe swore up and down that he had bought the ring weeks earlier and was just waiting for the right moment to pop the question.

But Elliott wasn't Joe. As far as I knew—and I was pretty sure I would, since this was not a topic on which Maisie would hold back—Joe had never been caught fucking a blonde with concrete tits in their master bedroom.

And what was up with that sexual position, anyway? Maybe it was an irrelevant and even inappropriate point to dwell on, but Elliott and I had never had sex like that. He'd always been solidly in favor of the missionary position and hadn't even liked it when I was on top. Once, when we'd both had a few too many Bloody Marys over brunch, he'd plucked up the courage to suggest anal sex. Actually, he didn't so much ask as just head in that direction. I'd shrieked, jumped off the bed, and spent the next two weeks wondering if he was really a closet case.

Maybe the blonde has anal sex with him, I thought bitterly. *Maybe she likes anal sex. Maybe that's why he cheated on me. And what the hell are they doing back there? They couldn't possibly be trying to finish . . . could they?*

Just when I was contemplating this horrifying thought—really, how could they? It would be the very worst of manners—Elliott finally appeared. He had taken the time to button up his oxford shirt, tuck it into his pressed chinos, and put on his shoes. As he stood in front of me, he bowed his head, which made him look like a little boy who'd been caught being naughty.

"Lucy . . ." he began, and then—apparently having no idea

what to say next—stopped. He stood silently, staring down at his feet.

"You're not going to tell me that this isn't what it looks like, are you?" I asked acidly.

"God, I'm so sorry. I didn't mean for you . . . Well, I didn't want you to find out like this," Elliott said haltingly.

I stared at him. "Find out?" I repeated.

Elliott looked anguished. His face was pale and drawn, and he kept running one hand through his hair. If I didn't hate him so much, I might have almost felt sorry for him.

"What?" I asked.

"I think it was all just happening so fast. Moving in together, all the talk of getting married. It was just . . . too much, too quickly," he said.

"Too quickly? Elliott, we've been together for three years!"

"I just think . . ." Elliott let out a low groan and rubbed his head with both hands, as though to loosen his thoughts. "If it's right, it shouldn't be so hard to move forward, should it? It should just . . . well, flow. Don't you think?" He looked expectantly at me, as though hoping for understanding.

"Flow?" I repeated.

"That's how it is with Naomi," Elliott explained. He suddenly seemed eager to discuss it, as though this were a theory he'd been working on for a while and was excited to finally be able to share it with me. "It just . . . flows. Do you know what I mean? Flow."

He made a swimming-fish movement with one hand.

This was too much. As if it weren't bad enough that, in the course of one day, I'd been falsely accused of sexually harassing a student, lost my job, had my car die and be towed off to the repair shop, fallen to pieces in front of a police officer, *and* walked in on my live-in boyfriend screwing a woman who had much nicer hair than me, now on top of all of that I had to listen to pathetic excuses about how we didn't flow?

It's really quite amazing how you can go from loving someone so much you can't imagine your life without them to hating them with every last molecule of your being, all in the space of a few moments. A white-hot burning anger lashed up within me, electrifying me out of my dazed stupor.

"Get out of my house," I said, spitting the words at him. "And take Miss Fake Tits with you."

"They're not fake." This was from Naomi, who had apparently been hovering in the hallway, just out of sight. She now stepped forward into the living room. She was dressed in head-to-toe white—a fitted T-shirt, linen trousers—and had taken the time to put on lipstick.

I stared at her, and she had the grace to blush.

"Look, I'm really sorry you had to find out about us like this," Naomi said.

She looked at me beseechingly—as though she had inadvertently cut me off in traffic and saying sorry might fix things. I guessed Naomi was one of those women who can't stand anyone not liking her. Which probably made her the perfect match for Elliott. They could trip off together into the sunset, as shallow as puddles and both convinced that they were nice people.

"It's not okay, and you're certainly not forgiven," I said.

Naomi looked hurt. "I think you should know—we're in love. We didn't mean to hurt anyone. It just happened."

"I don't care," I said. Which was a lie. Of course I cared. Her declaration made it just that much worse. The idea that they'd been at it long enough to fall in love—

No. I couldn't think about that now.

"Leave your key," I said to Elliott.

"My key?" he repeated.

"Your house key. The key to my house. The house you no longer live in," I said.

"Oh... right," Elliott said. He fumbled for his key ring, looking a bit confused, as though he hadn't thought ahead to all of this ending up with him homeless. Well, what did he expect? That we'd continue to live together, with him in the spare bedroom and Naomi dropping by for sleepovers? I felt a stab of pleasure knowing that his condo was sublet.

"You and your commitment phobia can move in with Naomi," I said nastily. "She deserves you both."

There was an uncomfortable pause.

"I can't," Elliott finally said. Naomi looked at her feet. Another flash of understanding hit me.

"Let me guess: Miss Fake Tits is *Mrs.* Fake Tits," I said.

"I'm separated," Naomi said, a tinge of resentment creeping into her voice. "And my breasts are not fake."

"Give me a break," I said, rolling my eyes. "He may be stupid enough to buy that line, sweetheart, but I happen to know what real boobs look like. Those aren't even particularly good fakes. Breasts are supposed to move now and then. Jiggle a bit. Respond to gravity."

"Lucy, please," Elliott said pleadingly.

Suddenly I just went all flat inside. All of my anger and contempt fizzled out, and I wanted for the two of them to be gone, so that I could be alone to have the emotional breakdown I deserved.

I held out my hand, palm facing up. "Key," I said. "Now."

Elliott slid the key off his ring and handed it to me.

"When would be a good time for me to come by and get my things?" he asked.

I hated that he was sounding so reasonable and in control

of himself. I closed my eyes and silently counted. When I reached ten, I still felt like stabbing Elliott in the eye with a sharpened pencil; I counted to twenty.

"I'm just going to go," Naomi said, as I counted.

Then there was some murmuring—I couldn't make out what they were saying, although I wasn't really trying to—and the sound of the door squeaking open and then shut. I opened my eyes. Naomi was gone, but Elliott was still standing there, his hands thrust in his pockets. He was looking at me sadly, brown hair flopping down into his face.

"I really am sorry, Lucy," he said. "I'm sorry you found out this way. This wasn't how . . . well. I didn't mean for it to happen like this."

I stared at him, as the underlying message sank in. He wasn't sorry he'd been cheating on me. He was just sorry that I found out.

"I'll leave your things out on the front porch tonight. If anything is still there in the morning, I'm going to drag it out onto the middle of the lawn, douse it with gasoline, and set fire to it," I said.

I woke up the next morning on my couch with the worst hangover of my life. The light slanting into the living room through the half-open blinds seemed insanely, painfully bright. My head was simultaneously pounding and spinning, and my tongue felt thick and woolly in my mouth. And what was that smell? I cracked one eye open. Harper Lee was sitting so that her flat black face was about an inch away from mine, staring at me intently. When she saw the signs of life, she leapt into action, squirming with happiness and lunging at me with swipes of her wide pink tongue.

"No, girl," I said feebly, holding up a hand to ward off the attack. "I can't take you out now. I'm too busy dying. And no offense, but your breath is rank."

I'd found the case of warm cheap champagne in the office when I was clearing out Elliott's things. He kept it to give to clients when they closed on a house. I pulled a bottle out, ripped the black wrapper off, popped the cork, and guzzled it straight from the bottle while I dragged Elliott's files, clothes, laptop, and even his Nordic Track—which was heavier than it looked, and a bitch to move—out of the house and dumped it all on the front porch.

Part of me resented having to pack his things, but another part of me was glad to have a goal—ridding my house of all things Elliott-related. And between the labor of moving everything and the effect of the too-sweet champagne, the anger that had been buzzing in my ears and causing my hands to shake began to burn off. By the time I was finished, I felt calm enough to decamp to the sofa with the bottle of champagne, which I proceeded to polish off. Harper Lee curled up companionably next to me. She certainly didn't seem at all upset that Elliott was gone. Maybe she'd always thought he was an asshole too.

The worst of it was that I just felt so *pathetic*. Here I was, at the age of thirty-two, alone again. No, this was even worse than alone, thanks to the humiliation factor. How much longer would it be until I decayed into a sad, lonely old woman with cats and a collection of holiday sweaters? I could picture it with terrifyingly clear detail—an orange vest with embroidered ghosts for Halloween, Santas for Christmas, intertwined hearts for Valentine's Day. Harper Lee grunted and sighed as she relaxed against me, and I amended the cat part. I'd be a sad old woman with a dog. Maybe I could get Harper Lee a baby carriage and push her up and down the street in it.

And then when people would ask to see my baby, they'd look in and see Harper Lee's sweetly homely face instead and recoil in horror. Might be fun to watch.

This much I knew: This wasn't what was supposed to happen. The fairy tales never ended with Prince Charming riding off, leaving Sleeping Beauty to fill her days buying porcelain figurines off eBay. No. Loneliness was something that happened to the sad, the misfortunate, the unlucky. I held up the bottle of champagne and toasted the room.

"Here's to me," I said, and took another swig of cheap champagne.

I did realize I was wallowing. I thought about calling Maisie, but I knew she'd insist on coming over, and I wanted to be alone. So I just sat there, numbly reviewing the events of the day and wondering how it was possible that when I woke up that morning I hadn't felt even a hint of premonition about the disaster headed my way. I remember wondering whether there was any tuna salad left in the fridge that I could bring to work for lunch or if Elliott had eaten it the day before. (He had.) And I reminded myself that I had to make an appointment to have my teeth cleaned. (Which, obviously, I forgot to do. Which was probably a good thing. Now that I was unemployed, I couldn't afford luxuries like dental hygiene.)

And then, as I sat there swilling the champagne, I started to think about money. Which immediately caused the anxiety to roil up in my stomach. I'd taught for ten years, a profession not known for making anyone rich. And even though I'd made a point of adding to my small savings account every month, there wasn't a lot in it. How much did I have in savings? I tried to remember. Five thousand? Six? No, definitely five. The last repair bill for the Volvo had come to nearly a thousand dollars, and I hadn't had enough in my checking account to cover it. Which reminded me that I'd have yet another car repair bill to deal with soon, which would shrink my savings account even more. Five thousand dollars. How long would that last? A few months? Maybe a bit longer, if I lived on ramen noodles and boxed macaroni and cheese. And what then? What would I do? What kind of work could I possibly do now that I couldn't teach? Maybe I could get a job at the bookstore. I spent so much time there, I'd gotten to know the manager. She'd probably hire me. But how much could I possibly make doing that? Minimum wage? It wouldn't be enough to pay my mortgage.

What if I end up homeless? I wondered, my anxiety kicking up into hyperdrive. *What if I can't pay my mortgage, and the bank seizes my house, and I end up turning into one of those sad, aimless souls panhandling on the street corners?*

Then sanity returned. *Get a grip*, I told myself. *You will not end up homeless. If worse comes to absolute worst, you can always move back in with Mom and Dad.*

This thought was nearly as depressing as the image of myself living on the street. And that's when I popped the cork from the second bottle of champagne.

Now, the morning after, I was facing up to the consequences of consuming one-and-a-half bottles of champagne on an empty stomach, as I hadn't eaten since the grilled cheese sandwich I'd had at Maisie's. Thinking of food made my stomach turn queasily. Meanwhile, Harper Lee wasn't giving up her one-dog crusade to get me up.

"Please," I begged her. "Can't you grow an opposable thumb and let yourself out just this one time?"

Harper Lee pounced again and made another attempt to shower me with smelly dog kisses. It was more than I could take. I gave in.

"Fine," I groaned. "Fine. I'll get up."

Somehow I managed to ease myself into a sitting position. Once the initial wave of nausea passed, I stood. Slowly, painfully, I staggered to the front door. There I made the mistake of glancing at my reflection in the large mirror that hung next to the door. I looked like nine shades of shit. My skin was so pale, it was almost green. My dark curls were mashed up one side, making my head look like a poorly trimmed shrub. My eyes were puffy and red.

And then I realized: This was what hitting bottom looked like.

But before I could dwell on this grim thought, Harper Lee began to twirl in circles and bark out a series of high-pitched yelps. I knew that bark. It meant, *If you don't let me out right this instant, I'm going to pee on the rug*. So I turned away from the mirror and opened the front door.

Harper Lee shot out past me, moving like a black streak, and headed straight for her favorite patch of grass. I staggered back a little. If I'd thought the light had been bright in the home, where it was at least partially filtered through the blinds, then I was completely unprepared for the siege of blinding white sunlight that now hit me. I lifted my hand up to shield my eyes. Elliott had come by at some point and retrieved his things off the front porch. A pity, really. I would have enjoyed a good bonfire. I've always believed that the therapeutic effects of revenge are seriously undervalued in our modern culture.

Harper Lee finished her business and went to stand at the bottom of the driveway, just next to the plastic-wrapped newspaper sitting there. This was our daily morning routine—first a pee, then I'd bring the paper in to read over breakfast, then we'd go for a walk.

And then I'd go to work.

Well, that wasn't going to happen. We needed a new routine.

"Come on, Harper Lee," I said. "I don't want the newspaper."

Harper Lee didn't move. She stood her ground and stared balefully back at me.

"The news is depressing. It's all about war, and terrorism, and rampant crime. And I can't deal with any of that right now. I'm already all stocked up on depression."

Harper Lee barked once. She wasn't going to let this go.

I sighed and staggered down the stairs and driveway in my bare feet. As I passed by the hose, which Elliott must have left out the last time he watered, I stubbed my big toe on the sprinkler.

"Ouch!" I glared at Harper Lee, who had decided to sit and wait for me. She opened her mouth, unfurled her tongue, and began to pant unrepentantly. Limping now, I made my way down to her, muttering under my breath about how nobody likes a stubborn dog. When I finally reached her, I bent over—a painful move in my condition—and picked up the newspaper.

"Happy?" I asked Harper Lee. She jumped to her feet and trotted jauntily ahead of me on our way into the house.

When I got inside, I slid the newspaper out of its plastic sock and dropped it on the kitchen counter. Moving slowly, I got out the plastic container I kept Harper Lee's dog food stored in, dumped a half cup into her bowl, filled the other bowl with water, and then switched on the coffee machine. Then, remembering I'd been too drunk to grind beans the night before, I switched off the coffeepot and poured myself a glass of water instead. I took two sips and then ran for the bathroom, where I promptly vomited up the water, along with what felt like most of the champagne.

When I finally finished throwing up—I sat for a while on the floor, resting my throbbing forehead on the cool bathtub rim—I rinsed my mouth with mint mouthwash and staggered back out to the kitchen. Harper Lee had finished wolfing down her breakfast and was now nosing around her empty bowl, searching for any stray bits of kibble she might have missed. When she was satisfied that she'd gotten it all, she turned her attention to her water bowl, drinking noisily. Finally, with a contented sigh, she padded off to her wicker-basket bed by the back door, hopped in, turned three times, and settled down for the first nap of the day.

I worked up the courage to make coffee—grinding the beans was especially painful—and while it was brewing, I stood staring out the back window, my arms wrapped around myself, trying desperately not to feel anything, to push back the dark, fetid thought bog I'd sunk into the night before.

To distract myself, I glanced down at the newspaper, despite the pledge I'd made to Harper Lee that I had no interest in reading the news. The headline at the top of the paper caught my eye:

WINNING LOTTERY TICKET SOLD LOCALLY
SOLE WINNER TAKES 87 MILLION DOLLAR JACKPOT

Huh, I thought, wondering idly if I knew the winner. It was possible—Ocean Falls wasn't exactly a teeming metropolis, even when the town swelled with snowbirds escaping the northern cold for the Florida beaches and golf courses. They were already starting to stream in, even though it was only late September.

I bet it was a snowbird who won, I thought resentfully. One of the ruddy-faced men with a closet full of green pants and salmon-pink blazers, or women with curl-set hair, coral lipstick, and lined faces set in expressions of permanent irritation. The sort who played golf all day and then went to dinner at five-thirty and knocked back three martinis before the early-bird steak special arrived at the table. The generation who'd been able to buy a four-bedroom house fifty years ago for twenty thousand dollars and then resell it at current prices for enough money to fund a retirement full of Bahamian cruises and Las Vegas vacations.

There was just enough coffee in the carafe to fill a mug. I did so, feeling a rebellious stab of pleasure. Elliott always hated it when I interrupted the brewing cycle. "You have to let the carafe fill all the way," he'd complain. "Otherwise, the first cup is too strong and the rest are too weak. They need to mix together."

"Here's to you, Elliott," I said out loud, holding my mug up in a mock salute. "You selfish, cheating piece of shit bastard."

I took a sip of coffee and began to read the story:

> An $87 million jackpot fueled record high sales of Florida Lotto tickets Wednesday, reports the Florida Lottery Commission. But it was a local Ocean Falls Quik-Rite store that sold the winning ticket with the unusual numbers: 48, 49, 50, 51, 52, and 53.
>
> "I never seen nothing like it," reports Bernice Purcell, owner of the Quik-Rite, located on Hibiscus Lane. "All of those numbers coming up right in a row like that. It was spooky."

I dropped my cup of coffee. The mug fell to the ground and shattered into a dozen pieces. Coffee splattered everywhere, pooling on the beige tile floor.

"Shit," I said, bending over reflexively to pick up the pieces. But then I stopped, stood back up, and grabbed the paper.

Surely I hadn't just read what I thought I'd read—had I? No. It wasn't possible. I was just hungover and stressed out, and my eyes were playing tricks on me. I smoothed out the paper and began to read again, this time carefully taking in every word.

But the story stayed the same. The winning numbers were 48, 49, 50, 51, 52, and 53.

I spun around and ran out into the living room. The canvas tote bag I used for a purse was still there. I had a sudden irrational fear that the ticket wouldn't be there, that I'd lost it or, even worse, somehow accidentally put it outside with Elliott's things—and he and Miss Fake Tits would walk off with my multimillion-dollar jackpot. I scrambled for my wallet, yanking it out of the bag, and riffled through it, my heart pounding.

It was there. A thin white receipt with the two sets of numbers printed in black. The computer-generated quick-pick numbers . . . and the set I'd picked: 48, 49, 50, 51, 52, 53.

"Holy shit," I whispered, slumping back against the wall, the ticket clenched in my hand. And then my legs gave out. I slid down until I was seated with my knees bent before me. I don't know how long I'd been sitting there, stunned into torpor, when the phone rang. I ignored it. But then a moment later my sister's voice over the answering machine filled the house:

"Lucy, are you there? Please pick up if you are. Something terrible has happened!"

Four

FIVE MINUTES LATER I WAS HALF-WALKING, HALF-jogging to my parents' house, still wearing the gray T-shirt and blue-and-white-striped pajama pants I'd slept in the night before. No one had picked up when I called my sister back—my sister still lived with our parents in the house we'd grown up in—and I'd actually grabbed my keys and headed to my car before remembering that the Volvo was at the shop. They lived only a couple of miles away from my house, so I decided to head there on foot.

The fear was so palpable it was practically humming through my body. What was wrong? Was it my father? I'd noticed a marked increase in the number of prescription pill bottles lined up on my parents' kitchen counter, but when I'd questioned him about it, Dad had waved me off, insisting that it was just a side effect of getting older these days.

"Blood pressure, cholesterol, that sort of thing," he'd said, shrugging. And I hadn't pressed him on it, hadn't made him tell me whether it was more serious than that.

Why didn't I make him tell me? I wondered, furious with myself for not pushing him on the subject. *What if something is seriously wrong and he didn't want to burden me with the worry?* My stomach clenched at the thought.

Or maybe it was my mother . . . but, no, that was impossible. Mom walked five miles a day and ate a disgustingly healthy diet. She couldn't possibly be sick—could she? I'd always thought of her as invincible. But what if—and suddenly my thoughts veered to a dark, scary place—something had happened to her? What if she'd fallen down the stairs? Or gotten into a car accident?

I sped up to a jog, until my pounding headache and the lack of a bra forced me to slow down to a walk again a half block later. I hadn't wanted to waste time dressing, although I did take thirty seconds to hide the lottery ticket in the freezer, stashing it inside a box of frozen waffles, in case a criminal decided to burgle my house at seven o'clock on a Thursday morning and discovered a winning lottery ticket worth eighty-seven million dollars.

Eighty-seven million dollars.

I couldn't get my mind around the surreal number. It was as though I'd woken up in someone else's life. The life of an adrenaline junkie. The sort of woman who sleeps in black lingerie, likes to film herself having sex, and dreams of becoming a contestant on a reality television show.

When I finally turned onto my parents' winding tree-lined street, from which you could catch glimpses of the Intracoastal Waterway between the houses, I was sweating heavily and seriously considering throwing up again. I didn't know the etiquette for barfing on your parents' neighbor's lawn, but it was probably best avoided, if possible, so I powered on.

My parents' house was the fifth one on the right. It was a white two-story colonial with a glossy black door and black shutters. There were the ubiquitous palm trees gathered in the front yard, along with a huge, flowering hot-pink bougainvillea and a fragrant white jasmine vine my mother had trained over an archway. I hurried up the walk and burst through the door without knocking.

"Hello? Is anyone here?" I called out.

A pack of barking, whining, howling dogs surged toward me. They ranged in size from a tiny teacup Yorkie all the way up to a tall, rangy greyhound, and as a group they were an intimidating lot. Over the years, more than one delivery man had gotten sight of the pack and, with a look of terror on his face, stopped in his tracks, dropped whatever boxes he was carrying, and sped off in the opposite direction. But I knew that the dogs—which my mom, with my dad's grudging approval, fostered until she found them good homes—were for the most part harmless. My mom had strict rules barring aggressive or dangerous dogs from the pack, although we'd all lost a fair number of shoes to our canine guests. The dogs surged around me now, grinning and wagging their tails, but I didn't stop to pet them as I normally would.

"Mom!" I called out. "Dad?"

"Lucy? Is that you?"

My mom's voice. It sounded like she was in the kitchen. Heart pounding, I hurried back there—and found Mom and Dad sitting at the breakfast table, reading the paper and drinking coffee. There was a plate of blueberry scones and a carafe of orange juice on the table. They looked up with twin expressions of surprise on their faces.

"Hi, honey," Dad said. "To what do we owe this surprise?"

My mother smiled brightly. "I'm glad you're here. Your father and I were just talking about the Humane Society's Paws and Claws Ball. I'm committee chair, and I've been trying to think up something catchy and different to do this year. What do you think about a casino theme?"

The Humane Society was one of my mother's many

causes. Every animal-welfare group in the country had her on speed dial. She also fed feral cats, patrolled the beaches for turtles' nests so they could be cordoned off, and, of course, there were the dozens upon dozens of dogs she'd fostered over the years. Harper Lee had even spent a few days as part of the pack, until I saw her and fell instantly in love. The dogs followed me into the dining room and—apparently exhausted by their guard duties—flopped onto the floor. My mother suddenly frowned, looking me over.

"Are you wearing pajamas?"

My parents were both already dressed. My dad was wearing a blue button-down shirt, charcoal-gray slacks, and a red striped tie. It was a variation of what he always wore to the office, even though he was a dental surgeon and so could wear scrubs if he wanted to. My mother had on a gray track suit with navy-blue piping on the arms and legs. Her blond-and-gray-streaked bob was smooth, and she was wearing peach lipstick.

"Emma left me a message saying there was an emergency, and no one picked up when I called back!" I said. "What's going on? Is everyone okay?"

My parents exchanged an exasperated look.

"Emma," my father said wearily.

"Everyone's fine," my mother assured me. "Emma's just . . . well, she's a bit worked up over the wedding."

Emma, my little sister, was getting married in February and had been wedding-obsessed from nearly the moment her fiancé, Christian, had slid the princess-cut solitaire diamond onto her finger.

"She's turned into a bridezilla," Dad chipped in. I looked at him, nonplussed. I had no idea he'd ever heard of the term *bridezilla*.

"No, she hasn't, Richard. She's just having a hard time

seeing the bigger picture. It happens to a lot of brides," Mom said.

My father snorted and rustled his newspaper.

Mom looked at me, her brow furrowed in concern. "Are you feeling all right, Lucy? You look a little peaked. And why are you so sweaty?"

"Because I ran over here thinking that someone's arm had fallen off or something! My car's in the shop."

"Not again! It's time you traded in that old junker for a more reliable car," Mom said. "How are you going to get to work? I suppose your father can drive you in on his way to the office. Can't you, Richard?"

"Of course," Dad said.

"So everyone's arms are firmly connected to their bodies? No one's been mauled by a renegade dog? Or been electrocuted in the bathtub?"

"Don't be so dramatic, Lucy. Everyone's fine," Mom said calmly. "Sit down and have a scone. Do you want some coffee?"

I sat. And I accepted a mug of coffee and a scone, reasoning that even if I wasn't hungry, the dense biscuit would probably soak up some of the cheap champagne still sloshing around in my system.

"What's Emma all worked up about?" I asked.

"She thinks your father has set an unreasonable budget for her wedding," Mom said.

I looked at my mother. This was the emergency? A too-low wedding budget?

"What's the budget?" I asked.

"Fifty thousand," Dad announced.

I gaped at him, then at my mom. "Fifty thousand dollars?" I repeated.

"Fifty thousand dollars," Dad said again. He looked at my

mother. "What do you think your parents spent on our wedding? I bet it was less than a thousand dollars."

"Yes, well, inflation and all of that," Mom said vaguely. Finances have never been her forte. She looked at me. "What do you think, Lucy? Is that a reasonable wedding budget?"

"Reasonable? I think fifty thousand dollars is an insanely large amount of money to spend on a wedding," I exclaimed.

Which suddenly reminded me with an electric jolt: the lottery. I hadn't told them about my winning ticket. Or about losing my job. Or about Elliott.

"Hmmm. I agree that sounds like a lot of money, but I've heard these events can get quite expensive," Mom mused.

Dad snorted. "More than this house cost thirty years ago," he said.

"That can't be true," Mom exclaimed. "Can it?"

"It most certainly is true," Dad said. He peered at me over his reading glasses. "I hope you're not here to announce that you're about to get married too. I'll have to file for bankruptcy."

"No," I said carefully, trying to ignore the painful stabbing sensation brought on by thoughts of Elliott and the engagement that would never be. I wondered if every time I looked back on our relationship, I would picture him having sex with Naomi and her fake breasts. A wave of nausea swept over me. No, I couldn't think of him, not now.

"But I do have something to tell you."

But just then, Satchel—a furry mutt of undetermined parentage—began to hump Virgil the Yorkie, causing the latter to bare his sharp little teeth and growl ferociously. Undeterred, Satchel gripped on tighter, prompting Virgil to start barking hysterically. An elderly poodle and a Corgi mix enthusiastically joined in the howling, and Mom had to wade in and separate the dogs, hushing them. Dad, meanwhile, completely oblivious to the cacophony, continued to stew about modern wedding prices.

"We may have to take out a second mortgage to pay for this event," he said. "I don't know why they can't just exchange vows on the beach and then have a clambake or something. Why does it have to be such a production?"

"I don't think Emma is the type to get married barefoot on the beach," Mom said, as she reclaimed her seat. The Yorkie padded over and hopped into her lap. Mom patted the dog absentmindedly as she took another scone from the plate.

I drew in a deep breath. "I won the lottery last night," I said. "The eighty-seven-million-dollar jackpot."

My parents stared at me for a minute, and then, unbelievably, they both began to chuckle. I stared back at them, not sure why they were laughing. Maybe they'd both been teetering dangerously close to the edge of insanity, and my lottery news had pushed them over.

Oh, my God, I thought. *I've broken my parents.*

"That would be something, wouldn't it?" Dad said, still chuckling. "But all joking aside, the winning ticket was apparently sold somewhere in town."

"I wasn't joking," I said.

"I wonder if we know who won. Wouldn't that be exciting? Maybe I could get whoever it is to make a donation to the Paws and Claws Ball. Or get them to donate a new roof for the shelter!" Mom enthused.

I looked from her to my dad, stunned into silence. I couldn't believe this. They really thought I was joking.

"Where's Emma?" I asked, pushing away from the table. My hangover seemed to be getting a second wind. It felt like my sinuses had been stuffed with cotton balls and my eyes rubbed with sand.

"She's upstairs. Go talk to her, will you? Maybe you can calm her down," Mom said.

"I'll see what I can do," I muttered, as I turned and trudged out of the kitchen.

Emma was not crying, but she was lying on her pink canopy bed with Ginger—our ancient golden retriever and the one permanent fixture in the house's ever-changing dog pack—staring up at the ceiling with a morose expression on her lovely face. Her long, glossy hair—straight and naturally blond, like Mom's—fanned around her on the frilly shams. Emma's room was much as it had been when she was thirteen: the canopy bed draped in tulle, the pink walls, the framed black-and-white prints of ballet shoes.

"Hey," I said, walking in and sitting down on the edge of the bed. Ginger snuffled and opened one eye. When she saw it was me, she closed it again, but her tail thumped in greeting.

"Hey," Emma said in a flat monotone. "What are you doing here?"

"Are you serious?"

Emma glanced up at me, her delft-blue eyes widening. "You look awful. Are you still wearing your pajamas?"

I stared at my little sister. With her doll-like features and petite yet perfectly proportioned body, she was indisputably a lovely girl. But at the moment I had no interest in admiring her beauty; I was too busy trying not to strangle her.

"Emma," I said through gritted teeth. "Are you going to tell me what's going on and why you left me that message, or should I just go ahead and kill you now?"

"You sound mad."

"Look, you psychopath: I ran all the way over here—literally ran, on foot—thinking that something really awful happened, and then when I finally get here, Mom and Dad announce that everything's fine and that the only drama going on is that you're wigging out about the budget they set for your wedding. And I can't imagine that anyone in their right mind—even you—would consider that to be an emergency," I said.

She huffed out a sigh. "Okay, fine, so maybe I overreacted just a tad."

"A tad?"

"A little," Emma agreed. She clutched a hot-pink heart-shaped throw pillow to her chest. "I just can't believe I'm still living with my parents at the age of twenty-seven."

I blinked. "What?"

She made a weary gesture, meant, I think, to incorporate her bedroom.

"I'm twenty-seven years old, and I'm still living in the same room I had when I was in high school. And I still have to ask my parents for money," Emma said sadly. "It's incredibly depressing."

Considering all that had happened in my life in the past twenty-four hours, I was having a hard time working up any real sympathy for my materialistic little sister. I lifted a hand to my throbbing temple, and was just about to leave Emma to her sulk, when Emma—clearly sensing that she was losing my interest—sat up.

"I think I'm having a quarter-life crisis," Emma announced portentously.

"A quarter-life crisis," I repeated.

"Yes. It's like a midlife crisis, but—"

"It happens when you're in your twenties. Thanks, I worked that out on my own," I said.

"I'm just feeling so blue. Like my life is looming in front of me, with all of these choices and obstacles. It's overwhelming. And then there's the wedding."

I had a feeling we would be coming back to this.

"Just so you know, I think fifty thousand dollars is an insane amount of money to spend on a party," I told her.

Emma gave me an affronted look. "Do you even know what wedding dresses cost?"

I shrugged. "A few hundred dollars?"

"Maybe at the Bridal Barn!"

"There's really a store called the Bridal Barn?" I asked. An insane image of cows and pigs wearing white tulle veils flashed through my thoughts.

"If you want a good dress, a decent dress, you have to spend thousands."

"Thousands? Is that dollars or pesos?"

Emma gave me a dirty look. "Dollars. And that's just the dress. Then there's the caterer, and the florist, and the band . . . It all adds up."

"So why don't you and Christian pay for part of it yourselves? You were just saying that being financially dependent on Mom and Dad is getting you down," I suggested.

Emma had a full-time job with benefits—she was a flight attendant, and her husband-to-be was a pilot—and for the time being, she lived rent-free in our parents' house. After the wedding, she was going to move in with Christian, who had a condo in West Palm Beach.

"I would if I could. That's the problem—I don't have any money," Emma said.

Money—the knowledge of my winning lottery ticket hit me anew. Eighty-seven million dollars: Was it possible I was going to have that much money? Just the idea . . . It was absurd, like something you daydream about but know will never really happen.

"Lucy?" Emma was staring at me, a frown creasing her face.

"What?"

"You're not listening to me!"

I dragged my thoughts away from the lottery ticket—I couldn't process that, not now that my head was pounding and it was taking all my energy to keep from slumping down onto the laced-edged comforter and groaning softly—and tried to remember the last thing I'd heard her say. Money. That was it. She said she didn't have any money.

"What do you do with all of the money you earn from your job?" I asked. But then I looked around the room, taking in the vast assortment of shopping bags, some empty, some still full. Clothes were slung haphazardly on every surface—folded over chairs, piled up on the desk—and shoes were spilling out of the closet. And Emma had never had cheap taste in anything. If I knew my little sister, she had probably shopped away every last penny she'd earned. Clothes, shoes, bags, accessories.

Emma often accused me of being economical to a fault. I had to admit, she had a point. I shopped only when I needed something, never recreationally, and even then I mostly stuck to the sales racks. I viewed clothes as a functional necessity, not something to obsess over. Of course, I never looked as fashionable as Emma. But then, I also wasn't still living with our parents. On the whole, I preferred my way of doing things.

Emma suddenly brightened. "Anyway, I've already decided I'm going to talk Daddy into not counting my wedding dress as part of the budget," she said breezily, getting up from the bed. She went over to her closet and began riffling through the truly impressive amount of clothing packed in there. "I'm having lunch with Christian's mother today. What do you think I should wear?"

Irritation and exhaustion—both emotional and physical—competed within me for top billing. I dropped my head into my hands and massaged my temples. Ginger shifted next to me to lay her golden-red head on my thigh. I stroked her ears, and the old dog closed her eyes in bliss, sighing deeply.

"I don't know and I don't care," I muttered.

Emma turned and stared at me, frowning. "What's wrong?" she demanded.

"I had a bad day yesterday."

"Why? What happened?"

"For one thing, I was fired."

"No!" Emma gasped.

"And, on a somewhat related note, I was accused of sexually propositioning a student."

"Are you *serious?*"

"Then . . ." I took in a deep breath, as sharp stabs of pain hit me. "Then I walked in on Elliott having sex with another woman in our bed."

Emma was so overcome by the magnitude of this announcement, she forgot about her wardrobe concerns and sat down heavily next to me on her bed. Her round eyes were wide with shock, and her mouth gaped open a little. And then, unexpectedly, she put an arm around me and pulled me into a hug. Emma was not a physically demonstrative person, so this impulse first surprised me—and then moved me to tears. I hadn't thought I was going to cry any more. At least not over Elliott. But then, I don't think the tears were for him. Rather, I was crying for my old life, which was now suddenly, irrevocably, gone.

"Are you okay? No, of course you're not okay," Emma said, patting my head. "But you will be."

"You think?" I sniffed.

"I know," she said. And she sounded so sure, I almost believed her.

Five

I ASKED MY DAD TO DROP ME OFF AT THE CAR-RENTAL agency on his way in to work, and twenty minutes later I drove myself home in a dark-blue Honda Accord. I hadn't told Emma about the lottery ticket, nor had I tried to convince my parents that I wasn't joking. In a few days I'd take them all out to a celebratory dinner and tell them then. Surely the lottery commission would provide me with some sort of paperwork I could use as evidence. Maybe they'd even present me with one of those giant cardboard checks. I pictured myself showing up at the next family dinner with it tucked under my arm, and even in my current state, I couldn't help a small smile.

I needed to focus on getting myself together, cashing in the ticket, and figuring out what the hell I was going to do with the rest of my life. My late grandmother—my mother's mother, and one of my favorite people of all time—was fond of saying, "When a door closes, a window always opens." I wasn't sure what lay ahead of me, but eighty-seven million dollars should open a hell of a lot of windows.

First things first. I'd have to collect the money. And deposit the check. And hire a financial adviser. Maybe more than one financial adviser, in case one was a screwup or decided to run off to the Caymans with my money. The very idea was so weird. Having your financial adviser flee to the islands with your fortune was something that rich people had to worry about. It was not the sort of issue that comes up much when you're a high school teacher living paycheck to paycheck. What would I be fretting about next? That my new Brazilian playboy boyfriend was only trying to marry me for my money in order to fund his polo hobby?

When I got home, I greeted Harper Lee, who leaped and bounded around me as though it had been weeks since we'd last seen each other. Then I headed back to the office, which now looked depressingly bare with all of Elliott's belongings cleared out. Despair began to well in my chest, but I forced it down. *I am not going to think about Elliott,* I told myself sternly.

I sat at my desk, switched on the computer, and waited for the chiming sound it made when it was up and running. I pulled up the Internet browser, Googled the Web site for the Florida Lottery, and, once I'd found it, navigated to the frequently-asked-questions page. I began to read.

The rules were clear: In order to claim my prize, I had to go to the Florida Lottery headquarters, which was located across the state in Tallahassee. It was a six-hour drive from Ocean Falls to the state capital. Forget that, I thought. I was in no condition to tackle a road trip. But such was the beauty of the modern world—with just a few more clicks of the mouse, I was able to purchase a ticket on Continental Airlines, leaving that afternoon for a nonstop flight to Tallahassee.

I sat back in my seat. My hangover was starting to fade, or at least the nausea was going away. My head was still throbbing. And, when I allowed my mind to wander, the events of the previous day would start to flash into my thoughts, bringing back a surge of anger mixed with grief and disbelief.

Just focus on the next task in front of you, I told myself sternly.

So I showered. I shampooed and conditioned my hair. I brushed and flossed my teeth. I rubbed sunscreen on my face and applied mascara to my lashes and balm to my lips. I dressed in a short-sleeved rose sweater and khaki pants. I packed an overnight bag. Finally, I called Maisie.

"Would you mind watching Harper Lee for me tonight?" I asked when she answered the phone. The background noise of her house sounded chaotic, as usual—the boys were whooping, Fang was barking, the cable news was turned up to full volume.

"Sure," Maisie said immediately. Then, suspicion creeping into her voice, she added, "Why? What are you doing?"

"I just have to go out of town for the night," I said evasively. My mom would have been happy to babysit Harper Lee—what was one more dog among the pack—but I knew Maisie would ask fewer questions. I had considered telling Maisie the truth about where I was going and why, but I felt a little weird about it, knowing the financial strain she and Joe were under. I'd tell her eventually, of course . . . just not now. Better to wait until I'd had a chance to fully absorb the news myself.

"You're not suicidal, are you?" she asked sharply.

"What?" I was so surprised, I laughed. "No, of course not. Why would you ask me that?"

"Because you just lost your job yesterday. And now you sound a little out of it."

"Sorry. Hangover."

"I don't blame you. I'd have gotten drunk too," Maisie said. "Where's Elliott? Why can't he watch Harper Lee?"

My thoughts were so tangled up, I'd forgotten that Maisie didn't know about Elliott. "He's... well. I'm not sure where he is. We broke up last night."

Maisie gasped. "What? What happened?"

I knew there was no way around this one and that, if I tried to evade her, it would just bring out the prosecutorial pit bull in Maisie. So, even though it was the last thing I felt like talking about, I told her about walking in on Elliott and Naomi going at it in my bedroom.

"Bastard! The fucking bastard!" she shrieked. "Whoops. Boys, you didn't hear what Mommy just said, did you?"

"Bastard!" I heard the twins yelling in the background. "Bastard!"

"Oh, crap," Maisie muttered. "Hold on, Lucy. Hey, guys, if you go in the other room and forget that you heard Mommy say that word, I'll let you have some cookies." There was a rustling sound and shouts of exultation, and then Maisie was back. "Sorry, hon. I just bought them off with sugar. Am I the Mother of the Year or what? Look, why don't you come over here. Put off your mysterious trip for a few days, and let us take care of you. We have cookies! And red wine!" she said temptingly.

Despite the nauseated lurch that shuddered through me at the mention of alcohol, I felt a rush of warmth for my friend. "I love that you asked, but I can't put this off. It's sort of... important."

"Important, hmmm? Well, clearly you're not going to tell me, but at least promise me you're not hiring a hit man to take out Elliott. Not that I'd miss him, mind you, but I don't want you ending up in jail for the rest of your life. He's so not worth it."

"I promise I'm not hiring a hit man," I said, laughing again. This was another thing I loved about Maisie: She could make me laugh, even when my heart was breaking. "And I will tell you all about it when I get back."

"Okay, then. Drop off Harper Lee. The boys will be thrilled to have her, as will Fang," Maisie said.

"Thanks, Maisie. I owe you big," I said.

"I know," she said cheerfully. "And someday I'll make you pay by forcing you to babysit the two horrors while Joe and I take off for a romantic weekend."

"You've got it," I said sincerely. "Anytime."

Maisie just laughed. "Lucky for you we can't afford it, or else I'd hold you to that."

The Florida Lottery headquarters was housed in a nondescript state-government building in downtown Tallahassee, which I found fairly easily, aided by the map the car-rental agency had given me. I don't know what I'd expected—dollar signs etched on the glass doors or a burbling champagne fountain—but when I got inside it looked a lot like the motor-vehicles office in Ocean Falls where I went to file my car registration. Industrial-tile floor, pale-green walls, indestructible gray plastic chairs in the waiting area. A receptionist sat behind a faux-wood desk, working on a sudoku puzzle. She looked up when I came in.

"May I help you?" she asked, peering up at me through purple-framed bifocals perched on the end of her nose.

I drew in a deep breath. "Yes, I think so. I . . . well, I . . . won the lottery last night," I said haltingly. And I held out my ticket to her.

It all happened quickly. The receptionist escorted me to a conference room, where she deposited me at one end of a long table surrounded on all sides by black chairs, then left to find someone official to take care of me. A few minutes later another woman, a pretty redhead with milky white skin and wearing a charcoal-gray suit, came in.

"Congratulations, Ms. Parker," she said. Her lipstick was dark red, and there was a beauty mark just to the right above her lip. "My name is Mary Sylvester. I'll be walking you through your claim procedure today."

"Hi," I said. "Thanks."

"Yesterday must have been a very exciting day for you," Mary Sylvester said.

"Well..." I was about to explain that I hadn't found out about my winning ticket until that morning, but suddenly my mouth felt unusually dry. Too dry to launch into a long, drawn-out explanation about lost jobs, harassment allegations, cheating boyfriends, and champagne binges. I distantly realized that my hands were shaking. I folded them in my lap, nodded, and said, "Yes," in such a faint voice that Ms. Sylvester smiled.

"Don't worry. This is pretty painless. And at the end we'll be handing you a check for an enormous amount of money, so it's worth your while," she said.

I smiled back at her and felt foolish. "At least one of us has been through this before," I said. "I'm sorry. I don't know why I feel so freaked out. I mean... this is a good thing, right? An amazing thing."

"That's right. And you're doing great," she said. "Some people cry. I've even seen a few faint. One man had chest pains when he received his check. We thought he was having a heart attack and had to call an ambulance."

"Oh, no! Was he okay?"

"Yes, he was fine. And you will be too," Ms. Sylvester said reassuringly.

It was the second time that day someone had told me this. I wondered if I looked like as big of a wreck as I felt. I just wasn't used to having this much drama in my life. And in the past thirty-six hours, I'd been doing emotional loop-de-loops. At least I wasn't having a heart attack; that was something.

While I filled out the paperwork, Ms. Sylvester took down the details from my driver's license and then explained that I had two choices: I could take the payout in thirty yearly installments or I could opt for a one-time adjusted payment that would come out to roughly thirty-four-point-four million dollars after taxes. I thought about it for a minute, but my head was so woolly I was finding it hard to do the math.

"The one-time payment," I finally said, although I wasn't sure if this was the better of the two options. I wished I'd thought to bring my dad with me. He'd have known which I should choose.

"Fine," Mary said. "This one last paper is a release form for publicity purposes."

"Publicity?" I asked. Unease pricked at me.

She nodded. "We'd like to put a photo of you receiving your check on our Web site. And some of our former winners, especially big-jackpot winners like yourself, have agreed to be featured in television commercials. Most of them have had a positive experience with it, I think. It's a lot of fun."

But I didn't need any time to think this one over. "No, I

definitely don't want to do any of that," I said firmly. "I'd like to keep all of my information private."

"Well . . ." Mary hesitated. "We're legally obligated to disclose your name and hometown to anyone who requests it."

"That's fine," I said, although I really preferred to keep that private too.

"Are you sure?" Mary asked. "We wouldn't use your picture in a negative way. Our publicity people are always very respectful."

I distinctly remembered a commercial for the Florida Lottery that had featured a jackpot winner jumping feetfirst into a pool filled with dollar bills instead of water, a look of crazed glee stretched across her plump face.

"Yes," I said. "I'm sure."

"All right, then. We just have to verify the authenticity of your ticket before we can give you your check," Mary said.

"Okay," I said, wondering how they went about doing this. Images straight out of the crime-scene TV shows Elliott had been so addicted to flashed through my head—men and women dressed in immaculate white coats peering at my lottery ticket through complicated stainless-steel microscopes before running it through some sort of genetic spinning machine.

I waited for a long time while they made sure I hadn't forged the ticket. When Mary Sylvester finally returned, there was a man with her. He looked like a politician, with his carefully groomed dark wavy hair, yellow tie, and navy-blue suit.

"Hello, Lucy," he said. When he smiled, a dimple appeared in his right cheek. "I'm Bob Newton, the Florida Lottery secretary. And this"—he handed over a check to me—"is for you."

I stared down at it. The check had my name on it—and was made out for the amount of $34,438,521.82.

Holy shit, I thought, staring down at it. *$34,438,521.82.*

"Congratulations," Bob Newton said.

"Congratulations," Mary Sylvester echoed.

"Thanks," I said. My lips felt dry. I licked them, but it just seemed to dry them out even more.

"Any plans on what you're going to do with all that money?" Bob Newton asked.

"No," I said. "No plans at all."

And as I spoke, I had the sudden sensation that I had jumped from a very high altitude and was free-falling through the air.

I didn't sleep much that night. After I left the lottery headquarters, I checked in to a hotel I'd noticed on my way in from the airport. It was a standard business traveler's hotel—corporate and anonymous. The carpets and matching drapes were an ugly sea-foam green. The bed was comfortable; the pillows were not. I'd finished my book on the plane, so I sat up in bed, propped against the lumpy pillows, and watched a movie on TV. It was entertaining in a mindless way, which was all that I was up for. And afterward, when I finally did fall asleep, it was fitful and unrestful. I was already awake and dressed when my wake-up call came in the morning.

The flight back to West Palm—the nearest commercial airport to Ocean Falls—was mercifully short. And when I finally got to Ocean Falls, driving north in the blue Honda Accord rental, I headed straight to my bank.

I thought about going to the drive-through but then decided that depositing a thirty-four-point-four-million-dollar check probably called for a visit to the counter. Or maybe even one of those managers' desks lined up on one side of the bank.

The bank was quiet. There was only one person queued up ahead of me, an elderly man in golf clothes who had liver spots covering his shiny bald head. I glanced over at the desks, off to the right of the lobby. They were empty.

"May I help the next customer," the single cashier said in a bored voice. The elderly man shuffled slowly over to her window.

I waited while they transacted his business. A young mother came in, accompanied by her two young sons, and lined up behind me. The younger boy began hanging off the velvet ropes that marked off the area.

"Quit it," the mother said. "Wyatt, you'd better behave yourself or no *Backyardigans* when we get home!"

"You always say that," the older boy muttered. "But you never mean it. You always end up letting him watch."

"Well, I mean it now," the mother said menacingly. The younger boy, evidently not believing her, continued to hang off the rope.

"I'm a monkey!" he chirruped. "Look, Ma! Oo oo oo!"

His mother looked pointedly in the opposite direction.

"May I help the next customer in line," the teller said.

"I think she means you," the mom said to me, her voice sharp. I started and realized she'd caught me watching her.

I turned and quickly walked over to the teller. She was a bit older than me and was carrying an extra forty pounds on her short, square frame. Her features were small for her fleshy round face, although she had lovely eyes—blue and slanted with thickly fringed lashes.

"I have a check to deposit," I said. "But—"

"Into checking or savings?" she asked, cutting me off.

"Savings," I said. "But—"

"Did you fill out a deposit slip?"

"Yes, but the thing is, the check is rather large," I said.

The teller gave me a pitying look. *It may be a large amount to you,* the look said, *but I am a bank professional. I probably handle more money in one day than you make in a year.*

"I assure you, whatever the amount is, I am more than qualified to take care of it," she said. She put her hand out. Her palm was plump, and her fingers were stubby and tipped with long red nails.

Silently, I handed her the check and my deposit slip. She took them, snapped them down on the counter, and it was only when her fingers were poised over the keyboard, ready to enter in the total, that she stopped to look at the amount of the check. Her jaw dropped open.

"What the—" She leaned forward, peering down at the numbers. Then she gaped up at me. I smiled pleasantly.

"Is this supposed to be a joke?" she asked, scowling at me.

"No," I said. "I told you it was a large amount."

"Excuse me," she said. She turned, picked up a phone, and, after a moment, began muttering into the receiver. Then she turned back to me. "Mr. Culpepper, our bank manager, will be out to help you in a minute."

Unspoken were the words, *And then you're going to get it.* As though Mr. Culpepper were some sort of a bank ninja who would come cartwheeling in, legs kicking, arms karate-chopping, ready to take out anyone who wasted his teller's time.

"Thank you," I said. I stepped to one side so the teller could help the mom of the little boys, both of whom were now hanging off the rope, pretending to be monkeys. The cashier's large blue eyes kept sliding toward me and then at my check—which she'd kept—and then back at me again.

I had to wait only a moment before Mr. Culpepper came out of the office behind the lines of desks. He was fortyish and baldish, with an affable sunburned face. He wore a blue polo shirt tucked into pleated chinos, which made him look more like a golf pro than a bank manager.

"Yes, Angela, what is it?" he asked the teller.

She handed the check underneath the Plexiglas shield, which he took. I saw him glance at the amount typed out on the check. His eyes widened ever so slightly.

"It's a joke, right?" the teller asked aggressively.

"No, I don't think so," Mr. Culpepper replied. He pointed to the state agency typed at the top of the check.

"The lottery?" Angela squeaked, her eyes opening wide. She stared up at me, her mouth open. I could feel my cheeks flushing, but I smiled serenely at her.

The bank manager also turned to look at me, but he managed to maintain his professional decorum. "Please come right this way," he said, waving his hand in a flourish.

"Where are we going?" I asked.

"Back to my office," Mr. Culpepper said. He smiled broadly. "We handle all of our VIP clients back there. Just so you know in the future."

"Oh . . . okay."

"Would you like coffee? Tea? Pellegrino?"

"No, thanks," I said.

I had the feeling that Mr. Culpepper was expecting me to be impressed with this more personalized approach to my banking. I wasn't. In fact, after spending ten minutes in his corporate beige office, listening to him drone on about the various financial-advising services the bank offered, I was starting to think I'd made a mistake not going to the drive-through.

"No, really," I said finally. "I'm not sure what I'm going to do with the money yet. Right now I just want to deposit the check somewhere safe while I decide."

I had to say this three more times and assure him yet

again that, yes, I understood I wouldn't have access to the money until the check cleared and, no, I really and truly didn't want a Pellegrino, before the bank manager finally allowed me to leave. As I hurried through the eerily quiet bank lobby, I could feel the teller's eyes resting heavily on me. She'd been joined by two other employees, a young man and an older woman I hadn't seen before, and they were staring at me too. And suddenly all I wanted, more than anything, was to pick up Harper Lee, go home, change into sweats, and collapse on the couch. I'd been in the spotlight enough for three days. It wasn't a comfortable sensation.

Six

FOUR DAYS LATER, ALL HELL BROKE LOOSE.

I later found out that it was all started by a bored reporter on a slow news day. His name was Mitch Hannigan, and he was a prematurely bald, twice-divorced semialcoholic who normally worked the crime beat for the *Palm Beach Post*. But there wasn't any crime that day—or, at least, there weren't any interesting crimes. Just the usual gang violence, domestic squabbles, and nickel-and-dime drug busts. So Hannigan killed the time before cocktail hour by calling some of his contacts around the state—reporters at other papers, government lackeys, even a loan shark he knew—to see if there was any buzz floating around. The sort of buzz he could grab hold of and dress up into a real story. And it was in this way—not from the loan shark, but from one of the government lackeys—that Hannigan found out that the sole winner of Wednesday's eighty-seven-million-dollar Florida jackpot had claimed her money but had refused to allow the lottery office to release any personal information about her to the press. Not so much as a snapshot of her grinning as she accepted an enormous cardboard check. This was, apparently, unusual; most lottery winners welcomed their fifteen minutes of fame.

Sensing that there might be a story there, Hannigan began to dig. I have no idea how hard it was for him. Finding out that I'd been a teacher at Andrews Prep probably wasn't too difficult; my name and picture were still up on the school's Web site. Finding out that I'd been fired—and the reason why—must have been harder. Dr. Johnson didn't condone the Andrews Prep staff speaking to the press about school matters. But somehow he managed it. Maybe one of my former colleagues broke rank to tell him the salacious school gossip.

Or maybe it was Matt Forrester, taking one last vindictive swipe at me.

The night before everything exploded, I didn't sleep well. I knew why: Guilt was draped over me like a too-hot blanket. I hadn't yet told my family or friends about my lottery winnings. I didn't understand why exactly I was hiding it from them, since I knew everyone was worried about me. Emma had told my parents about my job and Elliott but when my mother called, I told her I wasn't ready to talk about it, buying myself more time before I had to face up to this new life I'd been thrust into.

Telling them would have made it real. All of it, not just the money. And I had been living in a bubble of denial ever since I returned from Tallahassee. I stayed holed up at home with Harper Lee, wearing sweats, eating ice cream straight from the container, screening my phone calls, and watching the never-ending parade of cooking shows, which for some reason I found soothing. I'd never been much of a cook. Maybe it was something I could take up now that I had all this money . . . and all this time.

I had talked to a financial manager the day before. One of my dad's golfing buddies, Mel O'Donnell, a former broker, had given me the referral. Mel hadn't questioned why a high school teacher needed a high-end financial whiz, but then, I had been deliberately evasive, insinuating that the referral was for a friend. In any event, Mel said that Peter Graham, located in Palm Beach, was one of the best financial strategists in the area.

Peter Graham had been professional and to-the-point when I talked to him on the phone. I had an instant picture of an elegant older man sitting behind a heavy mahogany desk, with gilt-framed oil paintings of hunt scenes hanging on the walls of his wood-paneled office.

"What we need to do is sit down face-to-face, talk over your long- and short-term goals, and then draw up a plan for your future," he said.

"Great," I said, wondering if my plans to watch an Emeril marathon on the Food Network counted as a long- or a short-term goal.

"How soon can you come in?" Peter asked. I could hear him typing on a computer. "How's next week for you?"

We set up an appointment for the following Friday, and then I returned to my favorite spot on the sofa, pulled an afghan over my knees, and lost myself in a haze of television. I spent the rest of the day there, getting up periodically to refill my water glass or let Harper Lee out to relieve herself. Despite my Food Network TV obsession, I hadn't been eating particularly well. Dinner that night was a Fluffernutter on stale whole wheat bread and the last dregs of a bag of potato chips. And then I went to bed and slept fitfully.

* * *

When I woke up, there was a phalanx of reporters camped out on my front lawn.

I hadn't known the press was out there. It did seem to be noisier outside than usual when I jolted awake, sitting bolt upright in bed, my pulse skittering. It took me a few deep breaths to calm down.

Bad dream, I told myself. It was just a bad dream.

In it, I'd walked in on Elliott screwing Naomi. (They might claim to be in love, but to me it was the harsh verbs—*screwing, fucking, banging*—that I'd walked in on; nothing as romantic as *making love* or even *sleeping together*.) But in my dream, they didn't stop when I opened the door. They just kept going at it while I stood there staring at them, frozen in place, and when they finally finished—a noisy, headboard-banging finale—Elliott informed me that he had just won the lottery and was going to use the money to buy Naomi a boob job. That was when I woke up.

Eventually, my breathing returned to normal and my body relaxed. At first I could hear voices outside and the sound of car engines starting and stopping. Harper Lee crouched at the edge of the bed with her shoulders hunkered up, growling softly. Suddenly the phone rang, causing me to jump. I fumbled for the handset and looked at the caller ID. The number was blocked, which meant it was a telemarketer, some asshole hoping to catch me half asleep so he could talk me into changing my long-distance service or signing up for a new credit card.

I hit the talk button. "Aren't there rules about how early you people are allowed to call?"

"Ms. Parker, this is Mitch Hannigan from the *Palm Beach Post*. I'd like to ask you a few questions."

"I already have a subscription to the paper," I said irritably.

I hung up on him. The phone rang again. Again, it was an ID-blocked number. I picked up, hung up, and then turned off the ringer.

Damned telemarketers. They all belong in hell, alongside terrorists and cheating boyfriends. I stared up at my ceiling, and wondered if I'd be able to fall back asleep. But Harper Lee was stirring restlessly—she kept turning in circles, a sure indicator she had to go to the bathroom—and then there was the racket outside.

What the hell is going on out there? Could one of the neighbors be having a party? I wondered. *Surely it's too early.* I glanced at the clock. It was only 7:04, definitely too early for a backyard barbecue.

Harper Lee growled again. The fur behind her neck had ruffled up in indignation at the ruckus.

"Okay, killer, settle down," I told her. "Shall we go investigate?"

Harper Lee obediently leapt from the bed and stood at the bedroom door. Her ears were pricked up, and her muscular little body was tense. Moving quite a bit slower, I got up out of bed, shrugged on my favorite old green terry bathrobe, and headed toward the front door, Harper Lee prancing along beside me. I opened the door—and my jaw dropped open.

Just outside my door, standing on my porch and spilling down onto the walkway, was a crowd of people. Some of them were wearing suits and holding microphones, others were dressed in T-shirts and jeans and had cameras hoisted up on their shoulders. Beyond, parked by the street, there was a fleet of white news vans. There was the briefest of moments where I stared out at them through sleep-fogged eyes and they stared back at me. And then, moving as one, they pressed forward and began to shout.

"Ms. Parker, is it true that you sexually harassed one of your students?"

"Are you worried that the student will sue you for your lottery jackpot?"

"How do you respond to the anger on the part of some that you were allowed to claim a multimillion-dollar jackpot in light of the accusations that have been made against you?"

"Ms. Parker, is this the first time you've been accused of soliciting sex from a student?"

I might have stood there forever, rooted to the spot in horror and mortification. But then Harper Lee began to bark, throwing her head back and baring her teeth in such an uncharacteristic display of ferocity, I worried that she might bite one of the reporters thrusting a microphone in my face. I knelt down, scooped her up in my arms, stepped back into the house, and slammed the door shut. I stood there for a minute, leaning back against the door, my breath rasping loudly. The reporters were still shouting, their voices only barely muffled by the door.

"Is there any truth to the rumors that you're pregnant?"

"How common is it for teachers to have sex with their male students? Is this an isolated occurrence or a cultural phenomenon?"

"Ms. Parker, how does it feel to be known as the Lottery Seductress?"

I blinked and shook my head, like a horse trying to dislodge a fly. This didn't work; the reporters were still out there, still screaming questions at me. Harper Lee continued to howl with outrage, her barks drowning out the yells of the reporters. And yet I just stood there, utterly dazed, wondering how it was possible that this was my life.

* * *

My parents arrived an hour later. The police had shown up by then and marshaled the press off my property. The reporters didn't leave, though; instead, they milled about on the sidewalk, trampling the petunias I'd planted at the edge of my lawn over the summer.

I stood at the window, peeking out through a starched cotton curtain, and watched as one of the officers escorted my mother and father up the front walk, while the press shouted questions at them. My father was holding my mother's elbow, and they both looked pale and stricken. I was at the door, opening it just wide enough for them to enter, before they had a chance to press the doorbell.

I heard one of the reporters' voices, loud and carrying over the rest, yell out, "How does it feel to have a sex offender for a daughter?"

"Jesus, Mary, and Joseph," my mother said, turning to look back at the reporters. Thankfully my dad was there to shoo her inside, and I was able to slam the door.

My parents and I stared at one another for a moment. I was suddenly acutely aware of the fact that I hadn't yet dressed or brushed my teeth.

"Lucy," Mom finally said. "What in heaven's name is going on?"

I bit back the hysterical impulse to start joking. *What do you mean what's going on? It's just a typical Tuesday in the life of Lucy Parker, the Lottery Seductress.* But I managed to restrain myself, for my father's sake more than anything. I'd never seen him look so shaken; he seemed smaller, as though the shock of seeing his daughter featured on the morning news had caused him to spontaneously shrink.

They had seen the news, of course. I'd watched a few minutes of it earlier, before shutting it off in disgust. The story that a disgraced local teacher had won the lottery was on every channel, accompanied by an unflattering photo of me taken from last year's school yearbook, while grim-faced anchors used words like, *serious allegations of sexual misconduct, multimillion-dollar jackpot*, and—my personal favorite—*as of yet, no comment from Lucy Parker*.

"So, I have some news," I said instead.

"You weren't joking when you told us you won the lottery," Dad said.

"No. I wasn't joking."

"And . . . it's true what Emma said? You were fired because a student claimed you sexually harassed him?" Mom asked faintly.

I nodded. "He was angry about a low grade he received, so he made up a story about how I'd offered to change the grade if he'd have sex with me."

"But that doesn't make any sense," Mom protested. "Why would your school fire you just on the word of a student?"

"The kid, Matt Forrester, is from a really wealthy family that's donated a lot of money to Andrews Prep over the years. I think they were worried that if they didn't fire me to placate his parents, the donations would dry up."

"But . . . but . . ." My mother struggled to get the words out, before she cleared her throat. "You really won eighty-seven million dollars?"

I nodded. "Yes. Well, sort of. I opted for a one-time payout, which reduced the total amount quite a bit, and then I had to pay taxes."

"So . . . ?" Dad began, but then stopped. He and my mother looked at each other and then back at me. I knew what it was they wanted to ask me.

"Thirty-four-point-four million dollars and change," I said

succinctly. It struck me as particularly ludicrous that I was in a position to refer to thirty-eight thousand dollars—roughly an entire year's teaching salary—as change.

"Thirty-four-point-four million dollars," Mom repeated. And then she swayed suddenly, so that my father had to grab on to her elbow again to steady her.

"I think maybe we'd better sit down. And then you can start over from the beginning and tell us everything," Dad said.

"Okay. But you know most of it," I said, shrugging. "I was accused of sexually harassing a student. And then I was fired. And then I won the lottery. And then the press found out about it. That pretty much brings us up to date. Oh, wait—Emma told you that Elliott and I broke up because I found out he was cheating on me, right?"

They nodded in unison.

"Then that's pretty much everything," I said lightly. I had no idea where this bravado was coming from. It was almost as though I were observing the whole nightmare from somewhere outside my body. I knew that I should feel horrified, should act horrified, considering that my entire life was falling down around me like a tower of toy blocks. But all I could muster up was a bemused distant interest.

"I think we should all sit down," Dad said again. He patted me on the shoulder. "I'll make a pot of coffee. And then we'll figure it all out."

"Okay. But I can make the coffee. I'm fine, really," I said.

My parents exchanged another look. I could tell they didn't believe me. It didn't occur to me until later, much later, that they were worried I was in shock—and that they were probably right.

* * *

I thought the press would get tired of sitting outside my house for hours on end. I was wrong. Not only did they not leave, but their ranks seemed to swell. More vans pulled up, and more reporters and photographers climbed out, carrying heavy-looking cameras and clutching paper cups of coffee. Some of the reporters stood off to one side, holding microphones and speaking directly into the camera. I didn't have to wonder what they were saying—all I had to do was turn on the television, and I could hear them updating the viewers on what they knew of the story. There were also reporters stationed at Andrews Prep, interviewing students and even a few parents. Most of those interviewed expressed concern; *very serious allegations* seemed to be the favorite sound bite. However, a few of my students did go on camera to defend me.

"There's no way Ms. Parker would ever do something like that," Amanda Franklin said. Amanda was a painfully shy sophomore—she was overweight and had terrible acne—and the bravery it must have taken for her to speak out on live television reduced me to tears for the first time that day.

But despite the scattering of support here and there, I had, overnight it seemed, turned into the town harlot.

"When it comes to these sorts of allegations, I believe a person is guilty until proven innocent," one of the interviewed fathers said, his jaw tight and his eyes flashing with anger.

I recognized him. It was Xander Lawrence's father. I'd had Xander in class last year. When he came down with mono, I'd stopped off at the Lawrences' house to drop off the books we were reading in class so that Xander wouldn't fall too far behind. Mr. and Mrs. Lawrence had seemed genuinely grateful at the time, thanking me over and over again.

"I'm horrified," a mother I didn't recognize said from behind the wheel of her Lexus SUV. The reporter was interviewing her right in the middle of the car line. "We trust the school to protect our children, and then we find out a child molester is teaching them."

Child molester. The ugly words hit me like a gut punch.

"It will all blow over," Dad said soothingly. He had taken the day off from work. He probably had no choice, I thought. The press would just camp out in his waiting room, scaring away all of his patients.

"You think so?" I asked.

"Yes," he said. "The boy's parents said they had no plans to press charges, right? Not," he hurried to add, "that there are any grounds for the allegations in the first place."

"That doesn't mean anything. It's my word against Matt Forrester's," I said bitterly. "And you heard that father. I'm guilty until proven innocent."

"I can't believe that after the ten years you've worked there, that school wouldn't back you up," Mom said hotly.

I shrugged. "I guess I see their point. What if it was true? Even if they couldn't prove it, wouldn't it be irresponsible of them to let me loose around kids again?"

Just saying this out loud made me shudder. My dad saw and hurriedly refilled my coffee cup.

"No," he said firmly. "What's irresponsible is ruining someone's life when there isn't a shred of evidence against that person."

"Well . . ." Mom said. "Lucy's life isn't exactly *ruined*."

"No, of course it isn't," Dad said quickly.

"I mean, thirty-four million dollars," Mom said. "That much money could buy a lot of happiness. Think of what she could do with that much money." My mom suddenly inhaled sharply and turned to face me, her eyes gleaming almost maniacally. "Lucy!"

"What?" I asked, startled.

"You could build a shelter! A no-kill shelter! The Humane Society doesn't have the funds to keep all of the stray dogs and cats indefinitely. But you could!" she announced triumphantly.

I stared back at my mother, utterly speechless. What could I say? Her dream of a no-kill shelter was a noble one. And of course I wanted to use this money to do something meaningful. But building an animal shelter—that was my mother's dream, not mine. And as much as I didn't want to disappoint her, I also wasn't ready to commit to such a huge project. My life had been turned so upside down, I was just barely managing to keep on top of brushing my teeth. My dad seemed to sense what I was feeling, for he quickly stepped in to save me.

"Kay," he said gently. "This is Lucy's money. We can't pressure her on how she should use it. She's under enough stress as it is." He nodded in the direction of my street, where the unrelenting press was clearly audible.

"But Lucy loves animals," Mom protested.

"Of course I do. And of course I'll donate some of the money to your rescue organizations," I said quickly, hoping to mollify her. "But I haven't thought through . . . I just . . . I don't know what I want to do yet." Suddenly I felt incredibly tired and overwhelmed. It seemed to take all of my energy to keep my head up. I sat down heavily on the sofa and pressed one hand to my forehead.

"Sweetheart, are you all right?" Mom asked. She rubbed circles on my back, the way she used to when I was a child.

"It's a lot to take in," I said faintly.

"You should talk to a financial adviser," Dad suggested. "Someone who can keep the money safe for you until you decide what you want to do with it."

"I have an appointment with a financial consultant next week." I looked at my dad. "Mel O'Donnell recommended him. I hope you don't mind that I called Mel without speaking to you about it first."

"Of course not. It's exactly whom I would have asked," Dad said approvingly. "I shouldn't have worried. You've always been a sensible girl. Now if it was Emma . . ." He looked at my mother.

"Oh, dear. *Emma.*" Mom shook her head. "Wait until she hears about this. She'll be after you to fund the Wedding of the Year. I wouldn't be surprised if she tries to book Madonna to play at her reception."

I laughed. That would be just like Emma.

"I should pay for her wedding, though," I said.

"Absolutely not," Dad said, so sharply that Mom and I both looked at him in surprise.

"Why not?" I asked.

"We're her parents. We'll pay for her wedding," Dad said stubbornly. "I don't want you wasting your money."

"Dad, it's a lot of money. One wedding isn't going to make much of a dent in it."

"No. I want you to save that money for something important. Something meaningful," he said.

I could tell from my mom's wistful expression that she was still envisioning a state-of-the-art animal shelter with my name blazoned across the front.

"You've been given a rare opportunity, sweetheart," Dad continued, his brown eyes intent on mine. "The chance to make your life whatever you want it to be. Please don't squander it."

"Okay, Dad," I said. "I won't squander it. I promise."

My dad smiled at me. Relief transformed his face, making him look years younger. I tried to remember when his hair had gone from brown with touches of gray to gray with touches of brown. I didn't know why it was so important to him to pay for Emma's wedding—or, perhaps, why it was so important to him that I didn't pay for it. But it started to dawn on me that this money was going to complicate every area of my life.

After my parents finally left, I started to prowl around the house, feeling caged. I couldn't go out, not with the press surging around. And I couldn't use my phone. When the reporters weren't calling, tying up the line, random strangers were getting through and leaving messages on my answering machine. Some called to request investment money. They had an invention that would make us both rich and just needed the seed money to get started, or they knew of some land for sale in Texas that was guaranteed to be oil-rich. Others had sad stories of sick children and unpaid hospital bills. One woman talked at length about her little girl who was on the transplant list for a new heart, until she broke down sobbing in the middle of her message. I wrote down her name and telephone number and decided that when I met Peter Graham, I'd ask him the best way to go about helping some of these people. Maybe he would know how to sort those who were in real need from the shysters.

More disturbing were the threatening messages I received.

"They should lock people like you up and throw away the key," one intoxicated woman slurred over my answering machine.

And then there was the creepy man whose low voice caused the hair to rise on the back of my neck: "I heard you like little boys, you filthy little slut. Just you wait, you'll get what's coming to you."

After that, I unplugged the phone.

Luckily, no one had yet tracked down my cell-phone number. Probably because almost no one had it; unlike my cell-phone-addicted students, who practically lived with their phones pressed to their ears, I kept mine only for emergencies. The night the story broke, I used it to call Maisie.

"Hey," I said when she answered the phone. "So what's new with you?"

I expected her to laugh. Instead, she said, her voice strained, "Lucy. Are you okay? What the hell is going on?"

"A little of this, a little of that," I said, still trying to keep up the joke, hoping she'd play along. When she didn't say anything, I said, "Maisie?"

"I'm here. I just—Christ, Lucy, I don't know what to say. This is all just so . . ."

"Surreal," I supplied.

"Yeah. Surreal. Did you know reporters have been calling my house?"

Guilt squeezed my heart. While I knew I couldn't control what the reporters did, and it was bad enough that they were permanently camped out in front of my house, it was even worse to know that they were harassing my friends. "I'm so sorry about that," I said.

"Yeah, well, I'm sure it'll die down. But the thing I don't understand is . . . why, Lucy? Why did you do it?"

"What? I thought—" I stopped and swallowed. My throat was suddenly painfully dry, as though I'd swallowed a fistful of sand. I took a sip of water and began again. "I thought you said you didn't believe Matt Forrester's accusations."

"I don't!" Maisie said, her voice sharp and spiked with . . . what? Indignation? Outrage? Anger? And if it was anger, then whom was she angry with? Matt Forrester—or me?

But then she continued. "I meant, why didn't you tell me you won the lottery?"

"Oh . . . that. I don't know, exactly," I said. It sounded feeble to me. And apparently to her as well.

"I thought you trusted me," Maisie said flatly.

"Of course I trust you! God, Maisie, you know that," I said. Color flared hot in my cheeks, and I shifted uncomfortably on my seat. Harper Lee, sitting next to me, gave a grunt of displeasure at being disturbed. She shifted her round, sleek body so that she was again slumped against my hip and let out a deep, martyrlike sigh.

"Then why didn't you tell me? I'm assuming that's where you went last week on your mysterious out-of-town trip."

"I had to go to Tallahassee to claim the money," I said.

"And that was, what? Five days ago? How many times have we talked since then? And you didn't think of maybe throwing out the news that you'd won ninety million freaking dollars?"

"Eighty-seven million dollars," I said automatically. "And it was only thirty-four point four after taxes and my opting for a one-time payout."

"Oh, *only* thirty-four point four," Maisie said sarcastically.

"Look, I'm sorry I didn't tell you. I've been in—" I didn't want to say shock. It sounded so dramatic, as though I'd suddenly turned into a Victorian-era woman taking to my bed with the vapors. "I've just been trying to absorb it all. I wasn't purposely keeping it from you. I just wasn't ready to talk about it."

"Right," Maisie said. Her voice was flat again. It made her sound cold and distant, like a different person from the warm, funny friend I'd known all these years. "Or maybe you were just worried that I was going to hit you up for some money."

"What?" I said blankly. "Of *course* I didn't think . . . Maisie, you're being—"

"You wouldn't have even known to buy a lottery ticket if I hadn't told you about it," Maisie burst out. And now her voice was so full of self-righteous fury that I could feel a small flame of anger suddenly lighting within me.

"What does that have to do with anything?" I asked.

"It has everything to do with everything," Maisie said, spitting out the words as though they tasted bitter in her mouth. "It should have been *me*!" She wasn't yelling, but her voice was much higher than usual and edged with steel. "I should have been the one to win that money!"

"What are you saying?" I asked quietly. "You think you deserve it more than I do?"

"Well, don't I? After everything that Joe and I went through to get the twins? And that on top of my student loans! We're up to our eyeballs in debt. We can't even afford to hire a babysitter so we can go out to dinner on a Saturday night," Maisie fumed. "Do you know how much it's going to cost to put two boys through college? Not to mention the cost of private school, since the public schools around here are all crap, as you well know. We needed that money more! And, yes, I do think we deserved it more!"

After she finished, we were both silent for a moment. I listened to her breath, ragged and angry, and tried to swallow back my own mounting fury. I knew Maisie wasn't being rational, that she couldn't really believe that I'd won the lottery just to piss her off. It wasn't Maisie saying these things—it was just an inner demon, summoned up by fear and stress and anxiety, that had broken loose inside her and temporarily taken over her body.

But at the same time, I was the one who had the press camped outside my house beyond the police barricade. Weirdos were leaving threatening messages on my answering machine, and I was suddenly reviled by everyone in town.

Surely my need to have my best friend be understanding and supportive was greater than her need to shout at me. And knowing this, the anger that had flickered inside me suddenly flared up, burning hot.

"It's not my fault you're having money problems," I said, and in my anger my voice rose to a near shout. "It's not my fault you had a hard time getting pregnant. My winning the lottery wasn't some sort of cosmic fuck-you aimed right at you, Maisie. So stop being so self-centered!"

That was when Maisie hung up on me. I stared down at my cell phone, which was flashing the message CALL ENDED.

"Damn," I said, dropping the phone onto the coffee table. And then I closed my eyes, pressed my fingers against the lids, and wondered when—*if*—my life would ever return to normal.

Seven

ELLIOTT SHOWED UP THE NEXT DAY. SOMEHOW HE managed to talk his way past the police—his driver's license still had our shared address on it, I realized—and was able to walk right up to my front door and ring the doorbell while the press grouped back on the sidewalk and shouted questions at him. I peered out the window, and then, seeing who it was, I cracked the door open just as far as the security chain would allow.

"What do you want?" I hissed.

"Lucy! Thank God! Let me in." Elliott peered at me through the crack, his long, narrow face anxious.

"I don't want to see you."

"Lucy . . . please. I need to talk to you."

"I've already said everything I have to say to you. Unless you want a few choice words on what exactly I think of you. You know, words like *rat bastard piece of shit* and *cheating ball of pus*. You get the general idea."

"Look, I'm sorry. It was a huge mistake. *Huge*. I think I . . . I must have panicked about how serious we were getting, what with moving in together and everything," Elliott said.

The one good thing about the tidal waves of fury that kept lapping over me was that I was pretty sure it meant I wasn't in shock anymore. I closed the door, fumbled with the chain, and then threw the door open, ready to expend some of that fury at my asshole of an ex-boyfriend. In my blind rage, I'd somehow momentarily forgotten that the press was camped out in front of my house and that I looked like hell. I'd managed a shower that day, but I was wearing my oldest and rattiest sweats and had my hair scraped back in the ponytail favored by depressives everywhere. The reporters pounced.

"Lucy, do you have a comment?"

"Lucy, would you like a chance to tell your side of the story?"

"What does your boyfriend think about the allegations against you?"

They roared out their questions and pointed their cameras at me. I snaked one arm out, grabbed Elliott by the wrist, dragged him into the house, and slammed the door shut behind him. And then I turned on my ex-boyfriend, even angrier at him than before, if that were possible. While it wasn't exactly his fault that I'd let my guard down and allowed the press to get me on camera, he hadn't helped matters either.

"Wow. This is insane," Elliott said, running a hand nervously through his hair. "How long have they been out there for?"

"Two days."

"Do you need anything? Or do you want me to go out there and tell them to go away?" Elliott asked.

I laughed without humor. "It doesn't work. My dad tried that yesterday."

"And this is all because of what that student said about you?"

"Yes. Well, that and my winning the lottery." I folded my arms over my chest and stared coldly at Elliott. "That is why you're here, isn't it?"

"No! Of course not. I just wanted to check on you," Elliott insisted.

"Mission accomplished. Now you can leave," I said, turning toward the door.

"Wait. That's not all. I also wanted to talk to you," Elliott said. He reached out, presumably to touch my arm, but the look I gave him made him think twice about it. His hand dropped limply to his side.

"I don't have anything to say. It's done. It's over. We're over. There's no point in discussing the details," I said.

I glared at him through narrowed eyes. I noticed that he'd recently had his light-brown hair cut and there was a small shaving nick on his jawline. He was wearing a navy-blue polo shirt, pressed khaki pants, and, inexplicably, leather thong sandals. I'd never seen the sandals before. Elliott had always been a confirmed penny-loafer man, insisting that sandals for men were "very, very gay." I wondered if they were a gift from Naomi.

"I know I hurt you," Elliott said. "I made a mistake. A stupid, idiotic mistake. I fully admit that."

"That's big of you," I said sarcastically.

"You can't tell me you really want to throw away three years of shared history over one mistake?" Elliott's eyes were soft and pleading. His expression reminded me of Harper Lee when she's begging at the table, ever hopeful that a forkful of my dinner will come her way. "Because I think what we have is worth saving. I love you. And I know you still love me. That doesn't just go away overnight."

"Seven nights," I said.

He blinked. "What?"

"It's been seven nights since I found you in our bed with your new girlfriend."

"She's not my girlfriend," Elliott said quickly.

"I don't really care one way or the other. Your sex life is no longer any of my business."

"No, what I mean is, I've already told Naomi that it's over—because I love *you*, Lucy. It took losing you to make me realize that, to realize how much I've taken our relationship for granted. But now I know—you're the woman I'm meant to be with. You're the love of my life."

This speech was delivered with the same soft eyes and urgent, earnest tone. And then Elliott dropped to one knee and held out a white ring box I hadn't noticed in his hand. He opened the box, revealing a gorgeous, glittering two-carat diamond solitaire ring nestled on a bed of white satin.

"Marry me, Lucy. Let me spend the rest of our lives making it up to you," he said. A lock of light-brown hair had fallen forward over his brow, giving him a boyish air. With every gesture and every word, he was the very picture of repentance.

He had to be insane if he thought I was going to buy it.

"Did you practice that little speech?" I asked.

He hesitated for the briefest of moments. So I was right: He had practiced. Probably in front of a mirror.

"No," he said. "Of course not. Every word came from my heart."

With his ring-free hand, he patted himself on the chest, just over his heart. Or where his heart would have been if he actually had one. I looked down at his clear hazel eyes, narrow face, and thin, hard lips and wondered why in the hell I had ever wasted a single moment of my life with this man, how it was that I had failed to see what he really was. All along I'd always thought he was one of the good ones. I thought he only had a minor commitment hang-up and, despite that one flaw, he was worth waiting for. Now I finally saw Elliott for the selfish, manipulative jerk he really was.

Considering how wrong I'd been about his sense of loyalty, I probably shouldn't have been surprised to learn that he was a gold digger as well. Because it was blindingly obvious to me that there was one reason, and one reason only, that he was here now.

"The answer to your question," I said, "is a most definite *no*."

"No what?"

"No, I will not marry you."

Elliott's eyes widened, and I thought I could detect the faintest trace of sweat on his forehead. He was still down on one knee, and—as though suddenly aware of how ridiculous he looked—stood abruptly.

"But I thought this was what you wanted. To get married. For me to commit," he said.

"Oh, it was," I agreed. "But I've changed my mind. Thank God."

I could see something shift behind Elliott's eyes. I didn't know if it was anger, or frustration, or maybe even genuine disappointment.

"Are you saying no just because of Naomi? Because I promise, that's completely over," Elliott said.

"No, that's not it. Well, I mean, of course I'm *angry* about that. I did walk in on you screwing some random woman on my bed, after all. But that's not why I'm saying no to your proposal," I said.

"Then why?"

"Because you're an asshole, Elliott," I said gently. "And I'm well aware that the only reason you're proposing to me now is because of the lottery money."

"That's not true!" Elliott gasped. Two spots of red flamed suddenly on his cheekbones. I'd always envied him his cheekbones, which were high and prominent, like a model's. "I'm not here because of the money! I'm here because I love you."

"The thing is, I don't think you really *do* love me. I'm sure it must stick in your craw to know that if you'd been decent and kind and faithful, that money would now be yours too. But you weren't—and it isn't. And now I'd like you to leave," I said.

I turned and opened the door for him, taking care to step back so the photographers wouldn't be able to catch sight of me again. As if a switch had been flicked, the reporters immediately began shouting out questions. Elliott stood staring at me, not sure what to do. Then he blinked and looked down at the ring. With a decisive snap, he shut the box and thrust it into his pants pocket, where it made a noticeable bulge.

He left without saying another word.

Elliott got his revenge on me the next morning.

"Yes, it's been very hard," he said to Diane Sawyer, as she interviewed him on *Good Morning America*.

Diane was wearing a dove-gray suit and pearls, her lovely face frowning at him in concern. Elliott had on the blue sport jacket I'd bought him for Christmas last year over a white shirt unbuttoned at the neck. His expression was a perfect mixture of stoicism and sorrow. I even felt a little sorry for him, before remembering that he was, at that moment, betraying me for the second time in less than two weeks.

"I loved—no, I *still* love Lucy very much," Elliott said sadly. "I was prepared to stand by her through the stunning allegations made against her by this student. But then she won the lottery—and for whatever reason, she broke off our engagement."

"Engagement? What engagement, you lying turd," I muttered at the television.

"You believe she ended your relationship because she didn't want to share the money with you?" Diane Sawyer asked.

Elliott shrugged while tilting his head to one side. "I have to wonder if that was her motivation," he admitted, conveniently failing to mention how he'd cheated on me. The bastard.

"And what do you think about the allegations made by Ms. Parker's former student, claiming that she attempted to coerce him into having sexual relations with her?"

"At first I thought the allegations were ridiculous. The Lucy I knew would never have done something like that. But now . . ." Elliott looked right at the camera. "Now I'm starting to realize that I never knew the real Lucy Parker."

My jaw dropped open, and I shook my head silently. Which was worse: Walking in on your boyfriend screwing another woman . . . or having him appear on national television, telling the world that you're the new Mary Kay Letourneau? And then, to make matters just that much worse, *Good Morning America* flashed the most unflattering possible video of me. It had been taken as I was letting Elliott into the house, and featured me looking like a sloppy, guilty mess with my face twisted in an ugly expression of anger.

"Oh. My. God," I said. My legs felt suddenly weak, and I sank down on the sofa.

"Where do you go from here?" Diane Sawyer was gently asking Elliott.

He smiled bravely. "I'll be fine. It will just take a little while for my heart to heal, I think."

Diane Sawyer smiled warmly at him. "Good luck, Elliott."

"Thank you, Diane."

"And coming up on *Good Morning America,* we'll be taking a look at the epidemic of female teachers seducing their male students. It's an eye-opening story every parent of a son should hear," Diane Sawyer said seriously, as somber piano music played in the background.

I groaned softly and lowered my head into my hands. Without looking up, I lifted the remote in one limp hand and turned off the television.

By Friday afternoon, the reporters were still there, and I was still a prisoner in my home. The phone rang constantly whenever I plugged it in. They'd even somehow managed to track down my cell-phone number and began calling on that too. I finally turned off the cell phone and tossed it in the junk drawer in the kitchen.

I'd hoped that if I just ignored the reporters, they'd get tired of waiting and go away. But it had been a slow news week; there wasn't even a runaway bride or starlet heading to rehab around to distract the media. If anything, there were even more reporters camped outside than there had been the day before. I stood by the window, chewing on my lower lip and peering out at them from behind my curtains. There was a sandwich truck out there today, doing a brisk business serving BLTs and grilled hot dogs to the news crews.

I had to get away. I just wasn't sure where I could go. My parents' house was out of the question—it was far too crowded with dogs and wedding plans. And for the first time in our twenty-year friendship, Maisie and I weren't speaking. I'd always dreamed about traveling to Europe, especially to England, home of my beloved Jane Austen and Henry James. But when I'd pictured myself going overseas, it was a trip I thought I'd make with someone I loved. Going alone, and when my life was in a free fall, seemed somehow wrong.

The phone rang. I cursed myself for forgetting to take it off the hook after calling my parents' house, which I had immediately regretted when my little sister answered. As Mom had predicted, Emma was only too happy to let me pay for the wedding of her dreams. She was pointedly ignoring Dad's stubborn insistence that he and Mom were going to pay for the wedding and that she would have to make do with the budget he'd given her. This all put me rather horribly in the middle, and even though I'd begged to be left out of it until they'd hashed it out, Emma had taken to whispering her latest over-the-top ideas whenever we spoke. Today she'd gone on and on about releasing doves—real live, flying, cooing, shitting doves—just as the minister was pronouncing Emma and Christian husband and wife.

"And wouldn't it be fabulous to have my wedding at Pine Gardens? It's one of the nicest country clubs in the state." Emma burbled along enthusiastically. "There's just one problem."

"What?" I asked wearily.

"Owen Forrester."

I felt a spasm in the region of my stomach. Just hearing the name of Matt Forrester's father shook me. The money made me feel like I had a bull's-eye taped to my forehead. What if the Forresters did decide to sue me? Or, even worse, have me criminally prosecuted?

"What about him?"

"He's a member at Pine Gardens. In fact, he's the president of the board. I'm worried that he'll try to stop us from holding the reception there."

"He probably would," I said.

"If he finds out we're sisters."

There was something about Emma's tone—an offhand affectation that she always adopted when she was attempting to be sly—that caught my attention.

"If? Wait—are you saying you want me to pretend that I'm not related to you?"

"No, no, of course not!" Emma said in a way that made it perfectly clear this was exactly what she'd been contemplating. "I just wanted to find out what you thought I should do. But never mind." She scrambled to change the subject, although unfortunately not away from the wedding altogether. "Oh! I know what else I wanted to tell you. I had an *amazing* idea: I want to have a huge fireworks display at the reception! Doesn't that sound incredible? Tom Cruise and Katie Holmes did it at their wedding, and it was supposed to have been fabulous. But as it turns out, we need, like, ten different kinds of permits and a professional pyrotechnic. I found a guy, and he said he's going to need a deposit of five thousand as soon as possible."

"Emma, I've already told you. I'd be happy to pay for your wedding extravaganza, but I'm not going behind Dad's back. You need to work this out with him first," I said in my sternest teacher's voice.

This, of course, set Emma off on a hissing rant about how unfair and unreasonable Dad was being. I didn't disagree with her—I couldn't figure out why Dad was being so insistent that he pay for the wedding. He seemed to think that letting me pay for it would be taking advantage of me. But what was the point of having all this money if I couldn't help out my family with these sorts of unwieldy expenses?

By the time I finally got Emma off the phone, I thought that if I ever heard the word *wedding* again it would be too soon. Likewise, *fondant frosting, platinum eternity band, and darling little sterling-silver picture frames to hand out as favors.* As it was, my headache had returned, so I went off in search of the aspirin bottle and forgot to unplug the phone.

When it rang, I ignored it, assuming it was either yet

another reporter or Emma calling back to torture me with more wedding talk. Maybe she now wanted to give each guest a live peacock to take home as a wedding favor. Or maybe she wanted to arrive at the wedding ceremony in a gilded horse-drawn carriage.

But it wasn't Emma. The voice on my answering machine was lower and huskier than my sister's:

"Hey, Lulu, it's Hayden. Are you there? Or are you too busy seducing hot young boys to answer your phone? I just saw a story about you on Fox fucking News, and I damned near had a stroke. Pick up the phone right this minute and tell me what in the name of holy fuck is going on."

Eight

HAYDEN BLAIR WAS MY SECOND-OLDEST FRIEND. WE met our freshman year at Bates. She lived in the dorm room next to mine, and the first time I saw her she was sitting in the common room, her bare feet tucked up underneath her, while she watched a *Real World* marathon on MTV. I liked her instantly. She had sleek dark hair that fell halfway down her back, chic bangs, and wore dark-red lipstick without looking ridiculous. Her family was insanely rich, although for as long as I'd known her, Hayden had distanced herself from the silver-spoon lifestyle. She never hung out with the trust-fund brats at Bates, bought most of her clothes at thrift stores—although somehow still managed to look incredibly glamorous in everything she wore—and whenever the subject of her family's money came up, Hayden shrugged it off.

"Old money," she'd say, with a dismissive wave of her hand. "It's not like my parents earned it."

Hayden was the third of three daughters and not on great terms with the rest of her family.

"I'm my parents' Great Disappointment," Hayden had

confided to me that night, the first of many late nights we would spend sprawled out on the indestructible dorm couches. "My oldest sister, Evelyn, went to Wharton for her MBA, and Jezzy is going to law school next year after she graduates from fucking Harvard. I'm the only one who didn't go Ivy. My parents are still pissed about it."

"Bates is a good school," I said, feeling stung.

Hayden looked at me pityingly. "Yeah, well, it's not Harvard. And that's all my parents care about. I haven't broken it to them yet that I'm going to major in drama."

"Are you an actress?" I asked, impressed.

"Not yet," Hayden said, a small smile playing at her lips. "But I will be."

Neither of us was all that into the party scene at school—I was too shy, Hayden, a wild child who'd started clubbing at the age of thirteen, was too jaded—and so when the other girls on our floor left in a pack for the latest off-campus party, smelling of shampoo and floral perfume and wearing bodysuits and skintight jeans tucked into cowboy boots, Hayden and I would watch old movies and talk late into the night. Overnight, it seemed, we became the closest of friends.

"I've never really been friends with a girl before," Hayden had told me during one of our late night chatfests. "Girls don't usually like me."

I could see why some women would find Hayden threatening. With her strong features—the fierce tilt of her green eyes, the too-long nose, the almost masculine cut of her jaw—Hayden wasn't classically beautiful. But she was certainly very arresting; I got used to eyes following us when we went to dinner at the dining hall or walked across campus to class together. Men were particularly fascinated with her. It wasn't at all unusual for guys she didn't know to walk right up to Hayden and boldly ask her out. She never seemed surprised by the attention or even all that interested. She'd just smile and thank them politely but say no, she wasn't interested in dating anyone right now.

"Why aren't you interested in dating?" I asked her once.

I certainly was. Unfortunately, no one—neither random guys we met walking across campus nor anyone else—asked me out. The closest I'd gotten to a date was at the freshman mixer I'd attended on the first night at school, when a guy named Adam had staggered up to me and slurred that I was the most beautiful girl at the party. I knew that this declaration had probably been largely influenced by the amount of beer he'd downed at happy hour prior to coming to the mixer, but even so, I'd half-wondered if Adam and I might end up together. It would be a great story to tell our kids someday.

I met your mom on our very first night at college. She was so beautiful, she took my breath away. I just knew this was the woman I was meant to marry, he'd say, wrapping an affectionate arm around my waist and leaning down to kiss me on the cheek, while our children groaned at how sappy their parents were.

Taken with this image of domestic perfection, I'd let Adam walk me back to my dorm, where we engaged in a protracted kiss-and-grope session just outside the front door to Smith Hall. This included—at his insistence—an over-the-pants hand job, which was unfortunately witnessed by several of my new dormmates upon their return from the mixer and earned me the reputation of Dorm Slut on our very first night at school. I wrote down my phone number for Adam; he promised to call but never did. And for the next four years, whenever I saw Adam on campus—which happened with annoying frequency—he'd turn bright red and look away, making me feel as worthless and discarded as a used condom.

"What's the point?" Hayden said. "No one really dates here. We're in the middle of buttfuck Maine. There's nowhere to go. So when a guy asks you out, what he means is that he wants to hang out in your room or, even *worse,* his room."

"Why would his room be worse?"

"Have you ever been in a guy's dorm room? *Blech.* They smell disgusting: a combination of body odor and stinky feet."

I desperately hoped that I'd have the chance to smell that aroma at some point.

"And what's there to do in a dorm room but fuck? So all a guy is really doing when he asks you out is asking if he can fuck you," Hayden continued. She shrugged dismissively. "It's not like I'm anti-fucking—I'm extremely *pro*-fucking—just not on a narrow dorm bed with REM playing in the background and foreplay that consists of *you* giving *him* a blow job. No, thanks."

Hayden and I remained close during our four years at Bates and were roommates for the last three of those years. Despite Hayden's cautionary words, I eventually did visit my fair share of male dorm rooms, usually when I'd had too much to drink, and learned the hard way that Hayden was, for the most part, correct. College guys didn't have a whole lot of finesse in the bedroom; they came on strong and finished quickly. But I felt devastatingly sophisticated racking up some experience for the first time in my life, eventually even losing my virginity to Cole Willis after we'd been "dating" for three weeks.

Despite her wild teenage years—Hayden had endless stories about dropping acid at all-night raves and dating guys ten years her senior—she wasn't as impervious to romance as she pretended to be. During our sophomore year she fell pretty hard for Jason Downey, a senior with jet-black hair and smoldering dark eyes, who announced he was in love with her on their second date. That relationship lasted three whole months before Hayden broke things off. After Jason, there was a string of short, intense affairs, some with guys from our school, some with guys she knew from back home. All of these love interests shared a few things in common: The men were all incredibly good-looking and they were all madly in love with Hayden. And they were, every last one, devastated when she grew bored and broke things off.

I mostly observed Hayden's revolving door of eligible men with an amused yet detached interest. However, there was inevitably some overlap in Hayden's and my interests. Usually it was pretty simple: I would notice a guy—in class, in the dining hall, at a party—and would experience that small hormonal explosion of interest. We'd engage in some meaningful eye contact. And then he'd notice Hayden sitting beside me, with her elegant posture, glossy hair, and red, red lips, and, *poof,* just like that, I'd cease to exist.

A lot of girls would thrive on this sort of attention. I'd certainly known quite a few like that in high school, the sort who were never happier than when they were flirting with someone else's boyfriend. But not Hayden. She had so few girlfriends that she viewed our friendship as something worth protecting. If a guy she knew I was interested in went after her instead, all he would get for his trouble would be a contemptuous glare and a sarcastic comment from Hayden.

"Asshole," she'd say, tossing her hair back.

"Asshole," I'd confirm. And then we'd go outside, where I would keep her company while she smoked a Marlboro Light.

It was hard not to feel a little jealous. But Hayden's unwavering loyalty made it impossible to hold her popularity against her. There was only one time when my resentment boiled up and truly threatened my friendship with Hayden. And that wasn't even her fault.

"I met a guy," I sang out one night as I walked into the tiny living room of the off-campus apartment we shared. Hayden's mom had offered us her decorator to do the place up, but Hayden had flatly refused. So our apartment was kitted out like every other college apartment, featuring banged-up and mismatched furniture we'd scavenged from graduating seniors and Goodwill.

"At the library?" Hayden asked. She'd been lying stomach-down on a scratchy brown plaid sofa with sagging cushions and was marking pages in her psych textbook with a fat yellow highlighter pen. But upon my arrival, she turned over and bent up her knees to give me room to sit.

"At the library," I confirmed, as lit up inside as a Christmas tree. "He was in the reading room. I noticed him right away; there was something about him that I just instantly liked. But I didn't think he noticed me. I mean, why would he?" I added with a laugh.

"Don't do that. Don't put yourself down," Hayden said, frowning at me. "I don't know why you won't believe how pretty you are."

I snorted. "Maybe because it's a load of horseshit?"

"I'd kill to have your skin, not to mention your hair."

She reached up and pulled back on one of my long corkscrew curls and then released it, so it sprang back in place.

"You're more than welcome to it," I said. I had tried before to convince Hayden that curly hair was not a blessing but a particularly evil curse that I did battle with every day. She never believed me.

"And your boobs—you have the best boobs," Hayden said, looking down sadly at her own flat chest.

"Yeah, except you can wear whatever you want and always look like a fashion model. I can't put on a tank top without looking trashy," I said moodily. I could feel my inner Christmas tree turning brown and dropping its needles.

"Finish your story," Hayden said. "About Library Guy."

"Library Guy. That makes him sound like a superhero," I said, with a snort of laughter. I deepened my voice. "He can read faster than a speeding train and chases down patrons with overdue fines—he's Library Guy!"

Hayden laughed but nudged me with one sock-covered foot. "Come on, tell me what happened."

"Nothing happened," I said, grinning and hugging my arms around myself.

"Why do I not believe you?"

"Okay, something happened," I conceded. "But it wasn't that big of a deal."

"Just tell me already!"

"I'm trying! After I'd been there for about an hour, I went outside to get a coffee at Mo's." Mo's was a food-service van parked more or less permanently outside the library, ever ready to cater to students in need of cheese fries and caffeinated beverages. "The guy I'd noticed earlier came out too. He was standing in line right behind me. And we started talking—"

"How?" Hayden asked, clutching a pillow to her chest.

"He noticed the poli-sci textbook I was holding and asked me if I was in Kaplan's class. I said yes, and he said he was too."

"You'd never noticed him there?"

"No, but it's a pretty big class, and he said he sits in the back."

"Okay." Hayden made a rolling gesture with her hand, encouraging me to continue the story.

"We talked a bit about the class and both said we liked it. I got my coffee and he got his, and he asked if I wanted to sit down. So we sat on a bench, and we talked for a really long time. And it was . . . well, it was great. It was the first time in a really long time that a guy just wanted to talk to me. To get to know me."

"And?"

"And that's it. Then we went back inside, and I went to my reading table and he went to his."

Hayden pouted disappointedly. "I thought this was going somewhere good," she said.

"It was good. I think he really liked me," I said, remembering the warm brown eyes, the pink flush of his cheeks, the broad shoulders in the J. Crew barn coat. He was definitely sexy but not conventionally handsome. Which meant maybe I had a chance with him. "He asked if I was going to be at the library tomorrow night and suggested that we study for our poli-sci exam together."

"What's his name?"

"John."

"John what?"

"I don't know. He didn't say." I frowned. "Do you think that's a bad sign?"

"No, I don't. I think it all sounds very promising."

Promising. I liked the sound of that. And after a few study sessions at the library with John, I'd started to think that maybe Hayden was right. Maybe it—whatever *it* was we were doing—was promising. Because while John wasn't coming on hot and heavy, he also wasn't plying me with cheap beer and telling me I looked *just* like Julia Roberts only *prettier* (a line, I'm sad to say, worked on me one night after a few too many tequila shots). We'd study at the same table, take coffee breaks together, and gradually got to know each other. I learned that he was planning to go to medical school after he graduated. That his father and mother were both tax lawyers and were in practice together in Boston. That he'd spent his childhood summers on Nantucket. That he had dated his high school sweetheart for four years but that they'd grown apart after going to different colleges and eventually broke up the summer after sophomore year.

I kept waiting for something more to happen—for him to ask to see me outside the library or maybe to kiss me on one of those nights when we spent our study break sitting on a bench talking together. But he never made a move. At first I appreciated how slowly he was taking things; it seemed sweet and romantic, and I knew that if something did happen, it wouldn't be a disposable hookup. Then I began to worry that we'd crossed that invisible line from love interest to friendship.

"And once that happens, there's no going back," I said to Hayden a few weeks after the night I'd first met John. I was perched on the edge of the bed, watching her get ready for a semiformal mixer. She was wearing a short black fitted dress edged with white piping that she'd discovered at Goodwill and yet looked like couture draped on her tall, angular frame. She'd twisted her hair up into a neat chignon and was now carefully applying her signature red lipstick.

"That's not necessarily true. Remember *When Harry Met Sally*? They were friends who first met in college, and they eventually got together," Hayden said. She blotted her lipstick and then tossed the capped tube into her black satin evening bag.

"Eventually? Didn't they get together, like, fifteen years after they first met in that movie?"

"Something like that."

"I don't want to wait fifteen years." I sighed dramatically and traced one of the poppies on Hayden's Marimekko duvet cover with my finger.

"Maybe he's shy. Maybe you should make the first move."

Just the idea of this made my stomach twist.

"No," I said.

"Why not?"

Because I want him to like me enough to ask me out, I thought. *I want him to think I'm worth it.* And if I asked him out, even if he agreed, a part of me would always feel less valued.

I knew Hayden would never understand this, though, so I just shrugged and, to placate her, said, "I don't know. Maybe I will."

The doorbell rang then, Hayden's date arriving to pick her up.

"Would you mind getting it?" she asked. "I have to pee."

"Sure," I said sliding off her bed.

While Hayden ducked into the bathroom, I padded to the front door. I opened it and found myself face-to-face with . . . *John!* My heart gave an excited lurch and then seemed to zoom up into my throat. He'd come to see me! And since I hadn't given him my address, that meant he must have tracked me down! Which meant he must really, really like me! Joy bloomed inside me. It was finally, finally happening for me.

"Hey!" I said.

"Hey yourself," John said. He seemed confused. "Do you live here?"

Now I was confused too. Hadn't he expected me to live here? And why was he wearing a jacket and tie? He looked fantastic—his shiny dark hair curled back from his face, his brown eyes dark with excitement, and the jacket emphasizing his sexy broad shoulders—but it was a departure from the wool sweaters and beat-up Levis I was used to seeing him in.

"Jonathan!" Hayden said, gliding into the room, her face aglow. "Did you meet my roommate, Lucy?"

And it all became horrifyingly clear. His name wasn't J-O-H-N . . . it was J-O-N. Short for Jonathan. More to the point, short for the Jonathan that Hayden had been half in love with ever since she quite literally bumped into him on the quad a week earlier. She'd been gazing skyward, wondering if it was going to rain; he was looking back over his shoulder, talking to a friend. They'd had coffee twice, lunch once, and tonight he was taking her to the semiformal.

And I had convinced myself that he was falling for me. Shame and humiliation welled inside me, pressing upward.

"We already know each other," Jonathan said.

"You do?" Hayden asked, looking delightedly from him to me. "You didn't tell me that, Lucy."

I don't know how I managed to keep my face set in a neutral, pleasant expression that completely disguised what I was feeling inside. But somehow I must have, because Hayden didn't notice my distress.

"We have a class together," Jonathan said.

And before he could go on and disclose that he was the John I'd been mooning about for the past few weeks, I said quickly, "That's right. We're old buds."

This was patently untrue; we'd known each other for only a few weeks. But it was the sort of teasing patter the best friend of the love interest can get away with—Jonathan would just assume it meant I was giving Hayden a subtle thumbs-up of approval—so he grinned and said, "That's right. Lucy's saved my sorry ass. If it wasn't for her, I'd be failing poli-sci."

I was sure that would give it away, that Hayden would immediately figure out that Jonathan was John. And I didn't want her to know. Hayden was a zealot when it came to loyalty. If she even suspected that I had feelings for her Jonathan, she would immediately dump him. I didn't want that; it would make me feel even more pathetic and humiliated than I already did.

But Hayden was too smitten to notice. Her eyes seemed to drink Jonathan in, and an almost goofy smile played at her lips—something I'd never seen before. Jonathan was gazing back at her as though he couldn't believe his good luck. I had never in my life felt more extraneous.

"Have a great time," I said, backing away from the pair.

"Bye," Hayden said.

"Yeah, bye, Lucy," Jonathan echoed.

I spent the rest of the evening in my bedroom, curled up in a fetal position on my bed, my hands clasped to my stomach and my eyes sore and puffy from crying. I listened for Hayden's return. *Please don't let them come back here together,* I thought. *Meeting him by the coffeepot first thing in the morning is more than I can bear*.

But I didn't hear them return, and eventually I fell asleep. And the next morning, when I first listened at the door, then knocked softly, and finally—sure it was safe—cracked open the door to Hayden's bedroom, I discovered that she hadn't come back at all.

I never did tell Hayden about the John/Jonathan mix-up. Their relationship lasted longer than most of Hayden's flings; they were still together by the time we graduated. I got over Jonathan eventually, and the ache of seeing him regularly sprawled out on our couch, Hayden's head resting companionably on his shoulder, or, worse, the bitter jealousy that rose up in me like bile when I heard the soft, sighing sounds of their lovemaking through our paper-thin walls first lessened, then disappeared.

Jonathan and I were thrown together so often that we grew to be pretty good friends. And even after he and Hayden eventually broke up the summer after graduation—or, I should say, after Hayden unceremoniously dumped him, claiming that she wanted to transition into the next phase of her life unencumbered—Jonathan and I stayed in touch. He went on to med school at Dartmouth, eventually became a pediatrician, and was now married with two kids and living in Baltimore. I hadn't seen him in years, but we e-mailed back and forth occasionally, and every Christmas I received a card with a picture of his two adorable, dark-haired, apple-cheeked daughters, both of whom had inherited his smile.

After graduation. I moved back to Florida, got my teaching certificate, and applied for teaching jobs at a number of local high schools, including Andrews Prep. Hayden moved to Manhattan to pursue her acting career. Her biggest part was playing a golfer in a tampon commercial. In it, she pranced around in white shorts, taking graceful swings with a golf club.

I called Hayden the first time I saw the commercial air.

"Hey there, movie star!" I said, when she answered the phone. We hadn't talked in a few weeks, which felt like forever after having seen each other nearly every day for four years. I even felt a little uncertain about calling her. She'd been distant the past few times we'd spoken, and I'd never heard the whole story of why she and Jonathan broke up. But as soon as I heard Hayden's warm, rich chuckle and the deep exhalation of her cigarette smoke, it was as though no time had passed at all.

"Sadly, one tampon commercial does not make me a movie star."

"I thought you did a great job. You nailed the part. I totally believed that you had your period and yet felt secure wearing short-shorts."

"Not to mention that I actually played golf," Hayden said. "All of those years my mother dragged me to lessons paid off. Who would have thought?"

"I have a hard time picturing you being dragged anywhere you don't want to go," I said.

"I was madly in love with my golf coach. He had the best legs I've ever seen on a man," Hayden conceded. "So I didn't mind the lessons so much. But I never told my mom that. She would have stopped bribing me with Chanel lipsticks if she'd found out."

"Chanel lipsticks? How old were you?"

"Eleven," Hayden said. She laughed again. "Eleven going on thirty."

Hayden never did get her big break; after a few years she gave up acting altogether. She flitted from job to job, each time fizzing with excitement over the dazzling future she was suddenly envisioning for herself. For a time she worked as an assistant to a famous photographer and was convinced that it was only a matter of time before she'd become a photographer in her own right, with *Vanity Fair* and *Vogue* clamoring after her. Then there was her stint at an art gallery, organizing exhibits and acting as a liaison with artists. And then she landed a job as the assistant to a rising fashion designer.

I usually never heard why she'd left these jobs; Hayden called only when she was bubbling with excitement over her future prospects or when she had yet again fallen in love.

When she was licking her wounds over another job failure or breakup, she withdrew completely and wouldn't return my phone messages or e-mails for months at a time.

Although our lives couldn't have been more different in the eleven years since we'd left school—Hayden leading her glittering chaotic life in the big city, me teaching in quiet, sleepy Ocean Falls—we still managed to stay in touch. I called Hayden every few weeks, usually leaving her a message—she was never home—which she would eventually return. Twice I traveled up to Manhattan to visit her, and every year she came down to Florida to spend a few weeks at her family's estate on Palm Beach, and I would drive down to meet her there.

It had been over three months since I'd heard from her. I'd called and left messages, which went unreturned. I assumed she was in the midst of another of her withdrawn phases, which meant she was either out of work, or brokenhearted, or both. So I was thrilled to hear her voice on my answering machine. I fumbled for the phone, nearly knocking over a glass of water as I reached for it.

"I'm here, I'm here!" I said after I'd punched the talk button. "Don't hang up!"

"Stop yelling, I'm still here."

"I haven't heard from you in ages," I said, smiling for the first time in days.

"Is that what this is all about? A stunt designed to flush me out?"

"That's right. I won the lottery and got fired from my job just for you."

"That's what I thought. It's all about me, me, me." Hayden laughed her wonderful deep laugh, and then I heard the unmistakable sound of a cigarette being lit.

"I thought you quit smoking."

"I did. And then I started up again. It's like Kurt Vonnegut said—smoking is a socially acceptable form of suicide. Or at least it used to be, before all of the antismoking Nazis took over Manhattan," Hayden said.

"So, seriously, where have you been?"

"Vancouver."

"Really?"

"Yes, really."

"What were you doing there?"

"It was a business thing," she said vaguely.

"What sort of business?" I asked.

"You know: for my job."

I tried to remember what it was she was doing these days. PR for that record label? No, that was last year.

"You don't even know what I do, do you?" Hayden asked accusingly.

"Well . . . no," I admitted. "What are you up to these days?"

"It was really exciting. I got in on a new dot-com venture. A personal-shopping Web site for people who don't live near stores with personal-shopping services. Which apparently is most of the country. Customers could submit pictures of themselves, and then our personal-shopping experts would pick out the outfits for them from various online stores. And here's the best part: We'd get paid twice. Once from the customer for performing the service and then again from the clothes vendor for referring the business," Hayden enthused.

"That sounds great," I said. "Very inventive. Is it up and running now?"

"Well . . . no," Hayden admitted. "That's why we were in Vancouver. We were trying to get investors for the project. But the financing fell through." She sighed, and I could picture the smoke pluming from her nose. "So we couldn't move forward with it."

"We?"

"I was working with a partner. Craig Wilson. He's a whole other story."

I had a feeling I knew where this was going. "A new boyfriend, I take it?"

"No. A very ex ex-boyfriend."

"What happened?"

"He went back to his wife," Hayden said flatly. "The wife who he claimed had never understood him and who he was no longer in love with—and who, come to find out, is now pregnant with their second child. Yes, I really was that stupid."

"You're not stupid. He sounds like a creep," I said. "How were you supposed to know he was lying?"

"I don't know. I don't really want to talk about him. I want to talk about you—and whether that really was Elliott I saw being interviewed by Larry King last night."

He went on Larry King too? I wondered, as a wave of nausea washed over me. I'd been trying to avoid the television. Listening to reporters bandy my name around had felt surreal at first. Now it was just depressing. But this was the problem with not watching the news when you're at the center of the biggest story in the country—you don't know when your asshole of an ex-boyfriend is going to do yet another interview where he tells millions of people what a horrible person you are.

"Lulu?" Hayden asked, using her pet nickname for me. She was the only person I let get away with calling me that, having hated it since childhood. "Are you still there?"

"Yes," I said miserably. And then I burst into tears.

"Oh, my God! You're crying! What's wrong, sweetie?"

"You mean other than my boyfriend turning out to be a lying, cheating sack of shit, and getting fired from my job, and the entire town thinking I hit on teenage boys?" I bleated.

"But what about the lottery money?" Hayden asked, sounding surprised.

"What about it? It's just *money*. It can't buy me my life back."

"Oh, honey." Hayden laughed her slow, deep laugh. "Now, that's where you're wrong. That kind of money can buy you *anything*."

"I need to get out of town," I said. "There are reporters camped out in front of my house day and night. I can't even go to the grocery store. I've been eating frozen waffles for three days straight."

"That's easily solved: Meet me in Palm Beach. It'll be perfect! I'm sick of the city. A few weeks at the beach is exactly what I need."

"Aren't your parents there? I don't want to impose."

"Nope. They never go to Palm Beach before December," Hayden said. "We'll have Crane Hill all to ourselves!"

Crane Hill was the name of the Blair family's Palm Beach mansion. And, like all of the Blairs' houses, Crane Hill was huge and glamorous and subtly themed. Whereas the Connecticut estate was filled with Oriental rugs and Chippendale chairs, and their ski lodge in Vermont had massive leather sofas with nail-head trim and a chandelier made of deer antlers, the Palm Beach house was decorated with low sofas covered in pale-blue silk, bamboo tables, and enormous Art Deco mirrors, including one reportedly purchased from the Duchess of Windsor. It was located on the east side of the island, with stunning views of the white-capped ocean.

"Well . . ." I said slowly, the idea growing on me. "I do have an appointment with a financial adviser in Palm Beach on Friday."

"See? It's fate!"

"But how am I going to get there? I told you, the press is camped out on my front lawn. They'll just follow me."

"Luckily, you happen to be talking to the very woman who perfected the art of sneaking out of her house at the age of thirteen," Hayden said. "Give me a rundown of your basic house plans, including all possible exits, and I'll figure out a way to get you out of there. If I remember correctly, your back door is pretty well hidden from view, right?"

"Yes, my backyard is fenced in; I don't think the press can see back there. But how will I get to Palm Beach? My car's in the shop. I guess I do have the rental . . . but it's parked in my driveway. There's no way I can go out there without the press seeing me."

Hayden sighed. "Did you or did you not just come into a gazillion-dollar windfall? You can *buy* a new car. You can buy *fifty* new cars and hire drivers to chauffeur you around in them," she said.

Oddly enough, I hadn't considered this. Even though I certainly hadn't forgotten the money—the knowledge of it sitting in the bank thrilled me whenever I thought of it—I'd been so wrapped up in everything that was going wrong in my life, it hadn't really occurred to me that I could buy my way out of it. Of course I could easily buy another car. What had I been thinking?

"Okay," I said, my enthusiasm growing. "I think this could work!"

"Of course it will work," Hayden said confidently. "Now, let's figure out an escape plan and get you the hell out of there."

The plan was pretty simple. Once it was dark I'd sneak out through the back door, climb the fence into my neighbor's yard, and walk two miles to the Ocean Falls Marriott. There, I'd hire a car to drive me down to Palm Beach.

"A taxi?" I'd asked Hayden.

"A town car with a driver would be better. The hotel will know someone. They may even have a car and driver you can use," Hayden said.

"But why would they help me? I'm not a guest there."

Hayden sighed. "That's where the money comes in handy, Lucy. How much cash do you have in the house?"

"I don't know . . . maybe fifty dollars?"

"That's not nearly enough. Where's the nearest ATM?"

"There's a bank next to the hotel."

"Perfect. Stop there and get out as much money as the ATM will let you withdraw. Use that to bribe the desk clerk, the concierge, the driver, whoever. Just make it clear that you want them to keep quiet about it. And if they ask for your name, make one up. Or use mine."

"I've always wondered what it would be like to be you for a day."

"Have them take you to The Breakers on Palm Beach. They're used to dealing with high-profile clients there. Tip lavishly, and hopefully they won't tell the press you're there," Hayden continued. "I'll fly down tomorrow and meet you at the hotel."

On Hayden's instructions, I didn't bother to pack; a suitcase would slow me down. I just threw a toothbrush and change of underwear in my purse, and then stuffed Harper Lee into her hated black zip pet carrier. Then I went online and moved a sizeable chunk of money from my savings, where I'd deposited the lottery money, to my checking account. Once the transfer had gone through, I turned off the computer and called my parents. Thankfully, it was my father who answered.

"Hi, honey. How are you holding up?" he asked.

"Peachy keen," I said.

"Are the reporters still staking you out?"

"Yep. That's why I called: I'm going to get out of town until this blows over."

"Where will you go?" Dad asked, his voice infused with concern.

"Palm Beach. I'm going to stay at my friend Hayden's house. Let me give you the address."

"Hold on, let me get a piece of paper and a pen," Dad said. There was a brief pause. "Okay, go ahead."

I rattled off the address and phone number for the Blairs' beach house.

"Don't worry, I'll take care of everything here. Your house, your mail. What about Harper Lee?" Dad asked.

"I'm going to bring her with me," I said. "Would you mind returning my rental car for me, too?"

"Of course not. Give us a call when you get settled in, okay?"

"I will. Thanks, Dad," I said gratefully. "Give Mom my love."

"Take care of yourself," Dad said.

After we hung up, I sat down at my desk. I took out my checkbook—I had novelty checks with pictures of French bulldogs on them—and wrote out three checks for a half-million dollars each. It felt so weird to be writing out such an enormous sum, as though I were playing with Monopoly money. I addressed three envelopes—one for my parents, one for Emma, one for Maisie—and put a check in each envelope. Once they were sealed and stamped, I slipped them into the knapsack I'd be using as a purse, right next to my tattered copy of *To Kill a Mockingbird.*

I went into my bedroom and changed from my uniform of ratty sweats into black pants and a black T-shirt. Excitement skittered through me; this must be what it felt like to be an undercover spy. And in a sense I *was* going undercover. I was leaving my life behind and setting off on a new course. Before I switched off the light, I checked out my reflection in the mirror. The fatigue circles under my eyes were purplish, and my skin was wan—black has never been a good color on me—but I was still me. The same kinky out-of-control hair, the same too-round cheeks, the same boring brown eyes. Normally the sight would cause me to roll my eyes and curse the genes that had failed to give me the sleek hair and chiseled cheekbones I'd always coveted. But for some reason, seeing myself looking so normal, so ordinary, was reassuring. I turned off the light. Hopefully the reporters still camped outside would think I'd gone to sleep and would let their guard down.

I headed through the dark house toward the kitchen. I'd left my bag and Harper Lee, whimpering softly inside her carrier, there by the back door. I slung the knapsack over my right shoulder and Harper Lee's carrier over my left. I reached for the doorknob, but then hesitated and looked back at my modest little kitchen, which I could just barely make out in the dim light shining in from the neighbor's house lights . . . at the Formica cupboards, Corian countertop, and basic white appliances . . . at the vivid cornflower-blue walls I'd painted myself . . . at the oak Heywood-Wakefield dining table I'd discovered at a thrift store and spent three weekends stripping and restaining. It wasn't a glamorous room by any stretch; design snobs would probably look down their noses at it. But it was my home. And now I was leaving it. I didn't know when—or even if—I'd be able to return.

I opened the door, walked out into the darkness, and locked the door behind me.

Nine

I WOKE UP TO THE PHONE RINGING. IT TOOK ME A few beats to remember exactly where I was, although it all came back quickly—my nighttime escape from Ocean, Falls, the expensive, clandestine ninety-minute chauffered car ride to Palm Beach, checking into the glamorous Breakers hotel, where I'd handed the clerk my American Express card and a fifty-dollar bill when he asked what name I'd like to check in under.

"Hayden Blair, please," I said nervously, fully expecting to be refused a room and possibly treated as a national security threat. But the clerk just nodded, palmed the fifty, and upgraded me to a water-view room.

I switched on a light—the night before, I'd drawn the heavy blackout shades—and reached for the phone, which was still insistently chirping at me.

Please don't let this be a reporter, I thought. If it was, it meant our escape plan had failed. I braced myself and picked up the handset.

"Hello?" I said nervously.

"Is that the famous Hayden Blair speaking?" asked a familiar voice.

"Thank God it's you," I said, exhaling deeply.

"You know, I never tire of hearing that," Hayden said.

"Where are you?"

"I'm at home. There's a slight problem."

My heart sank. "You're not coming?"

"Of course I'm coming," she said.

"Oh, good, I was afraid you'd changed your mind."

"Nope. I just missed my ride."

"Your ride?" I asked. "What, were you planning on driving down?"

Hayden laughed. "Of course not. But I was supposed to catch a ride with a friend who was flying down there for some business thing, but I stayed out a little later than I meant to last night and ended up sleeping through my alarm. I'm going to have to fly commercial."

Since I lived in a world where commercial was the only choice, I wasn't sure what the problem was.

"So . . . can't you get a flight?"

"No, I did. I made a reservation. The only problem is . . ." Hayden's voice trailed off. She cleared her throat. "My credit card was declined. I think I must have maxed it out when I was in Vancouver with Craig." When she said the name of her ex-lover, her voice had a bitter bite to it. "He said his money was all tied up because of the divorce and that he'd pay me back once it was worked out."

"The divorce that never happened," I said. God, men really did suck.

"Right."

"Look, don't worry. Give me your reservation number. I'll call the airlines and give them my credit card."

Hayden sighed. "I was hoping you'd say that. You're a lifesaver, Lucy. I'll pay you back, of course."

"Don't worry about it. Just get packed and get to the airport. I'll see you when you get here. I'm in room fourteen-twelve."

"Room fourteen-twelve," Hayden parroted back. "Got it. See you soon!"

After Hayden and I hung up, I called the airline. I was a bit taken aback by the price they quoted—$1,408 for a one-way ticket—and then learned that Hayden had reserved a seat in the business-class cabin. I'd never flown anything but coach. Even now that I was a multimillionaire, it would probably never occur to me to fly first class. Why throw the money away when coach class will get you there just as quickly? But then I realized that it probably didn't even occur to someone like Hayden—with her family money and easy access to friends' private jets—to fly coach. She and I had been raised in such different worlds. I gave the airline my credit-card number—saying a silent prayer that the customer-service representative wouldn't recognize my name; luckily he didn't seem to—and then hung up and stretched out on my bed. My foot nudged against Harper Lee, who was curled up in a tight ball at the foot of the bed, although her eyes were open.

"I have to let you out," I said, and wondered where one went in a posh hotel to let a dog relieve herself. I slid out of bed, put on the white terry-cloth robe hanging in the closet, and called room service.

"I'd like to order some coffee, and . . ." I trailed off. For the first time in days, I suddenly felt ravenous. I looked at the room-service menu, helpfully positioned just next to the phone.

"Yes, madam?" a polite voice replied.

"And a ham and cheese omelet. And a muffin basket," I

said. "A glass of orange juice too, please." Harper Lee stared at me meaningfully. At times like this I could swear she understands English. "Also, an order of scrambled eggs." I started to mentally add up what I was spending—oh, God, was I really ordering a fifty-dollar breakfast?—but I tried to put it out of my mind. This was Palm Beach, after all. Home of the rich and famous. It wasn't like I was going to find a Denny's anywhere around here.

"Also, I need to let my dog out. Where should I do that?" I asked.

"I'll send someone up for your dog," the smooth voice said.

"Really?" I exclaimed. "Thanks, that would be very helpful."

"Of course, madam. May I assist you with anything else?"

"No, that should do it," I said, smiling into the phone. I went to the window and opened the coral drapes, which color-coordinated with the walls and patterned carpet. Sunshine streamed into the room, and I looked out at my upgraded ocean view. I inhaled deeply and felt my shoulders relax for the first time in weeks. I'd always loved Palm Beach. It was so beautiful, so glamorous. Even the beaches were more luxurious here—the sand was powdery white and the sea was a Caribbean blue, dotted with bursts of white foam.

"You know," I said conversationally to Harper Lee, "I think it's going to be a great day."

Service at The Breakers was a dream. A bellboy came right up to fetch Harper Lee, who was just starting to turn in circles and make her *I need to pee* face. He whisked her away, and by the time they returned, business completed, our food had arrived. I feasted as though I hadn't eaten in days. Which, I supposed, I really hadn't. The omelet was stuffed with shaved ham and oozing cheese, the juice was freshly squeezed, and the basket of muffins and rolls tasted as though they'd come straight from a Parisian bakery. (Or so I imagined, having never been to a real Parisian bakery.) Harper Lee gulped down her scrambled eggs, grunting happily as she ate.

After breakfast, I took a long, hot shower in the luxurious marble bathroom, which was stocked with private-label toiletries. Then I put the courtesy robe back on and got into bed with my book. I would have loved to lounge poolside, sipping a fruity drink, but I was too nervous that someone would recognize me after all of the television coverage. Still, I couldn't remember the last time I'd spent an entire morning lounging around in bed. It was deliciously decadent, and I enjoyed every minute. Despite my huge breakfast, I was famished by the early afternoon. I ordered room service again, this time a club sandwich with extra bacon. I gave one quarter of it to Harper Lee, who wolfed it down in one gulp.

"Don't get too used to it," I warned her. "We can't eat like this every day, or we'll both pork up."

Harper Lee grinned up at me and rested her paws on my knees. She folded her ears back fetchingly.

"You're not getting any more of my sandwich," I told her sternly.

Her little stump of a tail wagged furiously. I relented and handed over another stacked square of the club sandwich. Harper Lee lunged for it, narrowly missing taking a bite out of my hand with her sharp teeth, and retreated to a patch of sunlight by the window to eat her sandwich.

As the afternoon rolled along, I started to get bored and restless. I'd finished rereading *Mockingbird* and realized I should have packed a longer, denser book. Maybe one of the Russian novels that take weeks to read. I turned on the television and flipped through the channels. Thankfully, the talking heads on the cable news channels weren't covering the

Lottery Seductress story today. Instead, they'd turned their attention to another, more salacious story: an infamous Washington, D.C., madam who was threatening to reveal her client list. Everyone was speculating who the rumored clients were; the madam had hinted that they included several high-powered and well-known politicians.

I turned off the television and laid back in the bed. But now, instead of reveling in this new-found decadence, I noticed that my body ached from lying down for so long. Somehow, I eventually drifted off to sleep. While I napped, I dreamed nonstop. In one, I walked in on Elliott having sex with my sister. And when I asked what the hell they were doing, Emma looked up and began to tell me in excruciating detail about how she was going to have not one but *three* wedding ceremonies, each in a different country. And the entire time she nattered on about whether she should have the second wedding in Italy or France, Elliott stood there, his face tensed in concentration as he thrust his hips into her. It was an awful dream, and I woke from it with a start. It took me a long, groggy moment to realize someone was knocking on the door.

"Coming," I said groggily. I stood up, adjusting the robe around me. *It's probably the bellboy, ready to take Harper Lee out again,* I thought. Harper Lee clearly had the same thought; she was already by the door when I got there, her tail wagging and her body squirming happily.

I opened the door—and saw that it wasn't the bellboy after all.

"Ta-da!" Hayden cried out. She let go of her wheeled suitcase and threw her arms around me. She still smelled exactly the same as she had in college—a mixture of Fracas perfume and cigarette smoke.

"Happy to see me?" she asked, pulling back from our hug

to beam at me. She looked the same too—the glossy dark hair pulled back in a ponytail, the chic bangs, the ruby-red lips. She was thinner than she was the last time I saw her, though, and there were faint laugh lines just barely visible at the corners of her slanted, striking green eyes, which lent her a vulnerability she hadn't had before. It figured: Hayden was exactly the sort of woman who would manage to look even more glamorous as she aged.

"I've never been so happy to see anyone in my life," I said.

Hayden ordered up Bellinis from room service. "I need a drink after that flight," she said with a shudder, as she collapsed into a yellow chintz armchair. "There was a baby screaming back in coach the entire flight. Sometimes I think I'd like to have a baby, and then I meet one. Changes my mind every time."

"I don't know. I think it's different when they're your own," I said, thinking of Maisie's twins, sadness suddenly twisting in my heart. I missed Maisie and her boys. I wondered how she'd react when she opened the envelope with the check I'd mailed on my way out of Ocean Falls. I wished I could be there to see her face when Maisie learned that all of her financial problems would be instantly wiped out. She and Joe would finally be able to pay off what they owed and put aside college tuition for the twins. I imagined the tears shining in Maisie's eyes, gratitude mixing with guilt over having yelled at me during our last conversation.

"You think?" Hayden asked. She shrugged. "At the rate I'm going, I'll probably never find out."

"You and me both," I said, and we fell into a melancholy silence that was broken only when room service arrived with our drinks and a dish of shelled pistachio nuts. The sight of the slender crystal goblets filled with champagne and crushed peaches had an instantly buoying effect on Hayden's mood.

"I think we should make a rule right here and now: no sulking over men. They're not worth it. They're a waste of Kleenex," she announced.

"Hear, hear," I said. I raised my champagne flute to her. "Here's to a man-free life."

"Unless we're using them for sex," Hayden amended as she raised her flute too. We clinked glasses and then drank.

"Oh, my God," I said. "This is the best thing I've ever tasted in my life."

"I know," Hayden said, tossing a handful of pistachios in her mouth. Harper Lee had jumped into her lap, and Hayden stroked the dog's head absently. "We need a plan. First things first: We'll head over to Crane Hill." She looked me up and down. I was still wearing the hotel robe. "Do you have any clothes?"

"Just what I wore here."

"Good! I'll take any excuse to go shopping."

"You sound like Emma," I said.

"How is your sister?"

"She's fine. Well, insane but fine. She's getting married in February and won't be content until her wedding rivals Princess Diana's."

"Good for her," Hayden said approvingly. "Although I'm so over weddings. If I ever get married, I'm going to elope."

"Like to Las Vegas?" I asked. The incongruous picture of the coolly elegant Hayden in a tacky, over-the-top wedding chapel, complete with an Elvis impersonator officiating, amused me.

"No. City hall, I think. I'll wear a vintage Chanel suit and maybe even a little pillbox hat, just like Grace Kelly in one of those old movies from the fifties. Don't you think that would be sweet?" Hayden mused.

"I thought we were off men," I said.

"We are. I'm not talking *men*, I'm talking *weddings*. Totally different. Anyway, where were we? Oh, right: shopping."

"Okay. But nothing over the top. All I really need are some jeans, a few tops, a sundress, a bathing suit. Basic stuff. I'm pretty sure I can get it all at the Gap," I said.

Hayden ignored me. "We'll go to Neiman and Saks, of course. And there's a darling boutique on Worth Avenue that carries Tocca dresses. Those would look fabulous on you. And we'll have to do something about your hair."

I raised a protective hand to my hair, which was, as usual, rioting out of control.

"What do you want to do to my hair?" I asked nervously.

"Cut it. Something short and choppy, I think."

"My hair doesn't do short and choppy. You see these curls?" I held up a fistful of ringlets to demonstrate. "If you cut them short, they stand straight up, afro-style."

"You worry too much," Hayden said, with a dismissive flap of her hand. "You have to trust me."

"I do," I said. And I did trust Hayden; she had fabulous taste. But she was also naturally gorgeous. Unlike me.

"Maybe just a few inches," I said cautiously, touching my curls again. "And I've always wanted to try highlights."

Hayden shook her head dismissively. "Your hair is too distinctive. You've been all over the news, remember? You're the—what's that they're calling you?"

"The Lottery Seductress," I said miserably.

"Right. Well, everyone knows that the Lottery Seductress has distinctive brown curly hair. If you're ever going to be able to go out in public again, we're going to have to get you a new look. One no one will recognize."

I had to admit, this was sound reasoning.

"Maybe you're right," I conceded.

"Maybe? Please. I'm always right," Hayden said, giving me a saucy wink. She downed the rest of her Bellini. "Come on, let's get out of here. We have much to do!"

The sun was starting to sink down in the sky by the time we got to Crane Hill. Like many of the estates on Palm Beach, a tall, manicured privacy hedge surrounded the property. Hayden had rented a little red coupe at the airport, and she drove up to the front gate, leaned out the window, and keyed a four-digit code into the touch pad mounted there.

"Zero-four-two-three," she told me. "The birthday of Dad's favorite dog. Remember Pepper?"

I did. Pepper was a black standard poodle, with dark intelligent eyes. He died when we were in college; Hayden had cried for weeks. "Wasn't there a Salt too?"

"Yeah, but she was a submissive pee-er and had panic attacks whenever it thundered out, so everyone preferred Pepper."

"Poor Salt."

Hayden shrugged as if to say, *That's life*. The gates swung open slowly, allowing the red car to pass through. The driveway curved around in a circle under a portico, and just beyond was Crane Hill. The house was a sweeping two-story structure with a central building and two symmetrical wings. It had white stone walls, a classic red tile roof, and three grand archways over the front steps. Every time I saw it, I was newly impressed by the sheer grandeur of the place.

"It's smaller than I remember," I said dryly.

Hayden gave a snort of derision. "My parents have never believed in subtlety," she said. She parked the car and threw open her door. With a swing of long legs, which were still sporting the last traces of a summer tan, she was out of the car. I moved a little slower, making sure Harper Lee's leash was on before we got out of the car. In my faded black T-shirt and decidedly unhip black pants, I felt underdressed just to stand in the driveway.

As if she was reading my thoughts, Hayden glanced over at me and said, "It's going to be just us. I didn't even call the housekeeping service to let them know we'd be here," she said. "Is that okay?"

"Can I live without a maid, you mean?" I asked. I shook my head with faux regret; after all, my minuscule teacher's salary had never exactly stretched to include domestic help. When my toilet needed scrubbing, I was the one to do it. "I guess I'll have to find a way to manage."

Hayden ignored me. She was, oddly enough, crouching down behind the purple flowering bougainvillea bushes that bordered the front door; she appeared to be searching for something.

"What are you doing?" I asked, coming up behind her and peering over her shoulder. The only thing I saw was a long lizard scuttling along the white pebbled ground.

"Here!" Hayden said triumphantly. She seized one of the larger rocks and shook it once before holding it up to show me. "Ta-da! The key!"

"What, in there?" I asked.

But even as I spoke, Hayden had turned the fake rock over, popped off a plastic panel set in the bottom, and extracted a silver house key.

"Are you kidding me?" I asked incredulously.

"What? It's a key holder."

"I know what it is. I'm just stunned that anyone who owns a multimillion-dollar waterfront Palm Beach estate would hide the door key in a fake rock in the front garden," I said.

"Rich people get locked out too," Hayden said. "Besides, the house also has a state-of-the-art alarm system. This is just to get through the front door."

She stood, dusting off the skirt of her immaculate white sundress, and headed to the door. I followed behind her, pulling the suitcase she'd abandoned in the driveway. Hayden unlocked the door and then hurried through it to turn off the now-beeping alarm.

"It's the same code as the gate," she called back over her shoulder to me.

"Pepper's birthday."

"Right. Well, don't just stand out there—come on in!"

The front door opened onto a vast airy foyer with a vaulted frescoed ceiling, black-and-white-checked marble floor, and a huge round table in the middle. The last time I'd been here, there had been an enormous arrangement of pink and white roses displayed on the table; now there was only an empty crystal vase.

Hayden and I took a quick house tour. There was the living room, with the pale-blue silk couches and wing chairs; the cozier wood-paneled den, featuring a built-in bar and a flat-screen television; the modern kitchen with slate-tile floors, granite countertops, and stainless-steel Sub-Zero fridge; and my favorite feature of the house: the back lanai, which curved around a huge kidney-shaped pool and had a breath-taking view of the ocean. The lanai was scattered with teak lounge chairs outfitted with teal cushions that exactly matched the color of the pool tile.

I breathed in deeply, relaxing fully as I looked out at the

ocean. The water was calm as it rippled up toward the sandy beach. Even though the sun was setting behind us, the sky over the water was a glorious pink and ribboned with clouds.

"Wow," I said softly.

"I know. This is exactly what I needed," Hayden said, sighing deeply. "Do you want to go for a swim?"

"I don't have a suit," I said. I let Harper Lee off her leash, and she made herself at home, settling in on one of the chaise lounges.

"Go look in the cabana. There are usually extra suits in there," Hayden said, nodding to a pool house that was about as big as my actual house back in Ocean Falls.

But even as I headed off to change, Hayden just stripped off her dress. She wasn't wearing a bra; just the smallest wisp of a thong, which she stepped out of. Naked, she looked even thinner. I could see her ribs standing out prominently under her pale skin. But her small breasts were high and taut over a nipped-in waist and rounded hips. I couldn't help noticing that she had waxed away most of her pubic hair, leaving behind only a narrow strip. Hayden didn't seem at all self-conscious of her nudity. She strode casually to the edge of the pool, raised her arms overhead, and dove in. I wondered what it must be like to go through life so confident, so self-assured.

"How's the water?" I asked, when she'd resurfaced.

"Amazing," she said, dipping her hair back into the water, away from her face. "Absolutely perfect."

"I'll be right in," I said, as I ducked into the cabana. It was possibly the prettiest room I had ever seen. The walls were painted a soft azure blue, and a pair of identical sofas covered in white linen faced each other. A canopy bed that arched up like a birdcage was framed with frothy white panels and piled high with a fluffy snowy-white duvet and pillows. I felt an impulse to jump in it and burrow down under the pristine bedding. *If I could have any bedroom in the world, this would be it,* I thought.

I opened a huge armoire with intricately carved doors and inside found an armful of towels and a dozen bathing suits in various sizes, all with the tags still on. I tried not to gape at the prices, which were each over a hundred dollars. And for guest-room bathing suits! I bought my bathing suits at Target, and even then I usually waited for a sale.

I found a suit in my size—a one-piece in cherry red cut much lower in front and higher in the legs than I would ever have picked out for myself—and put it on. Then I grabbed a few towels and went back out to the pool, where Hayden was now swimming laps, her long legs scissoring effortlessly through the water. She looked up when I approached and smiled approvingly at me.

"That suit is hot," she said. "Red is definitely your color."

"Really?" I looked down at myself. "I never wear it."

"Well, you should. You coming in?"

"Yes." Instead of diving in, as Hayden had, I walked around the shallow end and slowly descended the tiled stairs. "Brrr! It's freezing! I thought you said it was nice."

"It is if you jump right in. The heater hasn't been turned on. We'll have to figure out how to do that," Hayden said.

"Would your parents mind if they knew we were here?" I asked tentatively.

"Why would they? They're not using the house."

"You don't think we should call and tell them?"

Hayden rolled her eyes. "Hell, no. Then I'll be stuck talking to them. Or, even worse, Mother might get it into her mind to nix her White Christmas plans and come down here instead."

"It's only October," I said. "The Season hasn't started yet."

Even though I was not a Palm Beach native, I was—as all Floridians are—well aware of the Season. From November to April, snowbirds flocked down to the Sunshine State, seeking an escape from the chilly northern climate. Ocean Falls attracted well-to-do retirees, who rented villas on the golf course or owned smallish second homes kitted out in shell- or palm-tree-themed decor. Palm Beach, of course, attracted a wealthier crowd. But the calendar was still roughly the same, with the population swelling over the winter months and then ebbing in the late spring.

"Even so, I'm not risking it," Hayden said firmly. "My mom and I aren't exactly getting along at the moment."

"Why? What happened?"

"Nothing new. I'm still not measuring up to my sisters. You know—they both had high-powered careers, married investment bankers, then downshifted onto the mommy track. And then there's little old me."

"What's wrong with being you?"

"Everything, according to my mother. It wasn't so bad when I was in my twenties, but now that I've reached the ancient age of thirty-two, she has informed me that enough is enough. It's time I give up my bohemian ways, find a rich husband, and get down to the important business of producing grandchildren." Hayden was drifting around the pool, inclined back, and occasionally pushing off the bottom to propel herself slowly through the water.

"Have you explained to her that modern feminism has given women choices? That we can be strong, secure, independent women of substance all on our own?"

Hayden snorted at this. "No. But I'd love to be there when you try to explain that to her."

"You're on," I said. "Because I'm in a very anti-man phase at the moment. I'm practically bursting with girl power."

"I'm pretty sure my mom thinks that's code for lesbianism," Hayden said, laughing. "After we dry off, we should pick out bedrooms. I always stay in the Yellow Room, but you can sleep wherever you want."

I remembered, from past visits to the house, that there were a seemingly endless number of bedrooms. And they all had titles: the Blue Room, the Chinese Room, the Rose Room, which featured a hand-painted mural of roses on every wall.

"Would you mind if I stay in the pool house?" I asked.

"What? You mean the cabana?" Hayden asked, looking surprised.

I nodded. "It's so fresh and airy in there. And I'd love to be able to wake up and jump right in the pool."

"Sure, whatever." Hayden shrugged. "I don't think anyone's ever stayed in there. But there's a first time for everything."

After dinner—the freezer in the kitchen was well stocked, so we defrosted a few steaks and a container of pesto to toss with tagliatini—Hayden appeared in the door of the pool house, armed with a pair of scissors.

"What are you planning to do with those?" I asked suspiciously, eyeing the silver shears. I'd been curled up on one of the white couches, reading a copy of *Rabbit, Run* I found on a shelf in the den.

"Cut your hair."

"What?" I shrieked. I jumped up and sidled behind the sofa.

"I have to cut your hair short enough so that it will fit under this," she said, holding up a hot-pink nylon baseball cap. The caption, *It's Five O'Clock Somewhere,* was blazoned across the front in black lettering.

"That's supposed to be my disguise?" I asked, eyeing the cap with distaste.

"Would you rather risk someone recognizing you?"

"Do you think anyone will really be paying attention to me?" I asked. True, I had been worried I'd be recognized while I was at The Breakers. But I'd been trying to convince myself that this was just paranoia and that, when you look as ordinary as I do, people tend not to remember you. Plus, the hat was truly awful.

"Are you kidding? Everyone checks out everyone here. Palm Beachers secretly love to spot celebrities, even if they pretend they're too jaded and sophisticated to care. So . . ." Hayden held up the scissors and snipped them menacingly in the air.

"But it will look terrible!" I wailed, raising a protective hand to my curls.

"It's just for a day or two, until we can get you in to see Frankie."

"Who's Frankie?"

"The best stylist in the world. I always go to him when I'm here. I'll call him and see when he can fit you in. He's normally booked up months in advance, but he always makes a special exception for me."

"And what if he doesn't?"

"He will," Hayden promised. "Come on. If you're serious about changing your appearance, you're going to have to get rid of those curls."

So I sat on a pool towel spread out on the middle of the floor and closed my eyes tightly. Hayden lifted up heavy sections of my hair and sawed away at them with the too-dull scissors. The sound of the clicking metal shearing through my thick curls caused goose bumps to erupt over my shoulders and arms.

"All done," Hayden finally said.

"How does it look?" I asked. I tried not to look down at the long strands of chestnut curls discarded around me on the towel.

She didn't say anything for a long moment. I turned anxiously and felt my stomach clench when I saw her doubtful expression.

"Well?" I said.

Hayden bit her lower lip. "I won't lie to you. It's not good. But don't forget, this is temporary."

I practically ran to the pool-house marble bathroom, took one look at myself in the enormous gilt-edged mirror, and burst into tears. I looked like a brunette Little Orphan Annie. My hair, freed of its weight, stood on end in a frizzy mess.

Hayden appeared in the doorway, brow knitted in concern.

"Frankie will fix it," she promised.

"I look like a poodle! I look like Pepper!"

I could tell what Hayden was thinking—that this comparison was really an insult to the lovely and graceful Pepper—but she was tactful enough not to say so out loud.

"Don't worry," she said, handing me the baseball hat. "When we're done with you, you won't even recognize yourself."

"You say that like it's a good thing," I muttered.

Ten

AT FIRST GLANCE, WORTH AVENUE LOOKED LIKE THE typical picturesque palm-tree-lined tourist-town shopping area. It was a narrow street between rows of charming one- and two-story Mediterranean-style buildings. Cars were parked along the curb beside meters. Awnings provided shade for the crowds bustling along with shopping bags. Purple bougainvillea had been trained to climb up arching columns.

But upon second look, there were some startling differences. The first hint that I wasn't in Ocean Falls anymore were the shop signs: Chanel, Gucci, Tiffany, Escada, Cartier. And the cars weren't just the usual Volkswagens, Fords, and Toyotas—here there were also Rolls-Royces, Bentleys, and even a vintage Aston Martin. There were plenty of camera-toting tourists out and about, but there were also very thin, very glamorous women strolling around in head-to-toe Lilly Pulitzer and equally glamorous men clad in linen. Dogs seemed to be popular among the Palm Beach denizens—pugs, whippets, and Jack Russell terriers wearing jewel-studded collars trotted smartly along by their owners' ankles. There were even doggy water fountains to keep the pampered pooches well hydrated.

I was all for strolling up and down the street, window-shopping and investigating the little vias that branched off from Worth Avenue and led to European-style courtyards, complete with fountains and decorative tile. But when it came to shopping here, I had no interest.

"I don't want to go in there," I said, when Hayden suggested we start off at an upscale boutique. When I peeked inside, I saw it was one of those minimalist stores where the clothes are all hung four inches apart on stainless-steel racks and nothing, not even a belt, costs less than three hundred dollars.

"Why not?"

"It's just . . ." I stopped and shrugged helplessly. "Can't we start someplace a little less scary?"

I watched as two terrifyingly thin women, one of whom was wearing a fur coat even though it was eighty degrees, teetered past us on four-inch heels and disappeared into the Gucci shop next door.

Hayden laughed. "These stores are scary only if you can't afford the prices. And trust me, *you* can afford them."

"Shhh!" I looked around nervously.

"No one can hear me. Come on, let's go in and look around." Hayden reached for the door.

I stalled for time. "I think I'd be more comfortable somewhere more anonymous. Like Macy's. Or we could try out the Bloomingdale's at the PGA mall," I said hopefully.

"Do you trust me?" Hayden asked.

"That depends," I said suspiciously.

"You're not supposed to say that! I'm one of your oldest

and dearest friends! You're supposed to trust me unconditionally," Hayden said in affronted tones. "Now, do you trust me?"

I sighed, martyrlike, puffing my cheeks as I exhaled. "Fine. I trust you," I said without enthusiasm.

"Good. Then we're going in to this store, and I don't want to hear another word about it," Hayden ordered. She held the glass door open for me.

I took one look back at the street, wondering if I could escape.

"Lucy!" Hayden hissed.

I had no choice but to follow her inside.

The sales clerk was very tall and regal, with perfectly coiffed short blond hair. She was dressed in a gray pants outfit made out of the sort of clingy material that would probably make me look like an elephant, showing every bump and lump, but it only served to highlight the sales clerk's itty-bitty waist and long, long legs.

"May I help you?" she asked politely, directing her comment to Hayden.

"Thank you, but we're just looking," I said.

The sales clerk glanced at me for the first time, and practically recoiled in horror. This is why I hate going into upscale boutiques: The sales clerks are always such snobs. Okay, sure, so I was still dressed in the same black clothes I'd snuck out of my house in, which admittedly were looking decidedly shabby after three straight days of wear. I'd topped it all off with the hot-pink baseball hat and a pair of cheap plastic sunglasses I'd picked up at CVS. I knew my outfit wouldn't land me on any best-dressed lists, but surely it wasn't *so* bad as to deserve this sort of reaction. I'd passed people on the street wearing fanny packs. *Fanny packs!* Even I, fashion-challenged as I may be, know enough not to wear a fanny pack.

But Hayden was undeterred by the snobby sales clerk's reaction. She grabbed me by one wrist and practically dragged me over to stand in front of the haughty woman.

"We're doing a makeover on my friend here," Hayden said. "Basically, she needs a whole new wardrobe."

"Hayden," I said, wriggling my arm in a vain attempt to shake off the death grip she had on me. "Don't you think that's a little extreme?"

"Are the rest of her clothes like this?" the sales clerk asked Hayden, as though I wasn't standing there, perfectly capable of fielding questions about my wardrobe.

"Yes," Hayden said. "Some are even worse."

The sales lady suddenly put a hand to her chest and gasped. My heart felt like it was seizing up in my chest. Oh, dear God, she'd recognized me as the Lottery Seductress. One call to the media, and news crews would be swarming all over me again. I looked around wildly, wondering if I should make a run for it.

"Is this for one of those television makeover shows?" the sales clerk asked excitedly. "Is there a camera crew hiding somewhere?"

I stared at her. "Makeover show?" I repeated. This was getting more and more insulting with every passing minute.

"Well . . . we're not supposed to say anything," Hayden said, leaning toward the sales clerk in a confidential way. She smiled. "I'll just tell you this: We need her transformation to be *spectacular*."

The sales clerk beamed at us as though this would be

her big break. "Leave it to me," she exclaimed, clapping her hands. "What size do you wear?" She eyed me critically. "Ten?"

"I wear an eight," I said, trying not to sound as sulky as I felt.

"Really?" The sales clerk obviously thought I was lying. But not to be deterred from her television glory, she marched determinedly off toward the clothes racks. She began pulling out dresses, skirts, sweaters, and trousers—it looked like one of everything in the store—and hanging them up on a rolling clothes rack that had materialized as if out of nowhere.

"Hayden," I whispered furiously. "Why did you lie to her?"

"I didn't," Hayden said, with absolutely zero shame. "I told her we can't tell her what we're doing. That's the truth. If anyone finds out who you are and what you're doing here, your cover will be blown."

"But she thinks she's going to be on TV!"

"Don't worry. I'm sure she works on commission, and we're definitely going to make this worth her while," Hayden said. She gave me a nudge. "Now, go on, get into the changing room, strip down to your underwear, and start trying things on."

I spent the next few days playing Eliza Doolittle to Hayden's Henry Higgins. It was exhausting. We shopped for hours at a time, with Hayden pushing me from store to store with the ruthless determination of a general launching an armed invasion.

And shopping on Worth Avenue wasn't like any shopping I'd ever done before. In the past, I'd always stuck to T. J. Maxx and the sales racks at Macy's. The boutiques that lined Worth Avenue were sandwiched between jewelry shops that buzzed customers in one at a time and antiques stores that didn't have prices on any of the merchandise.

"Two hundred thirty-five dollars for a pair of jeans?" I hissed at Hayden, as she worked through the racks at one of the boutiques, pulling out the garments she wanted me to try on. "I've never spent more than forty dollars on jeans!"

Hayden handed me the jeans and a periwinkle-blue short-sleeved cashmere sweater to try on. "You can afford this now, remember?"

"Not if I keep shopping like this," I grumbled. But I tried on the jeans, and, I had to admit, they did look pretty fabulous.

"See? Told you," Hayden said, adding them to our pile by the register. The sales clerk, a cool Asian girl with silky dark hair that cascaded down her back, could barely contain her excitement as she mentally calculated what her commission would be.

Up and down Worth Avenue we went. Almost everything I picked out Hayden dismissed as being too old, too frumpy, or generally unacceptable. And almost every time she'd hold something up to me, narrow her eyes, and thoughtfully say, "I think this will work," she would be right. It did work—the Versace blouses, the Gucci shoes, the Diane von Furstenberg dresses. We spent a day in Saks alone, where we shopped for shoes, handbags, and makeup, and where Hayden insisted I buy an evening gown.

"You never know when you'll need something formal—and when you do, it's usually too late to go shopping for one," she said in Saks, handing me a Badgley Mischka silk chiffon gown, the purple-black shade of an eggplant. "And, look, it's on sale!"

"For a thousand dollars!" I said incredulously. "That's almost as much as my first car cost!"

"Hmmm. A car. Have you thought about buying a new one?" Hayden said. We were driving around in a zippy BMW Hayden's parents kept on the island, having returned the red coupe to the car-rental agency the day after Hayden arrived.

"No cars. Not yet," I said. "At least not until I talk to my financial adviser."

"When are you going to see him?"

"Friday," I said.

"The day after tomorrow?" Hayden looked horrified. "You can't go with your hair looking like that."

"Maybe I can get a nicer hat. They do sell hats here, don't they?"

But Hayden had already pulled out her cell phone.

"Who are you calling?" I asked.

She didn't answer me. Instead, she said, "Frankie! It's Hayden!" Pause. "I know! It's been ages." Another pause. "Uh-huh. Uh-huh. Great! Look, I need a favor. I'm here. Yes, here-here. The island. And I need you to make a house call tomorrow." Pause. "I wouldn't ask if it wasn't important." She was using her stern, I-will-not-be-disobeyed voice. It had worked on me to tremendous effect in the past. "Yes, tomorrow. Yes, as in tomorrow-tomorrow." Another pause. Then she smiled. "Good. We'll expect you at the house at three o'clock." Pause. "See you then. Bye."

Hayden closed her phone with a click and smiled triumphantly at me. "You're on with Frankie for tomorrow." Then she narrowed her eyes, as she looked from me to the evening dress I was still holding. "What are you waiting for? Go try on that dress!"

On Thursday morning, we drove over to CityPlace, an attractive outdoor mall in downtown West Palm Beach. It was a popular area—the sidewalks were cluttered with shoppers—but it had a decidely more democratic demographic than Worth Avenue. There were a lot of national chains represented there—the Gap, Ann Taylor, Pottery Barn, Williams-Sonoma.

But Hayden dragged me past the Gap. She had a specific destination in mind: the Anthropologie store. "It has cute basics," she explained. "Ts, skirts, little cotton sundresses you can throw on with a pair of sandals."

"Isn't that what we've been buying?" I asked. I had, over the course of several days, accumulated a wardrobe that was easily five times the size of what I had in my closet back home in Ocean Falls. And one hundred times as expensive. I didn't want to think about how much I'd spent, although it was hard not to be all-too-aware of it, since I'd insisted on paying for everything in cash. I worried that if I used credit cards, someone would eventually recognize my name.

After lunch—Cobb salads at a little café, where we ate outside on a balcony that overlooked a fountain-filled square—we headed back to Crane Hill. Frankie arrived promptly at three, carrying what looked like an enormous tackle box and a canvas tote bag that was bursting to full with beauty gear.

"Frankie!" Hayden said when she opened the door. She threw her arms around him, and he set down his gear and hugged her so effusively, he lifted her off the ground. Harper Lee, who was skittering around at Hayden's feet, looked up at them and whimpered, unsure if Hayden was being greeted or mauled.

I could see why Harper Lee was concerned—Frankie was a big bear of a man. He was massively overweight, had a jowly face that was flushed an unhealthy shade of pink, and was sweating as though he'd just run a marathon. His hair was dark and even curlier than mine, and he sported a closely trimmed goatee.

I've noticed that all of the rich girls I've known—at Bates, I met more than a few—have oddly close relationships with their stylists. And while Hayden was never the type to run with the trust-fund brat pack, at least she seemed to have this unusual rapport with stylists in common with them. I'd been going to the same hairdresser for the past five years in Ocean Falls—Farrah, a dour girl with unrealized ambitions to move to Manhattan and style the fashion shows—and I wasn't sure she even remembered me from visit to visit. She'd certainly never hugged me in greeting.

"This is Lucy. Lulu, this is the fabulous Frankie," Hayden said, gesturing to him with a flourish.

"Fabulous? Please," Frankie said. His voice was low and growly, also like a bear.

"What? You are fabulous," Hayden protested.

"It's just such a gay word," Frankie said.

"So? You're gay," Hayden said.

"Which is even more reason not to use the word *fabulous.* It's a cliché," Frankie complained.

"So what should I call you? Furry? Hirsute?" Hayden teased.

"Better than fabulous. Besides, I am hairy. You should see my back," Frankie said, grinning. His teeth flashed white against the dark hair of his beard.

"I thought it was illegal for gay men to have hairy backs. Isn't there some sort of mandatory-waxing statute?" Hayden asked.

"Since I don't think I'll be dancing topless at the South Beach nightclubs anytime soon, I should be safe from the fag police," Frankie said. He turned a critical eye on me, and I self-consciously ran a hand over my shorn curls. "What the hell happened to your head?"

"It's Hayden's fault," I said.

Frankie looked at Hayden. "And I suppose you called me in to fix your mess?"

"Not fix her—*transform* her," Hayden said. "I hope you brought all your stuff, because I have big plans."

Frankie picked up the enormous tackle box and the tote bag. "Where do you want me to set up?"

It took hours for Frankie to complete Hayden's big plans, but it was a success: After it was over, I didn't look anything like myself. The Lucy Parker of old had disappeared, left behind in a trail of shorn curls and a pile of highlighting foils.

"Wow," I said, staring transfixed at myself in the hand mirror Frankie had produced from his tote bag. "I look so . . ."

"Gorgeous," Hayden said.

"Really freaking hot," Frankie added.

"Different," I finished.

"But in a good way," Frankie said.

"In the best possible way!" Hayden exclaimed.

I continued to stare at myself. Gone was my shorn, curly dark-brown hair; in its place were short choppy layers, straightened and bleached to a pale blond. I'd never been blond before, and it was bizarre to see my ordinary old face surrounded by lemon-hued locks. I looked like a different person. Which, I supposed, was the whole point.

"I've gotta get out of here," Frankie said, checking his watch. "I was supposed to meet some friends for drinks twenty minutes ago."

I handed Frankie back his mirror, which he packed away with the rest of his gear. After we said good-bye—Hayden and Frankie embraced again and talked about getting together for drinks sometime—and Frankie left, Hayden turned to me, her face flushed prettily. She was wearing her hair back in a ponytail today, which looked incredibly chic on her. When I wore a ponytail, I always looked like I was on my way to the gym.

"What do you think? Do you love it? Because I love it!"

"I do . . . It's just . . ." I ran a hand through my hair. It felt insubstantial and was so short, it left my neck vulnerable. "A big change," I finished lamely.

"You'll get used to it. I think we should go out to celebrate."

"Go out? But what if someone recognizes me?" Nervousness rippled through me.

Hayden laughed. "Trust me, there's not a chance. You look like a completely different person."

After ten more minutes of coaxing, I reluctantly agreed to go out. I even let Hayden pick what I was going to wear and do my makeup for me, so by the time we left, I really was transformed. We headed to Ta-boó for steak salads and then afterward went to a bar called the Drum Roll.

The bar was achingly hip. The walls were a calming dark gray-green that contrasted with the glossy white floor. Huge circular paper lanterns were suspended from the ceiling, filling the space with a filtered, ethereal light. The bar, which took up the length of one whole wall, and the rectangular tables bolted along the opposite wall were all made out of an exotic striped wood. Even though it was still fairly early on a Thursday night, the bar was already half full with glamorous, lithe club kids. Clothes were minimal, and nothing on anyone seemed to be sagging. I immediately felt ancient.

"Isn't this crowd a little young for us?" I murmured to Hayden.

She looked about in genuine surprise. "They're all about our age, aren't they?"

I wondered what sort of mood-altering drugs Hayden was taking that allowed her, at the age of thirty-two, to look over a room of twentysomethings—and young twentysomethings at that—and think they were her age. But before I could press her on this point, she headed over to a pair of unoccupied bar stools. Somewhat reluctantly, I followed her.

I was glad that we had, at Hayden's insistence, dressed up. I was wearing a gauzy orange-and-white sundress I'd bought at Anthropologie that day. Hayden had on a black linen shift she'd brought with her from New York. Despite our shopping marathon, she hadn't bought a thing. I remembered what she'd said about her ex-boyfriend running up her credit card and wondered if she'd be offended if I offered to give her some money. It was such a touchy subject, especially since Hayden had always been so fiercely proud of her financial independence from her parents. Over the years they'd tried again and again to help her out—even offering at one point to buy her an apartment in Manhattan—but she'd always rebuffed their offers. When I once asked her why, she'd shrugged and said, "I don't care for the strings that come attached."

Once we were seated on the tall stools, the bartender came over.

"What can I get for you?" he asked, smiling broadly at us.

"A Ketel One martini for me. Straight up with an olive," Hayden said promptly.

On the rare occasion when I go out for drinks, I normally order something boring, like a glass of chilled white wine. But that seemed too bland for this newly transformed Lucy.

"A vodka tonic, please," I said.

"Coming right up," the bartender said. He turned away

from us, grabbing bottles and emptying out a martini shaker. Hayden elbowed me hard in the side.

"Ow! What?" I exclaimed.

"Shh!" She frowned disapprovingly for a moment, but then her mouth transformed into a sly smile. "What do you think?" she asked softly.

"Of what?"

"Of *him,*" she hissed, nodding in the bartender's direction. "Isn't he hot?"

I looked at the bartender, who had turned back to face us as he fixed our drinks, and sized him up. Hayden was right—he was good-looking. He was in his twenties, and tall, with a muscular build very much in evidence under the thin fabric of his T-shirt. His features looked as if they'd been painted with strong, wide strokes—the broad cheekbones, the long nose, the generous lips, the square jaw.

"I thought we were off men," I said. "Men suck, remember? It's our new anthem."

"We're off *relationships.* Casual sex with hot guys is always acceptable," Hayden said. "Consider it a caveat to the original no-men rule. So you're not interested in him?"

I shook my head definitely. "He's all yours," I said.

And, of course, he was. The bartender, whose name was Ian, found reasons to hover by our end of the bar. He chopped limes there, arranged the fancy foreign beers in the cooler, wiped down the counter. And as he hovered, Hayden flirted. I had to admire her technique, which was smooth and subtle. She was friendly without ever being forward, managing to casually loop Ian into our conversation, which just happened to be a topic on which he was knowledgeable: the relative merits of various vodka brands.

Not a vodka connoisseur myself, and also aware that Hayden was reeling Ian in, I mostly just listened as the two of them debated Ketel One and Grey Goose, swirling the ice cubes in my drink around with a plastic swizzle stick. Then they easily moved on to the getting-to-know-you topics—where they grew up (he was from San Diego), where they went to school (Ian was a UCLA alum), and whether they had any pets (no, on both counts, although Hayden made a big deal over how much she adored Harper Lee, which I would have appreciated had I not known she was using my dog as boy bait). Ian had moved to Florida to take a job with an insurance company, but he'd gotten sick of the nine-to-five grind, so he quit and ended up tending bar instead. I noticed that Hayden slipped easily past questions about what she did—"I'm still trying to figure out what I'm going to be when I grow up," she said, flashing a charming smile at Ian—and was purposely vague about dates that would allow him to pin down her age, which I guessed was at least five years older than his.

While they chatted, I managed to finish not one but three vodka tonics, thus ensuring that I would wake up tomorrow feeling as though someone were attempting to split open my head with an ax. Eventually I excused myself and went to the ladies' room. As I washed my hands, I examined my new reflection in the mirror, wondering when the sight of the blond me staring back would stop surprising me. This new Lucy wore cherry-red lip gloss, so I touched up my lips before leaving the restroom. I could see across the bar that Hayden and Ian were talking intently, their heads bowed toward each other. I stopped and watched them for a moment, not wanting to interrupt them but not sure where else to go. Then I got the weirdest feeling that I was being watched. I glanced around at the now even thicker crowd of glamorous twenty-somethings—the later it got, the more of them seemed to arrive, which was the exact opposite of what happened to a crowd of thirtysomethings—and then nearly jumped out of my skin. I *was* being watched by someone.

The man was lounging in one of the spare booths toward the back of the bar. He was startlingly good-looking, which made me instantly distrustful of him. I'd never liked handsome men. Then again, maybe it was that handsome men had never liked me. No, that wasn't it. Handsome men had never *noticed* me.

This had never bothered me. There's something one-dimensional about the beautiful people, as though they're all walking, talking toothpaste advertisements. I much prefer the character of imperfect features.

This man, the one watching me, was older than the rest of the bar crowd—he had to be at least my age, maybe even a bit older. He had blond sun-streaked hair, pale eyes, and elegantly chiseled features. The chin was a bit too long and the nose a touch too broad, but even with these minor flaws, the overall effect was devastating. He was gorgeous, even considering his scruffy, beach bum appearance. His face had that golden hue that self-tanners aspire to and yet never manage to replicate, and his face hadn't seen a razor in at least a few days. He was wearing a T-shirt with a beer slogan across the chest over faded Levis. He smiled at me suddenly, a surprisingly sweet smile.

He thinks I'm checking him out, I thought, instantly mortified. I could feel my face burning.

I turned away quickly, and crossed the bar, back to where Hayden and Ian were still engrossed in conversation. But then one of the leggy young women leaned over the bar and called down to him.

"Ian, sweetie, I need a drink!" She held up her empty glass and rattled the ice cubes inside to illustrate.

Ian smiled apologetically at Hayden. "Sorry."

"Don't be silly. You are working," Hayden said flirtatiously. "Someone has to keep all these girls afloat in cosmos and apple martinis." Once Ian had moved off down the bar, she turned to me. "So? What do you think?"

"I think he seems like a really nice guy," I said honestly. I liked Ian. It would have been hard not to. He had the personality of a puppy and the abs of an underwear model, as we'd seen when he lifted his shirt and used the hem to untwist the cap off a bottle of beer.

"I do too. After Craig, I think maybe I should try dating a nice guy. Just for the sake of variety, if nothing else," she said.

"Dating? So you're going out?"

"Tomorrow night." Then she looked suddenly anxious. "If that's okay with you. I don't want to desert you."

"I'll be fine," I assured her. I was looking forward to a quiet night in. I'd stretch out on my dream of a bed, read, and listen to the ocean rumbling up toward the beach. "Where is he taking you?"

"Dinner somewhere, and then we're heading down to the Hard Rock Casino."

"Casino? I didn't know you gambled."

"Me? I'm all about taking risks, baby," Hayden said, winking at me. "But you should come with us. It'll be fun."

"Thanks, but no. I really am off men, no caveats. In fact, I just had a run-in with a creepy guy back there," I said, gesturing toward the back of the bar, in the direction of the bathrooms.

"What happened?"

"Nothing, really. Just a guy who thought I was checking him out. You know the type—the kind who thinks he's Brad Pitt and one smile will cause all women everywhere to throw their panties at him," I said bitterly.

"Did he say something rude to you?"

"No. He just smiled at me," I said.

"The bastard!" Hayden joked.

"No, seriously, it was the *way* he smiled at me."

"Like in a creepy way?"

"No. In a self-satisfied way," I said.

"Oh, I hate smugness. Which guy was it?"

He hadn't been smug, not really, but I didn't bother to correct her.

"The blond guy in the back booth. He's wearing a Budweiser T-shirt and looks like he hasn't showered in a week," I said.

"The really hot one coming this way?" Hayden asked.

"What?" I asked, looking up. But she was right, he was heading our way. I felt a nervous shock of excitement—was he coming over to talk to me?—before remembering who I was sitting next to. If he was crossing the room for anyone, it would be to talk to Hayden.

Or, even worse, what if he had recognized me? What if he remembered the face of the Lottery Seductress from one of the many news stories about me? At this, my stomach gave an uneasy lurch.

But, as it turned out, he hadn't crossed the room to speak to either of us. Instead, he nodded at Ian and said, "I think we're going to head out."

"We?" Ian said in a teasing way that made me know they were friends. He looked back—as did I—to see a stunning young woman standing behind the scruffy blond guy. She had stick-straight brown hair streaked with chunky patches of blond, and she was wearing a lemon-yellow halter sundress that showed off lots of toned shoulder and tanned thigh.

The scruffy blond guy smiled that sweet, lazy grin again. It wasn't a lascivious smile—he wasn't winking and smacking his lips—but it was still painfully obvious that the gorgeous girl was a conquest.

"Later, bro," he said.

"See you tomorrow, Mal."

So the blond guy had a name: Mal. *What kind of a name is Mal?* I thought, as I began to stir my ice aggressively. *Is it short for Malcontent? Maladjusted? Malodorous?* I snorted with laughter at this, which caused a few of the thin, leggy girls waiting at the counter to place their drink orders to glance sideways at me, before rolling their eyes at one another. And for some reason this caused me to feel a fresh wave of irritation at the womanizer Mal.

Why am I letting this guy get under my skin? I wondered. I didn't even know him and would in all likelihood never see him again. So why should his promiscuous lifestyle matter to me? But I thought I knew: Elliott. My anger at my ex wasn't so much displaced—I would happily poke out Elliott's eyes with kebab skewers if given the chance—as it was leaking into all of my other emotions. Which was annoying. I should be enjoying a fun night out with one of my oldest and dearest friends. I had a beautiful new dress, a sexy new hairstyle, and piles of money. I should be giddy, not fuming with cuckolded fury.

And right then and there I made a decision: I wasn't going to let Elliott bother me ever again. I wasn't going to mourn our lost relationship; I was not going to let myself become embittered with anger. From this moment on, I was going to be completely impervious to all of the emotional fallout of our breakup—the anger, the self-pity, the sorrow. None of it would affect me.

In fact, I thought, as I watched Hayden slide off her bar stool and exchange a flirtatious good-bye with Ian, there was no reason to swear off men. That had been the old Lucy—the angry, bitter Lucy with the long, dark hair and the easily broken heart. The new me—blond me, glamorous me, rich me—would flirt and date and maybe even have a torrid affair or two. If I could change my hair and my wardrobe, there was no reason why I couldn't transform my personality as well.

It's just mind over matter, I told myself, as I set some cash down on the bar to cover our tab. *Mind over matter.*

Eleven

PETER GRAHAM WAS NOT WHAT I EXPECTED. I'D PICtured him as a tall, elegant patrician with graying temples and a fondness for blue blazers with gold buttons. Instead, Graham was bald and probably five feet five inches in his stocking feet. He had a strong, stocky, pugilist's build, which he had stuffed sausagelike into a charcoal-gray three-piece suit. His entire body seemed tensed with a coiled, contained energy.

His office also wasn't done up in the clubby style I'd expected, with heavy mahogany furniture and hunt prints on the walls. Instead, it was very modern, with lots of Lucite and sharp stainless-steel edges. A large abstract painting featuring blood-red and violent purple blobs hung on the wall behind his glass desk. He gestured me to sit in one of the low-slung leather guest chairs.

I wasn't the only one with unfulfilled expectations.

"You look different in person," Graham said. "I saw a story about you on CNN the other day. I thought you had dark hair."

I lifted a self-conscious hand to smooth back my new hair. "I changed it so no one would recognize me," I said.

"Good idea," Graham said approvingly. "You might want to consider using a different name too."

This hadn't occurred to me. I wouldn't be Lucy Parker anymore? The very idea was both liberating and frightening. "You mean for good?"

"Just until the news stories about you die down. It will also help keep the profiteers away. Our first goal is to protect your assets. Our second goal is to grow your assets." He ticked these off on his fingers as he spoke. "So your jackpot was, what, thirty-five million after taxes?"

"Close," I said. "Thirty-four point four and change."

"And have you made any large purchases that I should know about? Cars, houses, that sort of thing?" Graham spoke quickly, a bullet spray of words.

"Just some clothes," I said. Then, remembering the checks I wrote before leaving Ocean Falls, I said, "Wait, no. I gave my sister, my parents, and my best friend each a half-million dollars."

I said this almost apologetically, as though Graham would scold me for my extravagance. But he just wrote down the numbers on a yellow lined legal pad with a black Montblanc pen without comment.

"I just thought I should give them something," I said, feeling compelled to explain even where no explanation seemed expected. "My sister's getting married, and my best friend is having some financial difficulties, and I wanted to help out. Was that a bad move?"

"Ideally, you want to keep the principal corpus intact. Invest it, protect it, live off the earnings. On the other hand, it's common for lottery winners to feel a lot of pressure from friends and family to share their wealth. There's the stigma that since the money was a windfall, rather than earned, the winner is not entitled to it," Graham said.

"Yeah, I'm starting to notice that," I said, thinking of Maisie's anger at me. It had been so unfair, so unjust.

"Yes, well, it's a rich person's problem. And, happily, you are now a very rich woman," Graham said, suddenly smiling approvingly at me. "And I'm going to do everything within my power to keep you that way."

An hour and a half later I left Graham's office, my head spinning with talk of portfolios, mutual funds, stocks, bonds, and lots of other financial jargon. It was a language that I'd never needed to speak before; now I was playing catch-up as fast as I could.

For the time being I was—unofficially, at least—no longer Lucy Parker. Instead, I'd adopted my mother's maiden name, Landon, although the tightening of Homeland Security meant that I had to keep my bank accounts and credit cards in my legal name. But socially I'd be Lucy Landon, at least until the stories of the Lottery Seductress died down. I would also have a new checking account and a debit card to go with it, which Graham would set up for me. Graham was in charge of giving me an allowance—a word I'd frowned at at first, as it reminded me of the spending money my parents had doled out when I was a kid. But he assured me that the accounts would always be topped up.

"Let's face it: With this much money, you can afford to buy whatever you like," he said, waving a hand in the air.

I couldn't help feel a thrill of excitement at this. *Whatever I liked.*

Graham continued, "But use your common sense. You'd be amazed at how many lottery winners there are out there who manage to blow through their winnings in a few short years and end up in bankruptcy."

"Don't worry. I won't be buying any jets or islands, or anything like that," I said.

"How about a house?"

I pictured myself owning one of the gorgeous Mediterranean Palm Beach estates, complete with a hedgerow fence, a swimming pool, and furniture right out of a glossy interiors magazine. I had to admit, I didn't hate the idea.

"I have a house," I said. "But it's in Ocean Falls. I don't know when—or even if—I'll be able to live there again."

Graham nodded. "Think it through. You might want to buy a second house, or sell that house and set up your primary residence elsewhere. But let's talk before you make any final decisions; we want to make sure your assets are protected from any litigation."

I knew he was being tactful, not wanting to mention Matt Forrester directly. I shook my head.

"The parents of the student who made those false accusations against me have assured Andrews Prep—my former employer—that they don't intend to sue," I said.

"That was before you came into possession of a large sum of money."

"Even so, he doesn't have a case. How could he? He made it all up," I said.

Graham looked at me almost pityingly. "Unfortunately, lack of proof does not preclude litigation. I'm not an attorney and so can't offer you legal advice, of course, but I think there's a chance—a strong chance—that the boy's family may sue you in hopes of forcing an early settlement."

"But Matt knows it isn't true! Surely he wouldn't be that stupid?"

But even as the words tumbled from my mouth, my stomach sank. Matt wasn't stupid, but he was lazy and greedy. And by all accounts, his father was a shark. Graham was right: They might try to go after my money. In fact, they probably would.

"As I said, I'm not a lawyer. But I think you should keep the possibility of a lawsuit in mind. Just so you're not surprised if it does happen."

"And if they do sue me?"

"Then you hire the best damned lawyer you can. And it just so happens that I know a few," Graham said.

"Okay," I replied, trying to ignore the sinking sense of anxiety this talk of lawyers and lawsuits was causing.

"Lastly—and I can't stress how important it is that you listen carefully, for this is probably the most important piece of advice I can give you." Peter Graham paused to let the weight of his words sink in. "From now on you must be very careful whom you trust."

"Whom I trust?" I repeated.

Graham nodded gravely. "Believe me, this sort of money will attract parasites. It's inevitable."

"Are you talking about con artists?"

"Sure, but it doesn't have to be that dramatic. Friends, lovers, even family members may come at you with an angle."

"So I can't trust anyone? That just seems so paranoid," I said with a nervous laugh.

But Peter Graham didn't even crack a smile. He just fixed me with a stern look. "I didn't say you can't trust anyone, but you should be careful and know that people aren't always what they seem. Proceed with caution, Lucy."

* * *

I didn't go straight back to Crane Hill after my appointment with Peter Graham. His talk of lawsuits and parasites had left me feeling uneasy, so I headed to my happy place where I always went when I needed to unwind: the bookstore.

I'd seen a Barnes & Noble at CityPlace the day before. It wasn't far away—just over the bridge, in downtown West Palm—and I managed to navigate my way back in the car I'd borrowed from Hayden and found a parking spot right in front of the store.

As soon as I walked into the cool quiet of the bookstore, my whole body relaxed. I looked around brightly, wondering whether I should start with the new biographies, which I'd always had a special fondness for. Or maybe I'd browse through the cookbooks. My brief but intense affair with the Food Network had kindled a desire to expand my culinary skills beyond heating up Lean Cuisines. But, no. What I needed, I realized with sudden certainty, was a novel. Something delicious that I could to sink into and lose myself in. I picked up a green plastic shopping basket from the stack beside the front door and headed straight for the literature section.

A sad reality of my life was that I had never been able to afford to feed my insatiable appetite for books. I read too quickly and too voraciously, going through as many as three or four books a week. The scan strip on my library card was worn down from use. But I'd always dreamed of having a copy of every book I really and truly loved—my own library, stocked to my exact taste. To me it would be the ultimate luxury, the way Louboutin shoes and Chloé dresses were to my sister.

And then it occurred to me: I could now afford books. I could buy all of the books I had ever wanted! More books than I could possibly read in a lifetime! Just the thought of this, of the stacks and stacks of volumes rising up before me like skyscrapers, a virtual city of literature, made me almost shaky with joy.

Seized with this image of my own perfect library and fueled by pure greed, I headed straight for a display table topped with a special line of classics in hardcover. *The Last of the Mohicans* went in my basket, followed by *Sons and Lovers, The Red Badge of Courage,* and *The Great Gatsby. The Grapes of Wrath. Jane Eyre.* And *Madame Bovary*—of course I had to have *Madame Bovary*! Everywhere my eyes fell, I saw another title I wanted. The stack began to grow, until the basket became so heavy in my hand, I could barely lift it.

Why don't they have shopping carts in this store? I thought desperately. I dashed up to the bank of cashiers by the front door.

"Is it all right if I leave this basket here while I shop?" I asked the nearest one. She was an attractive older woman with a kind face and short gray hair.

"Sure," she said, smiling at me.

I dashed off to grab another basket, which seemed to fill itself. Once I'd exhausted the display table, I moved on to the fiction section. *The Portrait of a Lady. Vanity Fair. East of Eden. Alice's Adventures in Wonderland.* And then another basket. And another.

It occurred to me then that I was starting to draw attention to myself. With every overflowing shopping basket I deposited on the counter, there were more looks, more murmurings between the cashiers. They were probably concerned that I was a crazy person with a disorder that compelled me to pull books off the stacks and that they'd be stuck reshelving them. I decided I should probably pay and leave before someone called store security.

As these anxious thoughts collided in my head like

bumper cars, someone tapped me on my shoulder. I started and spun around.

"Excuse me, I think you dropped this."

A man was standing there, holding out a copy of *A Farewell to Arms*. Without my noticing, the book had slipped out of my overflowing basket, the fourth one I'd filled.

"Thanks," I said, taking the book from him, averting my eyes in embarrassment at being caught in the middle of a shopping binge.

"Here, let me take that for you," he said, and without waiting for my answer, he plucked the basket from my arms. "Just a little light reading, hmmm?"

His voice was so light and playful that I found myself smiling up at him, despite myself. He was tall—very tall: I had to tilt my head back to look up at him—and attractive. Not gorgeous, not like the blond lothario I'd seen at the Drum Roll last night. This man's face was pale and a bit too narrow at the chin, a bit too fleshy at the neck. His dark hair, which he wore very short, was receding, exposing a wide expanse of forehead. He had friendly almond-shaped brown eyes, a prominent nose that ended in a sharp point, and when he smiled, he exposed a perfect set of straight white teeth. He looked unusually conservative for a sunny afternoon in south Florida, a place where most guys favored the American Jackass look: screen-printed Ts, cargo shorts, flip-flops, ridiculous facial hair. The man in front of me was dressed impeccably, in a navy-blue suit, a white shirt with gold cuff links flashing at his wrists, and a yellow silk tie. I liked how comfortable he seemed in himself. He neither slouched nor held his shoulders high and squared like he was trying to impersonate Superman. He looked to be in his late thirties.

"A little," I said sheepishly. "I guess I got carried away."

"No, not at all. I'm sure you're at least the tenth person today who came in to buy..." He leaned forward and riffled through the books in my basket. "*Middlemarch*. Alongside the perennial favorites *Don Quixote de la Mancha* and *Candide*."

Part of me wanted to yank the basket out of his hands—it was a well-known rule of etiquette that you never, ever commented on the contents of someone else's shopping basket. But there was something inherently affable in his nature—the wide eyes, the appealing grin—that stopped me. Instead, I smiled back at him, allowing myself to be drawn into his gentle teasing.

"I went a little crazy. I just kept finding more and more books that I had to have, and before I knew what was really happening..." I gestured helplessly at the basket.

"This isn't so crazy. There's, what—ten, twelve books here?" he asked.

"Yes, but..." I sighed, and lowered my voice. "This is my fourth basket. I sort of lost control once I got in here."

He laughed. I liked the open, ringing sound of his laughter and how his eyes crinkled at the edges. "I love it. A woman who loses control over books. I'd ask you to marry me right here and now, but I don't know if I could afford to support your habit."

"This is unusual even for me," I said. "In fact, I'm not exactly sure how I'm going to get all these into my car."

"Then it's a good thing you bumped into me," he said. He flexed his arms like a weight lifter.

I couldn't help it: I blushed. I knew he was just being nice and, yes, a bit flirty. But it had been a long time since a guy this attractive had paid so much attention to me.

"I couldn't impose," I protested.

"Sure you could," he said. "You'd be doing me a favor. I've

always regretted dropping out of Cub Scouts when I was eleven. This will help rehabilitate my reputation."

"Thanks..."

"Drew. Drew Brooks."

"I'm Lucy," I said.

"Just Lucy? One name, like Madonna?"

"Lucy... Landon," I said, tripping over my mother's maiden name.

"Are you sure about that?" Drew raised one eyebrow in mock query.

"Yes. Quite sure," I said brightly.

I could feel the cashiers' eyes on me as I stood in line. For all of Drew's jokes, it was clearly out of the norm for one person to buy piles and piles of books like this, all at once. It was a sad comment on our modern culture that the clerks in the Saks shoe department hadn't even blinked when I bought twelve pairs of shoes at three hundred dollars a pop, yet my book binge was causing a stir.

I began to worry about whether or not I had enough cash on me to purchase all the books. I knew I couldn't use my Visa. What if one of the sales clerks, interest piqued by my book-lust frenzy, recognized the name on my credit card and remembered that Lucy Parker was, in fact, the Lottery Seductress? And then alerted the press? Told them I was in the area, and had been miraculously transformed from a shy, retiring schoolteacher to a flashy blonde in designer clothes?

Oh, no, I thought, as my heart began to pound and I started to perspire. News of my transformation, of my new Palm Beach glamour, would just add fuel to the story. By this time tomorrow they might even have tracked down the name of my old college roommate and learned that her family owned an estate on the island of Palm Beach. And then it would be like Ocean Falls all over again, with the press camped out in our front yard. Crane Hill had the advantage of being surrounded by a fence and privacy hedge, but *still.* I'd be under virtual house arrest.

It was finally my turn to check out. The cashier scanned book after book, exchanging amused looks with Drew, who kept repeating the titles of every book as the cashier scanned it.

"*The Count of Monte Cristo,*" he said. "*Anna Karenina.* Hmmm, that's a thick one."

"Shhh," I scolded him. "Pack mules aren't supposed to comment on the contents of their load."

"Flatterer. Why am I getting the distinct feeling that you're only using me for my brute strength?"

"I thought that's what you were offering," I said, smiling despite the nerves wriggling in my stomach. What was the total now? What if I didn't have enough money with me? I supposed I could ask them to take some of the books off, but it would be so embarrassing, especially in front of Drew.

"No, it's just the first step in my master plan."

"Your master plan?" I repeated.

"That's right. First, I win your everlasting admiration by carrying your books for you."

"Everlasting admiration? Just for lugging some books out to my car?"

"Which softens you up and lowers your defenses, so when I ask you to have dinner with me, you'll have to say yes," Drew finished.

"Your total is $1,286.42," the cashier announced. "Do you have a discount card?"

"No," I lied. "I don't."

I did, but since it had my name on it, I didn't want to give it to her.

"You should get one. It's only twenty-five dollars, and you

save ten percent on book purchases. Even with the cost of the card, it would pay for itself with these books right here. And you'd still save a bundle."

"That's okay," I said.

"But, really, your whole order will be, let's see..." She pulled out a calculator and began to hit the buttons with the eraser end of a number-two pencil.

"Really, thanks anyway, but I'd rather not get a discount card," I said quickly.

"She likes to spend as much as possible," Drew told the clerk. "In fact, if any of these books are on sale, please waive that and charge her full price."

"Shhh," I shushed him. My heart beating a heavy *thunk-thunk-thunk,* I pulled out the cash envelope I'd gotten from the bank and began to slowly count out the bills.

Please let me have enough, please let me have enough, I thought. It would be close, I could tell. I counted out a thousand dollars in fifty-dollar bills and was then left with only twenties. One hundred. Two hundred. Two hundred sixty, two hundred eighty, three hundred. With a whoosh of relief, I triumphantly handed the clerk the stack of bills. She was much speedier at counting out the money, licking her index finger, and snapping the bills down in front of her. Once satisfied that it was all there, she punched some buttons on the register, deposited the bills in their proper slots, and then counted out my change.

"Thanks," I said.

I was so happy I hadn't blown my cover that I turned to beam up at Drew while the cashier bagged my books. Then what he'd just said suddenly hit me.

"Did you just ask me to have dinner with you?" I asked, genuinely surprised. Casual flirting was one thing—unexpected, yes, but not completely unheard of. But being spontaneously asked out on a date by a handsome stranger? That *never* happened to me.

"Yes, I did."

"You're not a serial killer, are you?" I asked, the words popping out of my mouth before I could stop them.

"Wow, that's even less flattering than being called a pack mule," Drew remarked, as he gathered several of the bulging plastic shopping bags.

"Sorry," I muttered. Then, to redeem myself, I grabbed a few of the bags. "You don't have to carry them all. Let me take some of them."

"If you insist. But the dinner invitation still stands."

"Well . . ." I stopped, thinking about it.

I had decided to abandon my no-men stance. And Drew seemed like a nice enough guy. But this gave me pause. I'd made the mistake of believing Elliott was one of the good ones and look how wrong I'd been there. But did that mean I was supposed to avoid all men who came across as decent and pleasant and only go out with the ones who were slimy right off the bat? Because that didn't seem like a great solution either. And there was no reason to think that Drew was anything like Elliott. Elliott had proposed to me in a transparent attempt to get his hands on my lottery money; Drew was gallantly carrying my shopping bags for me, even though he wasn't under any obligation to do so. Elliott wore those stupid leather thong sandals; Drew appeared to prefer classic lace-up dress shoes. They were nothing alike.

"Okay," I said. "I'd love to have dinner."

"Excellent," Drew said. He appeared to be struggling with the weight of the bags; the veins in his forearms were bulging with the strain, and a damp mist covered his face. "I'm glad to hear it. Now, why don't you show me to your car, so I can put down these bags before I end up with a permanent hunchback, and then we'll firm up our plans."

"Whoops, sorry!" I said. I held the door open for him. "Right this way."

"Please tell me your car is close by," he groaned.

Twelve

I ELECTED TO MEET DREW AT THE RESTAURANT rather than have him pick me up. He'd made a reservation for us at Morton's, a steakhouse in downtown West Palm Beach. The restaurant was darkly lit, which meant that I had to blink a few times after pushing through the wooden door so my eyes could adjust from the bright streaming sunshine outside. I glanced around and saw that Drew was by the bar, a clubby wood-paneled room off to the right, talking to an older, distinguished-looking man with short salt-and-pepper hair. Drew looked very handsome—and very preppy—in a blue blazer and khaki pants. His dark hair curled back off his face, exposing his high forehead, and his face was animated. I hesitated for a moment, not wanting to interrupt his conversation, but Drew looked up then and saw me. He grinned and stood, and when I walked over, he kissed me on the cheek.

"Lucy. You look lovely," he said.

I was rather pleased with my outfit—a red sleeveless shirt and long skirt, both made out of a flowy knit fabric that skimmed over my curves. When I saw it in the store, I thought it would look awful on me. But Hayden insisted I try the outfit on, and, as usual, she was right—it was perfect.

"Hi," I said, smiling at him.

"This is Ken Kramer. He's an old friend of my family," Drew said easily. "Ken, this is Lucy Landon."

Hearing Drew call me by my assumed name almost made me wince. *Lucy Landon.* It sounded so phony to my ears. But that was vastly preferable to Drew finding out he was on a date with the Lottery Seductress.

"Nice to meet you," I said to the older man.

"Hello. Well, Drew, give my best to your parents. Tell your dad I'll call him to set up a lunch sometime soon," Kramer said, before nodding to me and taking his leave.

"He looks familiar," I said, watching the maître d' rush up to hold the door for Kramer as he left the restaurant.

"He's the United States Congressman for this district," Drew said.

"Really? And your family is friends with him?" I asked interestedly.

"My family's pretty heavy into politics," Drew said, his tone casual. "Would you like a drink?"

"Just a glass of white wine, please," I said.

Drew signaled for the bartender to come over and placed my order. A moment later the bartender set the glass of chilled wine in front of me. I took a sip.

"Good?" Drew asked.

"Delicious."

"I don't know much about you, other than that you have fairly esoteric tastes in literature," Drew said. He had a habit of speaking quickly, I'd noticed, and everything he said sounded like it was a joke. "You're something of a mystery."

I felt a stab of panic at what I knew was a request for more personal information. I had expected this—it was a first date, after all; we were supposed to be getting to know each other. I'd even come up with a cover story, as though I really was a spy. I decided not to get too fancy, to basically stick to the facts and lie as little as possible.

"I'm not nearly that exciting," I said, covering my nervousness with a laugh. "I grew up in Ocean Falls. My parents and sister still live there. So did I, until recently. But I decided I'd had enough of small-town life, so I came down here to visit a friend and test-drive what it's like to live in Palm Beach."

"And what did you do back in Ocean Falls?"

"I worked as an office manager. For a friend's landscaping business," I said. It was part of the story I'd invented, a fictional job at Maisie and Joe's business.

"And are you planning on getting the same sort of job here?" Drew asked. He was drinking what looked like Scotch, served neat in a short, square glass.

"I'm not sure what I'm going to do," I admitted. This, at least, was the absolute truth. "I'm still trying to find myself."

Find my new self, that is, I added silently. The Lucy that couldn't be a teacher anymore.

Drew raised his glass to me. "Here's to finding oneself."

We clinked our glasses together. Just then, the maître d' came over to tell us our table was ready. Drew and I stood and, carrying our glasses, followed him to the table. It was one of those odd, crescent-shaped booths that force you to sit side by side, like in an old Hollywood movie. Not only was it awkward to sit that way, right next to Drew, as opposed to across the table from him, but in order to get into the booth I had to awkwardly scootch my bottom over bit by bit.

Drew took a few minutes to consult the wine list, asking for my input before settling on a bottle of cabernet sauvignon. He gave the bin number to the sommelier and then turned to me with a smile.

"What about you?" I asked. "All I know about you is that you're nice enough to rescue strange women in bookstores who've bought more than they can carry."

"I wouldn't necessarily say you're strange," Drew teased.

"Thanks a lot!"

"But I do get the feeling that there's something you're not telling me."

"What do you mean?" I asked, too nervously and too quickly. I could feel my skin heating up into an embarrassed flush.

"About the reason you're down here test-driving a new life, I mean. People don't normally make big changes, unless . . ."

"Unless what?" I asked. *Unless they've won the lottery? Been accused on national television of propositioning one of their students? Happening upon their boyfriend of three years in bed with a woman sporting fake breasts and a spray-on tan?*

And then, as if he could read my thoughts, Drew said, "What was his name?"

My jaw dropped open. "What?" I asked, in a strangled voice. "How did you know about Elliott?"

"Elliott, hmmm? I figured there had to be someone looming in the background. Let's face it—women like you don't rush off to start a new life unless some guy's been stupid enough to screw up their current one," Drew said, smiling at me. He really had a nice smile, accented by a set of dimples.

"Women like me?" I repeated. My voice was a bit higher and squeakier than usual, so I cleared my throat. "What do you mean, women like me?"

"Beautiful, charming, intelligent," Drew said.

Beautiful, charming, intelligent? I wondered, flabbergasted. No one had ever called me beautiful. Usually I got stuck with the dreaded *cute,* and that was on a good day. A guy I'd dated postcollege and pre-Elliott had told me several times that I had beautiful nipples, but as he said it in bed when he was approaching climax, I didn't take it too seriously.

I was still trying to digest Drew's compliment when the waitress arrived, pushing a cartful of raw steaks and produce in front of her.

"Hello," she sang out. "My name is Beverly. I'll be your server tonight. Have you dined with us before?"

Drew nodded, but unfortunately Beverly was looking at me as she spoke. I smiled and shook my head.

This prompted Beverly to launch into a bizarrely detailed explanation of every single dish on the menu, picking up various sample food items for a visual. I suppose this might have been useful if one really wanted to see the exact difference between a porterhouse and New York strip steak, for example. But when she held up a potato and a head of broccoli, I could no longer feign interest.

I glanced around the dining room . . . and there, sitting directly across from us in another one of the crescent-shaped booths, was the scruffy man I'd seen the other night at the Drum Roll. Only tonight he didn't look so scruffy. He was clean shaven and wearing a navy-blue polo shirt.

What is his name again? I wondered, but it came to me almost instantly: *Mal.* And Mal was looking right back at me. When our eyes met, my heart gave a nervous thump and then began to race, as though I'd had a shot of adrenaline.

In order to stop staring at Mal—which was difficult, considering I was facing him—I looked at his dining companion. She was very attractive, with delicate features and short dark hair, and was dressed in a slim-cut ivory dinner suit. She was also quite a bit older than Mal. She had to be in her late forties at least, or maybe a well-preserved fiftysomething. She also looked extremely annoyed. Her lips were pursed and her eyes were flashing: the very picture of a woman wronged.

How odd, I thought, as our waitress continued to natter on, now flourishing a bouquet of asparagus, while Drew listened patiently. *Why would a hookup artist like Mal be out with an older woman? And it looks like they're having some sort of a lovers' tiff.* That much was obvious from his date's thunderous expression and stiff posture.

The answer came to me in a flash of understanding.

Oh, my God, I thought. *He's a gigolo.*

I didn't even know that such a thing existed anymore. But that was stupid of me; of course it must. Wherever there was big money—and Palm Beach was certainly famous for its wealth—there would be opportunists sniffing after it. Hayden had told me that half of the shopgirls were just biding their time, until they could snag a wealthy husband. Obviously there would be a male counterpart—handsome men more than happy to squire rich divorcées or widows around town. Did he want to marry her, or was he just happy to get what he could off her? A nice watch, an expensive suit, a flat-screen television. The thought disgusted me. Mal was exactly the sort of man Peter Graham had warned me about.

It was worrying. Here I was, concerned that Drew would find out that I had this notorious and scandalous past, when what I probably should be worried about was if he, or any other guy I might ever meet in the future, would be after my money. At this thought, my resolve not to tell Drew the truth about my past hardened. I looked back at Mal, who was now gazing at me with an amused expression, and narrowed my eyes in dislike.

"Is something wrong?" Drew asked, leaning toward me in

concern. I started and realized that our waitress had finally finished her spiel with the tomato and broccoli and had pushed her cart away.

"No! Nothing's wrong," I said quickly.

"For a minute there, you looked like you were mad about something."

"Of course not." I was so flustered I started to blush again. "What would I be angry about?"

"I don't know. Maybe the waitress touched a nerve with her produce demonstration. Maybe you had a traumatic run-in with some asparagus in your past."

"Ah, no. What was up with that presentation anyway?" I asked, trying to push aside all thoughts of Mal the Gigolo. "Do you think they get many people in here who don't know what a potato looks like? Or did we just look particularly stupid?"

"No way. At least, you don't. You read *Madame Bovary*, after all. Maybe I'm the one dragging us down."

I laughed. "You still haven't told me what you do."

"I'm a lawyer," Drew said. "Commercial litigation at a midsize firm here in town."

"What were you doing at the bookstore yesterday?"

"I occasionally go there on my lunch break. I find it oddly soothing," Drew confessed.

"Me too!" I said excitedly. Not many people understood how comforting stacks and stacks of books can be.

"Plus, they have decent sandwiches in the café," Drew said. "So I'll go, browse a bit, then grab a sandwich. It's a good way to take a break from the stress of work."

"I totally get that. If I had a rough day at school, I used to stop at the bookstore on the way home just to unwind," I said. The words were out of my mouth before I realized what I'd said: *at school.* But Lucy Landon, the Lucy who was having dinner with Drew, hadn't been a teacher; she'd been an office manager. I could feel my cheeks flushing hot again, and I inwardly cursed my stupidity.

Thankfully, Drew didn't seem to notice my slip.

"Oh, really? Where'd you go to school?" he asked.

And I realized that he thought I was talking about college. I breathed a sigh of relief and resolved not to make any more mistakes. I liked Drew. I didn't want to jeopardize whatever this could turn out to be before I even had a chance to find out what that was.

At some point after the server had cleared away what remained of our steak dinners and before she'd brought out the hot molten chocolate cake (for me) and key lime pie (for Drew), I decided I was going to sleep with Drew. I didn't announce it, of course. One doesn't just casually say, *Would you please pass the cream? And do you have a condom on you, or should we stop at a CVS on our way back to your place?* But I was determined. The only sure way to get over Elliott would be to indulge in a good, old-fashioned rebound. And Drew—attractive, funny, smart Drew—would be the perfect guy to rebound with.

The new Lucy, I decided, the one with the blond hair and wardrobe of chic dresses, was just the type to sleep with whomever she wanted, whenever she wanted.

This was such a liberating thought, I got goose bumps.

We finished our desserts and coffee, Drew paid the bill, and together we headed out into the now dark evening to hand over our tickets to the parking attendant. I could feel the excitement fizz up inside me. How would this go down? Would he ask me over to his place? Or would we go to a glam hotel and order up champagne and strawberries to the room, as though we were characters in a Jackie Collins novel? I made a mental note to have Hayden take me lingerie shopping.

But when our cars pulled up—my borrowed BMW, his Lexus sedan—Drew just smiled down at me, his eyes crinkling at the corners. *This is it!* I thought, my pulse humming.

"I'd like to see you again," he said simply.

I stared at him, not sure what he meant. It had been so long since I'd done this, I couldn't get my footing. "You mean . . . later tonight?" I asked awkwardly.

Drew laughed. As though I'd just told a joke. Which I clearly *hadn't.*

"No. I meant next week. Are you free on Friday night? We could have dinner again."

"Um . . . sure," I said, hoping he couldn't tell how mortified I was. Was he ignoring my not-so-subtle suggestion that we not end the date now—or had he really not gotten that? Should I clarify what I'd meant?

"Great," Drew said. "I'll call you."

"Great," I repeated.

And then he leaned over and kissed me softly on the cheek.

"Bye, Lucy," he said.

"That doesn't mean he's not interested in you," Hayden said.

"Were you listening to the part where he kissed me on the cheek?"

"Mmm, I was," Hayden said patiently. "Pass me the sunscreen?"

I handed her the tube of SPF 15. Hayden squirted a white blob into her hand and rubbed the lotion over her bare shoulders and arms. We were poolside, reclining on the teak loungers. Hayden and I were both wearing bikinis and sipping from bottles of chilled water. Hayden's eyes were closed behind her sunglasses, but I was too captivated by the view of the clear turquoise water lapping up on the sandy white beach and the tall palm trees swaying gently in the breeze.

"And you don't think that's bizarre? That he'd pass up on a night of no-strings-attached sex?"

"You're overthinking this. He asked you out for another date. Obviously he wants to see you again."

"Maybe he just panicked and said that in order to get away from me," I said darkly.

"Yeah, because guys always do that. They ask out women they're not interested in, just to avoid an awkward moment."

I decided to change the subject. "I take it your date last night went well." When I'd gone into the kitchen to make coffee that morning, I'd run into Ian foraging for cornflakes. He'd had that cheerful, rumpled air that spoke all too clearly about how he and Hayden had spent *their* postdate night. Obviously Hayden hadn't been foisted off with a cheek kiss and plans for a future dinner.

"Mm-hmm," Hayden murmured. "I like Ian. He's a lot of fun."

"Did you two end up going to the casino?"

"Yes. And I was on a lucky streak. I won five hundred dollars playing blackjack."

"Wow!" I said admiringly. "That's amazing. I've never won anything in my life."

Hayden pushed her sunglasses up on top of her head and stared at me in disbelief. "You mean other than a multimillion-dollar jackpot?"

I blushed. "Oh, right. I keep forgetting about that," I mumbled.

"Lucky you," Hayden said, laughing, as she resettled the sunglasses on her nose.

* * *

Over the next few days I felt, in turns, apprehensive and annoyed every time the phone rang and it wasn't Drew. I tried to put him out of my mind, remembering that the new Lucy wasn't supposed to care about such things. And in the meantime Hayden and I settled down into lives of leisure, a well-honed pastime in Palm Beach.

We spent most mornings lounging by the pool, sipping iced coffees and taking lazy swims. Then we'd shower and head out for a late lunch at Ta-boó or the Palm Beach Grill. After lunch we'd shop at the boutiques on Worth Avenue, go to a matinee, or head back for more poolside time, depending on how ambitious we were feeling. Then, at around seven or so, we'd doll ourselves up and head out on the town. We'd have dinner at one of the many fantastic restaurants on the island—Cucina Dell'Arte, Trevini Ristorante, 264 The Grill. Then we'd usually end up at the Drum Roll so Hayden could see Ian. They were ridiculously cute together. And although I wondered if she was a bit too worried about the age difference—she'd even taken to wearing her hair in two low pigtails, like the young twentysomething hippie chicks—she did seem genuinely happy. Ian was equally smitten with her. Creatures of habit that we were, Hayden and I always sat at the same two stools at the end of the bar, and whenever there was a lull, Ian would hang out with us, leaning forward on the polished bar, gazing devotedly down at Hayden.

"It's not going anywhere, of course," Hayden said, when Ian went off to fill a drink order. She popped an olive into her mouth. "But it's fun to be with someone who likes me so much."

"Must be nice."

"Don't worry. He'll call. Your date isn't until tomorrow night. He still has time."

"I hate being in this position," I grumbled. "I don't like waiting around for a man to call me. It makes me feel pathetic, which I swore I wouldn't do anymore."

"You're not waiting around. You're out at the hottest bar on the island," Hayden corrected me. "You just need someone cute to flirt with." She glanced around, looking for contenders. "Look, there's Mal. You can flirt with him."

It annoyed me that I felt compelled to look. But, yes, there he was again, looking scruffily sexy and surrounded by a bevy of very young, very pretty girls skimpily attired in halter tops and miniskirts. Hayden had met Mal a few nights earlier at an after-hours party she'd gone to with Ian. I'd begged off going with them—after all those years of keeping teacher's hours, parties that began at two in the morning were just too late for me—and instead escaped home to bed.

"Yeah, he's just my type," I said sarcastically.

"I didn't say you had to marry him. But I bet he could get your mind off Drew. Have you seen his thighs? They're gorgeous, all tan and muscular," Hayden said dreamily.

"I hadn't noticed," I said, which was not strictly true.

The night passed pleasantly enough. Hayden and Ian filled me in on their casino trip the night before.

"Hayden is the Golden Goddess of Blackjack," Ian said. "She's amazing, a total natural."

"A natural card shark," I said, grinning at Hayden. "Why am I not surprised?"

Hayden rolled her eyes but smiled. "I think Lucy's luck must have rubbed off on me."

I froze, while Ian looked at us, puzzled. Hayden had promised me she wouldn't tell Ian—or anyone else—about my lottery winnings. She instantly realized her mistake and hurried to fix it.

"Lucy's always been lucky," she lied blithely. "She's just one of those people who was born under a lucky star."

Ian grinned at me, buying the lie. "Well, the next time we head down to the casino, you should come with us."

I smiled back at him but shook my head. "Not my scene," I said.

"Then you'll have to let me rub your belly for luck before I go," Ian said.

"Like a Buddha statue," Hayden said, delighted with the idea.

"Wow, how flattering," I said sarcastically. "A fat Buddha statue. Just what I've always wanted to be compared to."

"Don't worry," Hayden assured me. "The only stomach Ian will be rubbing is mine."

I pantomimed gagging, but Ian and Hayden were too busy exchanging smoldering looks to pay me any attention. I sighed and ate some peanuts. Nothing like being a third wheel.

"Hi."

I turned in the direction the voice had come from, and found myself face-to-face with Mal.

"I thought that if we're going to keep bumping into each other, it was probably time we officially met," he said. He smiled a lazy, lopsided grin. "I'm Mal."

"I know," I said irritably.

His sudden appearance beside me, when I hadn't even noticed that he'd crossed the bar, annoyed me. I knew it was irrational, but I couldn't help it—I instinctively didn't like the guy. Not only was he a player, which was bad enough, but he was also too damned pleased with himself, which was in my eyes an even greater failing. I didn't like cocky guys, didn't care for their swagger, their conviction that they were God's gift to the world.

Mal whistled. "Tough crowd," he said. His eyes were a very pale shade of blue. Unusually pale, in fact. Almost gray.

"Really? They seem easy enough," I said, nodding over to the group of hippie chicks I'd last seen him with. They were looking back at us, swinging their hair and pouting glossed lips.

"No kidding," Mal said. His smile widened. "I prefer more of a challenge."

"Try a nunnery," I suggested.

"That might be too much of a challenge. Plus, I have a rule about never dating women who bring up religion when you first meet them. Not that I have anything against religion per se, but it's pretty clear that if it's a top priority in your life, I'm probably not the man you're looking for," Mal said.

"Really," I said. "What do you think about Jesus? Quite an extraordinary guy, all things considered. Water into wine, and all that."

Mal ignored my naked attempt to get rid of him. "I also stay away from women who bring up marriage, children, and puppies right away," Mal said. "For the same reason."

"What do you have against puppies?"

"When a woman starts gushing about how much she wants a puppy, what she's really saying is that she wants a baby. It's chick code."

"Oh, my God. You're like a stereotype of yourself," I said.

This seemed to interest Mal. "Is that possible? Can you be a stereotype of yourself? If a stereotype is defined as a simplified and standardized conception or image invested with special meaning and held in common by members of a group, that is."

"I supposed what I meant was that you're the absolute stereotype of a player," I said crossly.

This made Mal laugh. "Why? Because I don't date religious women?"

"*Because,*" I said, "every time I see you, you're with a different girl."

"Woman," he corrected me. "Calling grown women *girls* is misogynistic and condescending."

"You know what? I think I officially hate you," I said.

"Really? Huh. Women usually like me," Mal said.

"So I gather."

"Aren't you going to at least tell me your name?"

"Her name is Lucy," Hayden said, leaning over me to join our conversation. "Hi, Mal."

"Hayden," I said, turning to face my friend, "I'm going to head back to the house."

"Come on, Lulu. The night's still young."

"I'm tired."

"Twenty minutes," Hayden compromised. "And then I'll go with you."

"Okay," I said, checking my watch so I could hold her to it. Ian appeared and set a bottle of Amstel down in front of Mal and fresh vodka tonics for Hayden and me.

"Not for me, thanks," I said, pushing my drink away.

But Ian, who'd been caught in Hayden's force field and was gazing down at her with a familiar love-struck grin, ignored me.

"Looks like you're stuck with me," Mal said. "We could try small talk."

"Or I could just sit here quietly by myself," I retorted.

"What do you do when you're not playing the girl about town?"

"I thought you just said calling women *girls* was misogynistic," I said.

Mal grinned so mischievously, it was hard not to smile back at him. I compromised by frowning severely.

"So I did," he said. "I'm sure you meant to ask me what I do."

"No, I didn't," I said.

"I'm a tennis pro."

"You are?" I asked.

"Why does that surprise you?"

"I just . . . I don't know," I said. In truth, it made all the sense in the world. What better job for a gigolo to have? It was the perfect way to find rich women to take advantage of. A few sets of tennis, a steam bath, a quick rendezvous in the clubhouse . . .

"What's it like to be a multimillion-dollar-lottery winner?" Mal suddenly asked.

I let out an involuntary gasp and my entire body went cold with fear. I could feel the fine hairs on my arms and neck stand up on end.

"What did you say?" I asked in a strangled whisper.

"I recognized you from TV," Mal said. "Although your hair is different." He narrowed his gray eyes critically. "To be honest, I liked it better before, when it was all long and curly. It suited you more."

"But . . . but . . ." I looked around wildly, half-expecting to see the phalanx of press suddenly appear in the bar.

"Don't worry. I don't think anyone else recognizes you," Mal said. Thankfully he was keeping his voice low. "You do look different."

"You did!" I hissed.

"I have an eye for faces. And I remembered your eyes."

"What about them?"

"I liked them," Mal said simply. "They're pretty. And honest. Not a combination I see a lot of."

"They're just ordinary eyes," I protested. But, despite my shock at being outed and my fear that this meant I'd have to find a new town to hide in, just when I was starting to get used to it here, deep down I couldn't help feeling a flicker of pleasure that Mal thought my eyes were pretty. And I got the feeling that he meant it too, that it wasn't just a line. . . .

Oh, good God, get a grip, I told myself sternly. *Of course it doesn't sound like a line. The best lines are the ones that don't sound like lines. This guy is a pro. He's exactly what Peter Graham warned me about.*

"Look, I have to get out of here," I said, and started to push away from the bar, ready to slide off my stool. The sudden weight of a hand on my wrist stopped me—Mal's hand, gentle but insistent.

"Don't go," he said softly. "I didn't meant to freak you out. Really, no one else knows who you are. And I'm not going to tell anyone."

"Why should I believe that?" I asked, my voice shrill. "I don't even know you."

"You didn't have to know me before you decided to hate me. So why do you need to know me before trusting me with your deepest, darkest secret?"

I frowned at him. "Are you insane? It's not the same thing at all!"

But Mal was laughing now, and my lips curved up into a reluctant smile.

"Ha-ha," I said. "And it isn't a dark secret—just a deep one."

"I think you're smart to stay undercover. This town is full of opportunists."

"And you'd know all about that, huh?" I snapped.

Mal grinned at me. It was an appealing grin, I had to admit. I could see why the girls—*women,* I corrected myself—

flocked to him. He might be a player, but he wasn't cheesy about it: no stupid lines, no heavy-lidded stares, no clumsy lunges. But I had to make it clear to him right here and now that I wasn't going to fall for his act.

"Look," I said. "I'm not interested. No offense. I'm sure you're a really fun guy, and obviously you're very popular around here even if you are unbelievably cocky, and you seem to have..." I tried to think of something nice to say. "Well... good hygiene, I guess. But I'm not into boy toys. It's just not my thing."

Mal leaned back on his stool, looked at me for a long moment, and then, to my astonishment, he started to laugh. It wasn't a chuckle but a full-out, belly-deep laugh. He was even wiping tears from his eyes.

"Boy toy?" he repeated.

And then he laughed some more.

Perplexed, I stared at him under furrowed brows. I had no idea what he thought was so funny. People around us were looking over at him, many of them smiling at the sight of his hilarity, even if they had no idea what had caused it.

"Good hygiene?" he finally asked, when he'd stopped laughing enough to speak. "That was the best you could come up with? *Good hygiene?*"

I couldn't help smiling at this, even though I did so rather sheepishly. "Well, I don't know you very well. But you smell nice enough. Or, at least, you don't smell bad."

And then we were both laughing.

"Talk about damning with faint praise," Mal said.

"I'm sorry," I said. "I wasn't trying to insult you. I was just trying to... well, to make it clear that I'm not interested in you. Not in that way. Although we can be friends, if you want."

"Lucky me," Mal said, still grinning. "Don't worry, sweetheart. You're not my type."

"I'm not?" I asked, surprised.

"And you call me cocky?" Mal asked, raising one eyebrow.

I blushed, realizing that I had sounded arrogant. And I couldn't exactly ask him why he wasn't interested in romancing me for my money. That would be even more insulting than telling him he had good hygiene. "It's just . . . you came over here to talk to me," I tried to explain.

"No, I didn't. I came over here to get a beer. And then stayed for the insults."

"I'm sorry," I said. "I'll try not to insult you anymore."

"I'm sure it'll be a struggle for you." Mal laughed. "Anyway, as illuminating as this conversation has been, I've probably neglected Melissa for long enough."

"Melissa?" I asked.

"The redhead in the green T-shirt," Mal said, nodding toward the back of the bar.

The redhead, I noted, was gorgeous. She had long, luxurious hair the color of copper and a golden tan, and what Mal had called a T-shirt was a very skimpy—and probably very expensive—silk sleeveless blouse in a gorgeous shade of jade green. I also noticed that she looked extremely pissed off.

"I think Melissa is bit peeved at you," I said.

"Melinda," Mal corrected me.

"You just said her name was Melissa."

"I did? Damn. Which one is it? Melissa or Melinda?"

"How should I know?" I laughed, and Mal shot me a dirty look.

"You're a lot of help," he said as he turned to leave.

"Hey, wait a second." Mal turned back to face me, his eyebrows cocked. "What is Mal short for?"

"Malcolm."

"Really?" For some reason, this surprised me. "You don't look like a Malcolm."

"Maybe that's because I'm not a seventy-year-old Scotsman."

I laughed. "Maybe so."

"I should get back to my date."

"Whatever her name is."

Mal looked uneasily over at Melissa/Melinda. "Right." But then he nodded genially at me and extended a hand, which I shook. "Lucy, it's been a pleasure. Sort of."

I watched Mal make his way through the crowd at the bar to rejoin the hippie chicks. The redhead—whatever her name was—made a big show of pouting, but then one of her friends seized the opportunity to start flirting with Mal. The redhead quickly took his arm possessively in hers and curved her body against his.

Hayden poked me in the side. "Are you ready to go? Ian's getting off soon, and he said he'll meet me back at the house. I want to take a shower before he gets there. I reek of smoke," Hayden said, wrinkling her nose. She stabbed out her Marlboro Light.

"Yes, I'm ready. Let's get out of here," I said.

Thirteen

DREW PHONED THE NEXT DAY.

"I'm calling to see if we're still on for tonight," Drew said. He sounded a bit distracted and was talking faster than usual. "I'm sorry; I meant to call you yesterday to confirm, but I was in meetings all day and didn't get the chance."

"It's fine. And, sure, we're still on," I said. After all, the new Lucy wasn't going to act sulky over not having heard back immediately from a guy she'd been out with only once. Then I wondered if maybe the new Lucy shouldn't be so readily available, should not have kept her night open, should in fact be so busy, it would be a *struggle* to fit Drew in. For no reason at all, I remembered Mal calling me a "girl about town," and the memory made me smile. That was certainly as far from the old Lucy as it got. That Lucy spent her nights at home, ensconced on the sofa with a cup of herbal tea and a good book.

"Fantastic," Drew said, and he sounded so pleased, I was glad I hadn't played hard to get. "Should I pick you up? Say about seven?"

"Sounds great," I said. I gave him directions to Crane Hill, and then we said good-bye and hung up. And I couldn't stop smiling. Two dates in one week!

Take that, Elliott, I thought, and pictured myself knocking him over with a well-placed karate kick to the stomach. *Hi-ya!*

That evening, before my date, I called my parents from the pool house. It had been too long since I'd talked to my family, and I didn't want them to worry. Emma answered the phone.

"Hey. It's me," I said. I was sitting on one of the white linen sofas, and I tucked my feet up underneath me. Just hearing my sister's voice suddenly made me homesick. Harper Lee, who was curled up on the sofa next to me, settled against my thigh with a heavy sigh.

"Lucy?"

"Yes. Of course it's me," I said.

"Hey! How are you? I'm so mad at you, by the way. I can't believe you ran off to Palm Beach and didn't take me with you. I could have used a little R-and-R right about now."

"Why? What's going on?"

"Well, the wedding planning is extremely stressful, of course. And Mom's been in a tizzy. Do you know who called her?"

"Who?"

"Oprah Winfrey. Well, not Oprah herself, but one of the producers from her show. Can you believe that?"

"What did they want?"

"What do you think? She wanted to do an interview with the Lottery Seductress. In fact, she wanted the whole family on her show," Emma continued. "Mom said no, of course."

Good old Mom, I thought. She'd never sell me out.

"But then she started to think about it and decided she made a mistake turning it down."

"What! Why?"

"Because of the publicity she could have gotten for whatever her project *du jour* is. Spay and Neuter Week, maybe? Or maybe it was Save the Sea Turtles. Anyway, she called the producer back to discuss it."

"Oh, no," I groaned. "First Elliott was on *Good Morning America* and *Larry King*, now Mom's going to be on *Oprah*?"

"No, she's not. They told her they wanted to do a show just on you. You know, the Lottery Seductress."

"Please don't call me that. And there's not a chance in hell I'm going on *Oprah* to talk about it."

"That's what Dad said you'd say," Emma said. "Where are you staying, anyway? Hayden's house?"

"Why? Are you going to sell me out too?" I asked suspiciously.

"No," Emma said. "Not even for Oprah." Then she reconsidered. "Well. Probably not for Oprah."

"Did you get the check I sent you?"

"Oh, my God! I totally forgot to thank you!" Emma exclaimed. "Thank you, thank you, thank you! I'm going to have the most amazing wedding ever!"

"Look, Em, it's your money to do with what you wish. But please don't spend all of it on the wedding," I said. "I want you to save it for your future with Christian."

But Emma wasn't listening to me. "Actually, we were a little confused. You sent a check to me *and* one to Mom and Dad. Were they both supposed to be for the wedding?" she asked.

"What? Of course not!" I said, thinking not even Emma could come up with a way to spend one million dollars on a wedding—could she? God, I hoped not. "I thought Mom and Dad would use the money to do something fun. Take a great trip somewhere, or maybe buy a second house. Dad's always said he'd love to spend his summers in Maine. They could use the money to buy a cottage up there."

"Dad won't accept the money," Emma said, suddenly serious.

"Won't accept it?" I repeated, confused. "But why?"

"He said he won't have you supporting him. Mom's ticked off at him. She said you wouldn't have given it to them if you didn't want them to have it. She wants to use it for one of her causes."

"I was hoping they'd spend it on themselves," I said. As much as I respected the animal-rescue work our mother did, I wanted my parents to put the money toward something fun. And the last thing I'd intended was for it to be a source of conflict between them. "I should talk to them. Is either of them home?"

"No. Neither one. Dad's still at work, and I think Mom went to feed the feral cats."

"Tell them I called. And that I'm fine," I said.

"Will do. Hey, wait, before you go, let me ask you something," Emma said.

I smiled. Emma might be self-centered and wedding-obsessed, but when it came down to it, she was a good sister. She probably wanted to know how I was dealing with the breakup. Or whether I was worried about the allegations Matt Forrester had made against me. And the truth was, I was still feeling a little shaky. So much had changed in such a short time, and I was still trying to get used to this new life I'd suddenly been thrust into. I could use some sisterly support right about now.

But then Emma continued: "What do you think about blush?"

"Blush. What about it?"

"Should I wear it?" Emma asked patiently.

"Um, are we talking makeup?"

Emma laughed. "No, silly. I always wear blush. You should

too, you know. You should try Nar's Orgasm. It would be perfect with your skin tone."

I looked wildly around the pool house, as if the answer to what the hell my sister was talking about was floating there in front of me.

"Did you just tell me you think I should have an orgasm?" I asked slowly. "Because you know I love you, Emma, but that's sort of personal."

"It's a shade of blush, you idiot. That's what the color is called: Orgasm."

"Lovely."

"It is. But that's not what I was talking about."

Does the sudden desire to pound your head against the wall until you manage to knock yourself unconscious happen to everyone when they're talking to their family? I wondered. Or was it just me?

"I'm talking about wedding dresses. Do you think they have to be white or ivory, or do you think it's okay to go with blush instead?" Emma continued.

"I think I have no opinion on this subject whatsoever," I said. I stroked Harper Lee's head, and she snorted appreciatively.

"Because my wedding is going to be very traditional. A five-course dinner, a jazz band, huge silver urns of white and pale-pink roses on the tables. But I thought maybe if my dress was a little untraditional, a bit unexpected, it would make more of an impact, especially against the traditional background."

"Uh-huh," I said, wondering if I could just hang up on Emma and pretend that we'd been disconnected. Although then I'd just have to call back, and she'd probably insist on continuing with the wedding-dress talk. She might even start over from the beginning.

"At first I thought I'd just go with a more modern dress. Strapless, maybe. Or shorter, with a really full, knee-length skirt. But the problem with that is that I've always dreamed about wearing a real wedding gown on my wedding day. And then I thought, what if I got a really traditional gown *but* in a nontraditional color? I was thinking something shocking, like red or fuchsia, but that seems like *too* much of a statement, if you know what I mean. So then I thought maybe blush would work—"

That was it. I couldn't take it anymore.

"Emma. I have to go," I said, cutting her off mid-rant.

"What? Why?" she asked, suddenly sounding hurt and very young. Like a little girl who'd been told she couldn't have ice cream for dessert because she didn't finish her Brussels sprouts.

"I'm sorry. It's just . . ." I cast around for a reason. I had a feeling that it wouldn't help matters to tell her if I ever heard the word *blush* again, my ears would start to bleed. Then inspiration struck. "I have a date tonight, and I have to start getting ready."

"A date! With who?" Emma asked eagerly, immediately ready to forgive my lack of interest in her wedding plans.

"His name is Drew," I said, feeling another rush of girly stomach squirms. "He's a lawyer. We went out a few nights ago, and he asked me out again for tonight. He's . . . well, he seems really great. He's very smart and witty."

"Way to go, you!" Emma said. "Is he cute?"

I attempted to take the high road. "You know, there are more important qualities in a man," I said loftily.

"So he's not cute. Well, that's okay. Looks aren't everything."

"For your information, he happens to be *very* attractive," I said. "Tall, dark hair, broad shoulders. And he has really great eyes. All sexy and squinty when he smiles."

"Mmmm. Have you slept with him yet?" Emma asked.

"None of your business!"

"So you haven't. Well, do yourself a favor."

"What's that?" I asked.

"Two words: Nar's Orgasm," Emma said. "Trust me, it'll do wonders for your face. You'll look like you have cheekbones."

"And on that note, I'm going to hang up," I said.

"Bye, Lucy."

"Bye, Emma. Give my love to Mom and Dad," I said.

"Knock knock," Hayden said, opening the door to the pool house and sticking her head in.

"Come on in," I said. "I'm just getting ready."

"Hey, look at you, gorgeous girl!" Hayden said, beaming at me.

"You like?" I asked, smoothing down the black strapless dress. It was made out of a surprisingly comfortable and flattering stretchy cotton sateen that somehow sucked in my stomach and yet still allowed me to breath.

"I *love,*" Hayden said. "You should wear those long red beads we picked up the other day."

I rummaged in a carved ivory box on the coffee table. The box was probably meant to be decorative, but I'd been using it to store the jewelry—mostly costume, although still jaw-droppingly expensive—Hayden had insisted I buy. I pulled out the beads, and Hayden took them from me, looped them around my neck twice, and fastened the clasp.

"Turn around," she instructed me. When I complied, she

adjusted the beads so that one loop was up high on my neck, like a choker, while the other dipped down low over the bodice of the dress. "There. Perfect! And wear the Jimmy Choo shoes. No, not those. The tan ones. He's very handsome, by the way. If you go for that blue-blazer-and-chinos sort of guy."

"Who? Drew? He's here?" Hayden nodded, and I felt a tingle of nerves, which I tried to smother by taking a deep breath.

"He said he's taking you to Chez Jean-Pierre," Hayden said approvingly. "Very nice. Obviously, he likes you."

"You think?"

"Either that or else he's just hoping to get you into bed by buying you an expensive dinner," Hayden teased.

I rolled my eyes. "Somehow I don't think so. Not after the cheek-kissing fiasco."

"Maybe he's just shy," Hayden suggested. "Or maybe he was nervous. Anyway, tonight will be your night. And if not, come meet Ian and me at the Drum Roll later on. Mal will be there. I bet he'd be more than happy to step in if Drew doesn't want to put out."

I swatted at her, and Hayden ducked, laughing.

"Sleeping with Mal would just be asking to contract a scorching case of gonorrhea," I said.

Hayden snorted. "Yeah, Mal does seem to subscribe to the theory that variety is the spice of life, doesn't he?"

"I thought he might be a—" For some reason, the word *gigolo* sounded too ridiculous to say out loud.

"What?"

"I thought he might sleep with women for, you know, money."

"You think Mal's a *prostitute?*" Hayden practically screamed the word, before dissolving in a fit of giggles.

"No! Not a prostitute! More of a . . . gigolo. In it for what he can get," I said sheepishly.

Still laughing, Hayden shrugged. "Maybe. But isn't everyone, to a point?"

"I'm not," I said.

"You, my dear, are worth thirty-four million dollars," Hayden reminded me. "You don't need anything."

"That's not true. Everyone needs something. Friendship, companionship, love."

"Well, maybe this Drew guy is the man for you."

"I doubt it. He doesn't know about my . . . situation," I said delicately. As though being accused of making a pass at a student, getting fired unceremoniously from my job, and winning a multimillion-dollar jackpot all at once was the sort of medical condition that couldn't be mentioned in polite society. I shrugged. "I'm not thinking of him that way. He's my rebound guy."

"Rebound guy or not, you'd better not keep him waiting. Dinner at Chez Jean-Pierre is a real treat. You don't want to miss it."

Hayden was right—dinner was spectacular, easily one of the best meals I'd ever had. I ordered the Dover sole, and Drew had the rack of lamb. And as we ate, and sipped chilled white wine, the conversation flowed easily between us. Drew told me a funny story about a client of his who went out on a day fishing trip with two business associates. All three of them proceeded to get bombed on mojitos and were so drunk they didn't realize their boat was sinking until they were ankle deep in water.

"So what did they do?" I asked.

"Put out an SOS call. And even though they immediately got in touch with the Coast Guard, they started talking about the movie *A Perfect Storm* and managed to scare themselves so badly, they had another round of mojitos to calm down. When the Coast Guard finally got to them, one of them was unconscious and the other two puked on the rescue helicopter on the way back to shore."

"And the boat?"

"Sank. It's somewhere on the bottom of the Atlantic Ocean, along with the *Titanic* and the *Lusitania,*" Drew said with a grin, as he took a swig of his wine.

"Who's your client suing? The company who insured his boat?" I asked.

"Oh, no, that's completely unrelated. The lawsuit has to do with the dissolution of a corporation he was a minority shareholder in. But that doesn't make for as good a story."

"No, I guess not," I said, smiling back at him. "Do you like practicing law?"

Drew shrugged. "Sure. How about you? Did you enjoy being an office manager?"

"I guess," I said. The problem with living a lie is that it requires a certain amount of proficiency in dishonesty. And I've always been a terrible liar. I tried to remember tips for sounding more believable while lying. Was I supposed to include more detail—or less? More, I thought. "It was pretty boring. Lots of . . . paperwork," I finished lamely. I had no idea what sort of paperwork I was supposed to have been performing at my fictional job and hoped that Drew wouldn't press the point.

"You prefer what you're doing now?"

"Right now I'm not doing anything, other than loafing around, shopping, swimming in the pool, and going out to dinner," I said. "Actually, what am I saying? This is paradise; of course I prefer it!"

And who wouldn't prefer a vacation in one of the most glamorous spots in the world over teaching English to a class full of overprivileged brats? I thought defiantly. And if I kept telling myself that, maybe I would eventually believe it.

Throughout dinner, Drew kept finding excuses to touch me. He patted my hand for emphasis as we talked. He brushed a loose hair from my bare shoulder. His calf pressed against mine under the table. And although he was never overt—he didn't run his hand up my thigh or squeeze one of my breasts—the physical connection between us hummed along with a low-key sensuality.

Drew kept me laughing. He told me stories about growing up with his two sisters, both younger, and how they had all terrorized one another, or how when he went to college he had no idea that he was supposed to change his own sheets and so had slept on the same stale, grimy bed linens for an entire semester.

"That's revolting," I said, wrinkling my nose in disgust.

"Yeah, well, I was an eighteen-year-old male. Revolting was par for the course," Drew said. "I won't even tell you about what it was like living in a frat house. We didn't do the dishes for weeks at a time, and by the time we got around to it... Well, I won't give you the details. It'll put you off your dinner."

"I can't eat another bite anyway," I said, putting down my fork with a groan. "That was fabulous."

"I'm glad you liked it," Drew said. When he smiled, his eyes crinkled up at the edges, and suddenly I felt a nervous flutter ruffle through me. We were almost at the end of our dinner, and unless I was completely illiterate at reading the signs, this date wasn't going to end as innocently as our first.

"Dessert?" Drew asked softly. I had the distinct feeling that he was wondering the very same thing I was.

The old Lucy would have waited for him to make the first move. So I banished that instinct and instead looked Drew straight in the eye.

"I have a great view of the ocean from my room," I said.

The sex was weird. Nice—but weird. Or maybe *weird* wasn't the right word, as it tends to conjure up images of whips and squeaking black vinyl and demands that your partner bark like a dog. Sex with Drew wasn't weird-kinky, just weird-different. More specifically: different from how it had been with Elliott. Which wasn't a bad thing. It wasn't as if Elliott had been the world's greatest lover. He'd treated my orgasms like they were a baton handoff in a foot race, asking me, "Did you come yet? Did you come yet?" over and over again, until I wanted to scream, *No, but I might manage it if you'd shut up for two minutes.*

Ironically, one of the things that was different with Drew was how vocal he was. I've never been much for dirty talk, finding it awkward and silly. And other than Elliott's orgasm watch, he never made a sound during sex, not even when he climaxed. He'd just grunt and then go very still and slack, until I gently pushed him off me.

But Drew kept up a stream of chitchat while we made love: "Do you like this?" and "Yes, keep doing *that,* that feels great," and "Ouch! Was that your fingernail?" He didn't wait for me to climax, the way Elliott always did—as though he'd receive a plaque engraved with LOVER OF THE YEAR on it—which was both a relief to have the pressure off and a bit of a disappointment. I'd gone through a period when I was twelve where I'd been obsessed with the sort of romance books that had covers featuring women whose breasts were a millimeter away from popping out of their bodices and that were filled with steamy and incredibly graphic sex scenes, during which the heroine always orgasmed, even while losing her virginity. This had set up unrealistic expectations in my young, impressionable mind that even sixteen years of dating had not fully dispelled.

And then, when it was over, Drew rolled over to the other side of the bed, sighed happily, and said, "How was your sole? I think I might order that the next time I go to Chez Jean-Pierre."

"It was delicious," I said, wondering how the male brain could go from sex to food so quickly. Maybe it never fully got off either topic but kept them running along in the background, like the headline ticker on CNN, even while the rest of the brain was occupied with more mundane tasks like work or teeth-brushing.

Drew turned back over on his side and grinned at me. His face was damp with sweat, and his chest hair was dark and thick. He reached over and squeezed my arm.

"You okay?" he asked.

"Yes, of course. Wonderful." Although to be honest I was now a bit sexually frustrated but couldn't think of a way to say this without hurting his feelings.

"Good. What do you want to do?"

"Do?" I repeated.

"We could go for a swim," he suggested.

"Did you bring a bathing suit?" I asked.

"Well, no, but you have seen me naked." Drew grinned. We were both well aware that at that very moment his penis—now somewhat deflated—was lying against my thigh. "Unless skinny-dipping offends your sensibilities."

I smiled back at him. "I haven't gone skinny-dipping since . . . Wait. I don't think I've *ever* gone skinny-dipping."

"Never? We'll have to remedy that immediately," Drew said. And then he stood and scooped me up in his arms.

"What are you doing?" I squealed, clutching at his shoulder. I'd always thought it would be romantic to be swept up in the arms of a hunky guy, like something out of a Regency romance. Willoughby carrying Marianne home in *Sense and Sensibility*. Or Colonel Brandon carrying Marianne in from the storm in *Sense and Sensibility*. Now that it was happening to me, however, I was just hoping he wouldn't drop me.

"I am taking you out for a swim," Drew said, grunting a bit from the effort of carrying me, which further tarnished the luster of romance from the gesture. And made me feel fat. Then, when he got to the door, he couldn't manage to grab the handle. "Can you open it?" he asked.

"Sure, just turn me around a bit," I said. "A little closer . . . little closer . . . there!"

Drew carried me outside, kicking the door closed behind him, and then strode up to the edge of the pool and—I couldn't believe this—*threw me in the water.*

The pool was cold—very cold—and as my entire body plunged down into the water, there was a frightening second where it felt like the breath had been knocked out of me. And I was just sinking, sinking, sinking down to the blue tiled floor. But then, before I could really panic, my body regained its buoyancy and I popped back up to the surface, spluttering with outrage. Drew was laughing so hard, he had to brace his arms against his thighs.

"You bastard!" I screeched.

"Bastard? That's a bit harsh, don't you think?"

"No, I do not!"

I splashed toward Drew, intent on pulling him in after me. But before I came within grabbing distance, he jumped into the pool, pulling his legs up in a cannonball. When Drew resurfaced he was still laughing, and he ducked my attempts to whack him. Instead, he grabbed my wrists in his hands and pulled me toward him, planting a kiss on my lips.

"Mmmm. You look sexy when you're all wet and your hair is plastered to the side of your face," he murmured.

"Hey!" I said, and was about to recommence my attempts to hit him, but then Drew kissed me again, this time with a surprising amount of heat. I could feel my insides melting as he wrapped his arms around me, and I stopped struggling against him.

"I think we have some unfinished business to take care of," Drew said in between soft, lingering kisses.

He ran his hands over my body, and everywhere he touched felt warm for just a moment, until his hands moved on and the cold water lapped back against me. I was half anticipating where the delicious warmth would come next and half worrying that Hayden would return home and find us naked and entwined around each other in the pool.

And then Drew's fingers were sliding down and inside me, and I stopped thinking altogether.

Fourteen

"I TAKE IT YOUR DATE LAST NIGHT WENT WELL," Hayden said the next morning, as she came out on the lanai, mail in hand. She'd arranged to have her mail forwarded from her New York apartment. I was sitting poolside in my Breakers bathrobe—a bargain at only ninety dollars—with a mug of coffee. I was taking in the view of the morning sky, still pink and hazy where it hung over the ocean. Harper Lee was milling around, sniffing at the ground, as though she expected a croissant would suddenly appear there.

"How did you know?" I asked.

"One, you're grinning like an idiot. Two, I just saw Drew on his way out," Hayden said, dropping the mail on a short teak table beside the lounger. And then she smiled wickedly. "And three, I glimpsed a bit of the action last night. Way to go, Lulu. In the pool. I didn't know you had such a wild side."

The smile slid from my face, and I could feel my cheeks burning with mortification.

"You saw us?" I bleated. "Just you . . . ?"

"Nope," Hayden said cheerfully. "Ian too. In fact, I have

to thank you. It turns out Ian really gets turned on by voyeurism."

I covered my face with my hands. "Please tell me you're kidding."

"Of course I'm kidding," Hayden said, smirking. "Like we'd watch you have sex. I just heard you splashing around out there and thought we'd best stay inside and leave you to your privacy. But you should see your face. I didn't know anyone could turn that shade of red."

"Harper Lee, please bite your Aunt Hayden," I ordered. Harper Lee ignored me, choosing instead to lean against Hayden's leg and stare worshipfully up at her.

"You wouldn't bite me, would you, sweetie girl," Hayden crooned, stroking Harper Lee's head. "What if I hadn't been joking? Would you be totally freaked?"

"Yes, I would. And I'd never have been able to look Ian in the eye again. Or you either."

"That would be awkward, considering we live together," Hayden pointed out. "Speaking of which, I got an e-mail from my parents this morning. Turns out they're not coming down here at all this winter. They're staying in Connecticut for Christmas, and then they're going to Hawaii in January. So we can stay indefinitely."

"Is that because we're here?" I asked worriedly. "I hope we're not putting them out."

Hayden snorted. "They have no idea I'm even here. It was a mass e-mail they sent to all interested parties—daughters, relatives, business associates, society reporters."

"Don't you think we should tell them?"

"No, I do not," Hayden said firmly. "I have always lived by one rule: When it comes to my parents, the less they know about my life the better. Anyway, now we have the whole

Season to hang out here in Palm Beach. Soaking in the sun, partying, living it up. It'll be great."

I smiled fondly at my friend. This was exactly what I needed—an indefinite break from my old life. *Who knows?* I thought, recalling the feel of Drew's hands roaming over my body the night before. Maybe it would turn into a permanent break. Maybe I could stay here forever, living in a big house by the ocean as the glamorous Lucy Landon. She was certainly having more fun than Lucy Parker ever had.

"At least let me pay rent," I offered.

But Hayden waved me off. "Please," she scoffed. "The house would just be sitting here empty. But I wouldn't say no if you offered to hire a cleaning service."

"You've got it," I said immediately. "A weekly service?"

"The house is so big, we really should have someone come in a few times a week, don't you think? I'll arrange it, don't worry. So? How was last night?"

"Well, I'm not giving you details—" I began.

"Not that I need them. You weren't exactly quiet," Hayden interjected.

"*—but,*" I continued, choosing to ignore her, even though my cheeks were flaming red again, "it was really amazing."

"I'm so glad," Hayden said warmly. "Drew seems really cool. Very charming."

"He is. Nice, and charming, and really funny. He makes me laugh. I haven't had so much fun with a guy in a long time."

"Just be careful," Hayden advised. "Flings are great, and sometimes they develop into something more. But sometimes they're just flings, and once the fling has . . ."

"Flung?" I suggested.

Hayden smiled, as I knew she would. "Right. Once the fling has flung, that's it. And that's okay too."

"You're absolutely right. Don't worry, I'm a big girl. I'm just enjoying this for what it is," I said.

"I hope so," Hayden said, although she didn't look convinced. She picked up the mail and riffled through it. Most of it she discarded to one side, unopened, but she did tear into a large bulky-looking manila envelope. Inside, there was a stack of letters, which Hayden flicked through. "Looks like this is for you," she said, handing it to me as she stood. "I'm going to shower. Do you want to go shopping later?"

"Sure," I said distractedly. Hayden disappeared back into the house as I examined the manila envelope. It was addressed in my father's handwriting. He'd sent it to Hayden, obviously not wanting to tip off even the mailman to where I was. Inside, there were mostly just bills, which had gone to my Ocean Falls house and my dad had collected for me—power, cable, Visa. I put those to one side. Peter Graham had told me he could arrange for an accountant to pay my bills; I would take him up on his offer. But besides the pile of bills and junk mail, there was a smaller envelope with a handwritten address.

I tore open the envelope. Inside was a note card with a watercolor of hydrangeas on the outside. A check fluttered out, spiraling down until it landed in a potted hibiscus. I plucked it out and saw that it was my check—the one I'd sent to Maisie. I stared at it for a moment. Then I looked down at the familiar slanting handwriting and began to read.

Dear Lucy,

Hallmark doesn't make a card for this occasion. I know, I looked. They actually have an I'm Breaking Up with You card (nice, huh?) and an Even Though You Gave Me Up for Adoption, You'll Always Be Like a Mother to Me card but, sadly, not a Thank You for the Ginormous Check but I Can't Accept It card. I guess it wouldn't be a big seller.

As you've no doubt figured out by now, I'm returning your check. And, knowing you as I do, I'm pretty sure this is going to royally piss you off.

First of all, thank you. It was a lovely thing to do, especially in light of how badly I behaved the last time we spoke. I was just so damned jealous that you won that money instead of me. And the worst of it is that I know if it had been the other way around, and I'd been the one to win, you would have been happy for me. Or maybe I'm wrong. Maybe you would have boiled over with jealousy too. Somehow I doubt it, though.

But, putting our argument aside, I just can't accept this money. I don't know why exactly, but it feels wrong. It's not money I'm owed, or money I earned, or money I have any rightful claim to. And I know—and I know you know, even if you won't admit it—that it's pity money. You feel sorry for Joe and me. I get that, I do; we're up to our necks in debt. I'm on a first-name basis with the asshole who calls every day from the credit-card company to harass me for the minimum monthly payment. And it would be so easy to cash this check and wipe out all of that debt once and for all.

But here's the thing: I can't let you make this go away. It's our debt, and we took it on—and took it on gladly—in order to get the twins. And they're worth it. If I had it to do all over again, I wouldn't change a thing. (Except for the birth. If I'm ever again pregnant with six-pound twins, I promise I will listen to my doctor and opt for the cesarean rather than insisting on a natural birth. Madness.) This is our burden, Lucy. If I let you step in and erase it for us, I would always feel uncomfortable about it. More than that, I would feel uncomfortable around you. You'd no longer be Lucy, my best friend; you'd be Lucy, my benefactor. And I think that would change our relationship permanently.

So I'm sending this back to you. I hope you're not too angry at me.

Love,

Maisie

P.S. Call me.

I read the note twice more, and each time my feelings turned and shifted like a kaleidoscope of changing colors. Maisie's letter had made me laugh, and tear up, and want to throttle her, and—finally—made me feel lonelier than ever before.

This is our burden, she wrote. And I knew what she meant by that. She meant, *This is our marriage. Our twins. Our life.* Ours . . . not yours.

It was one thing to call me the twins' aunt, to pretend that I was a member of the family, to include me in birthday celebrations and give me the bright watercolors the boys painted just for me. But when it came down to the nitty-gritty of it, no matter how close I was to Maisie, to Joe, to their boys, I would always be on the outside looking in. I wasn't a part of their family, not really. And Maisie worried that, by taking my money, this barrier would be forever breached.

Would I ever again have a relationship with anyone that wasn't influenced by this money I'd won? Would everyone I loved in my life always be wary that I was trying to buy them? Or, even worse, would I always have to worry that the people getting close to me were just doing so because of the money?

I picked up the French bulldog check and stared at it, wondering how some numbers on a piece of paper could have such power. And then I ripped it into tiny pieces.

* * *

"I don't think I like the way these Chip and Pepper jeans fit me," I said, staring at my reflection in a three-way mirror. "The 7 For All Mankind ones suit me more, don't you think?"

"Yes, but I like the Paige ones on you too," Hayden said, coming out of her dressing room. She was wearing an apple-green halter gown with a long flowing skirt that fit her like a dream. I nodded approvingly.

"That's gorgeous. What is it? Gucci?"

"No," Hayden said, adjusting the bodice. "Rebecca Taylor. But still, very impressive. A few weeks ago you wouldn't have known a Gucci from a Gap."

"I have a good teacher," I said.

"Yes, I've taught you well. For the first time you didn't immediately head back to the sales racks when we walked in the store," Hayden said. "And you haven't hyperventilated over the price tags once. I call that definite progress."

I shrugged, again checking out how my bottom looked in the jeans. No, these definitely weren't as flattering as the 7 For All Mankind jeans I had tried on earlier, I decided. I headed into my dressing room—which had walls draped in pink silk and a mirrored stool upholstered in cowhide—to take them off.

"The last pair of jeans I bought came from Old Navy," I called to Hayden through my door. "It takes a little while to get out of that mind-set."

"What do you think about this dress?" Hayden called back. "Yes or no?"

I opened my door a crack, while I stepped out of the jeans, and looked her over appraisingly. "Definitely yes."

"How does it compare with the yellow Chaiken dress?" she asked.

"I liked that one too. Why don't you get them both? It'd be a fun way to spend your blackjack winnings."

Hayden made a face at herself in the three-way mirror. "No. I can't afford them both. Hell, I can't even really afford one. We're not all billionaires, you know," she said. She pulled her hair back and used one hand to pile it up on top of her head, then examined the effect in her reflection.

"I'm not a billionaire," I said, laughing, as I stepped back into my skirt.

"Okay, Miss Literal, then we're not all multimillionaires," Hayden said.

Now that I was fully dressed, I opened the door to the fitting room all the way. I looked at Hayden, wondering if I could ask her what I wanted to without offending her. Because while it certainly wasn't any of my business how much money she had, I was in the position to help Hayden—if she needed my help.

But Hayden seemed to know what I was working up the nerve to ask her. She sighed and let her hair go. It fell back down to her shoulders with a silky, glossy swish.

"I'm a bit strapped at the moment," she admitted. "I lost some money—well, a lot of money—on that Web site deal Craig and I were putting together. And, even worse, I borrowed some money from my dad to finance it and now I can't pay him back."

"Is he angry?"

"Angry, disappointed, generally fed up with me. He said my mother is right, and it's time I grow up and settle down."

"You mean he wants you to get married too?"

"No, not necessarily. Not the way Mom is pushing it, anyway. He just wants me to get my shit together and figure out what I'm going to do with my life. His exact words were: 'Now you're not just wasting your time, you're wasting my money.' "

She mimicked her father's low, gruff voice, and then rolled her eyes.

I squeezed her arm. "I'm sorry, sweetie," I said.

"Don't be. He's right. I'm thirty-two years old. Really, it's pathetic that I'm still so rudderless. I do need to get my shit together."

"Are you really okay staying here in Palm Beach for the next few months?"

I wondered if, under the circumstances, maybe Hayden should head back to New York to look for a job. But I felt like I couldn't voice this opinion, especially in light of my new financial independence. Who wants to be told they need to get a job by a lottery winner?

"Yes, this is just what I need. A vacation from my life," Hayden said, smiling suddenly. "A few months of sun and beach and a fling with exactly the sort of man my parents would hate before I head back to reality."

"Who, Ian? Why would your parents hate him?" I asked, surprised. I thought Ian seemed like a pretty sweet guy. He was polite, good-looking, and didn't have an obvious drug problem or a wife and kids stashed away in the suburbs.

Hayden laughed at my naïveté. "A twentysomething bartender who spends all his free time gambling in Indian casinos? Please. He's not exactly the sort of guy they're hoping I'll end up with," she said. She took one last look at her reflection in the mirror and then shook her head sadly. "I'd probably better not buy anything. If I'm going to take a few months more of vacation, I have to make my money last."

"Absolutely not," I said firmly. "I'll buy that dress for you. And the yellow one too."

"I can't accept that," Hayden said, frowning at me.

"Of course you can. Look. I'm staying at your house, and you won't even let me pay you rent. And I just got this huge windfall. More than enough for both of us. So let me share some of it with you. At least while we're here," I said.

"It's nice of you to offer, Lucy, but totally unnecessary," Hayden said. Her voice sounded normal, but her shoulders had stiffened. I reached out and squeezed her hand again.

"Let me do this. Just think of me as your sugar mommy," I joked. "And you don't even have to sleep with me."

Hayden laughed, and as she did, she visibly relaxed. "Good thing. No offense, Lucy, but you're not my type."

"You'll let me buy you the dresses? And help out in general?" I asked.

Hayden hesitated, but then finally nodded. "Well . . . okay. But just so you know, I feel weird about it."

"Yay!" I cheered. "And you shouldn't feel weird. I *want* to do this." I thought of the check Maisie had returned to me, and a surge of bitterness rose up in me. This is what friends did: They offered to help out one another in need.

It was odd, really. A month ago if I'd been asked which friend, Maisie or Hayden, I could count on in a crisis, I'd have picked Maisie every time. I'd thought of her as my rock, the one person who was always there for me. But when my life had imploded, when everything had been turned upside down and shaken like a snow globe, Maisie hadn't been there for me. But Hayden had. Sweet, flighty, unpredictable Hayden.

"Come on, let's buy these and then go get an iced coffee. I need some caffeine," I said.

"Okay. Just give me a minute," Hayden said, disappearing into her changing room. She emerged a moment later wearing the aqua-blue tank top and floaty white linen skirt she'd worn out shopping, the two new dresses folded neatly over her arm. She smiled shyly at me.

"Thanks again," she said, making an awkward gesture

toward the dresses. "I know I shouldn't let you buy these for me, but . . ." Her smile widened, and her green eyes shone with pleasure. "I *so* want them."

"It's my pleasure," I said sincerely. It felt good to do something nice for a friend, I thought. It made me happy. And if Maisie didn't want my help, I wouldn't bother her with it again.

That night we had drinks at The Breakers, sitting at the aquarium bar with its spectacular ocean view, and then sushi at Echo. My alcohol tolerance was getting stronger. Another point in favor of the new Lucy, I thought. Old Lucy would have gotten sloppily drunk after three dirty martinis, while the new Lucy was just pleasantly relaxed, without a worry in the world. Actually, that wasn't entirely true. . . .

"I hope I'm not turning into an alcoholic," I said to Hayden, as we walked in to the Drum Roll and took our favorite seats at the end of the bar. Hayden waved at Ian, who grinned and winked at her. Then, finally registering what I said, Hayden let out an incredulous bark of laughter.

"You? An alcoholic? Somehow I can't see that," she scoffed.

"I've already had three drinks tonight," I said.

"So? It's a Saturday."

"And I normally spend my Saturdays grading papers, or watching a movie, or reading," I said. "Not glugging down dirty martinis."

"That was then. This is now," Hayden said simply. "It's about time you lived a little."

"I just hope I'm not living too much, too fast."

"I think you're sublimating. You're not really worried that

a few drinks over several hours on a Saturday night has turned you into an alcoholic. What you're really worried about is that Drew didn't call you today," Hayden said.

Ian appeared with two mojitos and set them down on the bar in front of us with a flourish. Hayden blew him a kiss in thanks.

"You think?" I asked.

But I knew she was right. Despite my best efforts to convince myself that Drew was a fling and that the new Lucy wouldn't sit around waiting for phone calls from a man she was casually involved with, I had still spent a good part of the day alternately staring at the phone and asking Hayden if anyone had called while I was swimming or in the bathroom.

"Yes, I do," Hayden said.

"But I don't want to be that woman, the one who sits around waiting for some guy to call and then getting pissed off when he doesn't."

"Then don't be that woman."

"I know. I just think it's rude not to call someone you just had sex with," I said, hating that my voice sounded so petulant. "It's bad manners."

It was only when I heard Mal laughing softly that I learned he was standing right behind us and had overheard everything Hayden and I had just said. I swiveled around in my chair and scowled at him.

"It's also bad manners to eavesdrop on other people's conversations," I said severely.

"I'm not eavesdropping. I'm just standing here innocently waiting to order a beer," Mal said, grinning at me. He was sporting his beach-bum unshaven look again today.

"Forget to shave?" I asked rudely.

Mal ran a hand over his scratchy beard growth. "Nope. I

have sensitive skin. I don't like to shave every day," he said. He placed one hand over his heart. "In fact, I'm a sensitive guy in general."

"Ha," I said.

"I am. At least I always call the day after," he said, which made Hayden snort in appreciative laughter before she turned to talk to Ian.

"Do you really?" I asked.

"You sound like you don't believe me," Mal said, smirking as he accepted a bottle of beer from Ian's outstretched hand. He took a swig.

"I just would have pegged you as a love 'em and leave 'em kind of a guy," I said.

"You're big on making assumptions, aren't you?" Mal said. His pale gray eyes stayed locked on mine as he drank some more beer.

"No, I'm not," I said, feeling suddenly stung. "Really. Your love life is none of my business."

"And yet it seems to interest you so," Mal said. He slid onto the empty bar stool next to mine. "In fact, we talk of little else."

To disguise my discomfort at his noticing this, I rolled my eyes. "Whatever," I said.

Mal snorted. "So tell me: Why do you assume that I'm the kind of guy who doesn't call the day after?"

I shrugged. "I don't know."

"Sure you do."

"Okay. Well. I think it's a matter of quantity. That's a lot of phone numbers for you to remember."

Mal snorted with laughter. "Have you heard of a nifty invention called pen and paper?"

"Okay. Point taken."

"No, I'm not done yet. So this guy you got together with. The one who didn't call you. Did you think he was the type who wouldn't call the day after?"

I stared at my mojito, willing myself not to blush. But I could feel the hot red flush creeping up my throat, spreading over my chest.

"No," I admitted. "I didn't."

"There you have it," Mal said triumphantly.

"There I have what?"

"You just proved that you don't have the best judgment on this subject. You thought I was the sort of guy who doesn't call the day after, and you were wrong. And you thought your . . ." He waved an airy hand. "Friend?"

I shrugged. "Sure, why not."

"*Friend,*" Mal continued, "was the kind who would. And in both cases you were wrong." He finished on a triumphant, almost smug note.

I stared at him. "And your point is . . . ?" I asked.

"You should be sleeping with me instead," Mal said.

I spit out the mouthful of mojito I'd just sipped.

"Sleeping with *you*?"

"You know, that's why I like you," Mal said. "You're good for my ego."

"Who's sleeping with whom?" Hayden asked, leaning over to hear our conversation.

"I was suggesting that Lucy here sleep with me," Mal said.

"You're not her type," Hayden said.

"I'm not?"

"Definitely not. She goes for preppy, clean-cut guys," Hayden said.

"Those guys are usually pricks," Mal said.

Hayden shrugged. "True, but what can you do? The heart

wants what it wants. And Lucy's heart yearns for Mr. Prep. You'd have better luck if you shaved and put on a pink polo shirt."

"Too bad. I don't wear pink," Mal said with a shrug. He took a philosophic swig of his beer. I looked from him to Hayden, not sure with whom I was more annoyed.

"First of all, my heart does not yearn for Mr. Prep. It doesn't yearn for anything. This," I said, pointing to my heart, "is a yearn-free zone. And second of all, I wouldn't be interested in Mal even if he were the last preppy clean-cut guy on earth. No offense," I added in Mal's direction.

"Hey, why start taking offense now?" Mal said.

"It's not personal, really. But I just got out of a relationship with a guy who had a loose definition of what monogamy means. I wouldn't get involved with another guy like that," I said.

"That's true. Her ex-boyfriend was a prick," Hayden said philosophically. She raised her mojito glass in mock toast to me.

Mal's gray eyes were suddenly not laughing anymore. "Why do you think I have a loose definition of monogamy?" he asked.

"I just . . . well, it's none of my business . . . but you do seem to be with a lot of different women," I said awkwardly. I had been sort of joking—thought we were all joking around—but now I had the impression that I'd really offended him.

"And I'm not having a relationship, monogamous or otherwise, with any of them," he said.

I shrugged, uncomfortable in the knowledge that I'd probably stepped over a line, even if I hadn't known the line was there. "Whatever you want to call it."

"Not just what I call it, Sunshine. It's what it is. I don't lead women on."

I turned to Hayden, hoping she'd step in, make a joke, and

defuse the situation, but Ian had reappeared at our end of the bar and was bent over, talking softly to her. She was no longer paying any attention to Mal and me whatsoever. I was on my own. I turned back to Mal and inhaled deeply.

"Look, I'm sorry if I offended you," I said. "Really, I am."

Mal looked at me for a long moment, then he grinned, and the tension was broken. "Don't worry. I'm getting the impression I'm going to have to develop a thick skin if I keep hanging out with you."

I laughed, more with relief that the tension had passed than anything.

"Besides," I said, "you already told me I wasn't your type."

"When did I say that?"

"The other night."

"Oh." Mal considered this. "It's true. You're not."

"Then why did you say I should be sleeping with you?"

Mal shrugged. "Diversity?" he suggested.

"Tempting—but no."

"Damn," Mal said, grinning at me in a way that made me suddenly aware of just how close to me he was sitting. I decided it was time to steer the topic away from sex.

"So, you give tennis lessons?" I asked.

Mal nodded. "Do you play?" he asked.

"I used to, years ago. I've been meaning to take it up again. Would you be willing to give me lessons?"

I wasn't sure whom this request startled more—Mal or me. I hadn't known I was going to ask him this. Although once I did, I realized it was true: I *would* like to take up tennis again. It was one of those things I never used to have time for, between work and Elliott and life in general. But now I had all the time in the world.

"Sure, anytime, except Tuesday and Thursday afternoons," Mal said.

"Why? What happens on Tuesday and Thursday afternoons?" I asked.

Mal looked at me as though he was trying to decide whether or not to tell me.

"I have another commitment," he said obliquely. "But any other day would be fine."

I was suddenly dying to know what his so-called commitment was. Did it have to do with the elegant older woman I'd seen him having dinner with? But I knew I couldn't ask him, especially not now, right after I'd insulted him by basically accusing him of being a slut.

"How about tomorrow morning?" I asked instead. "Ten o'clock?"

"Ten it is," Mal said. He smiled at me, and I felt a keen sense of relief. I had no idea why it was important to me that I be on good terms with this guy. Maybe it was just the effect of the dirty martinis and mojito. And speaking of the martinis and mojito . . .

"Maybe we'd better make it eleven," I said, pushing my now-empty glass away with a frown. "I'm probably going to wake up with a headache."

"Hey, Ian," Mal called out. "Bring Lucy a glass of water, will you? We need to get her hydrated for her tennis lesson tomorrow morning."

I laughed and accepted the glass of water Ian brought me. And it only then occurred to me that the last half hour, which I'd passed talking to Mal, was the first time all day I hadn't spent obsessing about Drew.

Fifteen

I WOKE SUDDENLY THE NEXT MORNING, ALERT AND uneasy. And then I remembered the plans I'd made the night before. Tennis lessons! What had I been thinking? I didn't even have the equipment to play tennis. I had an old racquet rattling around somewhere at my house in Ocean Falls, but I wasn't sure where it was, not that I could get to it. And although I now had a wardrobe to rival Nicole Ritchie's, I didn't have anything appropriate to wear on the tennis court.

But that's what money does, I remembered. It solves problems.

The thrill this realization brought me was still fresh. I wondered if I would ever get used to the idea that I could buy whatever I wanted, whenever I wanted.

I drove to the Rushes Tennis and Country Club in Hayden's car. I was going to have to arrange for my own car soon, I thought, and spent a pleasant ten minutes daydreaming about whether I should opt for a high-tech luxury car or one of the gorgeous old vintage ones I kept seeing parked along Worth Avenue. I thought briefly of my old yellow Volvo, which was probably still languishing in the mechanic's shop in Ocean Falls. I'd have to do something about that. Arrange to pay the mechanic, have the car sold. And at this, I felt an unexpected pang. I'd miss that car, even if it had been clunky and unreliable.

But I quickly shook off this regret. Who wouldn't prefer a sleek new Jaguar to an old, worn-down Volvo? I had to stop thinking like a teacher on a budget.

The Rushes was gated with a security checkpoint. I gave my driver's license to the uniformed guard at the gate, and for a tense moment I worried that he might recognize my name. But he just checked that I was on the approved visitors' list, wrote down the car's tag number, and then with a courteous nod waved me in. I exhaled gratefully, only then conscious that I'd been holding my breath.

The country-club grounds were immaculate. The grass was very green and precisely cut. The bushes were trimmed into twisting topiary shapes, and white and lavender snapdragons and purpled-edged petunias bloomed in artistic clumps. Golf carts zipped around, their drivers calling out and waving to one another as they passed by. I followed the signs directing me toward the clubhouse and parked in the visitors' lot. The clubhouse was very modern looking from the outside—two stories of pink stucco shaped like a hexagon, with a glass-domed roof—and decorated tastefully on the inside, from the patterned sage rug, to the muted cream walls, to the sconces with black shades that glowed next to oil paintings of the various golf-course holes.

The pro shop was just to the right of the entrance, and I headed straight for it. There were a few men browsing halfheartedly through a selection of sorbet-hued golf shirts. The sales clerk led me over to the tennis section.

"What are you interested in?" she asked. She flourished a

hand toward the racks. "We have just about everything you could possibly need. Racquets, clothing, accessories."

"I need it all," I said. "I need something to play in, sneakers, a racquet. I even need socks. Do you have everything?"

If the clerk was surprised, she had the grace—or the training—not to show it. She selected a few outfits for me: a white dress with black stripes down the side; a shirt and skirt in a bright ocean blue; a cherry-red skirt with a white sleeveless top.

"I'll take them all," I said, without bothering to try them on. During my brief yet intense tutelage under Hayden, I'd quickly learned how to eyeball what cuts and colors best suited me.

The sales clerk proceeded to help me pick out tennis sneakers—these I had to try on—socks, tennis underwear, and a simple white Lacoste visor. The clerk was young and bubbly and was giggling as I kept exclaiming, "Oh, I want this! And this!" And she'd pull the items down and add them to the growing pile on the glass display counter.

Picking out a racquet was a bit trickier. It had been so long since I'd played that when she questioned me about what brand and style I was interested in, I had absolutely no idea.

"What sort of surface do you normally play on? Is there a particular brand you're interested in? How important is spin to you?" The young woman peppered me with questions, none of which I had a ready answer for.

"It's okay, Dana, I'll take over from here," a male voice said. I turned and saw Mal standing there. He was wearing a white polo shirt and white tennis shorts, which made his tan look even deeper. His hair was damp with sweat and pushed back off his face, and there was another day's worth of stubble spread over his jaw.

Because I have a genetic predisposition to humiliating

myself, I said the first inane thing that popped into my head: "You still haven't shaved."

"Why are you so obsessed with my personal grooming habits?" Mal asked. His expression was quizzical, but his voice was edged with humor.

I could feel my face go hot and red. "I'm not," I muttered, looking down at the last racquet Dana had given me to try. I swung it around a bit, wondering if a racquet found its owner in the same way that wands did in the Harry Potter books.

"It's just something you comment on with alarming frequency," Mal continued, although he smiled at me.

"I... well. Can we just forget that I said that and start again?" I asked sheepishly.

"Okay. Are you in the market for a new racquet?" Mal asked.

"Yes. I think. I mean, if I'm going to take tennis lessons, I'll need a racquet, right?"

"It usually helps. I don't think that one's a good fit for you, however. Look, the grip is too small."

Mal plucked the racquet out of my hand and replaced it with another. The grip on this one felt a bit better, but Mal frowned at it, shook his head, and handed me another racquet to try. I held it, but he shook his head again and, holding my hand in his, turned the racquet to adjust the grip. I had a brief but intense reaction to his touch, which vividly reminded me of when I was a flat-chested thirteen-year-old with a crush on a lifeguard at the beach who was six years older than me and didn't know I existed. Every time I saw the lifeguard—even after he began dating a curvy, bikini-clad beauty—I'd feel a hot rush flood through my body.

"That grip looks good. How does it feel?" he asked, seemingly unaware of the physical flutterings his touch was causing me. I wondered how many times he had held a woman's hand while he adjusted her grip and how many women had responded to his touch with the same breathless excitement I was feeling. This thought—that I was one of many—annoyed me. I abruptly pulled my hand away.

"Fine," I said shortly. "Shall I buy this one, then?"

Mal's eyebrows rose. "Is that lottery cash burning a hole in your pocket?"

"Shhhh," I hissed, looking around. Luckily, Dana was at the register totaling up my haul and too far away to eavesdrop. "What if someone hears you?"

"They would probably think I'm joking."

I considered this. He was right; I was overreacting, which made me feel foolish.

"Look," I said. "Just tell me which racquet to buy, and I'll buy it. It's as simple as that."

Mal regarded me for a long moment. I didn't know what was going on behind those pale eyes and found it unnerving.

"I'll tell you what. Why don't you try this racquet out today, and if you like it then you can buy it," he finally said, taking it from me.

"Oh. Okay," I said. I gestured to the stack of tennis clothing, socks, underwear, and accessories piled up on the glass display counter. "I have to buy all of that stuff, though. And change clothes."

"I'll meet you on court three when you're ready," Mal said. He left, carrying the racquet tucked under one arm. I noticed the sales clerk's eyes following him until Mal was out of her sight. She sighed.

"Isn't he gorgeous?" she said to me.

"I hadn't noticed," I lied.

"Oh, my God, are you serious? I always get tongue-tied when I'm around him. I can't say hello without sounding like an idiot."

"I'll pay for this in cash," I said abruptly.

"What?" The girl was still so caught up in her Mal-induced reverie that she stared blankly at me for a moment. "Oh, right. Sorry." Then, with an apologetic smile, she turned to ring up the items I was purchasing. But the smile lingered on her lips.

And for some reason, this made me all the more irritated with Mal. I stared down at the pile of tennis gear, the pleasure of buying it suddenly dried up.

"What have I gotten myself into?" I muttered to myself as I swung—and missed—the tennis ball Mal had just lobbed over the net at me.

"What did you say?" he called out.

"Nothing," I said.

The weather was idyllic: sunny and warm without being too hot, and the sky was such a pure and brilliant blue, it was hard not to stare up at it. The outdoor tennis courts at the Rushes were red clay, the kind that leave a rust-colored residue on everything that comes in contact with them. The courts were enclosed with a metal fence painted a tasteful shade of green, to blend in with the perfectly manicured golf course just beyond. Flowers and shrubbery were planted along the outside borders of the fence. I'd never played tennis anywhere so lovely. And I'd never played worse.

"Damn it," I said through clenched teeth, as another ball bounced lazily past me. It wasn't even as if I could blame it on Mal slamming the balls at me in a play of macho domination; everything he hit gently arced over the net in my direction.

"Just relax," he called out. "Take a deep breath, draw your racquet down and back like I showed you, then follow through."

He demonstrated his perfect technique as he hit another ball to me. This one I managed to hit, but in my frustration I swung too hard, and it ricocheted over the fence.

"I suck at this," I commented. "I don't remember being this bad. I guess it's been so long since I've played, I must have forgotten my degree of suckage."

Mal laughed and shook his head. "You're doing fine. Just a bit rusty."

He lobbed another ball at me. I swung, hit it, and—amazingly—the ball bounced back into Mal's court.

"Good!" he said encouragingly. He hit it back at me. I swung and missed.

"Hold on, I'm coming over there," Mal said.

I glowered at him, in case he was even considering laughing at me, but Mal didn't tease me the way he might have if we were hanging out at the Drum Roll. Instead, he was in professional mode, his expression pleasant and not at all mocking.

"What I want you to work on," Mal said, when he reached me, "is bringing your arm down and then following through. Don't worry about hitting the ball. That will come. Just keep your focus on getting your swing right."

And then he stepped behind me, reached his arms around me, and, holding his hands over mine on the racquet, demonstrated the proper swing. I recognized it for what it was—an effective teaching device. Now my arms would hopefully retain the memory of how they were supposed to reach down and then swing through. But, unfortunately, the rest of my body immediately disconnected from the process. Instead, all I could focus on was Mal's chest brushing my back and his hands gently clasped over mine. He wasn't pressing against me, and his touch was as nonsexual as that of a gynecologist. But my body didn't seem to understand that. My throat suddenly felt thick, my skin flushed and tingled, my nipples hardened under my sports bra.

"You lower your arm and then swing through," Mal said, repeating the movement. "Think of it as drawing a question mark in the air with your racquet."

Please don't let him notice my nipples, I thought desperately, all too aware what fresh mortification this would bring. *I have to think of something else. Something nonsexual. Like . . . Harper Lee. Or features I'd like in my new car. Or Elliott, since he's the last person in the world I'll ever imagine sexually again.*

Unfortunately, thinking of Elliott caused me to flash to the scene of his infidelity, standing and thrusting into the blonde with the concrete tits. And then my thoughts rebelliously jumped to an image of Mal standing naked and thrusting—

My arm spasmed, and I dropped my racquet. Mal looked down at me quizzically.

"Are you okay?" he asked. Mal picked up my racquet and handed it to me. I reached to take it, but he didn't let go right away.

"Something's percolating in that head of yours," he said.

"No," I said, shaking my head. I attempted a smile but then worried that it would look like I was leering and stopped. "I'm just frustrated with how badly I'm playing."

"How long has it been since you played?" he asked.

I thought about it. "Five years? I can't remember exactly. It could be longer."

"That's a long time to be away from the sport. Don't put so much pressure on yourself. You'll pick it back up again. You just need practice," Mal said with an encouraging smile, releasing my racquet.

I'd have preferred it if he reverted back to the smart-alecky

Mal of the Drum Roll. It was easier to resist the crinkle-edged gray eyes and devastating smile when he was mocking me.

Before I could respond, I heard someone—a male someone—calling out my name.

"Lucy?"

I turned in the direction of the voice, my stomach clenching nervously. Was it someone from my old life who'd recognized me, despite the new hair? But then I saw who it was, and my entire body went rigid.

Drew.

I now remembered why I stopped having one-night stands. It was absolutely mortifying seeing someone who had slept with you once and then decided that the experience was so mediocre, it wasn't worth repeating.

"Drew," I said without enthusiasm. "Hi."

"What are you doing here?" he asked, drawing closer.

Since I was holding a tennis racquet, wearing a tennis outfit, and standing on a tennis court, this seemed like a silly question.

"I'm simultaneously solving a quadratic equation and composing a symphony," I said. I tapped my head. "All in here."

"Ha-ha," Drew said. He leaned down and kissed me full on the mouth. Which took me aback.

"What are you doing here?" I asked.

"My weekly golf game," he said. He grinned and winked at me. "It's in preparation for my retirement years. I want to kick serious ass at the old folks' home."

"It's good to have goals," I remarked. I nodded toward Mal, who was waiting patiently, observing us. "This is Mal. My tennis instructor."

"Hi, Mal. Drew. Drew Brooks," Drew said, holding out a chummy hand to Mal.

Mal hesitated for the briefest of moments and then took it. "We've met before," Mal said.

"Have we? Sorry, I have the worst memory for faces," Drew said cheerfully.

"Numbers too," I said, and then, worried that I was coming across as shrewish—surely not something the new Lucy would ever be—I smiled. I thought I heard Mal snort, but when I looked over at him, he seemed to have himself under control.

"I was going to call you after my golf game," Drew said. He either hadn't heard Mal's snort or he'd chosen to ignore it. "Are you free for dinner tonight?"

"Tonight?" I repeated. Part of me had leaped up in delight at the suggestion, thrilled that Drew hadn't seen me as just a one-night stand. The other part of me held back, whispering that I should play it cool and not let him think I'd be available for last-minute dates.

But then, before I could say anything, Mal stepped in. "She can't tonight," he said mildly. "A group of us are going out for drinks."

I managed not to let my jaw drop open as I turned to stare at Mal.

"Didn't Hayden tell you? She and Ian organized it last night," Mal said.

"Oh . . . right," I said. I had no idea what he was talking about; in fact, I was fairly sure Hayden had said something about Ian being on a lucky streak, so the two of them were heading back down to the casino tonight. But I had a feeling I should go along with Mal's story. I turned to Drew. "Another time, maybe?" I said.

The affable grin had vanished from Drew's face, replaced with a quizzical frown. He looked from me to Mal and then back at me again.

"Okay . . . well, I'll call you later, Lucy," he said. "Sorry I interrupted your lesson."

"No problem," Mal said.

"Bye," I said, and as Drew strode off toward the country club, I wondered if I'd hear from him again.

"He'll call," Mal said, as though he were reading my thoughts.

"He will?"

"He's the type who always responds to some competition."

"What? Competition from *you*?"

Mal laughed and shook his head. "Did it ever occur to you I might suffer from a fragile ego and that with every insult you're just pushing me closer and closer to the edge of despair?"

"No, I didn't mean it that way," I said, feeling my cheeks burn with embarrassment. "I didn't mean that he couldn't possibly be threatened by you. I mean . . . look at you."

Mal's eyebrows rose. "From anyone else, that would sound suspiciously like a compliment. But knowing you as I do, I have a feeling there's an insult hidden in there somewhere."

I rolled my eyes. "Please," I said. "If you can't take a compliment, don't blame it on me."

"Then what exactly did you mean?"

"Just that you're my tennis instructor. I'm taking a lesson. Why would Drew assume there was anything more to it than that?"

"Don't forget you're going out with me tonight too," Mal reminded me. "I think that got his attention."

"Yeah, what was that? Did Hayden really organize drinks tonight?"

"Nope," Mal said. "But I know his type. And I knew that if he thought there might be a rival for your affections, he wouldn't make the mistake of not calling you the day after again."

"Oh." I absorbed this. "But... why?"

"Why what?"

"Why would you do that for me?" I asked. I twirled my racquet in my hands.

"Because we're friends."

"We are?"

"There she goes again," Mal remarked dryly.

"No, I mean... I'm sorry. I don't know what it is about you, but I always manage to say just the wrong thing when I'm around you," I said.

"So it's my fault, huh?" Mal grinned at me.

"That's not what I meant."

"Maybe I should just start ignoring everything you say," Mal said. "Now come on. You still have ten minutes left in your lesson."

I groaned but held my racquet up in a halfhearted ready position, while Mal jogged back around to his side of the net.

"That's what I like to see," he said. "The eye of the tiger."

"Oh, shut up," I muttered. But this time, when he lobbed a ball at me, I managed to hit it back. The ball striking against my racquet gave a satisfying *thwack*, and it cut across the court at a sharp angle. I had a feeling Mal could have gotten it if he'd really run, but he let it whiz past.

"Good shot," he cheered me. And I felt my spirits lift. Maybe I wasn't so bad at this stupid game after all.

Mal was right: Drew called later that afternoon. In fact, he must have phoned directly after his golf game. I was still wearing my tennis dress, sitting on a chaise longue by the pool, chatting with Hayden, when the phone rang. Hayden answered, and then, her eyebrows arched meaningfully, she handed the phone to me.

"Hello," I said.

"Hi," he said. "It's me. Drew."

I smiled at Hayden and tried to ignore the excitement bubbling up inside me.

"Hey you. How was your golf game?"

"Terrible. I couldn't play worth a damn. All of my hopes and dreams for my retirement years are crushed."

"That does sound bad."

"Look, I know you said you had plans tonight, but I'd really like to see you." Drew's voice deepened, somewhere between playfulness and urgency in tone. "In fact, I'm *dying* to see you. Is there any way you can cancel on your friends?"

I was quiet for a moment as I deliberated on the best tack to take. As much as I wanted to say yes, I didn't want to undo Mal's good work.

"Well..." I said slowly. "I don't think tonight's going to work."

"Tomorrow then," Drew said eagerly. "I'll take you out to dinner."

I smiled into the phone. "Tomorrow," I agreed.

Sixteen

OVER THE NEXT FEW WEEKS, MY LIFE FELL INTO A PREdictable pattern. The days were spent shopping or lounging by the pool with Hayden, or taking tennis lessons with Mal at the Rushes. My tennis game was slowly improving, enough so that, without causing too much embarrassment to myself, I was able to join a women's round-robin doubles league that met at the club on Thursday mornings. My nights were divided between dates with Drew or, if he was busy, hanging out at the Drum Roll with Hayden, where we were often joined by Mal and Ian, when the bar wasn't busy. On the nights when Drew and I went out, he usually stayed over at the pool house with me.

"It's weird. The last thing I wanted was to get involved with anyone right now. But somehow this thing with Drew seems to have evolved into an actual relationship," I said to Hayden one morning after Drew left.

She and I were walking slowly along the beach. The tide had just gone out, leaving the sand cool and damp, and our feet made a trail of deep prints. Harper Lee jogged along beside us, panting with the effort. My French bulldog had been getting a bit tubby lately. Hayden was incapable of resisting Harper Lee's melting stares and was forever sneaking her extra treats.

"Why is that weird? That's how it always happens. When you're least expecting it, Prince Charming comes along and sweeps you off your feet," Hayden said.

"Hmmm," I said.

"What?"

"Prince Charming? I don't know. I don't think there's any such man. In fact, I think fairy tales are socially irresponsible. Last year I went to Disney World with Maisie and the twins, and you should have seen the princess crap they were selling. They had a parade where all the princesses were on floats, dressed up as brides and standing next to their princes. As though that should be every little girl's fantasy. I can't believe this is what we're selling our daughters. It's nauseating," I ranted.

"So instead, parents should read little girls stories about a princess who falls in love with a handsome prince, and then have the prince mutter something about not wanting to get serious, get back on his white horse, and ride off as fast as he can?" Hayden asked.

"Why not? At least we wouldn't be brainwashing them into thinking that the perfect man will come along and be the answer to all their problems."

"I take it things aren't going all that well between you and Drew after all," Hayden commented.

I sighed. "No, that's not it. Drew's great. He's thoughtful and funny, and I'm happy when I'm with him."

Ever since that first weekend, Drew had made a point of calling every day. When I reported this to Mal, he got a smug expression on his face and said, "Told you so." I'd rolled my eyes, but secretly I preferred Mal when he was being smug and sarcastic. It made it easier to resist the physical attraction. The last thing I needed right now was to develop a crush on a gigolo. Not, I quickly reminded myself, that Mal had done anything to encourage me. Either he had his hands full with his current conquests or, somewhat less flattering, he found me too repulsive to pursue.

"Sounds awful," Hayden said dryly.

I continued, ignoring her. "I just feel like I can't trust it, that I'm constantly waiting for the other shoe to drop. That one day Drew will suddenly announce that he's really a woman living in a man's body and has decided to have a sex-change operation."

"Or that one day you'll walk in to find him having sex with another woman on your bed?" Hayden asked.

I was silent for a minute, listening to the rhythmic roar of the water as it lapped toward the shore. "I guess. Elliott left me with some baggage."

"Elliott was baggage," Hayden said firmly. "And just because you fell for one guy who turned out to be an asshole doesn't mean that every man you date from now on will be one."

"But how do you tell the difference? I like Drew. He seems to like me. I want to think that he's a good guy. But..." My voice trailed off, and I shrugged, remembering yet again Peter Graham's warning to be careful whom I trusted. "I don't know absolutely for sure that he is. I don't know if I'm capable of judging that."

"I have the opposite problem. I tend to delude myself into thinking that even the assholes are Prince Charmings. Look at Craig. I knew he was married and cheating on his wife with me. And yet I convinced myself that he was an amazing guy who'd just made the mistake of marrying the wrong woman." Hayden rolled her eyes. "It's hard to believe I was really that stupid."

"You're not stupid. You're just . . . optimistic," I said.

"Yeah. I really need to work on that," Hayden said. "Being naturally pessimistic would save me so much trouble." She picked up a piece of driftwood from the sand, shook it off, held it out to Harper Lee, who eagerly sniffed at it, and then threw it. "Go on, girl! Go get it!"

Harper Lee stared after the piece of driftwood and then looked up at Hayden. Perplexed, she sat down and panted.

"You're confusing her," I said.

"She doesn't like to play fetch?"

"I think she finds it beneath her."

"Good girl, Harper Lee," Hayden praised, leaning over to pet the dog's head. "Don't ever take orders from anyone."

"Please stop corrupting my dog. What's up with you and Ian?" I asked, as we resumed our walk. "It seems like things are going well with you two."

"Actually, I'm thinking about breaking it off," Hayden said.

"Really? But you seem so happy together."

Hayden turned to grin at me. "I thought you just said you didn't believe in true love," she said.

The sand was softer at this part of the beach, sinking beneath our feet and then making a sucking sound when we pulled our feet back up.

"I didn't say I don't believe in love," I corrected her. "I just don't believe in the Prince Charming myth."

"Well, whichever way you phrase it, I don't think Ian's a good long-term prospect. He's a great guy, and we're having fun, but he's just so . . ."

"Young?" I suggested.

"Poor," Hayden corrected me.

"Hayden!"

"It's true. And I don't see bartending making him rich anytime soon."

"But that shouldn't matter," I protested.

"So says the woman with thirty-four million dollars," Hayden countered.

I wasn't sure how to respond to this. I'd never known Hayden to be so mercenary. In fact, I'd assumed that coming from a wealthy family made it unnecessary.

"I'm not saying money doesn't matter," I said. "But if you love someone, isn't that more important than a fat bank balance?"

"Jesus, Lucy, I didn't know you were such a romantic. Especially with all of that fairy-tale bashing," Hayden said with a laugh. "Look, all I'm saying is this: It's just as easy to fall in love with a rich man as it is to fall in love with a poor one. And think of how much easier the relationship will be if you don't have to worry about where the next month's rent is coming from. Did you know that money is the number-one issue married couples fight about?"

I decided to point out the obvious. "But you haven't fallen in love with a rich man."

Hayden smiled enigmatically. "I haven't fallen in love with a poor one either. Ian and I are just having fun. What's wrong with that?"

"Nothing," I said. I nudged a clump of dried seaweed out of my way with one foot. "Nothing at all."

When Drew called, I was curled up on one of the white linen sofas in the pool house, paging through a copy of *Vogue* that Hayden had left behind. I'd been trying to reread *Mrs.*

Dalloway earlier, but I couldn't seem to get into it. In fact, with all of the going out I'd been doing lately, I barely had time to read. The piles of books I'd bought at Barnes & Noble on the day I met Drew were stacked in a corner of the pool house, spines still uncracked. I'd resolved not to feel guilty about that. I'd spent most of my life with my nose stuck firmly in a book. It was about time I lived a little, even if that meant less time for reading.

"I have to go to a cocktail party for the Young Lawyers' Association after work. Can you live without me for a night?" Drew asked.

"If I must."

"What will you do?"

"The usual. Sex. Drugs. Rock 'n' roll," I said.

"Good, good. That all sounds very wholesome."

"I think Hayden wants to go over to the Drum Roll," I said. "Ian's working tonight."

"Is that Mal guy going to be there?" Drew asked.

"I don't know," I said, surprised. "Why?"

"I don't like him."

"You hardly know him."

"I know of him," Drew said, with a snort. "He has a reputation around the club."

"What sort of reputation?" I asked, although I had a feeling that I already knew.

"Let's just say that he entertains quite a few of the wives," Drew said delicately.

"You mean he's having affairs with them," I said slowly.

"No. I mean he's screwing them."

"What's the difference?" I asked, intrigued.

"Money," Drew said, this time much more to the point. "Apparently it changes hands. At least, that's the rumor."

I'd already guessed this about Mal, but hearing it confirmed was unsettling. My mouth suddenly tasted bitter, as though I'd taken a bite from a rotten apple.

"Oh," I said. And then, for some reason feeling as if I should rise to Mal's defense, I continued, "But you don't know that for sure?"

"No," Drew admitted. "But even so, I still don't like the guy. I'm not a big fan of adulterers."

"Can you be an adulterer if you're not married?" I asked. "Wouldn't the cheating wife be the adulterer, and he's just the accomplice?"

"I don't know," Drew said, suddenly impatient with the conversation. "Does it matter? Either way, it's not cool."

"No," I agreed. "It's not."

"What are you up to for the rest of the day?" Drew asked.

"Well, speaking of Mal—I have a tennis lesson this afternoon," I said. "It's a makeup from yesterday's lesson, which got rained out."

Drew made a harrumphing noise.

"What?" I asked.

"Can't you find another tennis instructor? Someone who doesn't have a reputation of sleeping with his clients?" Drew asked.

I laughed. "Don't worry. I think I'm safe. I'm not Mal's type."

"That's true. You're not old and rich," Drew joked.

I swallowed. I still hadn't told Drew about the lottery money. Or my real last name. Or why I had run away to Palm Beach. At first, I hadn't known him well enough to trust him. But now that I did know him—and thought I could trust him—I still hesitated. I knew Drew wasn't after me for my money—after all, he had no idea just how much money I had—and I doubted he'd believe Matt Forrester's ridiculous fabricated allegations. Or, at least, I hoped he wouldn't believe them. But he might mind—and mind very much—that I'd been lying to him all this time. That was the problem with lies: They were hard to keep up but even harder to come clean about.

Mal served the ball, and I returned it with a sharply angled cross-court shot that he had to run for—and missed! I was so delighted, I held my racquet up over my head in triumph, as though I'd just scored the winning shot in the finals of the Wimbledon championship.

"Did you see that?" I crowed.

"I did! It was a fantastic shot," Mal called back.

"You gave me an easy serve," I said graciously. I'd seen Mal play competitively a few days earlier and knew he was capable of a fast, spinning serve that I'd never have a prayer of touching, let alone returning. I had assumed Mal was a good player—he was a pro, after all—but even so, I'd been surprised by the grace and skill with which he played. He'd easily beat his opponent, who I later found out was twenty years old and played on his college's tennis team.

"It was still an excellent return," Mal praised me. "Your form was perfect. Did you feel the difference when you followed through on your swing?"

I nodded. "I really did!"

Mal glanced at his watch. "We'd better stop here. I have somewhere I have to be."

"Really?" I frowned. "I was hoping we could hit for a little longer. I need to work on my backhand."

"We'll tackle it at your lesson on Friday."

"Okay." We walked over to the table that was off to the side of the court, shaded by a jasmine-covered pergola. I zipped my racquet into its padded bag, while Mal poured us each a paper cup of water from the cooler. Mal tipped his head back and closed his eyes while he drank. There was a faint sheen of sweat on his brow, but otherwise he gave no sign that he'd been out in the sun for the past hour. I, on the other hand, was sweating like a pig. My white shirt stuck to my back, and beads of sweat trickled down my neck and cascaded into my cleavage.

"Where are you off to?" I asked.

"An appointment," Mal said enigmatically.

It was pretty clear he didn't want to go into any more detail. Which, of course, just inflamed my curiosity. Was this an assignation with one of the country-club wives? Maybe the gorgeous brunette I'd seen him out to dinner with?

"What sort of appointment?"

Mal looked at me, his face inscrutable. "The private sort," he said.

"Ohhhh," I said knowingly. "A hot date, huh?"

"Something like that."

"And who's the lucky lady?" I pressed on.

"You don't think it's a bit ironic for someone leading a secret life to pry into someone else's private business?"

I flushed. "I'm not leading a secret life."

"What's your last name again?"

"Well . . . it's not a secret to you."

"If I hadn't recognized you, would you have told me?" Mal countered.

"No," I conceded.

Mal nodded, as though he'd proven his point.

"But, wait, why won't you tell me what you're up to?"

"Because it's none of your business."

"Are you afraid I'll disapprove?" I asked.

Mal frowned. "What?"

"I'm not a prude, you know. It's not something I would do personally, but I'm sure you have your reasons," I said.

This was an outright lie. It horrified me that Mal was sleeping around with the married ladies of the Rushes Country Club, especially if he was doing so for financial gain. But for some reason that I couldn't put my finger on, I wanted him to admit it to me.

But Mal continued to look puzzled. "What? No, never mind, don't tell me." He crumpled up his paper cup and tossed it into the wastebasket. "I don't have time."

"So, fine, don't tell me," I said, irritation rising. "But you don't have to pretend that you don't know what I'm talking about."

"Maybe you should get out of the heat. Have some water. Rehydrate. Regain your sanity," Mal suggested. His lips twitched up in a half smile. "Bye, Lucy." And then he turned and walked off.

I glowered at his departing back. Matters did not improve when a curvy redhead—whose very long and very shapely legs were shown off to great advantage by a short white pleated tennis skirt—stopped Mal by practically throwing herself in his path. She looked like she was in her early thirties, which probably meant she was really a decade older. The money that flowed around this club went a long way toward buying the services of dermatologists, nutritionists, personal trainers, and plastic surgeons.

"Ma-al," I heard her squeal. "I've been looking *every*where for you. I want you to look at my swing."

She twirled her tennis racquet in one hand, but from her flirty tone and the slight tilt of her head, it was clear that she was interested in Mal for something other than his tennis expertise. My eyes narrowed with dislike. The rich thought they could buy anything and anyone. Then I remembered: I was rich. Maybe even more so than the redhead, although in a town like Palm Beach, where most of the residents were millionaires, it was impossible to know for sure.

But I'm not like her, I reassured myself. *I don't use my money to buy people.*

Although wasn't that exactly what Maisie seemed to think I was doing when I sent her that check? No, I thought, pushing away this unwanted thought. If she did think that, she was wrong. That money was meant as a gift, no strings attached. And if Maisie couldn't accept it in the spirit with which it was given, that wasn't my fault.

The redhead was now wantonly stroking Mal's arm. She'd lowered her voice, so I couldn't hear exactly what she was saying, but it wasn't hard to figure out the meaning. I found myself wishing I was a better tennis player so I could launch a few balls in their direction, hopefully beaning each of them on the head.

"I'm sorry, Liza, I can't work with you right now," Mal said, extricating himself from her clutches. "There's somewhere I have to be. Why don't you check my schedule in the pro shop? They'll set up a lesson for you."

If I hadn't known what he was up to, I would have enjoyed the look, first of surprise, then anger, that flashed across the redhead's pretty face as Mal moved on down the path. But then her gaze shifted to me and I started, realizing she had just caught me staring at her.

"Oops," I said under my breath, as the redhead shot me a filthy look and stalked off toward the back courts. I shook my head ruefully. Mal certainly seemed to be leaving a string of broken hearts behind him.

* * *

"How was your lesson?" Hayden asked when I got home. She was in the kitchen, eating Cheez-Its straight from the box. Marta, our new housekeeper, was there too, wiping down the counters. She was short and comfortably plump and didn't seem to speak a word of English. She smiled her greeting, and I smiled back.

"Why do you look so grumpy?" Hayden asked.

"I'm not. I'm smiling."

"You're smiling in a grumpy way."

"It's nothing, really." I opened the refrigerator door and rummaged around for a bottle of water. Water bottle in hand, I closed the door with unnecessary force. "It's just Mal—well, it's more something Drew said about Mal."

"What's that?"

I told her what Drew said about the rumors swirling around Mal. "And that fits with my original gigolo theory. Remember that woman I saw him out to dinner with weeks ago? She was older, very attractive . . ." I trailed off and circled a hand in the air.

Hayden shook her head. "I asked Ian about that. He thought it was hilarious. He said that Mal's not at all the type to run around after married women, rich or otherwise."

"Really? Hmmm," I said, considering this. Ian and Mal were close friends. Surely Ian would know if Mal was sleeping his way through the Rushes. "Unless Mal doesn't want Ian to know about it."

"But why keep it a secret?" Hayden shrugged. "He hasn't exactly hidden his other conquests."

"The girls at the bar, you mean?" I asked. Hayden nodded. "Please tell me he doesn't go into detail about that with Ian. I know Mal can be obnoxious, but bragging about his sexual conquests is beneath even him."

"No, of course he doesn't. But he was pretty obvious about leaving with a different girl every night," Hayden pointed out. "Until recently, that is. I haven't seen him there with anyone in a long time. Have you?"

I considered this. It was true: I hadn't noticed Mal leaving the Drum Roll with a pretty young thing on his arm recently—not that I'd been watching. Well. Not closely, anyway.

"So either he's a male slut *and* a gigolo," I said, "or he's just a male slut who's possibly reforming."

"Or he's a gigolo who's so overworked, he's decided to drop all extracurricular activities," Hayden said, grinning. "Oh, hey, I forgot to tell you, your sister called while you were out."

"What did she say?"

"She sounded upset. Said she really had to talk to you. Something to do with her wedding."

I groaned and slumped back against the counter. "No! No more wedding talk! I love my sister—really, I do—but I cannot handle one more minute of listening to her obsess about dresses, and flowers, and bridesmaids, and God knows what else. I don't have it in me."

"Hey, I'm just the messenger." Hayden held up her hands in mock defense.

"I'll call her back later," I said. Much, much later.

Seventeen

I PUT OFF RETURNING EMMA'S CALL FOR A FEW DAYS. I kept meaning to get around to it, but something always came up—a rough nail needed filing, or a movie I'd seen only two or three times before was on cable. When the guilt finally overcame my lack of enthusiasm for the task, I called home one evening while I was waiting for Hayden to get ready to go out to dinner. My dad answered the phone.

"Hi, Dad. It's me. Lucy."

"Lucy? Hi, honey! How are you? We hadn't heard from you in so long, your mother and I were starting to worry."

"Didn't Emma tell you I called a few days ago?"

"No."

I sighed. Typical Emma. "I'm fine. Why wouldn't I be?"

"Trouble seems to have a way of finding you," Dad said dryly.

I couldn't argue with him on that point. "Yeah, well. Bridezilla called me. So what's the wedding crisis this time?"

"I don't know. I've learned to tune your sister out whenever she gets on the topic," Dad said.

"But that's all she talks about."

"Exactly. I'll have to have her call you back, though. She's not here now."

"That's fine. Actually, Dad, there's something I need to talk about with you too. My financial adviser told me that you and Mom haven't cashed the check I sent you."

There was silence on the other end.

"Dad?"

"I'm still here. I just . . . well, I don't feel like we should take that money from you."

I sighed impatiently. "I want you to have it. I want you and Mom to use it to do something amazing."

"And I want you to save that money for your future," Dad insisted. His voice took on the steely tone that, when I was growing up, meant I was wandering dangerously close to trouble.

"I have lots of money. Lots and lots of money. Piles of it, in fact."

"You can't think of it that way. If you start spending the capital—" Dad began.

"Then I'll still have more," I said. "I couldn't possibly burn through all of that money. Not in my lifetime."

"Lucy, you've always been very careful with your finances. I want you to promise me you won't let this money enable you to slip into bad habits."

I wondered if he'd consider my recent splurges on Worth Avenue to fall under the heading of *bad habits* and thought I'd probably better not mention them.

"I'll tell you what," I said. "I will promise you on one condition."

"What's that?"

"You cash the check," I said.

"Lucy—"

"Consider it a quid pro quo," I said. My dad had been very big on the concept of quid pro quo when Emma and I were growing up. Whenever we wanted something, from a Bonne Bell Lip Smacker to car privileges, Dad would say, "And what's the quid pro quo going to be?" And we'd end up having to do a chore to earn it.

"Blackmail wasn't exactly the lesson I was trying to teach you."

"*Blackmail* is a bit harsh, don't you think? Especially since I'm trying to give you money, not get it out of you," I pointed out.

"I'll think about it. I'll talk to your mother about it."

"I thought Mom was all in favor of taking the money."

"Yes," Dad said. "Your mother wants to build a kennel in the backyard. I have mixed feelings about it. On the one hand, she says it will mean fewer dogs in the house."

I laughed. "Fat chance. Knowing Mom, it will just mean more dogs, inside and out."

"That's what I was afraid of," Dad said, sounding resigned to this inevitability.

"I meant for that money to be a good thing for you two. I didn't mean for it to be the source of conflict," I said.

"I know you didn't," Dad said. "Will you think about what I said about not overspending?"

"Of course," I said. I decided this wasn't a good time to mention that I had an appointment that afternoon to test-drive a car. And not just any car—a 1963 Porsche 356 Cabriolet. Frankie—Hayden's and now my stylist—had heard I was in the market for a car and had put me in touch with a client who was selling it. It would certainly solve my problem of needing to buy a car but not wanting to go through a dealer, who would almost certainly insist upon seeing my license and might recognize my name. I knew I would still need to arrange for the title transfer and insurance, but that was the sort of thing Peter Graham had said he could do for me.

"It's easy. I'll create a corporation, name you the sole shareholder, and the corporation will buy the car," he'd said the last time I'd seen him. And I had thought for the hundredth time in recent weeks that having money really does solve most problems. The old saying *Money doesn't buy happiness* really should be *Money may not buy happiness, but it can solve all the problems standing between you and happiness.*

"I should get going. I have to get to the office," Dad said. "I have three back-to-back root canals."

"Okay. Tell Emma I called. And say hi to Mom," I said.

"Will do. Bye, honey. I love you."

"I love you too, Dad."

The car was amazing. Not being a car person myself, I've never really understood how people can get excited about a machine that has the dull if necessary job of ferrying you from place to place. But as I gazed at the cherry-red Porsche convertible, I felt it for the first time: car lust.

"It's gorgeous," I breathed. And it was. The car was a sporty little two-seater with an elongated front, round headlights, and buttery-soft brown leather seats.

"I know," Sherman said sadly. "I hate to part with it."

I walked around the car slowly, trailing one finger on the shiny lipstick-red paint. "Why are you selling?"

"My company is transferring me to Paris," Sherman explained. He was about my age and height and had dark hair with blond highlights, thick eyebrows, and even thicker lips.

He was wearing a skintight blue T, flowing linen pants, and leather thong sandals. "I thought about taking it with me and having it shipped over—"

"I'll take it," I said quickly, before he could change his mind.

Sherman laughed. "You don't know how much I'm asking for it."

"Whatever it is, I'll take it," I said. And then, realizing that this was perhaps not the best negotiation tactic, I added, "How much are you asking?"

"I'll tell you what. You take the car for a test-drive, decide if you like it, and if you're still interested when you get back, we'll talk about the price," Sherman said. He walked over and opened the driver's side door for me.

"Really?" I asked excitedly.

"Hop in," Sherman said. Then, with the furrowed brow of a worried parent, he patted the car protectively. "Just be careful with her."

Five minutes later, cruising down South Lake Drive, I was convinced: I had to have this car. It didn't matter what Sherman was asking for it, I was going to buy it. Everything looked better from behind the wheel. The sky was an even deeper azure blue, the whitecapped ocean looked even more lovely, the mansions were even larger and more imposing. And I was sure the car made me look better too—prettier, sexier, more glamorous. The knowledge that I was going to own something so beautiful, so luxurious, made my pulse hum with excitement.

I put on my turn signal and was about to turn right and loop back around to Sherman's condo when I saw Mal drive by. At least, I thought it was Mal. Yes, it definitely was, I decided. That was his car, a little silver Mazda. I'd seen him getting in and out of it at the club. Mal was now driving west on Royal Palm Way, about to head over the bridge.

Palm Beach really is a small town, I thought. *A very rich town, but small nonetheless.*

And then suddenly I remembered: It was Thursday. And if I remembered correctly—and I knew I did—Mal's secret assignations, the ones he refused to talk about, took place on Tuesday and Thursday afternoons. Without thinking it through, I turned left instead of right and followed him.

Mal drove over the bridge to West Palm and took a right on South Flagler, driving along the water. I followed as far behind as I could without losing sight of him, realizing belatedly that a red Porsche convertible is not the best car for going undercover in. Mal made a left, then a right, and then another left, and suddenly the surroundings took a sharp turn for the worse. Gone were the waterfront mansions and towering office buildings. Here the houses were small and shabby, often with boarded-up windows and lawns that had more weeds than grass.

This is where Mal goes on his romantic trysts? I wondered. It didn't seem possible. There wasn't a luxury hotel in sight.

Ahead of me, Mal turned into a school parking lot. The sign in front read, LEEANDER HIGH SCHOOL. The school was two stories high and painted royal blue. Along one wall there was a mural of a majestic yellow lion, his head raised and turned so that he was staring out at the street. Above the lion, THE LEEANDER LIONS was painted in red block letters.

I hesitated, not wanting Mal to see me but not wanting to lose him in case he was just cutting through the parking lot. I watched him turn right into a looping driveway, which he followed around toward the back of the school and out of my sight. I drove slowly after him. A minute later his Mazda was back in view.

I came to a full stop and watched Mal pull into a spot in the school's rear parking lot, just next to the asphalt tennis courts. Like the rest of the school, the courts looked taken care of—the net was hanging straight and the lines were freshly painted—but it was utilitarian and designed for wear, not aesthetics. A group of girls, mostly black and Hispanic, were assembled on the court, some sitting, some standing. A few of the girls were hamming it up as they waited, dancing and wiggling their hips from side to side, as they waved their tennis racquets around overhead.

Mal jumped nimbly from his car and pulled his tennis racquet and a hopper of yellow tennis balls out of the trunk. When the girls saw him, they let out a loud cheer that I could hear, even at a distance.

"Mr. Mal's here! Mr. Mal's here!"

Mal waved his racquet in greeting, and one of the girls—tall and dark-skinned, with white beads braided into her hair—dashed out to greet him. He gave her a high five and handed her the ball hopper. The girl carried it easily and followed after him, beaming.

I stared openmouthed at the scene before me, as it began to dawn what exactly was going on here. Mal was *coaching* these girls. Yes, there was no mistake about it. After he'd greeted them—which seemed to involve some good-natured ribbing on both sides—the girls lined up on one side of the court, Mal on the other, and he began hitting balls to them. I recognized the drill—it was one he'd done with me. A forehand shot, then a backhand, a jog up to the net to take a volley, and then back for an overhead smash. The girls knew the drill, and the line moved quickly as each one stepped up to the baseline to take her turn.

I wasn't close enough to hear what Mal was saying, but the girls looked intent and focused, breaking into smiles only when they'd finished and been rewarded by a cheer from Mal.

And all the while I just sat there, staring at the spectacle and wondering how I could have gotten it so wrong. Even though I'd befriended Mal and spent hours with him, playing tennis or hanging out at the Drum Roll, I had never really given him a chance. I'd always assumed that *that* guy, the one I was getting to know, was really just a frothy whipped topping over a more mercenary and shallow core. And all along, I had misjudged him. He wasn't having sordid afternoon assignations with married women. He was doing something meaningful, something that had value.

Mal was, I realized, doing exactly what I most loved—teaching. Sadness pressed like a cold stone in my chest. I missed my job. It didn't matter how much money I had—after Matt Forrester's accusations against me, I would never be able to teach again. And if I wasn't a teacher, then who exactly was I?

My cell phone rang, startling me out of my reverie. I fumbled for it and quickly hit the talk button, while I crouched down behind the steering wheel. Thankfully neither Mal nor the girls seemed to have heard the ring tone, for no one even glanced in my direction.

"Hello," I whispered into the phone.

"Lucy? Is that you?"

I didn't recognize the voice. I was immediately wary. Had the press finally tracked me down? Had they somehow gotten hold of this number?

"Who's this?" I asked, my voice sharp and cold.

"It's Sherman. You have my car."

"Oh! Sherman! Right . . . sorry. I got . . . distracted," I said.

"I was about to call the police," he said testily.

Yikes, I thought. "Don't do that," I said. "I'm coming right back. And I definitely want to buy it."

"You do?" Sherman asked. He still sounded suspicious, but the prospect of the fat check I was about to write him seemed to dampen his anger.

"Yes," I said. "I do. Hold on, I'll be there in five minutes." Then, looking around and realizing that I wasn't entirely sure where I was, I said, "Better make it ten."

I took one last look at Mal. He'd broken the girls up into teams of two for doubles practice. On one side of the net the girls were serving, while the girls on the opposite, cross-court side returned service. Mal was jogging up and down the courts, trying to watch four sets of players at once, pausing occasionally to adjust a grip or correct a swing.

Wow, I thought, shaking my head. It was still hard to fully comprehend just how wrong I had been about Mal. It made me wonder: What else had I gotten wrong?

I made a neat three-point turn and drove slowly back down the driveway and off the school grounds.

Mal and his high school tennis team were still very much on my mind that evening while I was having dinner with Drew. We were dining at Café Boulud at the Brazilian Court hotel. I was having the grilled tuna; Drew had opted for the lamb chops. Drew was telling me a story about a client, an elderly woman who had been ripped off in a security-fraud case. I was half listening to him and picking at my fish.

"Is everything okay?" Drew finally asked. "You seem a bit preoccupied."

"I guess I am," I admitted. "I'm sorry. I don't mean to be such lousy company."

Drew smiled and shook his head. "You're not. Just more quiet than usual. Sometimes I wonder what you're thinking. You can be a bit mysterious, Lucy Landon."

Lucy Landon. How could I be in a relationship with a man who didn't even know my real name? It was ridiculous and, frankly, insulting to Drew. He deserved better than being deliberately misled. No, *misled* was too mild. I had lied to him. And the time to stop lying had finally arrived. I drew in a deep breath and exhaled slowly.

"There's something I've been wanting to—" I began.

But Drew was so intent on his own news, he didn't hear me. "I was thinking it's about time you met my family," he said.

This startling announcement chased all thoughts of confession out of my mind.

"Your family? Really?" I asked.

Drew nodded. "My parents are hosting a fund-raiser for the local children's hospital. It's being held at Mar-a-Lago—black tie, thousand dollars a plate. My mother has told me in no uncertain terms that I am to show up with a date. And so I told her I'd been seeing someone. . . ."

"Me," I said, smiling.

"You," Drew agreed. "She said that it was about time they met you. And I agree. What do you think?"

"I think I'm a little nervous," I said. "Will your parents like me?"

"Of course they will. But I should warn you: My mother is on a one-woman mission to become a grandmother. My sister Josie got married last year, and our mother's been driving her crazy, demanding to know when they're going to start a family."

"Does your sister want children?"

Drew laughed. "I have a hard time seeing Josie as the maternal type. She doesn't like kids. And my baby sister, Delia, hasn't ever been in a relationship that's lasted longer than a few weeks, so she's not going to settle down and start popping them out anytime soon. I think our mother sees me as her best chance for grandchildren. So don't freak out if she interrogates you about your readiness and ability to bear children."

"Are you serious? She'd really ask me about that?"

"Oh, yes," Drew said. "Perfectly serious. You don't know my mother."

"Maybe I should get a letter of reference from my gynecologist."

"You joke, but sadly I wouldn't be surprised if she asked for one," Drew said with a sigh.

"When is this fund-raiser again? I think I might be having a migraine."

"I just want you to know what you're getting into." Drew smiled and reached across the table to squeeze my hand. "Don't worry. They're all going to love you."

That word—*love*—hung there between us. It wasn't a word that we had said to each other before. By telling me that his family would love me, was Drew implicitly telling me that he loved me too? And was I in love with him? I wasn't sure. I certainly liked him and enjoyed spending time with him. But I'd been holding a part of myself back. Maybe it was because I hadn't yet told him who I really was. Or maybe my bad breakup with Elliott had damaged that part of me that was capable of falling in love.

But then Drew gave my hand a final squeeze and went back to his lamb chops and the story of his swindled client. And I had the distinct feeling that I'd been granted a reprieve.

Eighteen

"DAMN," I SAID, AS I RIFFLED THROUGH MY NEW mustard-yellow shoulder bag.

"What's wrong?" Hayden asked. She was peering at her reflection in the foyer mirror and, after a few minutes' deliberation, applied a final swipe of lipstick.

"I have to stop at the ATM before we go to the Drum Roll. I only have eight, no, wait, *nine* dollars on me. I thought I had more than that."

"I have cash," Hayden said. She dropped her lipstick into a miniclutch and then pulled out some bills from the bag. "Eighty bucks. That should be enough, don't you think?"

"I'll get some more out just in case," I said. I doubted we'd drink through eighty dollars' worth of cocktails at the Drum Roll, especially since Ian comped us free drinks whenever he could. But I also didn't want Hayden financing our night out, should we decide to get a bite to eat somewhere. As promised, I'd been picking up the house expenses—I paid Marta's salary, the groceries, the incidentals—and I hadn't failed to notice Hayden frowning when the mail arrived, always with a pile of bills forwarded from her Manhattan apartment.

Maybe I should swipe them and pay them off for her, I thought, and wondered if that would anger Hayden. I'd never known having money would be so complicated, but every time I tried to share it, I ended up pissing off the person I was trying to help. Only Emma had accepted her check without an argument. Which reminded me: My little sister had phoned again while I was out with Drew the night before, and I hadn't yet called her back.

I'll call her tomorrow, I decided, and promptly put Emma and whatever wedding-related hissy fit she was having out of my mind.

"Shall we take the Porsche?" I asked.

"If you don't mind driving," Hayden said.

"I love driving that car," I said dreamily. I looked in the mirror, and fluffed up my short crop of hair. "I'd better have Frankie come over and touch up my highlights soon."

"Why don't you just go into the salon?" Hayden asked.

I shrugged. "It's easier to have him come here."

"And more expensive," Hayden said. "He charges outrageously for house visits."

"Maybe I'll get him to come over on Saturday. Then he can do my highlights and style my hair for that benefit I'm going to with Drew," I said.

"Look out, I've created a monster," Hayden joked. "Dressed in head-to-toe Marc Jacobs and arranging for home visits from her stylist. Who would ever have thought this is where Lucy Parker would end up?"

"Who would have thought," I echoed. But as I spoke, I looked at myself in the mirror again. And for the first time, seeing the glossy woman with the sexy haircut and expensive clothes reflected there made me uneasy. I didn't recognize her—no, that wasn't quite it. The problem was that I didn't recognize *me* in *her.*

I gave myself a mental shake. I was being ridiculous; that *was* me in the mirror.

"You ready to go?" Hayden asked.

"Yep," I said, turning away from the mirror. "Let's go."

The Drum Roll was more crowded than I'd ever seen it.

"I guess the winter crowd has arrived," Hayden said.

"But it's only November."

"Just think of what it's going to be like after Christmas. The whole island will be chock-full of rich men," Hayden said.

"*Old* rich men," I said.

"Old rich men with grandsons who'll come down on the weekends to visit," Hayden countered, flashing me a sly grin.

I shrugged and nodded. Hayden hadn't yet broken up with Ian. But I didn't know how much longer their relationship would last, especially if a crowd of eligible men was about to descend on the island. Palm Beach was known for its wealthy retirees, but there were attractions for the young too. The golf courses, the tennis courts, the beaches, the polo grounds in Wellington. The island was a playground for the wealthy.

I didn't know why it should bother me that Hayden planned to dump Ian. It wasn't any of my business, and, besides, I was starting to suspect that Ian might have a gambling problem. He and Hayden were spending more and more time at the casino on the Seminole reservation. Hayden thought it was just good fun—apparently her lucky streak was still going strong—but she'd confided to me that Ian lost more often than he won. Much more often. I hoped he wasn't developing a full-blown gambling addiction. Despite the gambling, Ian was a sweet guy, and I suspected that no matter what she claimed, Hayden was fonder of him than she let on.

She still got that dreamy, unfocused look in her eyes whenever she saw him, and when they were together they constantly found reasons to touch each other. It probably should have been annoying but instead was sweet.

We pushed through the throng of people and made our way to the bar. Our usual bar stools were taken, and we couldn't even find a spot along the bar to lean on.

"Maybe we should just go," I said. This wasn't my sort of scene. It was one thing to hang out in a half-filled bar but quite another to be fighting our way through hordes of young girls in halter tops and the men who were trying to hit on them.

"But what about Ian?" Hayden asked. She was standing on tiptoe, trying to get a glimpse of her boyfriend.

"Hayden!" Ian shouted to make his voice heard over the din. "Over here!"

Hayden immediately began to push through the crowd. She jostled a thin woman with very long, dark hair, who was wearing a bikini top over skintight cropped capris.

Who goes out for a night dressed in a freaking bikini? I wondered. Even if you were twenty years old with an amazing body. Or maybe this was a sign that I was too old—and too out of touch—to be out clubbing. I certainly felt ancient, as old as dirt, surrounded by the lissome, fresh-faced youngsters.

"Hey," the sluttily dressed woman whined. "Watch where you're going."

Hayden, intent on getting to Ian, ignored her. I'd noticed that Hayden somehow always managed to avoid conflict. It wasn't that she was a pushover—far from it—more that she had an innate ability to tune out unpleasant people. It was as though she came equipped with an asshole-avoidance system.

Not having an asshole-avoidance system myself, I hung back and watched as she reached the bar. Ian leaned over and planted a kiss on her lips.

With Ian's help Hayden climbed gracefully up on the bar. The crowd applauded her, and Hayden gave them an airy wave before gracefully falling down into Ian's arms. They kissed again, and then Hayden got to work pulling out bottles of beer for the thirsty crowd.

"I see the Drum Roll has a new bartender," a voice behind me said. I turned around and saw Mal standing there. He smiled at me, his pale eyes crinkling. Annoyingly, I felt a stab of excitement.

Bad idea, I told myself.

"Hayden's been looking for a new career. Maybe she's finally found her calling," I said.

"It looks like it," Mal agreed. "What are you going to do while Hayden mixes martinis?"

"I think I'm going to head back home. This," I gestured around at the large crowd and loud music, "isn't really my scene."

"You want some company?" Mal asked.

No, I thought. *No, no, no.*

"Why? What do you want to do?" I asked.

"Do you feel like taking a walk?" Mal said.

No.

"Okay," I said.

We walked along the beach, our way just barely lit by a low-hanging moon and the lights blazing from the waterside mansions. I kicked off my heels and held them dangling from one hand, and the sand felt cool and dry shifting under my bare feet. Snatches of music drifted over—from house parties, from the nearby bars—but they were mostly muffled by the steady roar of the water lapping up on the shore.

"How long are you going to stay here?" Mal asked.

At first I wasn't sure exactly what he was talking about. How long was I staying where? Here on the beach? Out for the night? But then he clarified: "In Palm Beach."

"I'm not sure. I haven't really thought it through," I said.

"You're not going home?"

"To Ocean Falls? No. I don't see that happening anytime soon," I said. "I'm not exactly a beloved member of the community there anymore."

"You mean because of the allegations that student made against you?"

"Yeah. Funnily enough, people tend to disapprove of teachers trying to seduce their students."

"What actually happened?" Mal asked. His voice was mild and not at all judgmental, but even so, I bristled.

"Nothing happened. Do you really think I would do something like that?"

"No, I don't. But, then, people aren't always what they seem."

"I am," I said.

"Are you?" Mal asked.

I opened my mouth, ready to say, *of course I am*, but then I remembered looking in the mirror just that evening and not recognizing the woman staring back at me. Irritation rose up in me.

"If you think I'm such a fake, why would you take my word on what really happened anyway?"

"Because I don't think you're a fake, and I choose to believe you."

"Oh," I said, feeling somewhat mollified. "Well . . . thanks."

"No problem."

We walked in silence for a moment before I spoke again.

"I gave the student a failing grade, and because of that, he lost his eligibility to play on the school's soccer team. He begged me to change the grade, and when I refused, he made up the story about me propositioning him to get back at me," I finally said.

"Sounds like one screwed-up kid."

"I guess." It was hard for me to muster up much sympathy for Matt after what he'd put me through. I decided to change the subject. "Can I ask you a question?"

"You can ask. I can't promise I'll answer."

"Who was that woman I saw you out to dinner with at Morton's?" I asked. The elegant older woman was the one piece of information that no longer fit with my newly revised impression of Mal. Then again, maybe she had been a bona fide date. People dated outside their age bracket all the time. There was nothing wrong with that.

"Who? Do you mean my mother?" Mal asked.

"Your *mother*?"

I was so shocked, I stopped in my tracks and stared open-mouthed at him. Mal turned to face me. Through the dim light, I could tell he was frowning.

"Why do you sound so surprised?" he asked.

"I just . . ." *I thought she was an older woman paying for your sexual services.* Probably best not to mention that. "I never thought of you as having a mother," I finished lamely.

At this Mal laughed. "Did you think I spontaneously sprang into being?"

"No . . . I don't know." I took in a deep breath, inhaling the sea air. "Honestly? I thought she was your date."

"My *date*?" Mal sounded horrified. "You thought I was on a *date* with my *mother*?"

"I thought we established that I didn't know she was your mother." I started walking again, and after hesitating for a minute, Mal joined me.

"You did notice that she's sixty, didn't you?"

"Is she? Wow, she looks amazing for her age," I said.

"I'll tell her you said that. She'll be thrilled," Mal said dryly.

"Does she live here?"

"No, she was in town visiting. My parents live in Maryland, outside D.C."

"Is that where you grew up?"

Mal nodded. "Yep."

We walked in silence for a few minutes. Finally Mal burst out, "I can't believe you thought I was on a date with my mother! That's so *wrong*."

"Well, she's a very attractive woman," I said defensively.

"Even so."

"Why was she mad at you?"

"You know, for someone living a secret double life, you're inexcusably nosy."

"Fine, don't tell me," I said petulantly. Then, not able to resist, I added, "Unless you want to."

Mal sighed a deep, world-weary sigh. "If you must know, she'd been sent on a mission by my father to talk me into moving back home."

"Back home?" My forehead wrinkled. "You mean, moving back in with your parents?"

"Not exactly. It had more to do with going to work in the family business."

"Which is?"

"Construction," Mal said briefly.

"What, your dad is a contractor?" I asked. That would certainly explain his mother's expensive clothing and the meal at Morton's.

"In a manner of speaking."

"What does your dad want you to do? Join a work crew? Or be a project manager?" I persisted.

For some reason, though, this made Mal laugh. I had a feeling I was missing something—a crucial piece of information, or the punch line to the joke—but what that was, I had no idea.

"What?" I asked. "Why is that so funny?"

"You'd just have to know my dad to understand," Mal said. "But to answer your question: yes. He wants me to work for him, in a management position. I declined his job offer. My mother was not happy to hear this. Suffice it to say, they're not thrilled I'm living the life of a tennis instructor-slash-beach bum in Palm Beach."

This wasn't surprising. If his dad was a contractor, he probably had an old-school, blue-collar background—the sort of man who believed in hard work, buying not renting, and marrying young. A son who lived among the jet-set crowd, giving tennis lessons to the Ladies Who Lunch, would not impress him. But then I thought of the afternoons Mal spent working with the inner-city girls' tennis team, and I felt a flash of anger at his parents.

I was about to ask if his parents knew about his coaching but then remembered that I wasn't supposed to know either.

"You never told me how you ended up in Florida," I said instead.

"Old story. I came down here for spring break, got really drunk one night, and woke up on the beach. No clothes, no wallet, no friends. I couldn't even remember the name of our hotel. I didn't have any money to get home, so I just got a job and ended up staying," Mal said, his voice deadly serious.

My mouth had dropped open as he talked, and when he

finished, it was a long moment before I could speak, and even then it came out as a sputter.

"Are you . . . oh, my *God* . . . are you *serious?*" I yelped.

"Nope," Mal said, and he snickered. I whacked him on the arm. Hard.

"Ow!"

I took another swipe at him, but this time he sidestepped me.

"See that? I'm like a cat. Nimble even in the dark," Mal bragged.

"Lucky for you I've never been particularly athletic," I said.

"I guess so."

"Are you going to tell me the truth?"

"It's not a great story. Not as good as waking up on the beach naked and hungover."

"Try me."

"I made a go at playing pro," Mal said.

"Tennis?"

"Duh."

I rolled my eyes, although it was too dark for Mal to get the full effect of this. "You have such a way with words."

"Yes, tennis. I dropped out of school my sophomore year at the University of Georgia—I was on the tennis team there—and came down here to train at a tennis academy in Fort Lauderdale. The guy who runs it—Mick Beaufort—has helped launch a few of the top guys. He thought I had what it takes to go pro," Mal said. His voice was neutral, and when I glanced up at him, I could just see through the dim light that he was staring straight ahead.

"And?"

"And I screwed up."

"How so?" Then, worrying that I was prying, I quickly

added, "You don't have to tell me if you don't want to. If it makes you uncomfortable."

"Yeah, right. Like you'd let it go," Mal said, although the smile was back in his voice. "The crowd that hung around the tennis academy had a work-hard, play-hard mind-set. And I took that a little too far. I partied a lot, ended up missing a few too many practices, and got myself kicked out of the academy."

"Oh, no," I said. Which seemed a completely inadequate response, but I didn't know what else to say.

"I wasn't just being an asshole," Mal said quickly. "I mean, I was, considering I pissed away the opportunity of a lifetime. But I was pretty messed up at the time. It's why I left school when I did."

"Let me guess—there was a girl involved somewhere," I said, raising my voice to be heard over the wind, which was starting to gust up over the water.

"I thought we'd already talked about your unfortunate habit of calling women girls," Mal said in a mock severe tone.

"I forgot I was taking a walk with a militant feminist."

"See that you don't make that mistake again."

"So was I right? Was it a girl?"

"Yes."

"What happened?"

"Old story. Boy meets girl—"

"Now you're doing it too."

"Are you going to let me tell the story of my broken heart and subsequent lost dreams, or are you going to continue to tease me?" Mal asked.

"Sorry," I said. "Carry on."

"Where was I? Oh, right. Boy meets girl, they fall in love, talk about getting married. Then boy finds out that girl is messed up," Mal said.

"How so?"

"Honestly, I have no idea how much of what she told me was true. She told me that her last boyfriend had been abusive—"

"That's terrible!"

"I'm not sure if it was physical, or emotional, or both, or neither. Whenever I pressed her for more details, she'd shut down and refuse to tell me. And then she started to get seriously loopy."

"Loopy how?"

"Like stripping off her clothes and running naked out of her dorm. Or thinking that her sociology professor was out to get her—and I don't just mean giving her a bad grade but that he wanted to kill her."

"Did he?" I asked, horrified.

"No. It turned out she suffered from paranoid schizophrenia. It wasn't diagnosed until she was nearly twenty. Then she dropped out of school. Her parents took her home and basically told me not to contact her again," Mal said.

"But *why*?"

"I don't think they were bad people. Just very protective of their daughter. They lived in a small town, where her dad was a really big deal, and I think they wanted to keep her as sheltered as possible from local gossip. In my less magnanimous moments, I think maybe they wanted to keep her cloistered so that she wouldn't embarrass them," Mal said.

"That's awful," I said, crossing my arms in front of my chest as I tried to remember what it was like to be twenty, in love, and separated from that person. I couldn't. The truth was, I hadn't really been in love at that age. Infatuation, yes, but not love.

"Tell me about it." Mal paused. "You know, I've never told anyone about Jessica before. I guess I always thought talking about her problems would violate her privacy." He took a deep breath.

"Anyway, I dropped out too and took off for Florida, where I was going to become a world-renowned tennis star." Mal snorted a completely humorless laugh. "And instead, I was depressed and freaked out about what had happened to Jessica, and I dealt with it by getting drunk or stoned or both every night. Eventually I was kicked out of the academy, and it took me another five years to get my shit together."

"What did you do?"

"I bartended. And a few times, when the Season was over and the jobs dried up, I had to accept financial help from my parents just to pay the rent, which absolutely killed me. I swore I wouldn't be one of those jackasses who has to constantly call home to Daddy for help."

"Don't you think you're being a little hard on yourself?" I asked gently.

"No. I don't think I'm being hard enough. I'm not exactly proud of that phase of my life. But eventually I got a job as the assistant tennis pro for a tourist hotel in Fort Lauderdale. I was thankful enough for the break that I worked my ass off, and I traded up a few times to better and better resorts. Eventually I landed the gig at the Rushes Country Club," Mal said. "Which brings us up to the present." Apparently Mal had reached his limit on self-reflection, for he abruptly changed the subject. "So. What about your parents?"

"What about them?"

"Are they happy about how your life has turned out?"

"Sure," I said. But then I stopped to think about this question. Were they proud of me? I knew they had been when I was teaching. But I was also pretty sure that they wouldn't be thrilled with my new Palm Beach life of leisure. "I think they'd be happier if I was using my lottery money to do something meaningful. My dad especially seems worried that the money will have a corrupting influence on me."

"Are you corruptible?"

I was about to say, *No, of course not.* But then I thought about the past six weeks. The money I was spending, the late nights I was keeping, the fact that I couldn't remember the last time I'd picked up a book. I didn't know if that counted as corruption necessarily, but the money had certainly changed how I was living my life.

So instead I said, "Isn't everyone?"

Mal shrugged. "I suppose, in a really broad never-say-never sort of a way. But I believe in self-determination and taking responsibility for your actions."

"How exactly does that fit into your whole Peter Pan, beer-swilling, hookup-artist lifestyle?" I teased.

Mal feigned mock outrage. "Peter Pan? Hookup artist?"

"What would you call it?"

"My romantic nature, maybe? My poet's soul?"

I snorted. Mal laughed too, and then he did something startling—he took my hand in his and swung our arms lightly between us. Instantly, I tensed. It was one thing for two friends to opt to take a walk over sitting in a crowded, smoky bar; it was an entirely different situation when that walk involved holding hands on a moonlit beach.

Unfortunately, at that moment it felt like all my blood had suddenly rushed to my head, leaving me slightly dizzy. And rather than having a clear, precise idea of what to do, my thoughts were so jumbled, I couldn't grab on to any of them. Fuzzy notions that this was wrong, that there was Drew to consider, that even if Mal wasn't a gigolo, he was something of a player and quite definitely out of my league. But then there was the not-so-insignificant problem that I was attracted to Mal. And I very badly wanted to see where this moonlit walk was headed.

This is a bad idea, the logical, rational side of my brain cautioned.

Go for it, the emotional, irrational side countered.

Mal seemed to sense my growing agitation. He stopped suddenly and pulled my arm so that I was facing him. He was standing very, very close, his handsome face unreadable in the darkness.

"You're shaking," he said.

"I'm cold," I lied.

Mal's hands were suddenly on my hips, pulling me toward him. Before my mind could wrap itself around this startling development, Mal bent forward and kissed me. Any resistance I might have offered up instantly evaporated. Instead, my arms lifted, encircled his neck, and I kissed him back.

Everything around us receded—the sandy beach, the rhythmic roar of the ocean, the distant sounds of a house party at one of the mansions that lined the beach—until there was just Mal and me, touching each other. His lips were softly urgent as they pressed against mine, and I responded in kind, leaning up into him, wanting nothing more than to have this moment last into infinity. I still felt light-headed, but every last nerve in my body was tingling and on high alert.

But then Mal stepped back, breaking away. His hands slid from my hips to my arms and then to my hands, lacing my fingers with his.

"Come on, let's get out of here," Mal said. He dropped my left hand and turned, pulling me gently.

"Where are we going?" I asked. My voice was hoarse, and I cleared my throat.

"My place, your place, anywhere but here. I know the

beach looks deserted, but people are constantly coming out here," Mal said.

"Okay," I said. He was walking quickly, so even though we were still holding hands, I was a step or two behind him. "Wait a second."

What I meant was, *Wait for me*. But Mal apparently thought I was rethinking the situation, for he stopped in his tracks and dropped my hand.

"You don't want to do this?" he asked, turning to face me. I wished the light was stronger, wished I could see his expression. As it was, his face was shadowed. All I could make out was the white of his skin, the pale glint of his hair.

"I just..." I began, but then I stopped. Because now that he was no longer touching me, the warm fizzy sensation that had temporarily taken over my body was receding. Even worse, my thoughts began to clear. "Maybe...maybe we shouldn't."

"Okay," Mal said evenly. "If you don't want to."

"It's not that," I said quickly. Because I did want to. There was no point lying about it. "But there are reasons why we shouldn't. Drew, for one."

Drew and I hadn't exactly talked about whether or not our relationship was monogamous, mostly because up until now the conversation had seemed unnecessary. Drew and I saw each other almost every day. It would be an impressive feat if he was somehow able to fit another woman in between me and the long hours he worked. But while there hadn't been a formal commitment, there hadn't been a release of one either. And Drew and I had spent enough time together, and enough nights together, that if one of us was going to see other people, we ought to have that conversation first. I owed it to him and I owed it to myself. I wasn't the sort of woman who dated one man and then, behind his back, slept with another. A lot of things in my life—a lot of things about me—may have changed since the day I won the lottery, but this wasn't going to be one of them.

"Right. There's Drew."

I'd never heard Mal say Drew's name before, but I could tell from his flat tone that he didn't like Drew any more than Drew liked him. I wondered if it was just that they saw each other as rivals for the same woman—which, I had to admit, would be insanely flattering—or if they were just too dissimilar to get along. Drew was the buttoned-up country-club type, while Mal was the nonconformist who rarely shaved. They were both kind men, but still, very different.

"Yes, there's Drew," I said firmly. "He's a good guy, and he certainly doesn't deserve to have me sneaking around with other guys behind his back."

"Okay."

"I should at least talk to him first," I said.

Mal laughed. "Do you want to borrow my cell phone?" he asked, sounding almost normal, his tone losing the sharp edges.

"No," I said. "That's not what I meant."

"What did you mean?"

I sighed and closed my eyes for a moment. Then I swallowed hard, opened my eyes, and with as steady a voice as I could manage, I said, "I meant . . . this is probably a bad idea. I should go before this—well, I think I should just go home." I crossed my arms and began walking back down the beach, in the direction of the lighted parking lot, where my car was. I glanced back and realized Mal hadn't moved. "Come on, I'll drop you back off at the bar."

"That's okay," Mal said. "I'm going to walk on the beach for a while. Clear my head."

I hesitated. “How will you get home?”

“This is a small island, Lucy. I think I’ll manage.”

And then Mal turned and walked away from me. I watched him disappear into the darkness, and then, finally, I turned away too.

Nineteen

AS DREW STEERED UP THE DRIVEWAY BEHIND A LINE of Rolls-Royces and Bentleys, Mar-a-Lago loomed into view, looking like a tropical castle with its red-tiled Mediterranean roof and surrounded by palm trees.

"Your parents are having their party here?" I asked.

"It's not a private party. It's a fund-raiser," Drew said.

"Even so," I said faintly. Meeting your new boyfriend's parents was always potentially disastrous. Would you like them, or, more important, would they like you? This first meeting with the Brookses was made even more unnerving than most considering my assumed identity and accompanying cover story. What had I been thinking agreeing to do this at a black-tie event?

"Relax. You'll be fine. In fact, you'll probably be bored. This party is going to be full of stiffs in tuxes talking business," Drew said. He grinned at me and winked. Drew was wearing black tie, but he definitely didn't look like a stiff in it. To the contrary, the beautiful tailoring highlighted his wide shoulders and long legs.

"And your family," I pointed out.

"Just let whatever they say roll off you. Imagine you're coated in Teflon."

"You see, you say things like that and it makes me even more nervous. You make it sound like they're lying in wait for me!" I exclaimed.

"Yeah, well. That's because they probably are," Drew said. "Kidding! I'm kidding."

"Ha-ha," I said.

"Besides, you look fabulous," Drew said, casting me an appreciative glance. "I almost feel moved to break out in a chorus of 'Lady in Red.' "

"Please don't," I begged, although I was secretly pleased by the compliment.

My red silk Carolina Herrera gown was strapless, with a shirred bodice and a sweetheart neckline, and fell in an elegant column that just barely swept the floor. Best of all, there was a sexy slit up the front, exposing a sheer black underskirt. On my feet were a truly stunning pair of Christian Lacroix black satin strappy pumps encrusted with rhinestones. I'd worried that they were a bit over the top, but Hayden had insisted that if ever there was a time and place for rhinestones, this was it.

Frankie came by in the afternoon to touch up my highlights and blow out my cropped blond hair so that it was smoothed back from my face. Hayden had appointed herself my makeup artist. She'd done something with gray sparkly eye shadow and black mascara that made my eyes look darkly luminous.

And as Drew drove up the pebbled drive under the arching portico, where a troop of valets were waiting to take control of his car, I had my first look at what the other women were wearing. I was relieved to see that I had chosen my dress wisely. All of the women were dressed in floor-length gowns, and diamonds twinkled from necks, wrists, ears, and—in the case of one woman who clearly had a princess fantasy going on—a tiara. The vaults had been opened and the big jewels brought out for the occasion.

One of the valets stepped forward and opened the car doors. I waited as Drew stepped around and handed me out. As I stood, I heard a woman in head-to-toe plaid taffeta gasp and say, "What a fabulous red dress! Doesn't she look stunning!"

Stunning, I thought, feeling a bit dazed as Drew led me by the hand through the arched doorway. Had she really been talking about me? No one had ever called me stunning before. I again had the odd, detached feeling that I was no longer myself.

The fund-raiser was being held in the Gold & White Ballroom: aptly named, as the room was white with elaborate gold plasterwork covering the walls and ceilings. The windows were high and arched, with gold sconces featuring naked cherubs gleaming between them. Overhead, there wasn't just one large chandelier but rows and rows of them, filling the ballroom with a soft, glowing light.

There was already a large crowd gathered—the ladies in ball gowns, their husbands or escorts in black tuxedos. Chatter rose up, and perfectly whitened teeth flashed in social smiles, cheeks were put forth to receive kisses, and glasses of bubbling champagne were raised to glossy red lips. The room smelled strongly and pleasantly of mingled perfumes and colognes. There was a still-empty dance floor in the center of the room, where a jazz quartet was playing, and around the perimeter, round tables dressed in gold and white linens were set with bone china and crystal stemmed glasses. In the center of each table sat a gilded birdcage filled with twinkle lights and bunches of white peonies, tulips, and orchids.

"Drew!" The ringing voice was so imperious, I had to force myself not to cringe.

"Brace yourself," Drew muttered to me. Then he turned, smiled, and said, "Hello, Mother."

He called his mom *Mother*? That wasn't a good sign, I decided. It spoke of a stilted, formal relationship. The only time I'd ever called my mom *Mother* was when I was thirteen and in a particularly snotty mood.

"Mother, I'd like you to meet Lucy Landon," Drew said, placing one hand on my back. I think it was meant to be reassuring, but it might also have been to prevent me from fleeing.

Drew's mother was a formidable-looking woman. She was tall, with strongly etched features—a prominent aquiline nose, dark eyes that stretched up and out at the corners (*a face-lift?* I wondered), and thick blue-black hair that was cut in a blunt bob at her square jaw. She wore a floor-length white gown with a draped neck and long sleeves. A daring choice for an older woman, I thought, with the bridal and youthful implications of wearing all-white. But Mrs. Brooks had such a strong, grounded presence, she pulled if off magnificently.

"How do you do," Drew's mother said. She extended a limp hand to me. "Adeline Brooks."

"Hello, Mrs. Brooks. It's very nice to meet you," I said, smiling at her.

She inclined her head gracefully yet without losing her imperious air. Adeline Brooks was, I decided, a woman who was used to getting her way.

"I thought it was about time we met," she said.

I glanced quizzically at Drew. What had he told her about me? About us? He gave his head a slight shake.

"Mother, I told you Lucy and I have been dating for only a few weeks," he said gently.

"That's what you told me," Adeline said, in a tone that made it clear she didn't believe him. "But then, that's also what you told me about that girl—what was her name? It was something odd. Genevieve? Alessandra?"

"Her name was *Sadie,* Mother." Drew's voice now had an edge to it.

"Oh, yes, that's right. I've always been terrible with names," Adeline said, allowing herself a smile that did little to soften her stern face.

Drew shot her a look. "You never forget anything," he said pointedly.

"You give me too much credit, my dear," Adeline said serenely. "Anyway, Lucy, when we met Sadie, Drew said they'd been dating only a short time, but it turns out they were practically engaged." She gave me a conspiratorial look. "I think he was worried we'd scare her away."

"I can't imagine why," Drew said dryly.

Adeline chose to ignore her son. "So, Lucy, do you have any dark and lurid secrets I should know about?" she asked, turning toward me.

I had just taken a sip of champagne, but now, pinioned by Adeline Brooks's shrewd eyes, I started to choke on it. The bubbling liquid burned my throat, and my eyes watered as I coughed.

"Goodness," Adeline exclaimed.

"Lucy, are you okay?" Drew asked, leaning down worriedly to peer at me.

"Fine, fine," I managed, still coughing.

A man I presumed to be Drew's father chose this moment to join us. "Ah, Drew, nice to see you," he said. "What have I missed?"

"Oh, just Mother terrorizing my date," Drew said.

"Adeline," Drew's father chided her fondly. He turned to smile at me and held out his hand. I shook it; he had a much firmer grip than his wife. "You must be Lucy. I'm Hal Brooks."

Like Drew, Hal was tall with long limbs and wide shoulders. In fact, father and son looked much alike, although Hal Brooks's hair had gone gray and the flesh around his jaw had turned jowly.

I had finally gotten control of my coughing fit, although a tickle remained in my throat.

"It's nice to meet you, Mr. Brooks," I managed to say.

"Please, call me Hal," he said, and I returned his friendly smile. He gave me a conspiratorial wink. "Don't let Adeline give you a hard time. She likes to do that with Drew's girlfriends, and then she wonders why he isn't married and producing the requisite grandchildren."

"Yeah, it's a real mystery," Drew said, rolling his eyes. He drained the last of his champagne and set the empty glass down on the tray of a passing waiter. She handed him a full glass in return. "Perfect timing," he said gratefully.

"What do your parents do, Lucy?" Adeline asked.

"My dad is a dental surgeon, and my mom works with a number of animal rescues," I said.

"I like her already," Adeline said approvingly. "Where do they live? I think Drew said that you're a native Floridian."

"Yes, I grew up in Ocean Falls."

"Oh, yes, I know it well! We have some dear friends who live there," Adeline said brightly. "Owen and Cassie Forrester. Do you know them?"

My mouth literally fell open. I was distantly aware that gaping dumbly at Drew's parents would not make the best first impression, but I couldn't seem to help myself.

They knew the Forresters. As in Matt's parents. And if they knew the Forresters, there was no chance they hadn't heard about me. The real me, Lucy Parker. The teacher who, according to the Forresters, had sexually propositioned their son.

"They were supposed to be here tonight, but I suppose with one thing and another..." Adeline began, but then trailed off and waved a hand in the air. "They've had a lot to deal with lately, I suppose."

A lot to deal with. It wasn't hard to figure out what—or whom—Adeline Brooks was referring to, and I felt a familiar flutter of resentment. I was the one who'd had a lot to deal with, thanks to the Forresters' destructively dishonest son. But even so, the very idea that I had almost ended up in the same room with them...My knees went wobbly at the thought. That would have been so very, very bad.

"Lucy? Is everything okay?" Drew asked, leaning toward me, his brows furrowed with concern.

Calm, I told myself. *Be calm.*

I didn't want to lie to Drew's parents or to Drew any more than I already had, but I obviously couldn't blurt out the truth of exactly how I did know Owen and Cassie Forrester. I drew in a deep breath to steady myself.

"I'm fine," I said to Drew. Then, to his mother, "Yes, I've heard of the Forresters." Which was technically true. I *had* heard of them.

"I'll have to ask Cassie about you the next time I talk to her. Your last name is Landon, right?" Adeline asked.

I nodded, hoping that a lightning bolt wouldn't come streaking down from the sky to strike me dead on the spot. How many lies can you tell before officially arousing God's wrath?

"Oh, look, there's Bonnie Wilson. Her husband recently passed away. I think this is her first event out," Adeline said, looking concerned. "Hal, come with me to say hello to her, will you? Lucy, it was a pleasure meeting you. I hope I didn't scare you off."

"Not at all," I said faintly. I was still feeling a bit shaky and was glad to escape further questioning.

Adeline and Hal moved off to intercept the new widow—who looked remarkably well rested, radiant even, dressed in a dramatic floor-length violet sheath—leaving Drew and me alone.

"That went well, right?" I asked hopefully.

"Absolutely. I could tell my mom liked you."

"At least she didn't ask me if my ovaries are working."

"Miracles do happen," Drew said. "But the night isn't over yet. The fertility cross-examination could still come."

"Where are your sisters?" I asked, looking around, wondering if I'd recognize them. I'd seen them in the family photos scattered around his generic bachelor-pad condo but only had vague impressions of big smiles and pretty hair.

Drew looked around, but the ballroom was getting more and more crowded, and finally he shrugged.

"I don't see them. But I'm sure Mother put us all at the same table, so you'll meet them at dinner. And in order to prepare, I suggest we ditch this champagne and get something more potent. Like a few shots of tequila," Drew said darkly. He tried to take my champagne glass, but I held it back, shaking my head.

"First of all, I haven't had tequila since a very bad, very dark night back in college that ended with me so hungover I couldn't get out of bed for two days. And second, I don't want anything stronger. I don't want your family to think I'm a drunk," I protested.

"They won't notice. They're all drunks. It's a WASP tradition."

"Even so, after this one glass, I'm going to switch to club soda," I said.

"That's it, I'm going to have to break up with you," Drew said. "I can't date a teetotaler."

But he grinned and then leaned forward to place an impish kiss on my nose.

"God, Mother's on a tear tonight," Josie, Drew's younger sister, said. She was short and curvy, with elegant shoulders and luminous skin. Her husband, Todd, had boyish features and a bland personality. So far, after greeting us, he hadn't said a word.

"Tell me about it. She told me I was too old to be wearing this dress," Delia agreed.

Delia, the youngest sister, was taller and leggier than Josie, and her face had a rubbery, comical quality. I secretly thought her mother had a point about the dress, which was very short, strapless, and skintight. Delia certainly had the body to pull it off—she was thin to the point of gauntness—but it looked like something that had been designed for a teenage girl.

"You are too old for it," Josie said bluntly.

"Bitch," Delia said without rancor.

"Girls," Drew said with mock severity. "Behave."

"Anyway, Mother's just pissed that I didn't bring a date. I mean, it's not like I can wave a wand, say a spell, and—*poof!*—conjure up a boyfriend just to please her," Delia complained. "And what about me? I'm the one who's sexually frustrated. I'm at the point where I'm ready to start rubbing up against lampposts."

I laughed, and Todd perked up, but the fourth couple at

our table—I couldn't remember their names, but the wife had some distant connection to Josie—looked shocked.

"You shouldn't be allowed loose in public," Josie said, frowning at her younger sister.

"Like it's my fault I'm sexually frustrated. But all Mother cares about is how I threw off her table arrangement." Delia made a vague gesture at the empty seat next to her. "She said that if I had told her ahead of time that I didn't have a date, she would have arranged for one of the bachelors to sit here. Which, I informed her, was exactly why I didn't give her the advance warning. The last thing I want is to be forced to talk to some boring, balding guy. Whoops, sorry, Todd," Delia said, casting a guilty look at her brother-in-law, whose brown hair was noticeably thinning.

Todd looked up, confused. I had a feeling it was a common state for him. "Huh?"

"Never mind," Delia said. She made a face at me and whispered, "He never listens to me."

"Maybe that's because you never stop talking," Drew teased. Delia stuck her tongue out at him.

"Keep it up and no one's going to vote for you," Delia told him.

"Vote for you for what?" I asked, not missing the quelling look Drew shot his little sister.

"Wasn't I supposed to say anything?" Delia asked. Her brow wrinkled, she looked from Drew to me.

"Has that ever stopped you before?" Drew retorted.

"What?" I asked again.

"Drew's running for Congress," Josie informed me with obvious pride.

It was my turn to stare at Drew. He was *running* for *Congress*? Since when? And why was this the first I was hearing of it?

"I'm only considering it. I haven't formally decided," Drew said quickly, casting me an apologetic look. "I was going to talk to you about it. I found out our current congressman, Ken Kramer, is retiring. He's a close friend of the family."

"I know," I said faintly. "I met him with you."

"That's right. Anyway, he told me that if I run, he'll throw me his support. Which is pretty significant. He's very popular."

"Oh," I said. "Well . . . good for you."

Yet another lie. I didn't think it was good. Not at all. To the contrary, I thought it was a terrible idea. First of all, if Drew ran for Congress—and if we continued to see each other—there was no way I could continue to fly under the press's radar as Lucy Landon. He'd be under scrutiny, and so would I by extension. A new haircut wouldn't disguise me forever. And second, even if I told Drew the truth about who I was, and he was okay with that, and we somehow stayed together . . . the brutal truth was, I didn't *like* politicians, with their toothy smiles and empty promises. They were a squirrelly, slippery bunch.

Drew read the distress on my face. "Honestly, I haven't made a firm decision yet," he said. "And I'll tell you as soon as I do."

"Thanks," I said, smiling tightly. Drew reached under the table and squeezed my hand. I hesitated, irritated that I'd had to learn about his political aspirations from his sister. But then, warmed by the affection I saw in his dark eyes, I smiled for real and squeezed his hand back. Still, one realization became uncomfortably clear: I had to tell Drew the truth about who I was. Not now, not here, but tonight if possible.

"I like this one better than your last girlfriend, Drew," Delia said bluntly. "But, then, that wouldn't be hard. Sadie was a real bitch."

"Delia," Drew said warningly, with an apologetic—and somewhat sheepish—glance to me.

"She's right, Drew. We never liked Sadie," Josie concurred. "She wasn't exactly what you would call warm and fuzzy."

"Cold and pointed is more like it," Delia said. "She was also a gold digger. You're not a gold digger, are you, Lucy?"

"Delia!" Drew exclaimed, his eyes widening with anger.

"There's no point in asking," Josie said sensibly. "If she was a gold digger, it's not like she'd admit it to us."

"She has a point," I said, and despite Drew's glower at his younger sister—or maybe because of it—I started to giggle.

The absurdity of this conversation had suddenly hit me. Here I was, worried that they would find out that I was a lottery winner—that I was the infamous Lottery Seductress—while they were wondering if I was just after Drew's money.

"Oh, God, she's coming this way," Delia said, staring over my shoulder.

"Who?" Drew asked.

"Who do you think? *Mother!*" Delia hissed. She slouched down in her seat, as though hoping she could make herself invisible.

"And she's not alone," Josie commented. "Who are those people she's dragging after her? The Dunways?"

Drew glanced behind him. "No, those aren't the Dunways."

"How would you know?" Josie asked scornfully.

"Because Walter Dunway is a partner at my firm," Drew said.

"Oh. Well, I guess you're probably right," Josie conceded, rather ungraciously. "So who are they?"

"Aren't those the Forresters?" Drew said. "Mom was just talking about them to Lucy."

I dropped the fork I was holding. It fell on my plate with the sort of loud, resonating crash that causes all conversation around you to cease, while heads swivel in your direction. I couldn't confirm this was happening, as I was too horrified to look up. But I could practically feel the weight of dozens of pairs of sharp, judgmental eyes on me.

"Lucy? Are you okay?" Drew asked, leaning toward me.

I stared back at him, wondering what would have happened between us if I had just told him the truth from the beginning, back on our first date. Maybe I would never have heard from him again. That was certainly a possibility. But, then again, maybe our relationship would have still had a chance.

"I'm so sorry," I said, trying to convey all of my regrets into those simple words.

Drew rubbed my arm. "Don't look so worried, Lucy. It was just a fork."

And before I could say anything else, before I could offer up any last-minute explanations, Drew's mother was upon us.

"Hello, everyone," Adeline said, sweeping up to the table. I recognized her voice, although I hadn't yet turned around to face her.

"Hello, Mother," Josie said. "Nice dress."

"Thank you, darling. Drew, do you remember how I was just telling you and Lucy about my friends Owen and Cassie Forrester, who live in Ocean Falls? Well, guess who showed up after all! I didn't know they were coming, but here they are," Adeline said.

Her voice was pleasant, but there was just enough bite in the undertone to make it clear that she did not appreciate guests showing up to her fund-raiser without having properly RSVP'ed. I supposed it played hell with her seating arrangement.

But Adeline Brooks's hostessing challenges were the least of my worries, especially as she laid a manicured hand on my bare shoulder and said, "Cassie, Owen, I'd like you to meet

Drew's new girlfriend, Lucy. Lucy hails from your neck of the woods, Cassie."

This was it. I couldn't put it off any longer. I took a deep breath, said a silent prayer that the Forresters wouldn't recognize me, and turned to face them. My eyes fell on Owen Forrester first. He was a large, blustery man, his skin pink from the sun and his stomach round from too many steak dinners. His wife, Cassie, was so thin and frail, she looked insubstantial standing next to him. I supposed she was once pretty—Matt had inherited her finely boned, feline looks—but she now had a pallid, unhealthy look about her. And then, as Cassie stared down at me, her face sagged into an expression of horrified shock.

"You just moved here from Ocean Falls a few weeks ago, isn't that right, Lucy?" Adeline continued, oblivious to Cassie Forrester's reaction.

I don't know if it was Adeline's use of my first name without the added *Landon* to fake her out, or if perhaps Cassie Forrester had memorized the features of my face—the woman who had victimized her son, or so she believed—so that not even a different hairstyle would fool her. But Cassie Forrester knew exactly who I was.

"You," she said, her voice a gasp. *"You!"*

Owen Forrester hadn't bothered to look at me—the date of a friend's son not worth his attention—so he shot a confused look at his wife.

"Cassie? What's wrong?" Owen asked.

"It's *her,*" Cassie hissed. "It's *Lucy Parker.*"

Owen did a double take, turning to stare down at me. His thick lips gaped open.

"Lucy . . . Parker?" he croaked.

"No, this is Lucy *Landon,*" Drew said, standing to properly greet his mother's friends, although he was clearly confused about why the two of them were looking at me as though I were a giant, hairy rat scampering across the salad plates.

"I don't know what lies she's told you, but that woman is Lucy Parker," Cassie said, practically spitting the words out. "She's the teacher who victimized my son!"

"That woman on the news?" Adeline gasped. "Drew, what's going on here?"

Drew was shaking his head in confusion. "I have no idea what any of you are talking about," he said. He rested a heavy, supportive hand on my shoulder. "I told you, this is Lucy *Landon*. I think I would know her name. She is my girlfriend."

As much as I appreciated Drew's defense, I knew the time had finally come to confess. I wished it could have happened some other way—doing this in the middle of a crowded charity ball with his mother, sisters, and Matt Forrester's parents looking on was hardly ideal. But that was my fault. I hadn't trusted Drew with the truth. Instead, I'd lied to him over and over again. This was my payback.

I stood shakily. My face was burning—I could feel the blood rushing to my cheeks, pounding at my temples—and my limbs felt wooden and too heavy to move. Inhaling deeply, I turned first to Drew, whose hand had slipped from my shoulder to my waist as I stood.

"She's right," I said to him. "My name *is* Lucy Parker. I lied when I told you it was Lucy Landon."

"Why would you do that?" Drew asked, looking utterly bewildered.

"I'll tell you why," Cassie snapped. "It's because she tried to seduce my son! My *teenage* son, while he was her student! And she got caught, and the school fired her, and she slunk out of town in disgrace!"

"What?" Drew said. "But Lucy's not a teacher." Then, peering down at me, he asked, "Are you?"

I nodded. "I was. And she was right about one thing: I was fired." I turned to Cassie Forrester then, mustering up what dignity I could. "But I never tried to seduce your son. He made that lie up because he was angry over the failing grade I gave him."

"Matt would never do that!" Cassie's voice was shrill with anger.

"How dare you," Owen Forrester said, his fists curling at his sides. I wondered if he'd try to hit me and had to force myself not to step away, not to back down.

"He did lie. And those lies ruined my reputation and my career," I said. My voice was oddly calm, especially since my stomach was churning so wildly that I thought I might be sick right then and there in the middle of Mar-a-Lago's Gold & White Ballroom.

"My son doesn't lie!" Cassie shrieked.

"He did about this. And I think if you're at all honest with yourselves, you know that Matt is a troubled kid," I said.

"How dare you," Owen said again. This time he loomed toward me, as though trying to intimidate me. Drew moved in front of me. He had a good six inches on Owen Forrester, although Owen probably still outweighed Drew by forty pounds. But it seemed to do the trick. Owen took a hasty step back.

"I don't know exactly what's going on here. But I won't have you threatening Lucy," Drew said, his voice even.

"I don't need to threaten her. That's what I have lawyers for," Owen Forrester snarled. He was flushing too, his skin turning an unhealthy shade of tomato red. He glared at me. "And you'll be hearing from them."

Then, taking his wife's arm, Owen turned and marched off without a backward glance. Cassie, though, turned to look at me one last time. I could see rage twisting her lips and tears shining in her eyes, and I felt a stab of pity for her. If she really believed her son, then of course she thought I was evil incarnate. And if she didn't totally believe him . . . well, then, I was the woman who had punctured her fantasy of the perfect little boy who never tells a lie. Either way, if I were her, I'd hate me too.

Adeline Brooks was watching the Forresters leave, as were a number of people sitting at nearby tables who had heard enough to know that something was going on, even if they didn't know all the details. They stared at us with frank interest, delighted that the party had more to offer than champagne and chateaubriand. Adeline turned and gave her son a level stare.

"Drew," she said. "I think it would be best if you escorted Lucy home now."

It was an order, not a request. Drew nodded curtly at his mother. He turned to glance at his sisters, who were staring at us with twin expressions of shock, their eyebrows arched high and their lips rounded into Os. Even dull Todd seemed to have perked up with interest.

"Bye," I said faintly to them.

"Bye, Lucy. It was nice meeting you," Delia said brightly.

"Delia," Josie hissed at her.

"What? I like her."

But then Josie apparently stomped on Delia's foot under the table, for Delia let out a loud "Ouch!" and fell silent, glaring rebelliously at her older sister.

I turned to face Drew's mother. "Mrs. Brooks . . . I'm so sorry," I said, with as much dignity as I could muster.

She nodded once, her face like stone. Clearly, I was not what she had in mind for her son. I could hardly blame her for that.

"Let's go," Drew said softly. His hand had dropped from my waist, and I found that I missed its warmth. But he didn't offer me his hand or even his arm. Instead, he waited for me to walk ahead of him—*Is he worried I'll refuse to go?* I wondered—and then followed silently behind me.

I don't know if it was my imagination, but it seemed as though the room quieted as we exited, every table turning to gawk at me as I walked past. I did my best to lift my head and square my shoulders, but even so, it was impossible not to feel like the banished harlot.

Drew didn't say anything to me as we stood under the arched portico waiting for the parking attendant to bring around the car. I was glad. I knew Drew was going to have questions, and I would answer them all to the best of my ability, but it wasn't a conversation I wanted to have in earshot of the half dozen valets milling around.

Thankfully, Drew waited until we were safely inside his car and rolling back down the long driveway before he spoke.

"Is this one of those Candid Camera shows where you, my mother, and my sisters have teamed up to pull a prank on me? Is Ashton Kutcher going to be waiting for us at the end of the driveway to tell me I've been punk'd?" Drew asked. His voice was even and his expression inscrutable, but I could tell he was upset. Of course he was upset. I could hardly blame him for that.

"I'm sorry," I said. "I should have told you the truth from the beginning."

"Yes. You should have. But better late than never," Drew said.

And so I told him all of it. Palm Beach is not a large island, and so I was still explaining—all too aware how inadequate my explanations were—by the time we arrived at Crane Hill. We sat in his car in the gated driveway, the motor running, while I finished. Drew hadn't spoken a word since we'd left Mar-a-Lago. I found his silence unnerving.

"So that brings us to tonight," I said. "The party. The Forresters. Your mother."

Drew smiled wearily and rubbed at his eyes with one hand. "You know, you may have just succeeded in keeping my mother from ever again trying to marry me off. I think she'd probably prefer that I just stay single from now on."

"And do you want to know the ironic thing? Mothers usually love me," I said, managing a shaky laugh.

"Not my mother," Drew said ruefully.

"Yeah, I sort of figured. I won't be expecting a Christmas card from her," I said. Then, my smile fading, I said, "Please tell her again how sorry I am. I hope I didn't ruin her party."

"Are you kidding? Palm Beach socialites would pay to have that sort of scandal break out at their fund-raisers. Everyone will be talking about it for weeks. My mom's social calendar will be booked through April now," Drew said. "If it weren't for the fact that you were there with me, she'd probably throw a party in your honor to thank you." He grinned and shook his head.

"But I was there with you," I said, stating the obvious.

"Yes, you were." Drew's smile faded.

I forced myself to ask the necessary question. "Where does this leave us?"

Drew let out a long sighing breath. "If you and I continue

seeing each other, I'll basically have to write off any political ambitions I might have," Drew said. "And that's something my family wants for me."

"Is it what you want?"

Drew sighed, and for the first time that night he looked tired, almost haggard. "I don't want to disappoint them," he said simply.

"Oh," I said. I wasn't angry or even hurt—after all of the lies I had told him, I didn't have the right to be. But I was saddened. "I understand."

"I'm sorry, Lucy," Drew said.

"You don't have anything to be sorry for. I'm the one who owes you the apology."

"If I were really the white knight here, I'd be willing to ride into battle for you. I'd tell my mother to mind her own business and tell my dad I wasn't going to run for office and that, even if it makes them uncomfortable, I'm keeping you in my life," Drew said. He shook his head and looked almost disgusted with himself. "But I can't do it. I don't know why I can't . . . I just can't."

"I'm not asking you to," I said quickly.

"You shouldn't have to ask."

I stared at his profile, at the sharp angle of his nose, the blunt square of his chin. In the weak light pooling out from the wrought-iron house lanterns, his skin had an otherworldly green glow.

"You and I aren't in love," I said quietly. "Maybe if we were, you would want to ride into battle for me. And maybe I would ask you to."

"Maybe," Drew said. He smiled crookedly. "I'd like to think so, anyway."

I rested my hand on his for a moment, and he caught up my fingers and gave them a squeeze. I smiled briefly and got out of the car. I watched as Drew waited for the gate to slowly swing open, and then he drove out, turned onto the road, and disappeared into the night.

It was only then that I noticed there was another car parked off to the side next to the Porsche. Between the darkness and my emotional talk with Drew, I hadn't noticed it earlier when we first drove in. Now I took a closer look. It was a sleek black Mercedes that I'd never seen before.

Apparently we had company.

Twenty

"HELLO?" I CALLED OUT AS I OPENED THE FRONT DOOR. The house was dark, and it was so quiet the rhythmic ticking of the grandfather clock in the front foyer sounded as loud as a metronome. I kicked off my rhinestone-studded high heels, which were killing my feet, and padded off to find Hayden.

I wandered through the house, looking in all the likely places. But there wasn't anyone in the vast living room, or in the cozier wood-paneled den, or in the kitchen, which smelled of bleach and looked as if it hadn't been occupied since Marta left earlier in the day.

I heard voices outside on the lanai. I couldn't tell what they were saying, but there were the high lilting notes of Hayden's voice and a lower male rumble, and then the two mingled together in laughter. I hesitated for a moment, wondering if I should go out there or if Hayden would want to be alone with her guest. But I was still feeling shaky from my abrupt exit from the charity ball and less abrupt breakup with Drew, and I didn't want to be alone. Besides, it was probably just Frankie, or one of Hayden's other friends that I hadn't yet met, so I didn't think she'd mind if I joined them. I headed out the back kitchen door, one of several that opened up on the lanai.

They apparently didn't hear the door open and close, and—thankfully—I didn't say anything. Because the man with Hayden was definitely not Frankie—and it was pretty clear they wouldn't appreciate the interruption.

The man reclining back on the teak chaise was older, probably in his mid-fifties, although that estimate could have been off by a decade in either direction, depending on how well he'd aged. He had silver hair that contrasted with his dark eyebrows, a foxlike face with a sharp chin, thin lips, and a narrow nose. He was stark naked.

Hayden, whom I hadn't seen a moment before—one of the columns holding up the lanai's roof had been in the way—stepped forward into view. She was wearing a white G-string bikini. It was little more than three tiny triangles, barely large enough to cover anything. Hayden was swaying from side to side, in what was probably meant to be a seductive dance but looked a little silly from where I was standing, especially considering there wasn't any music playing. But then Hayden reached back and, with one swift move, untied the bow that was holding up her bikini top. It slid to the ground, and Hayden stepped forward toward the man, climbed onto the chaise, and straddled his body with her long legs. He fondled her breasts, and Hayden leaned forward to take him in her mouth.

I decided it was well past time for me to get the hell out of there.

Thankful that I was in my bare feet and could make a quiet retreat, I hurried back into the kitchen, closing the door silently behind me.

What the hell was going on? I wondered. *What is Hayden*

doing with that guy? I mean, I knew *what* she was doing, but why was she doing it with him? What had happened with Ian? Had they broken up?

Hayden had joked about finding a rich older man to marry, but that was just it: She'd been *joking*. Hadn't she? She wasn't really that mercenary, was she?

My stomach was grumbling—I'd been kicked out of the fund-raiser before dinner was served—so I made myself a peanut butter and jelly sandwich, poured a glass of milk, and took my meal upstairs. Since I obviously couldn't sleep in the pool house, I chose to spend the night in the Blue Room. It had a four-poster bed hung with heavy silk panels and busy navy blue and cream trellis-print wallpaper. I sat at the small, fussy writing table to eat my sandwich and then went into the bathroom to wash off my makeup. After listening at the door to Hayden's room—I wanted to make sure she and her guest hadn't moved the festivities inside and upstairs—I let myself in, planning to borrow a pair of pajamas.

I fumbled for a light switch, and once I finally found the one that illuminated the bedside tables, I saw that Harper Lee was there, curled up on Hayden's pillow. When she saw me, she jumped to her feet, gave her muscular little body a strenuous shake, and bounded over to me, snorting and yawning.

"Hi, girl," I said, leaning over to pet her. Which was harder than it sounded. My red evening gown was so tight through the bodice that it was hard to breathe, much less bend over.

I saw that Hayden's laptop, also on the bed, was open and on. When Harper Lee had bounced over to me, she'd jostled the computer enough to switch off its screen saver. I glanced at the screen and saw that Hayden had left her Internet browser open to the eBay Web site. Nosiness overcame me, and I looked closer, wondering what she was bidding on. But then I saw that she wasn't bidding on anything. Instead, under the handle *PalmBeachPrincess*, Hayden had two dozen items up for auction. Her Chloé handbag and Badgley Mischka Platinum Label black cocktail dress, both listed as being in like-new condition. A Cartier watch, which I knew had been a college graduation gift from her parents. Then I saw what else she was auctioning off, and my heart gave a lurch. A lemon-yellow Chaiken dress. A pair of dove-gray Christian Louboutin pumps. An Italian cashmere sweater. A white boatneck Escada sundress. All listed as new and never worn. And all of which I had bought for Hayden.

I walked over to her closet and opened the doors. And there were the clothes, all the things I'd purchased for her on our countless shopping trips—all of which she'd let me buy for her; although she'd stopped short of asking for the items, she'd made it clear she wanted them—and all of which still had the price tags attached. How had I failed to notice that she'd never worn any of them?

Then there was the bigger question: Why was she selling all of them? And had she planned on selling the clothes when I bought them for her? Because although it wasn't stealing—they were hers to do with as she wished—her actions certainly had a strong taint of dishonesty. It reminded me of Sarah Macleod, a woman back in Ocean Falls who had a little boy a year younger than Maisie's twins. Maisie had befriended Sarah through the vast mommy network in town and had given Sarah a big box of clothing that the twins had outgrown. Maisie later learned from a mutual friend that, rather than keeping the clothes, Sarah had taken them straight to a children's consignment shop and pocketed the money they'd fetched. Maisie had been infuriated when she found out.

"I just feel like I was taken advantage of," she'd fumed. "I was trying to do a nice thing for her. If I'd wanted to sell those clothes, I would have taken them to the consignment store myself."

Taken advantage of. Yes. That was exactly what I was feeling. But it wasn't like I could go talk to Hayden about it now, indisposed as she was. I tried to shake off my shock and, closing the closet door, I went to the dresser to find the pajamas I'd come to borrow. I started with the bottom drawer and worked my way up. The pajamas were in the top drawer, the last drawer I looked in, along with a tangle of bras and satin briefs—and money. Lots of money. Crumpled twenties, tens, and even fifty-dollar bills.

Where did Hayden get all this? I wondered, picking up handfuls of bills and staring at them as though they might hold the answers for me. Had she won it at the casino? And if so, why was she selling her clothes on eBay?

And then suddenly I remembered: How many times had I looked in my wallet recently, sure that I had cash, only to discover that I was completely out? Now that I thought about it, it seemed as if it had been happening quite often. I'd blamed it on the spendthrift habits I'd picked up since moving to Palm Beach, but maybe that had been a denial of sorts. Was it possible? Had Hayden been *stealing* from me?

I dropped the money as though it were burning my hands. My mouth tasted bitter, and fatigue pressed at my temples. Suddenly I wished I were anywhere but here, in this too-big house, having to sleep in a strange room, while a floor below, my roommate was making love to a man old enough to be her father.

What I wanted—what I wanted more than anything—was to be home. In *my* home, my little house surrounded by all of my shabby old things, where I could put on my favorite pajamas, which had been worn to the perfect degree of threadbare softness, and curl up on the sofa with my dog and a good book.

As if reading my thoughts, Harper Lee whimpered and looked up at me imploringly. I stared back at her and felt the tears start to well in my eyes.

"I wish we could go home, sweetheart. I wish we could," I said. "Come on. We're sleeping up here tonight."

With Harper Lee at my ankle, I walked out of Hayden's bedroom and closed the door firmly behind me.

"Lucy, wake up," a familiar voice said. A weight sagged down at the edge of the bed, and then a hand unceremoniously jostled me. "Wake. Up."

I opened my eyes to squint at the intruder. It was . . .

"Emma?" I croaked. I cleared my throat and tried again. "What are you doing here?"

"I came to find you," Emma said. "Oh, my *God*. What did you do to your hair? It looks amazing."

"What's going on?" My mind, still groggy, whirred to catch up with what was going on. "Is everything okay?"

"No. Everything is definitely not okay," Emma said flatly.

I sat bolt upright in bed, staring at her. "Is it Mom? Dad?"

Emma frowned and tossed her hair back. She was, as usual, looking stylish even at this early hour, dressed in an orange sweater and a short white skirt slung low on her hips. Wait, how early was it? I glanced at the clock: 10:08 a.m. Not exactly early, then, but I'd had a hard time falling asleep last night.

"Mom and Dad are fine. Well, they're still bickering about what to do with the money you gave them, but other than that they're fine," Emma said.

"So why exactly are you here? Not that I'm not glad to see you," I quickly added.

Emma sighed heavily. "It's the wedding."

I groaned and collapsed back on the bed. I should have known. In Emma's narcissistic world, a snag in her wedding plans equaled an emergency.

"Hold on, I have to pee," I said. I tossed the covers off and headed toward the en suite guest bathroom. Harper Lee, roused by Emma's entrance, had flopped onto my sister's lap, rolling over to expose her pink underbelly for Emma to stroke.

When I emerged from the bathroom, Emma was stretched out on the bed, Harper Lee cuddled up beside her. My sister looked critically around at the Blue Room.

"The wallpaper is a bit much, don't you think?" she asked. "What is it with rich people and ugly wallpaper, anyway?"

"How did you get in here?" I retorted grumpily. I sat at the foot of the bed, facing Emma, and wrapped my arms around my knees.

"Hayden let me in. She was on her way out to breakfast with some old guy."

Hayden. The memory of finding her eBay auctions and hidden stash of money came back to me with an unpleasant jolt, settling sickly in my stomach.

"I tried calling, but you didn't call me back," Emma said. "And I really needed to talk to you, so I decided to drive down and see you."

"So what's the current wedding drama?" I asked.

"I need more money," Emma said baldly.

I struggled for a moment to process this. Maybe it was just the early-for-me hour or the surprise at suddenly seeing my sister turn up.

"What happened to the money I gave you?" I said. A half-million dollars, to be exact. Not an insubstantial sum.

"I spent it."

"On what?"

Emma sighed. "I knew you were going to be difficult about this."

I bit back any number of angry retorts that surged up. But I somehow managed to stay calm and looked at Emma for a long moment, until she caved and, with a roll of her eye and a dramatic sigh, said, "Fine. Christian insisted that we spend the money you already gave us—gave *me*—on a house."

"That sounds like a sensible thing to do," I said. "Where did you buy?"

"We used it as a down payment on a house in Jupiter," Emma said, in a way that I knew meant she was holding something back.

"A down payment?" I asked. A half-million dollars was enough to buy a whole house, even in pricey Jupiter. "Where's the house?"

"It's . . . on the water," Emma finally admitted.

I gaped at her. Even with the recent spate of hurricanes that had blown through the state, oceanfront property in Florida was expensive. Very, very expensive. "How much was it?"

"Christian thought it was a good investment. He said you can't lose money in real estate," Emma said defensively.

"I don't think Christian's been watching the news much lately. Did you at least get a good deal on it?"

"I think so. It was only one point five."

"One point five—wait. *Million?* One point five *million?*" I asked, my jaw dropping open.

"Well, yeah. But with the money you gave us as a down payment, our mortgage was only one point one million."

"What idiot banker would give the two of you a one-point-one-million-dollar mortgage? No wonder all the mortgage companies are in trouble," I fumed. "And wait: What happened to the other hundred thousand I gave you?"

"I bought a few things," Emma said sulkily.

"Like . . . ?"

"Like my wedding dress. Oh, my God, you should see it. It's gorgeous. It's strapless and has a tiered skirt with these cool, modern ruffles around the waist," Emma said dreamily, her financial crisis forgotten for the moment.

"You spent all of that money on a dress?"

"No, of course not. We used part of it for our honeymoon—we're going to Peter Island Resort. The pictures look amazing. It's a private island, and the suites are all superluxe." Her tone turned defensive. "Don't we deserve to have a once-in-a-lifetime trip for our honeymoon?"

Deserve? I decided to let that pass. "And that's it? A dress and a vacation?"

"And I leased a Mercedes and bought some clothes. It actually went very quickly," Emma said, her tone defensive again.

"I bet," I said. And then, remembering my own shopping extravaganzas and the new Porsche parked in the driveway, I realized that it was true: It really did go quickly.

"Why don't you sell the house?" I suggested.

"Christian doesn't want to. But between the mortgage payments and the insurance, it's sucking up all of our money. I don't know how much longer we're going to be able to keep it."

I had a feeling I knew where this was going. And I had to stop it.

"Emma, I'm not buying you a million-dollar beachside home," I said flatly.

"I'm not asking you to!"

"Then what are you asking for?"

"I need money for the wedding," Emma said.

"I thought Dad wanted to pay for that," I said.

"So he says, but he won't give me nearly enough. I need at least another hundred thousand," she said.

I stared at her. I'd always known that Emma had no fiscal sense. If you gave her a nickel, she'd find a way to spend a quarter. But to think that even Emma, who was learning for the first time what it was to be house poor, would be stupid enough to spend that much money on a wedding when she couldn't even make her mortgage payments was incomprehensible to me.

I closed my eyes for a long moment and realized that if I gave in now, this would never end. Right now it was the wedding, but it wouldn't be too long before she'd ask me to bail her out on her mortgage payments. And what then? Visa bills she couldn't pay? Property taxes? Luxury vacations?

I drew in a deep breath, let it out in a whoosh, and said, "No. I'm not giving you more money."

"Why not?" Emma demanded, her voice suddenly shrill.

"Because I would just be enabling your out-of-control spending habits," I said.

"But that's not fair," Emma exclaimed. She jumped off the bed and glowered down at me, hands set on her narrow waist.

"It's my money. I can do with it what I wish," I said, crossing my arms and staring right back at her.

Emma snorted. "Please. It's not like you earned it."

"What does that have to do with anything?"

"I just don't think you have the right to be so selfish!"

"Right back at you, little sister," I snapped, anger fraying my already tattered nerves.

"What is that supposed to mean?" she asked.

"It means, I've already given you more money than you

deserve. And instead of being grateful, you're acting like a spoiled brat," I shot back. "I wish I hadn't given it to you. I wish I hadn't given you one single dime."

I had seen Emma angry before. When she was a little girl, she'd stick her lower lip out in a pout while fat tears trickled down her baby-rounded cheeks. And as a teenager, she'd had her fair share of temper tantrums that would end with her slamming a door behind her as loudly as possible. But I'd never seen her quite like this. It was as though all other emotions had been frozen right out of her. Her eyes narrowed, her jaw set, and she regarded me with cold hostility. I flinched; she was looking at me as though she hated me.

"If that's the way you feel, then I don't think I want you in my life anymore," Emma said.

"God, Emma, stop being so childish." I had wearied of this scene, and I turned away from my sister, wanting more than anything for her to just go and leave me in peace.

"I mean it. In fact, consider yourself officially uninvited to my wedding," Emma announced, as though this were the worst punishment she could think up for me. "I don't want toxic people around me on the happiest day of my life."

Toxic people? I thought. I felt like I'd entered a fun house, my world turned into one of distorted reflections. Small became large, thin became fat, and handing over a half-million-dollar gift made you toxic.

My sister could be selfish and exasperating, but now, for the first time, I felt an intense stab of hatred for her.

"If that's what you want, fine. And now I think it's time for you to leave. Past time, really," I said.

Emma stood there for a moment longer, bristling with anger. Clearly she wanted to say more, something that would wound me. But finally she just tossed her hair, turned, and stalked out of the room. I waited until she was gone, and then

I sank back down on the edge of the bed and rested my head in my hands.

I'm not sure how long I sat there. I breathed in deeply, willing my fury to die down. But instead of relaxing, I just grew more angry. It felt as if my friends and now my family had turned on me like buzzards feasting on roadkill.

My thoughts went to Hayden again and the stash of money in her drawer. I didn't know if I could bear finding out that one more person I'd trusted had let me down.

Twenty-One

I HAYDEN DIDN'T GET HOME UNTIL THE EARLY AFTERnoon, her breakfast out having extended into lunch and beyond. But despite the late night I assumed she'd had, Hayden didn't look tired. To the contrary, she seemed to radiate contentment. Her dark hair was shiny, her green eyes were gleaming with triumph, and her dark red lipstick was, as always, perfect.

"Hey," she said, as she burst out on to the lanai, where I was lying on a chaise with Harper Lee, rereading *Anna Karenina.* I was just at the part where Vronsky has followed Anna back to St. Petersburg, and I wondered what it must feel like to inspire that sort of love in a man who hardly knows you. Or maybe that's the point; maybe it's the mystery that attracts him. Would Vronsky continue to follow after Anna like a love-struck puppy if he'd seen her flossing her teeth or puking in the toilet with a stomach flu? Doubtful.

"Hi," I said, closing the book.

"You would not believe what I have been through in the past twenty-four hours," Hayden said, kicking off her heels and flopping down into the chaise next to mine. She closed her eyes and lifted her face up toward the sun.

"Ian called about ten times," I said.

"Ian! I totally forgot!" Hayden exclaimed, her eyes popping open. "I was supposed to meet him at the Drum Roll last night."

"That's what he said. He was worried about you."

Hayden didn't seem overly concerned. She waved a dismissive hand. "You're not going to believe this, but I met my future husband yesterday," she said, turning to look at me.

"I saw him."

"You did? Where?"

"The two of you were out here by the pool last night," I said.

Hayden let out a nervous giggle. "I was wondering why you slept upstairs. How much did you see?"

"Too much. I beat a hasty retreat," I replied.

"I should probably be embarrassed," Hayden said. She smiled and stretched. "But I'm too happy. Amazingly, incredibly, deliciously happy."

"Tell me about him," I said.

"His name is Hartford McAllister, but everyone calls him Trip," she said.

"Understandable with a name like Hartford. How did you meet him?"

"Actually . . ." Hayden hesitated. "He's sort of a friend of my father's."

My eyebrows arched about as high as eyebrows can go. "Are you serious?"

"It's not like they were boyhood friends or anything," Hayden said hastily. "They just know each other from around here." She circled one hand in the air to indicate the island.

"Uh-huh," I said. "So how old is he?"

"I don't know. I didn't ask," Hayden said. "But I don't think age is all that important in a marriage. What matters more is common goals and ideals." She smiled wickedly. "And lots and lots of money. Which, luckily, Trip happens to have."

I had a feeling that was the direction we were headed in. Trip was an attractive man, especially for his age, but he wasn't much competition for Ian's sweet smile and killer body. I'd seen Ian in a bathing suit; it was an impressive sight.

"How much money?" I asked.

"Big time. Oil money. His family's from Texas," Hayden said. "And Trip is part owner of a nationwide chain of restaurants."

"Which one?"

Hayden shrugged. "Something to do with hamburgers. I don't know. Anyway, I bumped into him at Ta-boó, and he said he remembered me from some cocktail party my mother threw a few years ago. To be honest, I didn't remember him at all, but we got to talking, and I found out he's newly divorced, and one thing led to another. . . ."

"Is he aware that he's going to be your future husband?"

Hayden's smile faded and was replaced by a concerned frown.

"What's wrong? You seem weird. Did something happen last night at the fund-raiser? Did you and Drew have a fight?"

Drew. Disappointment washed over me, followed closely by a chaser of shame. I'd badly screwed things up with him. But I couldn't think about that now.

"I went into your bedroom last night," I said, abruptly changing the subject.

Hayden stiffened visibly. With a studied casualness, she pulled a pair of sunglasses out of her bag and slid them on top of her head, holding back her hair. "Oh?"

"Your computer was on. I saw what you were auctioning off on eBay," I said.

"You were snooping through my private things?" Hayden asked sharply.

I stared at her, not quite believing that she was going to play the role of victim. It was a bit like a woman finding out that her husband is having an affair by checking the incoming and outgoing calls on his cell phone and then, when she confronts him, he gives her a lecture about respecting his privacy.

"No. I went in there to borrow pajamas, since I couldn't get into the pool house, and your computer just happened to be on. Why are you selling off the stuff I bought you?"

"That's none of your business," Hayden said. She folded her arms in front of her. Something was wrong here—very wrong—but I didn't know what. Yet.

"None of my business?" I repeated, staring at her in disbelief.

"Yes. Those are my clothes, my things, and I can do with them what I wish."

"But I *bought* them for *you*."

"I didn't ask you to."

"You didn't say no when I offered either," I retorted. "And even if you didn't ask, you made it pretty damned clear that you wanted them."

Hayden turned away, her shoulders stiff with anger. "Lucy, like I said, this is none of your business. So please butt out."

"What about the money?"

"What money?"

"The cash in your drawer."

"You went through my drawers too?" Hayden whirled back around and stared accusingly at me.

I squared my shoulders and stared right back at her. "I told you, I was looking for pajamas. So is that money mine?"

"What exactly are you trying to say, Lucy?" Her voice was like cut glass, sharp and cold.

My skin felt tight and hot on my face, and it took effort to keep my voice even. "I'm asking you if you took money from me."

"How dare you?" Hayden hissed.

Tension crackled between us, and I could feel the hair on my arms stand on end, as though electrified. For a moment I considered backing down. I could say I must have been mistaken, and apologize for bringing it up. But I knew it wasn't a mistake. I don't know how I knew—maybe it was the intensity of her anger, or maybe I saw shadows of guilt flickering behind the veil of her green eyes—but I knew: Hayden had been stealing from me.

"Tell me why," I pressed her.

Hayden's face suddenly twisted with fury. "Do you have any idea how much you'd have to pay in rent to live in a house like this in Palm Beach?" Hayden asked, her voice rising to a near-shout. "Try fifty thousand a month, at *least*. Yet you've been living here for *free*. And then you have the nerve to turn around and bitch about a couple of bucks here and there? Some clothes?"

I stared at her, not quite believing that this was happening. Hayden and I had never fought before, not even when we were roommates sharing a two-hundred-square-foot dorm room. I had certainly never seen her look at me like this—as if she wanted to strike me. Her cheeks had darkened, and her eyes flashed. Her red mouth curled into a sneer.

Be very careful whom you trust, Peter Graham had cautioned me. The memory of those words jolted me. I had never thought they could apply to one of my oldest and closest friends.

"Why?" I asked again, my voice choked with emotion. "What do you need the money for?"

Hayden's eyes slid away then, fixing on a spot on the ground. I half-expected her to tell me to mind my own business again, but it had gone too far: We were beyond denials.

"I've had a run of bad luck at the tables lately," she said.

It took a few beats for this to sink in.

"You mean, gambling?" I asked slowly. "But I thought you did that just for fun."

"It was. In the beginning."

"Beginning? But how long have you been gambling? Just since we came here, right?"

Hayden still refused to meet my eyes, and suddenly the truth of what was going on clicked into place, like pins in a lock, and it all became devastatingly clear. Ian wasn't the one who had a gambling problem. It was Hayden. And with this blinding insight, everything else began to make sense—Hayden's estrangement from her parents, her financial problems, even her failed Web site, which was probably just as much of a gamble as a hand of blackjack.

"How much do you owe?" I asked.

Hayden closed her eyes briefly. "Thousands."

"Like ten thousand?" I asked.

Hayden looked at me then, her expression no longer defiant. Instead, she looked beaten.

"All together, around two hundred thousand. Not including what I owe my parents. They paid for some of my debts before cutting me off," Hayden said. Her voice thickened, and tears glittered in her eyes. She tried to take a deep breath, but it caught in her chest and came out as a strangled sob.

I gaped at her, stunned by this enormous figure. "But... how? Where did you get the money to wager that much?"

"The casino advanced me markers. They knew who my family is and figured I was good for it. I thought that if I could just raise some capital and turn my losing streak around, it would all be fine. Then I was going to pay you back, Lucy, I swear I was. My parents too." The tears spilled out, trailing down her cheeks. Hayden's shoulders slumped forward in defeat.

As I stared at my friend, I was overcome by a deep rush of sadness. Hayden had everything—she was bright, beautiful, and had every advantage money could buy, the sort of privileges and education that most could only dream of. And she had pissed it all away. Thinking about this, about all that had been wasted, I suddenly felt as if a plug had been pulled, and all of the energy drained out of my body.

"I should leave," I said abruptly. "I'll make the arrangements as soon as possible."

"You don't have to go," Hayden said, wiping at the tears with the back of her hand. "Really, Lucy, I'm going to make this right. That's why I have to marry Trip. Then all of these problems will go away."

"Marrying Trip isn't going to make this go away," I said slowly. "Hayden, you have a problem. Surely you must see that. You need help, professional help, to deal with your gambling addiction."

Hayden looked at me blankly. "Gambling addiction? Jesus,

Lucy, I think you've watched a few too many episodes of *Oprah.* I've just had some bad luck, that's all."

"When you reach the point where you're auctioning off all of your belongings to feed your habit, it's not just a run of bad luck. It's a serious problem."

Hayden shook her head, her face hardening. I made one last try.

"I'll help," I offered. "I'm sure we can find a program designed to help people with this sort of problem."

"You, help me?" Hayden laughed scornfully. "That's a good one. You, the woman who wins millions and millions of dollars, the kind of money that can solve any problem, and yet acts like it's the worst thing that could've happened."

"No, I don't! I never said that!" I exclaimed, stung by this sudden attack.

"Please. How many times have you moaned about missing your pathetic job? As though not working when you don't even have to is some sort of tragedy. It makes me *sick.* You have no idea how lucky you are. So how *dare* you lecture me!"

I stared at my friend, so startled by her anger, her vitriol, that I couldn't speak. Is that how she really saw me?

Hayden seemed to realize that she'd gone too far. She stopped abruptly and covered her mouth with one hand. Her eyes, green and luminous, were wide with shock. "Oh, God, Lulu, I didn't mean to . . ." she began, reaching toward me.

I knew she was about to apologize, and I didn't want to hear it. For now I was angry, too, my rage rising up until I could feel the blood pounding in my ears. I stared at her, wondering if I was seeing the real Hayden for the first time. She'd used me, stolen from me, and then finally sneered at me, as though I were some pathetic loser, beneath her contempt.

"Don't bother," I said. And then I got up and walked away from her. As far as I was concerned, our friendship was over.

* * *

I spent an hour on the phone—making travel plans, touching base with my parents, letting Peter Graham know where I'd be—and then I dropped Harper Lee off at a luxury kennel, where she'd stay for only a few days, until my dad got the chance to drive down and pick her up. When I got to the Drum Roll in the late afternoon, the bar was mostly empty. Ian was there, cutting up lemons and limes, prepping for the crowd that night. And sitting at the bar, watching a football game playing on the television that hung over the liquor bottles, was Mal. They both looked up when the door opened, throwing a slice of bright sunshine into the room. My stomach gave a nervous wrench.

"Hi," I said, heading toward the bar, trying to quell my flutter of nerves. I hadn't seen Mal since the night we kissed, and I had no idea how he'd react to my suddenly appearing in the bar.

"Lucy!" Ian said. I saw hope and concern flash across his face and knew that Hayden probably still hadn't returned his phone calls.

"Hey, Ian," I said hesitantly.

"Is Hayden with you?"

"No, she's not."

"Is she okay? Why hasn't she called me back?"

I had no good answer for this question. *I don't know* would be a lie. But telling him that she was too busy giving blow jobs to an older and, more important, *richer* man seemed unnecessarily cruel.

"I think you need to talk to her about that," I said, earning a sharp look from Mal.

And even though my words were guarded, Ian wasn't stupid. His face darkened, and he looked away.

After a long, uncomfortable pause, Ian finally said, "I'll be back in a minute. I have to bring in a few cases of beer from the back."

I wasn't fooled, and I doubted Mal was either. Ian wanted to be alone, even if it meant sitting in the cooler behind the bar until he had a chance to collect himself.

"What are you doing here so early on a Sunday afternoon?" Mal asked casually.

"I was hoping to get a drink," I said. I glanced in the direction Ian had just disappeared. "Maybe I should have ordered first, before breaking the news about Hayden."

"What is the Hayden news?" Mal asked. He stood and walked around the bar.

"Are you allowed to be back there?" I asked.

"Desperate times," Mal said. He deftly mixed me a vodka tonic, put in two freshly cut slices of lime, and pushed it across the bar to me. "And you look like you could use it."

"You could say that," I said, taking a grateful drink. "In the past twenty-four hours, I've been accosted by the parents of the boy who got me fired from my school in Ocean Falls, I broke up with Drew, I was uninvited to my sister's wedding, and I found out that someone I thought was a good friend has been stealing from me."

Mal gazed at me with those disconcerting pale eyes and smiled slowly.

"At least your life doesn't lack drama," he said.

"That's just it. I don't like drama. In fact, I *hate* drama. I want my life to be drama-free," I said.

"So, let's take your problems in the reverse order. Who's been stealing from you?"

"Hayden," I said. I closed my eyes for a moment, and shook my head. It was still hard to believe.

Mal gazed at me, his expression sympathetic. "I can't say I'm surprised."

"You're not? I was. And I was especially surprised to discover that she has a gambling habit. That's why she stole from me. I know I can afford it, it's not that. . . ."

"No one likes being taken advantage of," Mal said.

"No," I agreed. I stirred my vodka tonic with a plastic swizzle stick.

"Why hasn't she called Ian back?" Mal asked. I looked up sharply, then glanced toward the door to the back.

"Don't worry. I won't say anything. Not that I have to. I'm sure Ian's figured it out," Mal said.

"Figured what out?"

"Rich man, probably a bit older. The type to be flattered that a younger woman would flirt with him."

"How did you know that?"

"Let's just say I know Hayden's type," Mal said.

"Apparently better than I did. I was shocked," I admitted.

"You tend to accept people at face value."

"What does that mean?" My two earlier confrontations had me on the defensive. I crossed my arms over my chest and glowered at Mal.

"You saw me with younger women and assumed I was a player. You saw me with an older woman and assumed I was a gigolo," he said.

"I did not!"

"Yes, you did." He held up a hand to ward off my protests. "Hayden told Ian. He told me."

My denials died in my throat. "Oh," I said. I could feel my face flaming. I stared down at my vodka tonic, too mortified to meet Mal's eyes.

"Don't look so traumatized," Mal said, a smile spreading slowly on his face. "I'm actually a little flattered."

"Yeah, right."

"No, I am. Just the idea that you'd think women would pay

to sleep with me. It's nice to be thought of as a sex god," Mal said.

"I never said I thought you were a sex god," I muttered.

Mal laughed. And then he did something unexpected. He leaned across the bar, tipped my face up to his, and kissed me full on the lips. I was now flushing with a very different sort of heat, one that was ricocheting around my body. His mouth was warm and tasted of beer and the lime juice he'd licked off his fingers after making my drink. My entire body suddenly felt liquid with need.

"What was that you said about breaking up with that asshole Drew?" Mal murmured.

"He's not an asshole," I protested. "He's really a pretty decent guy."

"I never liked him," Mal said. "Did you know he irons his jeans? They have *creases* down the front. What sort of a freak does that?"

"That's a pretty shallow reason not to like someone."

"That's me. Shallow Mal," he said. And then he went back to kissing me.

If it's decadent to drink a vodka tonic in the middle of the day, it's probably downright degenerate to have a one-night stand immediately thereafter. But that's exactly what I did. Mal and I could hardly keep our hands off each other long enough to get out of the bar and into my car and then back to his apartment on Cherry Lane. I was too busy kissing Mal and trying to pull off his clothing while he fumbled with mine to pay much attention to what his place was like, but from the brief glimpse I saw as we stumbled through the front door, it was more grown up and put together than I would have expected from Mal. A black leather sofa, a pair of boxy white chairs, a modern abstract painting hanging on the wall.

But the apartment decor quickly vanished from my thoughts as Mal pulled me into his bedroom and began to kiss my neck. I have always had a weakness for having my neck kissed, and Mal was particularly good at it—the perfect proportion of pressure and movement as his lips moved slowly from the hollow of my throat to the sensitive patch just under my ear.

"You have goose bumps," Mal said, running one hand down the inside of my arm to demonstrate. Which, of course, caused even more goose bumps to rise up.

I leaned into him, pressing my body to his. His response was gratifying. The way his breath grew shallow and his body curled into mine thrilled me. Then, suddenly, his touch wasn't so gentle. His kisses bruised my lips, his hands gripped at my wrists, his thigh moved in between my legs. I didn't mind. To the contrary, his need and want fueled my own excitement. I just wanted more of him.

More, and more, and more.

Later, as we lay side by side on his rumpled bed, I told Mal the rest of it. The Forresters yelling at me in the middle of the charity ball. My breakup with Drew. My sister's temper tantrum when I refused to give her more money.

"I've always had such an ordinary life," I said. "And you know what? I liked it that way. I'm not one of those adrenaline junkies who has to have everything topsy-turvy all the time."

Mal laughed softly. I liked his laugh. It seemed to rumble up from deep within his chest. And it was a very nice chest, muscular and pale compared to his arms and face. He had a tennis player's tan. We'd always called it a "farmer's tan" as kids, not that I'd known any farmers. I ran my fingers lightly over his chest hair, enjoying the soft feel of it against the hard ridges of his muscles.

"*Ordinary* is not the word I would use to describe you," he said without opening his eyes.

"But I am ordinary," I exclaimed. "Just look at me!"

Mal rolled over onto his side, his teeth flashing white as he smiled. He reached out and traced the curve of my side, from the swell of my hips to the indent of my waist, up one side of my breast, and then back down again. I closed my eyes, thrilling at his touch.

"No. Definitely *not* ordinary," he said.

I lay there silently, lost in the sensations of touch and caress, the clean male scent of his skin, the rhythmic rise and fall of his breath.

"Do you know what I'm in the mood for?" Mal asked, his mouth millimeters from my ear.

"I think I can guess."

"I meant after that."

"What?"

"A steak. Medium rare. And a Caesar salad. Doesn't that sound perfect?"

It did sound really good. What with all the drama, I hadn't eaten much today. "Okay. Where do you want to go?"

"How about Morton's?" Mal suggested.

"I don't know if I'm dressed for that," I said. Then, remembering I was naked, I blushed. "I mean, I was just wearing jeans before."

Jeans that cost more than my prom dress, but still. Morton's was a nice restaurant.

But Mal shook his head. "It's fine, I don't think anyone will care. And if they do, we'll eat at the bar."

"No," I said firmly. "I'll go home, take a quick shower, get dressed, and meet you over there."

The truth was, this would be our first real date, and I wanted to dress up for it. And while the logical part of my brain was still baffled that a guy like Mal—the sort of man whom women drooled over—could possibly be interested in someone as ordinary as me, the less logical side was over the moon. Maybe it was naive of me, but somehow I just knew—maybe from the way he looked at me, or the touch of his fingers against my skin, or how comfortable we were lying together—that he really did want to be with me. At least for now. The knowledge filled me with a pure, incandescent joy.

I started to sit up, ready to hunt down my clothing, which was scattered across Mal's apartment, when a hand snaked out and pulled me back.

"Not so fast," Mal said, rolling toward me, weighting me down with his body.

"I thought you were hungry?"

"I am," Mal said. The smile he gave me managed to be playful and wolfish at the same time. It was a heady combination.

The sun was still shining when I drove back to Crane Hill, feeling tired and boneless and so perfectly happy, I thought I might burst. My thoughts were full of Mal and what I should wear on our first official date. There was an olive-green Diane von Furstenberg wrap dress with short sleeves and a ruffled collar. Or I could wear the pretty floral silk sundress I'd picked up at Anthropologie, the pattern a mélange of bright greens and happy yellows.

I was so caught up in thoughts of my wardrobe as I pulled up to the gate outside Crane Hill, ready to punch in the security code on the keypad, that I didn't notice the man approaching me until he was right next to the car.

"Lucy Parker," he said.

Instinctively I stared up at him, startled to hear my real name after all these weeks. The man grinned down at me, pleased to have caught me off guard. This irritated me, and I wished I'd been more careful. For that matter, I was, for the first time, regretting the convertible. It left me too exposed. This was why movie stars rode around in dark cars with tinted windows, I thought.

"Who are you?" I asked warily.

"Mitch Hannigan from the *Palm Beach Post,*" the man said. "I'd like to ask you a few questions."

Twenty-Two

I STARED UP AT HIM, MOUTH AGAPE. WHEN I FINALLY found my voice, it was shaky with fear.

"How did you find me?" I asked.

"I saw your picture in the paper. Imagine my surprise. Everyone's looking for the Lottery Seductress and she turns up in the society section of my newspaper." Mitch Hannigan flashed an oily smile, and handed me a newspaper folded open to a collage of photographs. There I was at last night's fund-raiser, a candid shot taken while I was talking to Drew's mother. "The hair is different, but I recognized the face. It didn't take much digging to learn that you and Hayden Blair were roommates in college."

I didn't like him. I supposed no one in my position would, but even aside from the fact that he had me cornered, there was something unpleasant about Hannigan—a hard glint in his small brown eyes, the way that his smile looked more like a sneer, the goatee he wore in a failed attempt to disguise his weak chin.

Hannigan didn't wait for my response. Instead, he began to rattle off a series of questions. "Do you deny the allegations Matt Forrester made against you? Are you angry at him? Do you feel a sense of vindication at having won the lottery after being fired from your job?"

I looked at the front gate and tried to remember how quickly it closed. Would I be able to punch in the code and drive onto the estate without Mitch Hannigan following me? Doubtful. Hannigan's eyes followed mine, and he guessed what I was thinking.

"I'm not the only one who's going to find out you're living here, Lucy," he said. "The press is going to be all over you. You're going to have to face us eventually. So why not talk to me now and get it over with?" he asked. I think he was trying to make his voice silkily inviting, but I found him repulsive.

"So if I talk to you, the press is going to just go away? Somehow I doubt that," I said.

Hannigan shrugged. "As long as there's a story, there will be reporters sniffing around it. If you put your side out there, it may mean they'll leave you alone sooner."

I shook my head, not believing him.

"I just want to live in peace," I said. To my horror, I could feel tears stinging hotly in my eyes. I tried to blink them away. I didn't want to betray any sign of weakness in front of this man.

But if Hannigan noticed my tears, he wasn't moved by them. "You're a big story. People want answers to their questions."

"It isn't any of their business," I snapped.

"Have you ever read one of the gossip rags while you're in line at the supermarket? Clicked through to an entertainment story on the Internet? Sure you have. There's no point in pretending you're above it. And this is no different," Hannigan said.

"Of course there's a difference! I'm not an entertainer. I didn't willingly enter the public eye!"

"But you're there now. And this story isn't going to go away anytime soon. The woman who wins millions in the lottery turns out to have a dark past? That's huge. People love to see the rich and powerful take a fall," Hannigan said with obscene relish. He seemed to realize I was recoiling from him, for he made an effort to inject a wheedling tone in his voice. "Come on, Lucy. Don't you want to get your side of the story out there? Don't you want people to know the truth?"

"The truth as you report it," I retorted.

"I'll tell you what: You give me a statement, and I'll print it verbatim," Hannigan said.

I thought for a moment, drumming my fingers against the steering wheel. I could feel the muscles in my jaw tightening, clenching down until my teeth ground together. Hannigan and the other reporters were never going to leave me alone. They were going to hunt me and harass me until I buckled under the pressure.

"So what do you say, Ms. Parker?" Hannigan asked in a grating tone. "What do you want to tell our readers?"

I stared up at Mitch Hannigan and decided that I hated him. I hated his flat, soulless eyes, I hated his sneering mouth, and I especially hated his ugly goatee. And suddenly I was angry again. I was furious with Mitch Hannigan for tracking me down and yet again blowing my life apart. But I was also mad at Hayden for stealing from me. At Emma for being so selfish. At Maisie for letting me down. At my parents for letting the stupid money come between them. At Elliott for being an ass.

I took a deep breath and said through clenched teeth, "The only thing I have to say is this: Ruining someone's life should not be treated as entertainment."

I leaned out of the car and punched the code into the security box, taking care to shield the keypad from his view. As the gate slowly opened, Mitch Hannigan called out, "What do you mean by that, Lucy? Whose life was ruined? Yours or Matt Forrester's?"

I looked back at him. "Which makes for the better story?" I asked. And then I drove up the driveway without a backward glance at him.

I walked, zombielike, through the main house back to the pool house to get the bags I'd packed earlier. Because there was no doubt about it—I couldn't stay in Palm Beach. Not now that the press had found me. I had originally been booked on a flight down to Miami that night, and then on a connecting flight to Paris, but then I ran into Mal, and... well. Those plans had evaporated into smoke as soon as he kissed me. I checked my watch. There was no way I'd be able to make the flight out of West Palm. But if I could somehow get out of here without Mitch Hannigan seeing me, I could drive down to Miami and maybe still catch the flight to Paris. If I missed it, I'd hole up in a hotel for a night and take the first available flight out tomorrow.

This time, I wasn't traveling light. I guessed that Hayden would appropriate anything left behind to sell on eBay, and I didn't want to make any more contributions to her gambling problem. As for the money she'd taken, she could keep it all. The only thing I couldn't take with me were my books; they'd be too heavy to travel with.

I set down my luggage and took one last look around the pool house. The pale-blue walls, the ethereal white bedding, the sound of the ocean thrumming in the background. It was such a peaceful place. I was sorry to be leaving it.

"You're really going, then?"

I spun around to see Hayden at the door. I'd been so caught up in my thoughts, I hadn't heard her approach. Now that she was here, I found I didn't know what to say to her, so I just nodded stiffly.

"Did you know the press is out front?"

"Yeah. I ran into that guy on the way in," I said. "He's a reporter for the *Palm Beach Post.*"

"There's a crowd of them out there now. The news vans were arriving when I got home. I barely got inside, and they were all shouting questions at me," Hayden said.

"Great," I said curtly. I wondered how I was going to get to Morton's to see Mal and tell him I had to leave town, without the press following me there.

The corners of Hayden's mouth turned up in a humorless smile. "I guess my parents are going to find out we've been living here after all. They're going to be pissed. I lost house privileges when they cut me off."

I was still focused on the press, whom I could already picture swarming outside the gates. Just the thought made me feel claustrophobic, and I pressed a hand to my sternum, willing myself to breathe. The memory of sitting in my house like a prisoner was still fresh. In the distance I could hear the house phone ringing, and I knew it was them, starting to close in on me.

"What?" I asked distractedly, aware that Hayden had spoken but not focused on her words. It took a few beats to process what she'd said. "Your parents. Will they really be angry?"

"Furious," Hayden said, nodding. She shrugged. "But what are they going to do? Charge me back rent?"

"They could kick you out."

"Maybe. But probably not once I tell my mother about Trip," Hayden said.

I glanced at her sharply. "Speaking of Trip, I saw Ian earlier."

"Oh, yeah? Where?"

"The Drum Roll."

"You've been at the Drum Roll already?" Then Hayden suddenly frowned. "Did you go there looking for him?"

For a minute I thought she meant Mal, and my heart skittered.

"Looking for whom?" I asked cautiously.

"Ian! Who else?"

"No, of course not. Why would I?" I asked. "Oh, you mean to tell him about you?" I shook my head, disgusted that our friendship had unraveled to this point. "I wouldn't do that."

"What did you say to him about me?"

"Nothing. He wanted to know why you hadn't been returning his phone calls. I told him he should talk to you," I said.

Hayden made a face. "That's basically the same as telling him that I cheated on him."

"I'm not going to rat you out, but I'm not going to cover for you either," I said. I shrugged and turned away from her, tired of the conversation.

I liked Ian and felt sorry for him, but his relationship with Hayden was really the least of my worries at the moment. I was too busy wondering how I was going to get past the swarming mob of reporters and get to Mal so I could tell him in person that I had to leave.

Mal. The thought of leaving him caused a tight, painful sensation in my chest. I could ask him to come with me, and for a wild moment my hopes soared at the idea of Mal and me traveling through Europe together. I pictured us walking hand in hand through Paris, taking a gondola ride through the canals of Venice, staring up at the domed roof of St. Paul's Cathedral. It was crazy, we had only had that one afternoon together, but maybe . . .

No. It was crazy, I thought, and reality came crashing down with a thud. I was deluding myself. Who would leave his job, his friends, his whole life, to run off to a foreign country with someone he barely knew? I wasn't his girlfriend; I didn't know if he was interested in seeing me again. Hell, we hadn't even spent a whole night together. It was ridiculous. No, it was worse than ridiculous—it was *desperate.* Wouldn't it be better—much, much better—to remember our perfect afternoon together than to taint it with my sloppy neediness and his inevitable rejection?

"Lucy, look, I just wanted to say—" Hayden stopped and swallowed. "I'm sorry. I shouldn't have taken that money. I just . . . I guess I was scared. I got in too deep, and I couldn't see another way out. And I'm sorry for what I said. About how I didn't need advice from someone like you."

I nodded stiffly, not yet ready to forgive.

"Is there anything I can do to fix this? To make things better between us?" Hayden asked. There was a quaver in her voice, and she looked at me with wide, beseeching eyes.

I shrugged, feeling helpless. What could she do? Even if she repaid the money, the trust between us had been breached. "I don't know, Hayden. I really don't know."

It was Hayden's turn to nod. She looked as weary as I suddenly felt.

"So where are you going?" she asked.

"I don't know for sure. Right now I have to figure out how I'm going to make it past that mob of reporters."

Hayden brightened. "Oh, I can help you with that!"

"You can?" I asked doubtfully.

"Didn't I tell you I perfected the art of sneaking out undetected at the age of thirteen?"

"This is a little more complicated than getting past your parents' room without waking them up. There's a horde of them out there," I said, gesturing in the direction of the front gate.

Hayden smiled. "That just makes the challenge more fun," she said. "Don't worry. I'll take care of everything."

Hayden's plan was quite devious. She put on the clothes I'd worn home from Mal's house, wrapped her head in a scarf so that her dark hair was concealed, and put on a pair of huge sunglasses. Taller and thinner than me, she wouldn't fool anyone if we were standing side by side. But squealing out of the driveway and racing past the reporters in my little red convertible, the press would think she was me. Especially when she headed straight off the island, picked up I-95, and drove north toward Ocean Falls.

I watched her drive off, peeking out from behind the drapes in one of the upstairs bedrooms, and saw the reporters—Mitch Hannigan leading the charge—scramble to climb into their cars and news vans and peel off after her, all convinced their story was getting away. Ten minutes later the street in front of Crane Hill was empty. So empty that no one saw the black town car with the tinted windows pull up through the gate and then moments later depart, with me in the backseat.

"You're going to Miami Airport, ma'am?" the driver asked in a thick New York accent.

"Yes," I said. "I'm booked on a flight that's leaving at nine. Do you think there's any way I'll make it?"

The driver shrugged his square shoulders and looked up at me in the rearview mirror. "We can try. It'll be cuttin' it close, though. But maybe if the traffic's not too bad."

I thought of Mal, who was probably at Morton's by now, sitting and waiting for me. "Is there any chance we can swing by Morton's steakhouse on the way?" I asked hopefully.

"Not if you want to make your flight, lady," the driver said.

It was the moment of decision. Should I go see Mal, tell him what had happened, and take the ridiculously slim chance that he might want to come with me? Or should I try to make my flight before the press figured out that Hayden wasn't me and swarmed back to Palm Beach, ready to bribe the dispatcher at the car service I'd hired to find out where I was going?

I stared out the tinted window as the mansions standing aloof behind their high-hedged walls passed by. My mouth felt dry, and a trickle of sweat dripped from my neck down my back.

"What do you want to do?" the driver asked.

I swallowed. I knew what I wanted. I wanted Mal, wanted to be *with* Mal. I knew it the same way I knew myself. What I didn't know was how he felt about me. I knew Mal liked me, but that didn't mean he was falling in love with me. Or that he ever would.

I inhaled deeply and then released the breath slowly.

"Take me to straight to the airport," I said.

I pulled out my cell phone, called information, and got two numbers. First I called Morton's. Mal hadn't arrived yet, so I asked the hostess to tell him that I wouldn't be able to meet him after all and to please extend my apologies. Then I called Mal's condo. When the machine picked up—the sound of his warm, slow voice made the skin on my arms and chest break out in goose bumps again—I simply said, "It's me . . . I'm sorry."

I couldn't think of anything else to say. I pressed the off button and went back to staring out my window.

Twenty-Three

OVER THE FOLLOWING WEEKS I STROLLED THROUGH the streets of Paris, and then, when I tired of the city, I rented a car and drove south, heading for the picturesque scenery of rural Provence. From there I traveled to Italy, where I rode in a gondola in Venice, wandered through the Boboli Gardens behind the Pitti Palace in Florence, and spent Christmas Day sitting by the edge of Lake Como, staring off at the mountains in the distance, marveling at the breathtaking view. I spent a few days touring Berlin and Prague and then headed to Amsterdam, where I walked the canals and visited the Van Gogh Museum. Finally, I flew to London with plans to stay awhile. Peter Graham had arranged a three-month lease for me on a flat in South Kensington. I wanted to see everything—St. Paul's Cathedral, Buckingham Palace, the Tower of London, Westminster Abbey, and make day trips to the English countryside. It was the great European tour I'd always dreamed of taking.

The only problem was, I was miserable. I had never truly been lonely before—I've always been content to spend time on my own—so the force of the choking, desolate feeling surprised me.

I talked to my parents a few times, and I had a feeling they knew something had happened between Emma and me, even if they weren't sure exactly what it was. But they were both careful in what they said to me, confining their conversation mostly to local news and reports on Harper Lee, who was staying with them while I traveled. When I spoke to Peter Graham, he told me that my parents had finally cashed the check I wrote them, but when I asked my dad what they'd decided to do with the money, he simply said, "Nothing yet." It was clear he didn't want to discuss it further, and neither did I. I didn't have the energy.

I missed Mal more than I imagined possible. Thoughts of him were constantly with me. And it wasn't only in the romantic locales—Paris and Venice—that I keenly felt his absence. I wondered if he'd have also gasped in awe to see the ruins of Rome juxtaposed against the modern city, or if he, too, would have been moved to tears when touring the Anne Frank House in Amsterdam. Would he have insisted on seeing all of the sights of Florence, or would he have chosen—as I did—to spend an entire afternoon sitting by a fountain in a town square, eating gelato and people-watching?

By the time I finally arrived in the British capital, I was so tired that I spent three straight days in the flat, hardly mustering the energy to get out of bed. I ate cereal straight from the box and watched American sitcoms on the television. I didn't know if I had the flu, or if I was depressed, or both. I finally made myself get up, shower, and head out into chilly London and join the throng of tourists taking in the sights. But I tired easily and found it hard to work up much enthusiasm for anything I saw.

Happily, no one recognized me as the Lottery Seductress. The story apparently hadn't gotten any traction in Europe, and on the few occasions when I saw an American news broadcast, I wasn't on it. I stopped by an Internet café a few times to check my e-mail, and while I was there, I did a Google news search on my name; the posted stories were all over a month old, dating back to my flight from Palm Beach. As for my e-mail, once I cleaned out the 1,546 junk messages that had accumulated there, there were a few interesting items. Maisie had sent me a picture of the twins at Halloween, dressed as pirates and smiling their heart-melting grins, and another from Christmas morning, where they were still in their pajamas and surrounded by a mountain of discarded wrapping paper. Hayden sent me an e-mail that began with another apology, explaining that when her father had cut her off she'd gotten deeper and deeper into debt at the casino, which sent her into a spiral of anxiety and fear that eventually led to her stealing from me. Not that it excused what she did, she was quick to say, and she was again very, very sorry. I was surprised to find that I couldn't summon up much in the way of anger toward her.

Then there was the message I almost deleted, mostly because of the subject: *Gigolo for Hire.* I figured that it was a junk e-mail, one promising miracle cures to enlarge the penis I didn't possess. Also, I didn't recognize the address: *grandslam@gnet.com.* But something made me click on it anyway.

TO: litteach@mailso.com
FROM: grandslam@gnet.com
SUBJECT: Gigolo for Hire

So what now?

Grand Slam—as in tennis, not sex—and the gigolo in-joke. It was from *Mal.* He must have gotten my e-mail address from Hayden. I stared at the e-mail for a long, long time, as I tried to come up with a reply to this enigmatic question. I wanted to say something witty and sexy, something that would remind him of the afternoon we had spent tangled up together. But everything I thought of sounded cheesy or flat, overly sentimental or cold. So finally I hit the reply button and just wrote the truth: *I have no idea.*

And then I hit send.

A few weeks after I replied to Mal's e-mail—I hadn't heard from him since, even though I'd made a point of checking my messages a few times a day after that—I finally bottomed out.

It had been a particularly dismal day. First I mistakenly went to the Tate Britain, when I meant to go to the Tate Modern, and didn't figure out I was in the wrong place until I had walked twenty minutes in the rain, without an umbrella, from the Tube stop to the museum. Then, when I figured out my mistake and got back on the Tube, the train came to an abrupt stop in the middle of a tunnel, forcing us to sit there in the dark for a half hour while the driver made the occasional announcement that we would be delayed for only a few more minutes.

I finally made it to the Tate Modern, toured the exhibits without any real enthusiasm, and then had tea in the café. I sat next to a moony-eyed couple who proceeded to hand-feed each other bites of cake while I stared down at my tea feeling like the loneliest person in the world. To cap off the day, someone pick-pocketed me on the Tube on my way home, stealing my Oyster fare card and a twenty-pound note. Actually, I wasn't entirely sure I'd been robbed; it was perfectly possible that I had dropped them in the jostle of the crowd. But in the dark mood I was in, I felt completely justified in blaming the loss on theft.

When I got home to the flat, I curled up on the bed, and sank into my misery. I missed my home, my family, my life. It hadn't been perfect, but it had been mine. How had I ended up here, alone and far away from everything and everyone I loved? And yet, what right did I have to feel sorry for myself? I was in good health and had an obscenely large fortune; there were people out there who were sick or hungry and who had no real hope of things getting better for them. It was time to get my life together and move forward.

"Enough is enough," I said out loud.

And then I picked up the phone and made a call.

We arranged to meet for tea at the Ritz London. I was so nervous, I arrived ten minutes early and sat waiting in the extravagant Palm Court, with its decorative plasterwork, crystal chandeliers, and marble columns. I told the waiter I'd postpone the actual tea and sandwiches until my companion arrived, but I quickly regretted the decision. Tea would have given me something to do with my hands. So I played with my silverware, unfolded then refolded my napkin, and wondered how long I would have to wait.

Then I saw a familiar face, and another rush of nerves overtook me. My pulse jumped and skittered, my stomach twisted, my mouth went dry. I hastily stood up and tried to arrange my mouth into a smile, even though my face felt stiff. What would I say? How would this go? Would everything between us be permanently changed by the separation?

But then our eyes met.

"Lucy!" Maisie called out. She bounded toward me, looking much as she had when we were fifteen and she'd run across the lawn that joined our two houses to tell me that Jason Carlisle had kissed her, and suddenly I knew everything would be fine.

Maisie reached the table and threw her wiry arms around me.

"I can't believe I'm finally seeing you! I've missed you so much!" Maisie said, her voice muffled against my shoulder.

"I've missed you too," I said, and even though I couldn't stop smiling, my throat and chest tightened, and tears flooded my eyes. "Thank you for coming!"

"Are you kidding? A free trip to London! How could I say no to that?" Maisie said.

She laughed as she spoke, but her words cut too close to the reason we hadn't spoken for months: the lottery money. We both realized it at once and broke apart, staring at each other for a long moment.

"I'll tell you what," Maisie said. "Let's catch up first, before we get into everything else."

"Deal," I said. "I want to hear all about the twins."

Maisie oohed and aahed over the sumptuous surroundings of the Palm Court, and a pot of hot Darjeeling tea arrived, along with a three-tiered serving tray filled with tiny sandwiches, scones, and pastries. We ate and drank, and Maisie told me about the boys, who were resisting potty training and who had recently started swim lessons. Joe had acquired a landscaping contract for a large apartment complex. Maisie was considering returning to her law practice part-time when the twins entered pre-K next fall.

"So that's about it for us. Now it's your turn," Maisie said.

I shrugged. "I told you most of it on the phone. I've just been traveling."

"Oh, don't give me that 'I've just been traveling' garbage. I spent fifteen minutes telling you about the twins' pooping progress, and you can't give me any details about what you've been up to?" Maisie exclaimed.

I laughed. "But I'd so much rather hear about the boys."

"Start talking, Parker."

"Okay, fine, but you asked for it. Just be glad I didn't bring any travel slides with me," I teased. And I told her about France, Italy, and the other places I'd been, trying for her sake to make it all sound exciting. Maisie sat in rapt attention, her eyes widening as I detailed the sites I'd seen and museums I'd toured.

"But what about men?" she finally asked. "I was hoping you'd meet some gorgeous foreigner and have a torrid love affair."

"Torrid love affair?" I repeated, amused. "You mean like Lucy in a *A Room with a View*?"

"Did that Lucy get laid?"

"No. She was emotionally repressed."

"Then no, that's not what I meant," Maisie said.

"Well." I hesitated. "There was someone . . . someone I met back in Palm Beach."

"Oooh, tell me all about him!"

But thoughts of Mal—of his pale blue eyes, the angular line of his jaw, the sweet curve of his lips, the low rumble of his laughter—just depressed me. Maisie must have seen my face cloud over, because she leaned forward, her expression etched with concern.

"What's wrong? Don't tell me he turned out to be another Elliott," she said.

I laughed at this. "I don't think there could be another Elliott."

"Oh, there's always another Elliott out there. The world is thick with them," Maisie said darkly.

"How can someone so happily married be so bitter about men?"

"Who said I'm happily married?" Maisie asked. I couldn't tell if she was joking or not.

"Aren't you? No, don't tell me if you're not. I don't think I could bear it. You and Joe are my shining example of idealized couplehood."

"I hate to burst your bubble, but there's no such thing," Maisie said, popping a cucumber sandwich into her mouth. "Mmm, I like this one. Watch out for the salmon ones, though. They're a bit fishy."

"Huh. I didn't know that," I said.

"Maybe it's a cultural thing, and the English just don't mind fishy-tasting fish," Maisie said.

"No, I wasn't talking about the sandwiches. I was talking about your *marriage*."

"Oh, come on. Surely you weren't under any delusions about how perfect Joe and I are. Remember the fight we had at his Super Bowl party, where he asked if I was PMS'ing because I was so irritable and I dumped the bowl of Doritos over his head? I really wanted to dump the bowl of queso dip on him, but it was just a bit too hot, and although I was annoyed, I didn't want to send him to the ER," Maisie said.

"I remember." I started to laugh. "And you really were PMS'ing."

"He still shouldn't have mentioned it. We've been married for seven years; he should know better by now," Maisie said.

"I know you guys have the occasional fights and problems." I stopped; we were back to the money issue. I took a deep breath and soldiered on. "But the thing is, you're hanging in there together. Look at the sort of guys I end up with. Elliott, who cheated on me. Drew, who, okay, wasn't a bad guy, but he didn't love me either."

"Who the hell is Drew?" Maisie asked, wrinkling her brow in confusion.

"And then there's Mal," I continued, ignoring her question. "Who's out of my league."

"Of course he isn't out of your league!"

"You don't even know him," I pointed out.

"That doesn't change my opinion," Maisie said.

We smiled at each other. "Are we going to get around to talking about the money?" I asked.

"Do we have to? We're having so much fun. This is just like old times. Except for the part where we're in London and having tea at the Ritz," Maisie said, gesturing at the picturesque scene around her. As if on cue, a man in a tuxedo sat at the piano and began to play.

"Why didn't you take the money? I wanted you to have it," I said, my grin fading.

Maisie studied her teacup. "I felt like it would ruin our friendship if I accepted it," she finally said.

"But how would it do that?"

She looked up at me, her pixie face more serious than I had ever seen it. "Because from then on, we'd always be indebted to you. Every time I bought something stupid—a silk blouse I'd never wear because it was dry clean only, or a book I had no intention of reading—I couldn't tell you about it, because you'd think, *There she goes again, wasting my money,*" Maisie said.

"No, I wouldn't!" I protested. And I was just about to get angry when I remembered my last conversation with Emma and how, right before she attempted to wrangle more money from me, I had been critical of how she'd spent the money I'd already given her.

"Damn," I said softly.

"I'm sorry," Maisie said quickly. "I know it upsets you that I couldn't take it, and I know that not being able to accept it is a personal flaw of mine. How I always have to control everything, et cetera, et cetera."

"No, you're right," I said. I sighed deeply. "I am judgmental about how people spend money. I do it all the time."

"Everyone's judgmental," Maisie said.

"Not everyone. And even so, it doesn't excuse my doing it," I said. I glanced up at her. "How come you didn't mind accepting the plane ticket to London I sent you?"

"You said you needed me," Maisie said simply. "Of course I'd come."

I swallowed back the knot forming in my throat. "Thanks," I said hoarsely.

Maisie's grin turned impish. "And how could I say no to a first-class trip to London? Oh, and by the way? Flying first class has permanently spoiled me. I don't think I'll ever be able to fly coach again."

I laughed. "I'm glad you liked it."

"Liked it? My seat reclined into a bed! It was nicer than sitting in my living room. Although, considering my living room, that probably isn't saying much." Maisie beamed at me, and then her smile faltered. "Are we okay, then?" she asked tentatively.

I nodded. "We're great."

"Good. Because I just remembered I have some gossip to tell you," she said portentously.

"What?"

"Well... there's a rumor going around about Matt Forrester."

I stiffened. "What about him?"

"He's in *rehab*," Maisie said triumphantly. "His parents are trying to hush it up, but of course it's gotten out. That's one of the beautiful things about living in a small town—nothing stays secret for long."

"Rehab, huh?" I considered this. "I have to say, I'm not surprised."

"But don't you see? This totally vindicates you!"

"How so?"

"Who's going to believe the allegations he made against you now?" Maisie said.

I shrugged. "Everyone. People always want to believe in the scandal. And a teacher seducing her student is a much juicier story than a troubled kid telling a lie."

Maisie frowned. "When I was still at the prosecutor's office, this was the sort of news we'd love to get about an adverse witness. Evidence of drug or alcohol abuse always destroys credibility with the jury."

"Maybe. But this isn't a court."

"Haven't you ever heard of the court of public opinion?"

"Yes. And in that court, I've already been tried, convicted, and the angry mob is just waiting for me to be drawn and quartered in the public square," I said.

Maisie looked stricken. "Does that mean you're not coming home?"

I sighed, feeling weary again. "I don't know, Maisie. I don't see how I can. Could you live somewhere where everyone thought you were into seducing teenage boys?"

"No. But I can't imagine not living near you. You're the sister I never had," Maisie said earnestly, reaching across the table to rest her hand on my arm.

I looked at her. "Do you really think that?"

"Of course! You know that, don't you?"

"Well, to be honest, when you sent that money back . . . I

thought maybe it meant . . . that you didn't want me to be too close to your family," I said, stumbling over the words.

Maisie frowned, and then her face transformed into an expression of fierce intensity. "Lucy, you *are* a part of our family. I know Joe and the boys feel the same way. We all love you."

"Thanks," I said. But this time I couldn't keep back the tears. They spilled from my eyes and rolled down my cheeks, salty and hot. Maisie quickly handed me the white linen napkin, which I used to mop up the tears. I tried to smile at her. "Sorry. I'm just so glad you're here. I've been really lonely."

"I've missed you too," Maisie said. And then, both of us watery-eyed and sniffling, we hugged again.

Maisie stayed for a week, and for the first time since I'd arrived in Europe, I started to enjoy myself. We went to museums and churches and even took some day trips out into the countryside to see Bath and Cambridge. I'd booked Maisie a suite at the Ritz, thinking she could do with the time alone after three years of wrangling the twins, but she insisted on staying with me at my rented flat instead. I was glad. It took me back to our girlhood, when we spent nearly every weekend sleeping over at each other's house.

We enjoyed ourselves so much that, the day Maisie was leaving, I woke up feeling a sense of desolation that I couldn't shake.

"You should come home with me," Maisie urged, as she stuffed clothes into her battered suitcase.

Reluctantly, I shook my head. "I can't. Not just yet."

Maisie looked up from the sweater she was folding and shot me a shrewd look. "Because of the Lottery Seductress crap or because of the tennis pro?" she asked.

Caught up in the spirit of reconciliation, I'd told Maisie all about Mal, not bothering to sugarcoat the story to make myself sound better. Now I was starting to regret it. She was, of course, disapproving of how I'd run out on him without explanation. But, even worse, Maisie had—without ever having met Mal, as I kept pointing out to her—decided he was The One. I told her over and over that he was way out of my league, the sort of guy who dated thin girls with perky breasts. Men like that, I said over and over, don't end up with dowdy schoolteachers. Since it hadn't yet sunk in to Maisie's rocklike skull, I repeated it yet again.

"But you're not dowdy," Maisie exclaimed, tossing the sweater into her suitcase.

"That's only because of the hair," I said.

"No, it's not. Although, honestly, I think I liked you better with your curls," Maisie said. "You don't look like you with your hair blond."

"Dowdy, you mean."

"No. Honestly, Lucy, you are so hard on yourself. You never looked dowdy."

I snorted.

"Okay," Maisie said. "The new clothes are definitely an improvement, I'll give you that."

"Hayden gets credit for the wardrobe. She picked everything out for me."

Maisie scowled. "Don't even say her name. I still can't believe she was stealing from you."

I shrugged. "Hayden just got in over her head. She didn't mean to hurt me."

Maisie, not ready to forgive and forget, just rolled her eyes. "Have you heard from her?"

"Yeah, I got an e-mail from her yesterday. She said she's hoping to get engaged soon."

Maisie's eyebrows arched up and her eyes went round with surprise. "*Engaged?* To that old guy?"

I nodded.

"But didn't they just start dating?"

"I suppose it's been a few months now. And they were both spouse-shopping, so it's not that surprising it would happen quickly. He wants a trophy wife, she wants a fat bank account. Really, if you think about it, it's a perfect match."

"Please. I give it a year, tops."

"Don't you always say that all of the most successful marriages are based on shared goals?" I teased her.

"I don't think one spouse having money and the other spouse wanting money counts as a shared goal."

"Believe it or not, I hope she's happy," I said, shrugging.

"Why wouldn't I believe that? You're a nice person. Much nicer than I am. I hope she's miserable, the conniving little snake."

"She's not a snake. Not really. She just has a lot of problems," I said, thinking of the gambling debts and the fact that she'd traded in Ian, whom I thought she might truly have loved, for a man I knew she didn't. Life would not be easy for Hayden, even if she did marry Trip and his oil money. I wondered if, ten years from now, she'd still think it had been worth it.

"Don't think I didn't notice that you changed the subject away from Mal," Maisie said, zipping up her suitcase and tipping it upright.

"You're the one who asked if I'd heard from Hayden."

"Seriously, Lucy, don't you think you should at least call and talk to him?"

The truth was, I *did* want to talk to Mal. But every time I worked up the courage to call him—sometimes even going so far as to pick up the phone, my fingers poised over the numbers, ready to dial—my pulse would start to pound and my stomach would twist up, and I'd lose my nerve.

"The thing is, you don't know how he feels about you," Maisie continued. "You keep assuming that he was never interested in you—"

"I wouldn't say that. I fully acknowledge that there was chemistry there," I interrupted her.

"I think it sounds like more than chemistry. I think it sounds like the two of you fell in love," Maisie said, fixing me with a prosecutorial stare.

"Don't be stupid," I said irritably, my eyes dropping. "Sexual attraction is not the same thing as love."

"I didn't say it was. But I know you, and I can tell you thought of this guy as more than just a one-night stand."

"One-afternoon stand," I corrected her, my mouth twisting up into a humorless smile. "And even if I have feelings for him, that doesn't mean that he returns them."

"But you haven't given him a chance to tell you that he does!" Maisie exclaimed. "Or is that it? If you don't tell him how you feel, he won't have the chance to reject you?"

"I don't have such a great track record when it comes to relationships," I said, feeling anger corkscrewing up inside of me.

"You can't judge other guys by the Elliott standard," Maisie said flatly.

"That's the only standard I have to go by!" I said, flaring back at her.

We stood there, staring at each other—my arms folded protectively across my chest, Maisie's hands planted aggressively on her hips. Finally I shook my head and turned away from her.

"I don't want to fight. Your taxi will be here in a half hour," I said.

Maisie hesitated but finally relented. "Okay," she said. "I'll drop it—for now."

I decided it was time to change the subject. "Do you think the twins will like the toy rockets?"

"God, yes. They'll love them," Maisie said. "Is it terrible that I don't want to go back yet? I miss them terribly, Joe too, but it's been a dream being able to sleep in and eat out and swan around London with you."

"Then stay longer! Yay! We'll change your ticket!"

"I can't." Maisie sighed. "I have to get back to real life. And the boys have been staying with my mom while Joe's at work. I could tell when I talked to her yesterday that she's at the end of her rope. She started pushing potty training on them too hard, and the twins revolted and flushed their training pants down the upstairs toilet. They flooded her bathroom."

I laughed at the mental image, which, knowing the Wonder Twins, was all too easy to picture. "I understand. But I'll miss you."

Maisie hugged me. "Me too." She pulled back and looked up at me. "Come home soon, Lucy. Please."

"I'll think about it," I promised.

And long after Maisie left, carried off to Heathrow in a large black taxicab, I did think about it. I couldn't run forever. Sooner or later I would have to go home, wherever home ended up being.

I also hadn't told Maisie that when I checked my e-mail the day before, I'd finally gotten a response from Mal. He'd written simply: *Let me know when you figure it out.*

I'd stared at the e-mail for a long time before closing my inbox without replying. Before I decided whether or not I should go back to Florida, and if I should call Mal, I had to figure out what I was going to do about the lottery money. My father's words back at the very beginning, when he'd first found out I'd won, kept echoing in my thoughts:

You've been given a rare opportunity. The chance to make your life whatever you want it to be. Please don't squander it.

That's exactly what I had done. From practically the first moment I'd arrived in Palm Beach, all I'd done was shop and party, party and shop. I'd never even asked Peter Graham about putting aside part of the money for philanthropy, as I'd meant to. Instead, I'd used my winnings to fund the sort of glamorous lifestyle that I'd never aspired to in the first place. But now I knew: That lifestyle wasn't me. I wanted more from life. Or maybe it would be more accurate to say that I wanted less.

Twenty-Four

IT WAS A FEW DAYS BEFORE EMMA AND CHRISTIAN'S wedding, and I still hadn't decided if I would be attending. True, Emma had uninvited me. But then a creamy linen wedding invitation printed in an elegant engraver's font arrived at my London flat.

I spoke to my mother on the phone a few days after I received the invitation, and she urged me to come home for the wedding, but I'd been deliberately vague about my plans. The truth was, I didn't know if I wanted to go. Worry about the reaction I'd receive from the wedding guests and anger at Emma fought with my bone-deep desire to see my home and family. And, even if I was still upset with Emma, I didn't want to miss my little sister's wedding.

It was the letter that finally made the decision for me. I knew my parents had hoped it would; after all, they had sent it by overnight courier so that it arrived at my London flat on a cold, dreary February morning two days before the wedding, with a yellow sticky note attached: READ THIS. LOVE, MOM AND DAD.

I unfolded the single sheet of lined notebook paper and

began to read the unkempt handwriting that I recognized from a former life.

Dear Ms. Parker,

As part of the program I'm in, I'm supposed to make amends by apologizing to the people I've hurt. And the way I figure it, you're pretty much at the top of the list.

I'm so sorry. More sorry than I can say.

When I told my parents and Dr. Johnson that lie about you hitting on me, I was just hoping I'd be able to get back on the soccer team. But then it all got so crazy. First you got fired, and then suddenly it became a huge news story. I didn't know how to stop it. I should have said that I lied, but I guess I was scared everyone would be mad at me. Which isn't an excuse, I know.

I talked to my counselor about it, and he said that I had to set things right, so I've told everyone the truth—my parents, the school, even that reporter who kept calling to interview me. I told them all that I made the whole thing up. I was right—everyone is pretty pissed off at me. I was even expelled from school. I don't care. I figure I pretty much deserve it. The reporter said he'd write a story for the newspaper to set everything straight.

I wanted to apologize to you in person, but when I called your family to find out where you were, your dad wouldn't tell me. I guess I understand. I think he was afraid my parents' lawyer wanted to know so they could sue you. To be honest—and that's what I intend to be from now on, honest—my parents were planning to sue you, even after I told them that I made up the story about you hitting on me. They're not bad people. I think they thought I was lying about having lied because I was embarrassed and just wanted to get them to drop the whole thing. But I told them that if they sued you, I'd tell the judge and the lawyers and everyone else that I lied, and they wouldn't have a case. So they finally agreed to let it go.

I hope that I get the chance to apologize to you in person someday.

Yours truly,
Matt Forrester

I read the letter three times before the words sank in, before I let myself hope that it could possibly be true. And then I noticed that there was something else in the envelope—a newspaper clipping. My heart hammering, I pulled it out and read it. The article was written under Mitch Hannigan's byline.

LOTTERY TEACHER VINDICATED; STUDENT ADMITS HE LIED

In a startling reversal, Matt Forrester, the Andrews Prep School student who claimed that multimillion-dollar lottery winner and former English teacher Lucy Parker made inappropriate sexual advances toward him, has come forward to admit he lied.

"Ms. Parker never hit on me. I made up the story in order to get back at her for giving me a low grade," Forrester said. "I apologize for all of the trouble I caused Ms. Parker and hope that someday she'll be able to forgive me."

The article went on to give a recap of the story—how I was fired and went on to win the lottery, the media circus that followed, how I had stayed undetected in Palm Beach for several weeks. It concluded by stating that I was unavailable for comment and was believed to be traveling out of the country.

I read it over several times too, wondering if it could really be true. But the words remained the same. Matt had admitted he lied. Mitch Hannigan had published the story. It was finally over.

I picked up the phone and called British Airways. Once the cool English voice of the customer-service representative answered, I said, "Hello, I'd like to book a one-way ticket from London to West Palm Beach. Departing as soon as possible, please."

My house had an empty, neglected feel to it. The air was stale, and dust motes danced in the sunshine. I walked around, opening the windows to let in the cool late-winter breeze. I just missed tripping over two big boxes in the living room. When I bent down to look more closely at the boxes, I recognized Hayden's handwriting on the address labels and realized they must contain the books I'd bought in Palm Beach. My dad, who had been taking care of my house while I was away, had brought the boxes inside for me.

I stood back up and looked around. Everything was so familiar. There was the comfy chenille chair I had saved up for four months to buy, the beach-scene painting I'd discovered at a local thrift store, the silver candlesticks that had belonged to my grandmother. Everything had been picked out and bought by me, one piece at a time. When you don't have any money, every purchase takes on a new importance.

I finally wheeled my suitcase into my bedroom, where I looked longingly at my bed—it had been a long flight, and I hadn't slept at all on board—but I only had an hour to get ready for the rehearsal dinner. So I showered and changed into a simple silk midnight-blue dress with flutter sleeves and sequins glittering along the hemline. When I was finally ready, I headed to the garage. My Porsche and Volvo were both parked there; Dad had taken care of getting them home to me. I started to pick up the Porsche keys—I really did love that car—but then a wave of nostalgia for my beat-up yellow Volvo washed over me, and I instead grabbed for the familiar *I need coffee* key ring and square Volvo key with the rubber-encased head.

I slid behind the wheel of my old car and turned the key, wondering if the car would even start after so many months of inactivity. The engine had always been temperamental. But it roared to life, albeit vibrating so much it made my teeth rattle, and a moment later I was backing out of the driveway.

It was only a five-minute drive to the waterfront restaurant where the wedding-rehearsal dinner was being held, but as I turned down the familiar streets, I already noticed changes that had taken place in my absence. The house on the corner of Beach Street had been painted a pretty hydrangea blue, and the chiropractor's office on Porpoise Drive had closed, a sign in front announcing that a Montessori nursery school would be opening in the space. As I drove, my nerves felt as though they were stretching, growing more and more taut with each passing moment.

I knew my family would be happy to see me—well, perhaps with the exception of Emma—but what about the other guests? Which would they believe—the national story of the Lottery Seductress, or the much smaller, less publicized story that Matt Forrester had recanted his accusation? There was no way of knowing ahead of time.

I pulled into a parking spot in front of the restaurant and climbed out of the Volvo.

"Here goes nothing," I muttered to myself.

I saw a few people up ahead walking into the restaurant—Christian's mother, Judith, whom I'd met at various family functions, and two of Emma's best friends from high school. My pulse began to race, so I took a deep breath to steady myself and followed them inside. The hostess—a young girl wearing a black sundress—smiled at me in welcome.

"Hi, can I help you?" she asked. She didn't seem to recognize me, which I thought was a good sign.

"I'm here for the rehearsal dinner," I said.

"Oh, sure, it's right back here. I'll show you." She led me to a banquet room off to the side of the dining room.

The room was set up with round tables, dressed in crisp white linens. Most of the guests were already there milling around, drinking champagne from flutes and munching on the hors d'oeuvres being circulated on round silver trays by the waitstaff.

I saw Emma first. She was in the middle of the room, basking in the attention her bride-to-be status allotted her. She certainly looked the part. She was wearing a fitted gold sleeveless sheath that showed off her well-toned arms. Her blond hair was twisted up in a chignon, and she wore a gold bangle on each wrist. Christian stood behind her, looking as blandly handsome as ever in his blue suit. I'd personally never found him very attractive—his eyes were too close together—but he was an okay guy. Emma's friends certainly seemed to like him, laughing up at Christian flirtatiously and throwing their heads back to expose long creamy throats, like birds in the middle of a mating ritual. I knew that their obvious interest in Christian and jealousy that Emma had snagged him would please my little sister.

"Lucy!" my mother's voice called out, rising sharply over the din. I was still staring at Emma, and at the sound of my name my sister looked up. When our gazes met, her eyes narrowed slightly. Was Emma angry that I'd come? Worried that

I'd cause a scene? There was no way of knowing. A moment later I was engulfed in my mother's embrace.

"Hi, Mom," I said, suddenly fighting back tears I hadn't known were coming.

"I can't believe you're really here!" she said, sounding close to tears herself.

"Kay, I don't think she can breathe," Dad said mildly. "Hello, Lucy. Welcome home."

My mom let go of me just long enough for my dad to hug me, and then she wrapped her arms around me again. "I knew you wouldn't miss the wedding!"

"When did you get in?" Dad asked.

"Just a few hours ago. I stopped by my house before I came here. Thanks for watering my plants and taking care of everything."

"Happy to help," Dad said, smiling down at me. "Harper Lee will be thrilled you're back."

"I can't wait to see her."

My mom, now clutching at my hand, peered at me. "You look so different."

"It's the hair. I wanted to find out if blondes really do have more fun," I joked.

"Hi, Lucy."

I turned and saw my little sister standing there, viewing me with obvious suspicion.

"Hello, Emma."

"I didn't know that you were coming," she said.

"I didn't either. It was a last-minute decision."

Emma bit her lip and looked down, not meeting my eyes. Although she looked glamorous in her sparkling dress and razor-sharp high heels, I could see the little girl with the missing front teeth and scabbed knees she'd once been.

I smiled at Emma, and to my surprise she smiled back, tentatively at first, but then her face relaxed and her smile widened.

"I'm glad you're here," she said softly, and reached out to squeeze my hand. "Lucy, I'm sorry. I acted like a spoiled brat. You must hate me. I would if I were you."

I looked at Emma for a long moment, wondering if I could believe her apology. Sometimes it felt as if I'd never be able to trust anyone again. And yet I didn't want to go through my life twisted and bitter with suspicion.

I finally said, "No, I don't hate you. How could I? You're my little sister."

Emma sniffed and pressed manicured fingers into the corners of her eyes. "Don't make me cry," she warned. "I don't want my mascara to run. Wait! I have the most amazing idea: Now that you're here, you have to be my maid of honor!"

"Really?" I asked.

Emma nodded enthusiastically.

"Ashley can be a regular bridesmaid. I'm sure she won't mind," Emma said. "And all of the bridesmaids are wearing red, so as long as you wear red too, it won't matter if your gown is slightly different. We can go to the mall after this is over. I'm sure we'll be able to find something at Macy's."

"I have a red dress," I said, thinking of the red Carolina Herrera gown I'd worn to the fund-raiser at Mar-a-Lago.

"You do?" Emma asked.

I nodded. "Yes. And it will be perfect."

And it was. The whole wedding was pretty spectacular. Emma really was the most beautiful bride I'd ever seen, radiant in her Vera Wang gown. Christian's eyes actually teared up when she started down the aisle on our father's arm, and I found myself warming to my new brother-in-law. So what if his eyes were too close together? There were certainly worse flaws for a man to have. And Christian seemed to truly love my little sister.

The reception was held at a country club—not the Forresters' club, which was probably just as well—and it was lovely. Twinkle lights had been entwined around posts and potted plants, hundreds of candles lit the room, and tall vases filled with calla lilies were on every table. There was a band with a singer who sounded like Patsy Cline, her voice deep and molasses rich. The champagne flowed freely, and couples filled the dance floor, even during the dinner service.

The guests were for the most part very kind to me. The women noisily told me how different I looked and how much they liked my hair and how pretty my dress was, while their husbands kissed me chastely on the cheek. Not everyone was willing to offer public displays of acceptance, though. Christian's parents were very warm toward me, but his two aunts kept their distance, and I saw them muttering together, casting me dark looks that made it easy to guess what they were talking about. I just lifted my head high, smiled at everyone who smiled at me, danced with the groomsmen, and made a point not to drink too much. It helped that Maisie and Joe were there, flanking me like a pair of bodyguards until I made them go off and dance together.

Oddly enough, no one mentioned the lottery money. I don't know if it had become inextricably tangled in the Lottery Seductress story, so that one couldn't be mentioned without dragging up the other, or if it was simply a case of good manners trumping curiosity. Either way, I was thankful.

* * *

It wasn't until brunch the next day that the subject finally came up. The brunch was held at the hotel where Emma and Christian had spent the night in the bridal suite and where most of the out-of-town guests were staying. It wasn't a formal gathering, just a buffet of scrambled eggs and French toast, and the wedding guests, many of them pale with bloodshot eyes, trickled slowly in as they dragged themselves up and out of bed.

I was feeling virtuous for not having a hangover, so I indulged in a mimosa with brunch. I sat at a table with Christian and Emma, the parents of the bride and groom, and the groom's brother and very pregnant sister-in-law.

"Lucy, I heard you just got back from a trip to Europe," Christian's mother, Judith, said, as she stirred cream into her coffee. She had a friendly open face and short dark hair softened with highlights. "That sounds exciting."

I returned her smile. "I had planned to go backpacking across Europe after college with some friends, but I broke my ankle right before graduation and ended up having to bow out of the trip. It took me ten years to get around to making it up," I said.

"Well, I'm sure it was nicer to do it your way than to go backpacking," Judith said. "All of those awful hostels the kids stay in." She shuddered. "Give me luxury hotels any day."

"Richard and I are going on a trip," Mom announced, sipping a mimosa from a champagne goblet.

"You are?" I asked, surprised. This was the first I'd heard of it. "Where are you going?"

"A cruise through Alaska," Dad said. He crooked his furry caterpillar eyebrows at me, and I grinned back at him, knowing that this was his way of telling me that they'd finally decided to spend the money I gave them on the trip.

"That's great," I said warmly. "I'm so glad."

"We'll be gone for a month. And when we get back, we're going to break ground on our new kennel. We bought the lot next door that was for sale," Mom said happily.

"So a compromise was reached, then," I said, and my parents both beamed at me, clearly pleased with the solution. I noticed they were holding hands under the table.

I passed a few minutes of conversation with Judith about my trip to Europe, and when I mentioned the few days I'd spent on Lake Como, Christian's father, Paul, chimed in to tell me about his and Judith's trip there a few years earlier. The pregnant sister-in-law, Jenny, said she thought Lake Como was where George Clooney lived and asked if I'd run into him. Her husband, Scott—brother to Christian, and something of an asshole—rolled his eyes and told his wife not to be stupid. I shot him a dirty look and told her that, no, I hadn't seen George Clooney, but then again, I hadn't been looking for him. My mother, who had been only half listening to the conversation, suddenly leaned over and asked which George Clooney movie we were talking about, which then required a too-detailed explanation that we weren't discussing any of his movies, just the fact that I hadn't seen him in person.

This spurred a completely irrelevant conversation about Movie Stars One Hadn't Seen in Person, until we realized that the only movie star any of us had ever seen was Rutger Hauer, whom Judith swore she had passed in a Chicago airport six years earlier. Paul, who had been with her at the time, was just as sure it wasn't him and that Judith only thought so because she had watched *Ladyhawke* on cable the night before the supposed sighting.

And the whole time this conversation was going on, Emma and Christian were quietly gazing at each other with gooey expressions, which just reminded everyone at the table—or, at least, reminded me—that they'd spent the night before consummating their nuptials.

My jet lag was kicking in again, and I was just trying to think up a good excuse that would get me out of there so I could go home and snuggle up in bed with Harper Lee, when Judith suddenly leaned forward and said, "Lucy, what are you going to do with all of that money you won?"

Everyone at the table went instantly quiet.

"Judith," Paul said severely. She turned to look at him, and he shook his head at her. "Don't put Lucy on the spot."

"Oh! I'm sorry," Judith said, turning to look at me, her face creased with anxiety. She reached out a hand and patted my arm. "I didn't mean to upset you, Lucy."

"You didn't," I said quickly. "I'm not at all upset."

And then, since every face was now swiveled toward me—even Emma and Christian had snapped out of their newlywed love fog—I decided now was as good as ever to drop my big bombshell.

I took a deep breath. "Actually, I do have plans. I've decided I'm going to open a school."

The silence was so absolute, it was a bit intimidating.

After a few uncomfortable beats, Judith finally asked, "What kind of a school?"

"It's going to be a small, humanities-based program for at-risk teen girls. Academically, we'll cover the same subjects as a regular school, with an added emphasis on art, literature, and creative thinking. But there will be counselors to work on self-esteem, a mentor program to bring the girls strong female role models, and—most important of all—I want to stress the importance of foresight. How the decisions they make now really can and will affect their futures," I said, unable to keep the excitement out of my voice.

I hadn't meant to go into so much detail, but every time I thought of the school, I instantly got carried away. The idea had first popped into my head weeks earlier, while I was in London, and it refused to go away no matter how many times I tried to convince myself that it was too ambitious, too unwieldy, too unrealistic. It was the perfect solution. I wanted to use the money I'd won to make a difference. If I could make this work, then not only would I be able to teach again, I'd be helping some of the most marginalized members of society.

"Goodness! How wonderful!" Judith exclaimed. "I can't think of anything better!"

"Nor can I," Dad chimed in. I could swear he had tears in his eyes, and he seemed to be swelling with pride.

My mother was thrilled by the news too. "Even though I must admit I was hoping you'd use the money to build a new no-kill shelter, this is a fabulous idea too," she enthused. "And more in line with your interests, I think."

I nodded. "I really want to teach again. Only not at a school like Andrews Prep. Those kids have so much already. I want to be somewhere where I can really make a difference. I can help these girls get back on track and make something of their lives. There are so many negative influences out there. They need something to hold on to if they're going to make it."

"It's the boys. Girls start getting in trouble when they're trying to please boys," Jenny said darkly, her hands folded on her swollen abdomen.

"What about the troubled boys? Don't they deserve to have a program too?" Scott asked. I had the feeling he was speaking more to aggravate his wife—who was, indeed, shooting him a dirty look—but I decided to pretend he was genuinely interested.

"I thought of that, but I figured I should probably start

with the girls and then see how successful the program is," I said.

"I think that's smart. You can always expand later," Judith said.

"I was just reading a piece on single-sex classrooms," Paul chimed in. "I think it was in *Time* or maybe *Newsweek*. I'll try to find it and send it to you, Lucy. It was interesting and really supported the claim that kids—girls, especially—can flourish in a single-sex school environment."

"Thanks, I'd like to read it," I said. I looked over at my sister. "So . . . what do you think?" I asked.

"I think it's a great idea," Emma said unexpectedly.

"You do?"

Emma shrugged. "I'm not saying it's what I'd do if I had that sort of money. But I think this is right up your alley. It'll make you happy." She smiled at me, and I grinned back at her.

Emma picked up her mimosa and held it up to me in a toast. "To Lucy and her new project," she said.

Everyone followed suit, even those who were sticking to water or coffee. "To Lucy's new project," they chorused.

The next few weeks were a whirlwind of activity. My goal was to get the Bright Futures School up and running in twelve months' time, and I already had a to-do list that was a mile long. I had to find a location, figure out the licensing requirements, come up with a curriculum, hire a staff, handle all of the money issues—although Peter Graham, my financial adviser, had sweetly volunteered his time to help me with that—and a million other considerations that kept cropping up. My parents pitched in before they left for their cruise, and even Emma said she wanted to help, although between her honeymoon to Peter Island, work, and selling the beach house she and Christian had wisely decided they couldn't afford to keep, she didn't have a lot of extra time.

I suffered through an interview with Mitch Hannigan, who had seemed very keen on the Lottery-Seductress-turns-philanthropist aspect of the story. Just sitting across the table from him at Starbucks made my skin crawl, but I figured the publicity made it worthwhile. I had to admit that the article he wrote, which appeared on the front page of the local news section, was very positive, despite a few unsavory allusions to the wild socialite party life I'd supposedly led in Palm Beach.

A week later there was an article about Drew in the same section of the paper. I'd gotten used to seeing his name in print—news stories about his congressional campaign regularly appeared in the paper—but this story was more personal in nature. In it, Drew was interviewed about his life as the local boy made good, his prominent Palm Beach family . . . and his new girlfriend, who just happened to be a publicist. There was a picture of her sitting nestled in Drew's arms, both of them flashing toothy smiles. She was pretty much what I would have expected—attractive, polished, appropriate. She had an elegant, thoughtful face and long dark hair held back in a white headband. I'd be lying if I said I didn't feel a pang of regret, but that's all it was—a small ripple of wonder at what might have been had Drew and I met at a different time, under different circumstances.

After Hayden sent an e-mail saying that she thought Trip was about to propose to her, I'd e-mailed her back, asking for details. She never responded. From the silence, I had a feeling things hadn't gone quite as she expected. I made a point of regularly reading the society section of the paper, where the engagements of the moneyed Palm Beach community were always announced, but I never saw Hayden's name. I knew from past experience that Hayden always put out a radio silence when she was disappointed in love or business, but now I wondered if this silence spoke to even greater troubles. I hoped for her sake that she'd come out of it okay.

Mal didn't e-mail me again. It was probably for the best, I told myself. Cut things off in one clean break. It was dignified and mature and—when I was being honest with myself, which I tried not to do when it came to Mal—pretty damned miserable. But I knew I'd be okay . . . eventually. Both the old and new Lucys had taught me that.

And then, a few weeks after the article about the Bright Futures School appeared in the *Palm Beach Post,* an odd thing happened: I received a check in the mail. It had been sent in an ordinary business envelope, the kind that's printed on the inside for security, and was hand-addressed to me. When I opened it up, there wasn't a note, just a check that fluttered out, spiraling to the ground. I picked it up and then stared down at it, vaguely aware that my heart had started to thump loudly.

The check was from Mal, and it was made out to the Bright Futures School Foundation I'd set up, with a note on the memo line saying simply, *Donation.*

The check was made out in the amount of three million dollars.

Twenty-Five

I BROKE ALL SPEEDING LAWS AS I DROVE DOWN TO Palm Beach in my convertible. I hadn't been able to part with the car, although I kept the old Volvo too, to drive on rainy days. But I wasn't worried about it raining today. It was gorgeous out, like an advertisement for Florida vacations. The sky was an azure blue and dotted with swirling cotton-candy clouds.

In a little less than an hour, I was driving through the all-too-familiar streets of Palm Beach. I headed straight for the tennis club, hoping that Mal would be at work, although preferably not in the middle of a lesson. If I had to sit beside the courts, scuffing my toes at the red clay while I waited for him to correct a client's topspin and offer suggestions on how to improve their serve, I just might lose my mind.

I took a frantic turn into the gated driveway of the Rushes Country Club, followed the winding road through the carefully manicured grounds to the clubhouse, and pulled into the first open spot I saw. I forced myself to walk calmly and deliberately around the side of the club to where the tennis courts were. The courts were full. Men in white shorts and women in tennis skirts rallied back and forth, their conversations and occasional exclamations dotted by the pinging of ball against racquet.

I rushed down to the edge of the courts and, shading my eyes with my hand, scanned the players for Mal. His broad shoulders and sun-bleached hair were usually pretty easy to pick out. But I didn't see him. *Damn.*

"Can I help you?"

I turned and saw the perky sales clerk from the pro shop standing there, smiling politely at me. She had a name tag that read DANA pinned above her left breast.

"I'm looking for Mal. Is he here?" I asked.

"No, he's not. He's off this afternoon, but he'll be in tomorrow. Do you want to leave a message?"

Suddenly I realized I knew exactly where Mal was. It was Thursday, practice day for the girls' tennis team at Leeander High School.

"No, thanks," I said to the sales clerk, and turned and bolted for my car.

I tried to remember the way to the high school. The last time I'd driven there, I'd been following Mal and was paying more attention to keeping his car in sight than to all the twists and turns of the route. I had to stop twice and turn around to get back on the right track. But somehow—maybe through sheer dumb luck—I finally managed to find the school.

Wheels squealing as I made the turn, I drove around the building to where the tennis courts were located at the back. And, yes, the girls were there, hitting balls back and forth across the net. They were doing baseline drills, two on each side. And there was Mal—my heart gave a wild lurch—standing between the two courts and calling out to the girls, instructing them to get their racquets back, to follow through on their swings, to chase down balls out of reach. All instructions he'd given me during our lessons, right down to the way he called out playfully, "Chantal, are you trying to choke your racquet?" or "Sharise, if you don't start running for those wide shots, I'm going to set a fire under your feet!" or "Good hustle! That's what I like to see!" When one of the girls hit a winner, Mal would jump up and down, waving his hands in the air, making a complete idiot of himself. And the girls loved him for it.

So did I.

But, I reminded myself sternly, *that's not why you're here.*

"Who's that lady, Mal?" one of the girls called out. "Do you know her?"

All of the girls instantly stopped playing and turned to stare at me.

"Check out that tight whip," I heard one of them say. I had no idea what that meant—even after a decade of teaching, I wasn't fluent in teen slang—but I had a feeling they were talking about my car, since they all stopped staring at me and began eyeing the Porsche instead.

Mal turned to see what had distracted his girls. As our eyes locked, I felt a physical jolt of energy pass through me. Without looking away from me, Mal said, "Keep on going with the drill, ladies. I'll be right back."

"Is that your girlfriend, Mr. Mal?" one of the girls called out, which unleashed a torrent of giggles and catcalls that Mal wisely ignored.

He strode purposefully across the courts and up to where I waited on the sun-faded parking lot. My heart felt like it was hammering harder and louder with each step he took toward me. By the time he reached me, I thought it might burst right out of my chest.

"Hi," I said.

"Hi," he replied. His voice was calm and even. "What are you doing here?"

"I knew you coached the tennis team here."

"How? No one knows that."

"I do. In truth, I'm a CIA agent. The lottery-winning schoolteacher is just a cover."

Mal grinned. "Right. Because that's really flying under the radar."

"It's actually so high over the radar, no one would ever suspect. That's how the CIA works these days. Julia Roberts is an agent too. Although now that I've told you that, I'll have to kill you."

"I suppose you will," Mal agreed. "So, really, how did you find out about my coaching gig?"

"The old-fashioned way. I followed you a few months ago," I admitted.

Mal's eyebrows raised. "You were stalking me?"

"That's not the most flattering characterization," I said. "Why didn't you tell me you were coaching a girls' tennis team?"

Mal shrugged. "I didn't want anyone to know."

"Why? It's not like you're shooting crack into your eyeballs. You're giving some needy kids your time. That's a good thing."

"I don't like it when people make a big deal out of their volunteer work," Mal said. "They should just do it and shut up about it."

I nodded. "Okay. Fair enough."

"Why are you here now?" Mal asked. His tone was casual, but his face was guarded.

"Why do you think?"

"I take it you got my check."

I nodded. "If you were trying to get my attention, it worked."

"I just wanted to help," Mal said.

I frowned. "But it was a joke, right?"

"No, it wasn't a joke."

"But you don't have three million dollars," I protested.

Mal laughed. "How do you know?"

"Because you just don't. Wait—do you?"

Mal drew his eyebrows down and gazed at me contemplatively. He was wearing a bright white T and shorts, which highlighted how deeply tanned his arms and legs were.

"Do you?" I repeated, my voice rising.

"Why don't you try cashing the check? That's one way of finding out."

I just stared at him, mouth agape, while I tried to process this. *Mal was rich.* Oddly enough, this irritated me. It seemed like an awfully big piece of information to hold back.

"How rich are you?" I demanded.

Mal shrugged eloquently.

"But you never said anything!"

"What was I supposed to say?"

"I don't know. Maybe, 'Hey, Lucy, guess what? I'm really rich.' That would have worked for me. We certainly talked about my lottery money often enough."

"No, we didn't."

"Yes, we did."

Mal shook his head patiently. "No. We talked about how much your life had changed since you won the lottery, but we never really talked about the actual money."

"You're splitting hairs!"

"Why are you getting so angry?"

"Because you lied to me!" I realized how stupid this

sounded, but my anger, once ignited, had started to blaze out of control.

"I didn't lie to you. I never told you I was poor," Mal pointed out. He leaned against my car and smiled, which just pissed me off even more.

"But you *pretended* to be," I said.

"How so?"

"Your job, the way you dress, the way you live," I said—well, shouted, really—and waved my hands.

"I live on Palm Beach."

"You know what I mean!"

"Look: Yes, I have money. But it's not really my money. It's my dad's."

"But you said your dad is a builder."

"He is, sort of. He owns a company that builds houses."

"How big of a company?"

Mal hesitated. "The largest residential developer on the East Coast," he admitted.

I stared at him. "So if it's not your money, how were you able to write that check?"

"My dad set up a trust fund for me years ago."

"You're a *trust-fund brat?*"

"Really, Lucy, don't hold back. Tell me how you feel," Mal said with a snort of laughter.

But I wasn't in the mood to be teased. My entire body was prickling with anger. I felt duped, led on, lied to. It was like Elliott all over again. I turned on my heel, planning to march back to my car and drive off without saying another word, but a strong hand gripped my arm and spun me back around.

"Ow!" I said.

"Sorry," Mal said. He loosened his grip but kept his hand firmly on my arm. "But you're not leaving again. Not until we settle this once and for all."

As I stared at him, taking in the carved lines of his face—the prominent nose, the sharply angled jaw, the curve of his lips, the pale-gray eyes—I felt my anger fading. Why was I so mad? Had he really lied to me? Now that I thought about it, it didn't seem like he had. I'd just assumed, and when it came to Mal, my assumptions were usually wrong.

"The way I see it, if anyone should be angry here, it should be me," Mal said.

"Why?" I asked. "What did I do?"

"You left," Mal said simply. "In fact, you stood me up. You didn't even bother calling me."

"I did," I protested. "I left you a message. Didn't you get it?"

Mal just looked at me, and I could feel the flush creeping over my cheeks and spreading down my neck and chest. He was right—I had stood him up. And rather than having the guts to talk to him, I'd left a message on his answering machine. If a man had done that to me, I would have been outraged.

"You're right," I said softly. "That was a shitty thing to do. I'm sorry."

Mal didn't say anything for a long time. He just looked at me steadily, allowing my remorse to blossom into full-blown regret. I had screwed up, and badly.

"Thank you for the donation," I finally said, doing my best to sound grateful. "If you're sure you want to give that much, I'd be happy to accept it on behalf of my school."

"I wouldn't have sent it if I didn't want to," Mal said. "Besides, I had to get your attention. Nothing like making the grand gesture to do that."

At these words, hope bubbled up. "You wanted to get my attention?" I repeated slowly.

Mal gazed steadily at me. "What do you think?"

I stared back at him, determined not to look away. "I don't know what to think," I finally said.

"Yes, I was trying to get your attention," Mal said softly. Suddenly he seemed to be much closer than he had a moment before. Funny how that happened. I hadn't even seen him move.

"You were?" I asked, my voice almost a whisper.

Mal nodded. "Most definitely," he said. His lips were now so close to mine, I could feel the soft whoosh of his breath.

"Oh," I said.

Mal cupped one hand behind my neck and gently drew me toward him. I turned my face up to his, and then we were kissing. Lips, arms, hips, thighs pressed together, until I wasn't sure where I ended and Mal began. I wouldn't have minded if the kiss went on forever but, distantly, we became aware of the cheering, and we both began to laugh. We turned, breaking off our kiss, and were greeted by the sight of Mal's tennis team, clapping, cheering, and stomping their feet.

"You know, I am supposed to be a role model," Mal said dryly.

"You?" I teased. "Those poor girls!"

"Mmm, flattery will get you everywhere," Mal said, squeezing my waist in a way that made me jump. He laughed.

"What's so funny?" I demanded.

"It's just you're the only woman I've ever been involved with who was disappointed to find out I have money," Mal said, shaking his head. "You do insist on being different, Lucy Parker."

I smiled ruefully. "Being rich isn't all it's cracked up to be," I said. "I'm not saying I didn't enjoy the nice clothes and the dinners, and this"—I pointed to my Porsche—"is a seriously kick-ass car. But to be perfectly honest, living the life of the idle rich never suited me."

"I know. I wasn't really that surprised to read in the paper that you'd given it all up."

"I didn't give it *all* up," I said quickly. "I kept some to live on."

"Do you have any idea how few people would do that? How unusual you are?"

"A lot of wealthy people give their money to charities," I protested. "You did."

Mal shrugged. "It's easy to say money isn't important when you have it. But because of my background—where I grew up and the sort of people my family socialized with—I've also had a close-up view of how destructive it can be. Especially inherited wealth. I always knew I didn't want to be one of those guys—the sort who live off their parents, drink too much, and generally do their best to screw up their lives."

"Lottery money is even worse. It's all so sudden. Your life changes completely overnight, and not because of anything you did or made. Just because you bought a ticket and played some numbers."

"I think you did okay with it," Mal said.

I shook my head. "I let the money change me. Temporarily, at least."

"And then you learned your lesson and changed back to your old self?"

I shook my head. "No, not exactly. I think that Lucy had a little growing up to do. She wasn't always the best judge of character."

Mal smiled at me, and I thought I saw approval gleaming in those gray eyes.

"And now?"

"And now I'm learning to dig a bit deeper. It's a work in progress."

"Like life," Mal said.

"If you want to get all philosophical about it, yes," I said, smiling back at him.

"So now you know my little secret. Rather than the gigolo you thought I was—"

"You're never going to let that one go, are you?"

"Never. Anyway, instead, I'm a trust-fund-brat-slash-Palm-Beach-playboy. So which do you think is worse?"

"Please. What sort of a pathetic excuse for a playboy works even though he doesn't have to and spends his afternoons volunteering?" I asked, nodding toward the girls, who had finally given up on watching us and were back to hitting balls. "Although it's true you do spend quite a bit of time mooching around the Drum Roll."

"That's because I own it," Mal said casually.

My jaw dropped open. "You *own* the Drum Roll?" I gasped.

Mal grinned at me.

"But... but..." I sputtered. "You never said... and Ian never mentioned... but why would you keep that secret?"

"I'm an enigma wrapped in a riddle."

I gave him a playful push on the arm. "Come on, tell me why!"

"My dad kept insisting I invest some of my money in a business. And I wanted a place to hang out, somewhere with good drinks and a good atmosphere—"

"And lots of hot young girls," I added.

"Are there hot girls there? I hadn't noticed. Ouch, stop hitting me!"

Mal grabbed my wrists to prevent me from beating him about the head and pulled me close. "The truth is, I did it to get my dad off my back. I didn't expect it to be successful. I never wanted to be a businessman."

Our lips were close together again, as close as it was possible to be without touching.

"Oh, really? And what is it you want?"

"Haven't I made that perfectly obvious?" Mal asked softly.

I swallowed. "I'm not always the most perceptive person on these matters. Especially when it comes to you. Maybe you'd better just tell me straight out."

"You. That's what I want," he said.

Was this really happening? I wondered. Because it seemed so incredibly unlikely. Yet Mal was standing here in front of me. And those were his hands firmly pressing on my hips. And that was his face—wait. There was something different about his face.

"Hey! You shaved!" I exclaimed.

Mal rolled his eyes. "I pour out my heart to you, and this is what I get in response? More commentary about my grooming habits?"

I brushed the back of my hand against his smooth cheek. "I'm not complaining. I like it."

"I'm so glad," Mal said dryly. But he was smiling. And despite the fact that my heart was pounding and Mal was standing so close that I felt a little dizzy, I managed to smile back at him.

"Sorry," I said. "What I meant to say . . . I mean, what I want to say . . . is yes."

Mal's pale-gray eyes creased at the corners. "Yes? Yes to what?"

"Yes to everything," I said. I leaned forward, tipping my face up to Mal like a flower bending toward the sun, and this time, I kissed him.

ABOUT THE AUTHOR

Whitney Gaskell is the author of five previous novels, including *Mommy Tracked* and *Pushing 30*. She lives with her family in Stuart, Florida. To find out more, visit her at www.whitneygaskell.com.